Simon's Bridge

A Novel

Book 1 of 3 in The Simon Glenayre Trilogy

Imagined and Chronicled

by

D. Aaron Smith

DEDICATION

For my daughter, Abigail

With all my heart.

D. AARON SMITH

ACKNOWLEDGMENTS

You can visit D. Aaron Smith at

www.daaronsmith.com
www.facebook.com/AuthorD.Aaron.Smith
twitter.com/daaronsmith

The song "Power in The Blood," thoughtfully composed by Lewis E. Jones in 1899, resides within the Public Domain.

The author wishes to thank Barbara Andreasson of Harper's Magazine. It was Harper's Magazine where on December 1922, Mary Brent Whiteside's poem, "Who has known heights" was originally published. It is with great admiration that her poem is reprinted here. "Who has known heights" resides within the Public Domain.

The author is honored to include these fine works within this novel.

Alte Liebe rostet nicht.

(Old love does not rust.)

-*Old German proverb*

Where's the coffee? Didn't I buy coffee yesterday? I thought we had coffee.

-*D. Aaron Smith*

FROM THE AUTHOR

"Simon's Bridge" started out as one thing, but it became something else.

It began as a horror novel, you see. It really did. But it ended as something very different. I think Simon's life, as read through the pages of this book, reflect many of the changes experienced in the life of the author. No, this isn't a biography of my own life (thank goodness), but I can't help but think that like Simon, I entered into this story as D. Aaron Smith but emerged at its end a different person. Now this book is finished, I can't help but to feel somehow changed.

As I sit here and type this, I reflect on something I read once. It was a quote from Jim Morrison of The Doors and it came to mind frequently as I worked on this book. I am paraphrasing here, but in a nutshell, it went something like this: "I ask critical questions about myself and the world around me, and I try to find honest answers. To me, that's what 'art' is all about." Well there you have it. Thanks, Jim.

So that's what I did. I asked questions about myself, the world around me and I tried to find honest answers. I was honest with the characters in this book. I asked them to develop their own personalities. And they granted my wish, bless their little hearts. It came to the point where I was no longer telling Simon what to do and I didn't influence Bailey on whether or not to forgive. I wasn't the boss. The characters in this book decided the plot. Ultimately, I became only the conduit through which the story flowed. What was meant to happen, happened. And thank goodness for that because I couldn't come up with this stuff on my own.

Many readers may be surprised at the progressions this book takes. It was just meant to happen. How do I know? Simon said so. Bailey said so. Sure- Al, Ager and Valetta sure had their influence too. Again, I was only the author. I only did as I was told.

Would you please indulge me a bit longer? Please? I have a few people to thank. And for good reason. They are wonderful, blessed parts of my life.

Ten years ago, I got exactly what I prayed for. How many of us can say we got exactly what we wanted? I can. Because ten years ago I became the father of a little girl. Talk about grateful. To this day I still can't believe I was chosen to be her father.

Your daddy sure loves you, my sweetheart girl. I am so proud of you! I can't wait to see what kind of wonderful difference you are going to make in the world! You're fantastic!

Always in my thoughts is the proud memory of my father, Sfc. Jerry Wayne Smith.

I want to thank my mother. The reasons for this are legion.

To my brother, Daniel. I couldn't have found the ending if it weren't for you. Typical Dan: Always there for me when I need you.

Pam Meadows, RN, MSN, has proven to be a tremendous source of friendship and counsel as well as technical input for this book. You are a dear friend of mine. You have been an important influence in the crafting of Bailey Eden Piper. Like you, Bailey is steadfast in her beliefs and committed to the well-being of others.

Friends to thank? I got 'em: Jason and Doug. Being my lifelong friends, Jason and Doug agreed to let me use their names for the characters Hix and Hendricks (unlike the characters in the book that shares their good names, the REAL Hix and Hendricks are two of the most intelligent people I have ever known. They are also the most wonderful friends anyone could be blessed to have). We are brothers.

Roger, Cheri and their wonderful daughters- Natalie, Jo Ellen and Beth Ann as well as their own families

To Pat Koontz - I needed to talk, and you listened and you cared. I am grateful beyond words. But I'll try anyway. Thank you.

I am a proud Kansas Citian. Is that a word? Citian? Well I'm using it because this is my laptop and I type what I want. Kansas City is a great place to live. And in the heart of our city sits a jewel: The Nelson-Atkins Museum of Art, nicknamed "The Stone and The Feather," it sits right down the street from the historic Country Club Plaza. The original building, "The Stone," is a beautiful place. It houses my favorite painting: Caravaggio's "Saint John The Baptist in The Woods." I can't tally all the hours over the years I've stood in front of that painting. Next door is "The Feather," the new modern art wing of the museum. At night the walls light up from the inside and it is spectacular. Like its distinguished older brother next door, the inside of the building itself is also a beautiful work of art. Just to see the way natural light works off its walls and corners indoors is really something special. I love The Nelson. It is my home away from home.

I laugh as I extend this particular thank you: To Michael Cross and Alex Keyworth of The Nelson-Atkins Museum of Art. The enthusiasm you both have for our wonderful museum was inspiring. And fun. I enjoyed our conversation and appreciate your help. Like the art at the Nelson-Atkins, it is fine people like you who make my visits there a great experience, every time.

And to whoever you are, I want to extend my warmest greetings. I don't even know your name. But you are kind-hearted and will be beautiful in my eyes, and I can't wait to meet you someday. So until we meet, be safe.

And of course, thank YOU for buying this book. You took a chance with your hard-earned money, and have helped to make a dream come true. I know things are tough in this day and age and money is so terribly tight. But you took a chance on this book. And I thank you. I hope the words contained within these pages are worthy of your expectations. You are all a blessing. Again, I thank you, thank you, thank you.

To The Lord: I thank you for your love and forgiveness. For dying on the cross for my sins because you love me so. I hold you above all others. My daughter and I, we are yours.

So there.
DAS.

PROLOGUE

The morning sunlight shone through the stained glass windows, painting the piano keys red, blue, and gold.

Just nestled into their pews, the congregation's chattering simmered to reverent whispers. Hand-held fans could be heard shoving the thick, hot air from one side of the sanctuary to the other. Sitting to the right of the dais, the ivory of the piano's keys revealed the reflection of long graceful hands drawing near. The fate of those hands, like the generations before them, was that they be used to craft their own doom. The owner of these hands however, would have none of it.

This mettle now ran in the family, starting with her generation.

Instead of crafting their self-destruction, these hands were used this morning and like so many Sundays before it to create a sound that would swell and fill the room with melodic colors. Reverend Lighthouse cracked the door of his office just enough to see out into the sanctuary. And as he put on his vestments, he could hear the congregation flipping through hymnbooks. Their harmonies soon followed.

"When a body catch a body, a comin' through the rye."

The long graceful hands belonged to Samantha. She sat at that piano just as she had these last several years, playing hymns before the Reverend Isaac Lighthouse took the pulpit. The features of her face were delicate and angelic. Her skin, a soft, rich brown like fresh ground coffee and her eyes radiated tranquility from within their easy gaze. Reverend Lighthouse quietly observed from the crack in his office door as her left hand firmly, precisely forged the substructure of the hymn in the bass clef. The fingers of her right hand danced gracefully around the treble clef, as if they were sparrows playing on a breeze. The minister watched as she delicately swayed to the music in so subtle a way most people other than he would never even notice. He resisted taking pride in that he knew Samantha better than anybody, including her own husband. And he allowed himself a silent celebration that they were never separated by space and time.

The yellowed walls composing this place, built upon a foundation of Faith, Hope and Love, had been witness to many events these past several years. The countless unions of husband and wife, the christening of newborn children, and the gatherings to see loved ones off to the other side. Lighthouse went to his desk and reached for his Holy Bible. Dog-eared and worn, the sacred book seemed to leap from his desk and snuggle into his very hand. He walked past the overburdened bookcase of this dimly lit office and made his way back towards the light seeping in from the door. As he twisted the brass door knob to step outside, he paused to reflect on a piece of fabric that hung, framed and mounted beside his office door. The fabric had the words *"What are we going to do?"* written in black marker upon it. Those words served as a reminder of a different time and a far different place. Lighthouse gave a sigh and walked out the door.

Passing by Samantha at the piano, he stopped by her side and knelt down. "We've come a long way," he whispered into her ear, "haven't we, Sis?"

And with a peck on her cheek and a loving squeeze of her shoulder, he was off to the pulpit.

"Good morning brothers and sisters." He paused for a moment and looked around the room. "Now just when we think the good Lord couldn't make a more beautiful day," his voice rose in volume as he lifted his hands and smiled, "He again finds a new way to illuminate the sky with another fresh and beautiful morning. Can I get an 'Amen'?"

The congregation responded with a joyful "Amen" and a passionate wave of hands. Another service in this tiny whitewashed church, complete with its schoolhouse steeple and little picket fence had begun. The congregation sat absorbed in the moment before Isaac Lighthouse as he gazed into the eyes of his flock. The Reverend was well known for his smile. And he seemed to always wear that smile, as if he had a marvelous secret that was his very own. And his eyes, a long inappropriate gaze into them being the secret desire of many ladies in the congregation, seemed to go on and on as if they were a pathway to a new and wonderful place.

He continued.

"Now every Sunday is special, brothers and sisters, of course," he beamed, "but today is an extra special day…"

Lighthouse looked out at the people before him and secretly enjoyed the expressions of intrigue on their faces. Already they were captivated, and he knew it. "It was twenty years ago today that one man took a stand. Twenty years ago today that one man who thought he was worthless came to the realization that he was worth much, much more." Again, he paused to look out into the pews and then at Samantha at the piano. The expression on her face was tranquil, the look in her eyes, *knowing.* "This tale can be told now, brothers and sisters, because it is all said and done." He continued. "The ground beneath our feet has ceased trembling, the clouds above broken up, returning to us our beloved blue sky."His face abruptly turned serious. And the congregation noticed.

"Within the realm of what we know, or what we *think* we know, there is only one constant in this present world of ours. The existence of Good and Evil." The congregation nodded, fans waving. He leaned forward over the pulpit for maximum effect. "Friends, many of us spend our entire lives under the assumption that the sky will forever retain residence above our heads, the ground beneath our feet, forever granting us our beloved terra firma." Leaning forward again, he tapped on his Bible with his index finger, "Of course, nothing could be farther from the truth. Yes, Good and Evil are here. They're always here."

"Omnipresent. Ancient."

"Forever."

"Today's sermon is a story about Fear. It is a story about Hate. It is about the battle between Good and Evil, *and it is a story about the rediscovery of Faith…*"

"What in the world is goin' on with him today? He got a fever or somethin'?" The two round old women sat in the front row, exchanging awkward glances, little pillbox hats sitting skewed atop their very heads. Fans fluttering. Their lips whispering back and forth. "Think he's finally goin' crazy?" Orpha Mae, whose fan still flitted rapidly, kept her eyes locked on Lighthouse. Leaning over slightly, she could only murmur "uh-huh." The volume of the Minister's voice exploded. Both ladies jerked in their seats.

"*Faith.*"

"A word repeatedly lost and found in the annals of human history. A word cast into the gallows of slavery, long since soaked into the sands of Normandy and splattered from an exploding bus across the Holy Land..."

His eyes wandered off in the direction of a wall in the back of the sanctuary, as if it were flashing past events before his very eyes. For a never-ending moment, he stood silent. He scratched at the side of his neck. Somehow, Lighthouse shook himself back to the here and now.

The expressions on the faces of his flock were of bewilderment. Lighthouse found himself in uncharted territory. Reverend Lighthouse, always quick with a joke, a tall fishing tale, a big hearty laugh or the perfect Bible verse for any occasion, found he was *speechless*.

More silence. A distant cough echoed from the back of the church. He nervously fidgeted with his pen.

Mercifully, the soft "clink" of a middle C from the piano. The note was more than just a tone being played on an instrument. It was a lifeline being thrown from Samantha to her brother. That one note told him she was there for him. Turning to Samantha, he instantly knew the look on her face. "Say something, anything" she said with her eyes and soft smile. Lighthouse knew what she was thinking: Just start and the story will take over and tell itself. Her voice from past conversations over tea rang through his head. "This has to be told, Izzy. You made a promise."

He placed both hands on the edge of the pulpit and dropped his chin to his chest. He watched as a lonely drop of sweat landed on his open Bible. Lighthouse read the verse chosen by gravity. The moisture crept over the words of John 1:5.

"The light shineth in the darkness, and the darkness cannot overcome it."

Reverend Lighthouse lifted his head, took a deep breath and smiled.

The congregation was quiet. The only sounds created by those shuffling uncomfortably in their seats and the occasional clearing of the throat. The hand-held fans, usually flailing at full speed, were now still.

"Let me start like this," He then began.

"His name was Simon Glenayre."

"But you can just call him 'Simon.'"

CHAPTER 1

In the moon drenched darkness of their bedroom, he sprung up, wavy Adonis hair smeared across his forehead. Blood, glistening black in the moonlight, crept like a snake from his lip down to his chin.

He took in another desperate gulp of air as he scanned the room.

The silk sheets faintly squealed from within clenched fists, the bed gyrating while his eyes darted this way and that. And now she could be heard groaning and rumbling from the distant, foreign lands of their king sized bed. He tried to still himself.

Again, he scanned the bedroom.

Though he thought he had closed them before he went to bed, the windows now sat wide open. The sheer curtains whispered their secrets as they delicately floated atop the silky night breeze.

As Simon Glenayre leaned back towards the headboard, he could feel the pillow squish behind him. Again, he heard her groan. "Again, Simon?"

He found his wife, after being abruptly awakened again tonight, far from a mothering mood. Leaning back on her elbows, she ran her fingers through her mess of fiery red hair. It had just dawned on her that she had to get up even earlier than was previously thought. Enough time was needed to iron a blouse for her meeting. Seeing the time on the alarm clock, she realized that tomorrow's meeting was now this morning's meeting, the alarm just a couple hours off. She knew she stood little chance of getting back to sleep.

"Sometimes I hate your guts," she hissed. Simon Glenayre

closed his eyes and wished the moment away.

Simon held up his hand and looked at it in the hazy blue moonlight. Seeping in from the open window, the moonlight made his hand look as if it were dead. He refused to look at his image in the mirror across the room. He was fearful of what he might see.

His feet found their way to the cold of the hardwood floor. Once again and like many nights before, he would wander the long hallways of this place, this gilded cage with many rooms. They were rooms he would never again step foot in after tonight.

Simon passed through long, dark hallways and corridors. From outside of the house, his silhouette could be seen in the windows, disappearing and reappearing in each. He found his way to the kitchen and its stainless steel fridge, built into the wall. The small bulb flared bright in Simon's eyes when he cracked open the refrigerator door. His hand found its way to the middle shelf and a bottle of water. The cracking of the lid's seal echoed in the cavernous stainless steel and marble kitchen.

Before the bottle reached Simon's lips, he thought of his grandfather and cousin, Max. The longer he stayed away, the harder it was to go home and face them again. They gave him a home as well as an oasis from the anguish and guilt of losing his parents. To make matters worse, he showed himself a fool the way he stormed out of their lives. Together, his grandfather and cousin only expressed their love and concern for him. They saw he was getting worse. Like many addicts, Simon ran from those who loved and cared for him most.

He screwed the cap back onto the unused water bottle and placed it on the edge of the counter top. His silhouette disappeared around the corner.

Simon soon found himself back in the bedroom and standing at the foot of his bed.

Tonight in their bed, she vaguely innocent, lying there with her eyes tightly clenched. The luminescence of the moon masked the true color of her hair. There was a time when Simon would sit and run his fingers through her hair, as they relaxed in their den with the television turned down. Those evenings were in the past, forever it seemed.

The bed was long and wide. Silk sheets and several large pillows adorned it. The walls of the bedroom were scattered with paintings by the modern, trendy artists of the moment from London, New York, and LA.

But still, as he lay there on that night and like so many nights before, his thoughts turned to someone else. He was wrong to give up. She had such a delightful voice, shimmering blonde hair. She smiled with her eyes. He felt guilty for thinking of her. He'd hurt her so bad.

Looking up to the ceiling Simon found only the shadows of the curtains, splashing like dark waves upon a lonely shore. He yearned to reach out and touch Chloe's arm for comfort, but the risk of waking her was far too great. Her alarm clock would begin barking in less than an hour. She was best left asleep.

The massive fireplace was silent and dead. The crackling of the wooden logs had long since surrendered their last gasps with a final pop and hiss.

Looking out the open window one could see a long road in front of the three story house. The road twisted itself down into the city. Through the starlit darkness of the California night with its amber streetlights seen from the surrounding hills, Los Angeles looked like a lost universe. Or perhaps the inner workings of a human body. Stars flickering down in the valley, and the freeways pumping traffic into and out of the center of the city, like arteries providing lifeblood to the human heart.

Providing lifeblood.

Pumping life in and out of the city.

Endlessly, pumping.

Simon felt the tightness in his chest ease up, though he felt he didn't deserve it.

A look around the room revealed comfort and luxury. And all of it bathed in the hazy blue light from the open window.

CHAPTER 2

The walls of the structure shook and the floors vibrated.

The security personnel in the main vestibule watched with concern as the outer glass shell of the colossal building wobbled from the sound and fury, fearing the colored panes might shatter down upon them at any moment.

Their source of concern was not the shifting of tectonic plates, nor was it the heavens crashing down to Earth. The source was closer than that. For the power that shook this place was unleashed, not from the skies above or the ground below, but by a multitude of people who throbbed with a unified and potent heartbeat. A horde of people, tens of thousands strong who stomped on the floors of the arena. And they were chanting. They were chanting a word. That word was a name.

And that name was "Simon."

Entering the arena, past the guards who are frisking the ticket holders and searching hand bags for weapons, the main floor of the arena is soon exposed. The sea of stomping and chanting fans of the headlining act already find themselves packed like sardines at the front of the stage. Behind the five-story high curtain and across the enormous stage, roadies and stage hands frantically sort cables and make last-minute adjustments to the lights. Behind the stage is a hallway. It's a dimly lit hallway and it is long. Security guards sweep the hallway, verifying backstage passes of the groupies and contest winners, all wide-eyed and alert, hoping to catch a glance of one man.

Further down the hall, at the darkest end is a lone door. And upon that door is a name. The name is "Glenayre."

A guard stands irritably at his assigned post, beside this door.

He would much rather be out on the streets, catching bad guys, but instead he is here, and quite annoyed about it. He can smell the bluish smoke creeping down the hall and into his well-trained nostrils. Nothing would make this servant of the law happier than to sprint down the hall, apprehending the source of the drugs being used. But to do that, to apprehend each and every offender of the laws he holds so cherished, would take an army. And his shift was almost finished. His replacement would soon arrive and it then would be *his* problem to consider. Besides, his newborn daughter was waiting at home for his father as well as the embrace of his loving and tremendously patient and understanding wife.

They say the life of a man or woman in law enforcement is thankless and dangerous, but the life of their loved ones waiting for their safe return is said to be equally frightening. This particular policeman thought of his wife's smile. Once more, he considered the situation: drug usage down the hall that should be addressed as his conscience directs him, resulting in several hours of paperwork before he could finally go home, or- ignore the smell, end his shift and get home to his family who wait for him. The knot in his heart tightened as the rope of his conscience was tugged fiercely from both ends.

He felt the cross beneath his uniform and prayed silently for forgiveness. He would choose to rejoin his family sooner, rather than much, much later.

In the dressing room of Simon Glenayre, Chloe Glenayre, wife of the musician and poet, sat watching a bottle of Perrier vibrate upon the table top and rolled her eyes. She dangled a stiletto-heeled shoe from her French-manicured toes. She glared at the silhouette fumbling from behind the back-lit changing curtain.

"Simon," she said with a tone of boredom and dislike easily detected, "it's getting close to down-time."

"Step on it."

The figure behind the changing curtain froze.

The bare dressing room walls were painted sea-foam green and a large tray of meats and cheeses sat curled up and sweating in a distant, lonely corner. From above, the soul-drenching hum of fluorescent lighting droned on and on. The unnatural light from above robbed human flesh of all the hues of life, making one's skin look pasty and sad.

Chloe found the choices of places to sit frustrating, certainly not worthy of someone of her stature, being the wife of a rock star as well as the fastest-rising woman in the music industry. But still, her feet were killing her, so upon her arrival she assessed the situation, trying to choose the least-disgusting of her options: short and filthy trailer furniture by the food in the corner or the old wooden office chair by the desk. She chose the office chair. She could hear the occasional sigh of the policeman assigned to guard Simon's dressing room, as well as the ruckus down the hallway. Faintly, she could even hear the noise from outside the arena.

They'd begun to arrive days earlier, the fans of Simon Glenayre. Their days before the show were spent wandering around the acres of parking lot in search of lost friends as well as the always disgusting but desperately required portable toilet. Their nights were spent covered in blankets, trying to keep warm by one of several small fires burning throughout this rock n' roll shanty town. The flames could be seen from the interstate, sending orange embers up into the sky, like fireflies seeking to cool themselves in the misty haze of the moon.

Back in the dressing room, Chloe observed Simon emerge from behind the changing curtain, shirtless. He didn't look her way and was unaware of her forced smile. She looked at the musculature of his well toned body and admired the deep, shifting canyons of his back as he brushed his teeth. She continued to bounce her shoe from the tips of her toes, convincing herself that Simon was worth it. Worth the status she had commandeered at the record company, worth the admiration of her friends on Rodeo Drive as well as the collection of platinum cards in her wallet.

Chloe jerked in her chair, her shoe flopped off her toes and landed on the floor when the door to the dressing room was flung open. It slapped against the wall with a loud bang.

In the doorway stood a man. A large man, larger than most. His hair was wavy and black. A clump of oily hair fell down against the man's forehead. Laughably, he tried to slick the hair back but it fell down again. He gave up and scanned the room for Simon. His accent was thick and it boomed loud in this room made of cinderblocks, as if his voice was a cannon being fired in a high school gymnasium. He spotted Simon.

"Simon!" the man bellowed. "Whatcha doin'? You got twenty minutes before down time and you still ain't ready?" His laugh was long and thunderous. "You think the whole world is gonna sit around waiting for your lil' fanny to get movin'?" Simon stood leaning down over the sink. He didn't look up. He wouldn't turn

15

around.

"As a matter of fact, I think they *can* wait." No one else in the room could see his smile.

"Well look, Narayan and the other guys in the band have a couple of ideas they'd like to run by you," the big Italian said. "Just to get your approval. That is" he laughed, "if you can get your butt in gear!" The man felt another presence in the room, it was a presence he knew all too well and it always made him uncomfortable. He turned without surprise to find Chloe sitting behind him, glaring.

"Oh, hi Chloe," he said as nice as he could. "Howya doin'?"

"Fine Valletta," Chloe muttered in a hateful groan. She refused eye contact.

"You want me to setcha up a chair at the side of the stage for the show?" It pained Valletta to look at Chloe. Still, he tried to be nice, as best he could.

"No Valletta, thank you and goodbye."

Simon turned around slowly and grinned at the big Italian. "Thanks Val. And tell the guys I'll be there shortly," he said.

"Sure thing," Valletta looked at Chloe from the farthest corner of his eye as he made his way to the door, "thanks boss." He gave a look of dislike to Chloe who returned one of her own. He left the room quieter than he came in.

Simon could feel Chloe glaring at his back. His wife and alleged partner for life. To this day they remained the best of enemies, the worst of friends.

Simon resumed brushing his teeth. He rinsed out his mouth and spat into the sink and watched the toothpaste swirl down the drain. The sight of water running into the darkness of the drain brought to mind an unpleasant and unwelcome memory. Simon tried to block it out, but he would be unsuccessful. He braced his hands against the sink and recalled an incident, years ago when he was a boy.

Simon snuck into the kitchen for a soda in the middle of the night and witnessed something. It was his mother sitting at the kitchen table. She was auto-writing, again. So engrossed in what she was doing, Simon's mother was completely unaware of her son's presence. In her intensity, as she sat entranced and writing in a script that was distinctly not of her own hand, the pencil snapped. And what resulted horrified the young boy who would someday grow up to become one of the most recognized faces in popular music. Simon watched in horror as the pencil hemorrhaged blood upon the white tablecloth from within the grip of his mother's trembling hand. Simon would run down the dark hallway, turning just long enough to see the blood pouring from the edge of the table and onto the linoleum of the kitchen floor. That night he would pull the covers tightly over his head, weeping and praying that what he had witnessed was only a bad dream.

Simon's knees nearly gave out beneath him as Chloe screamed for his attention yet again.

"Simon!" she screamed. "Are you listening to me?" Simon jerked but continued to look down at the sink, refusing to look at himself in the mirror.

"No," he muttered. "I'm sorry, what'd you say?"

Chloe sprung from her chair, storming in Simon's direction. She grabbed him by his toned arm and snapped him around, as if he were an ill-behaved child. "Its Valletta," she hissed. "He has to go. And I mean it this time, Simon." Simon grabbed a wash cloth, soaking it in the hot, running water. Chloe jerked his arm again. "You're not listening to me. He has to go. He hates me, and I hate him. Who's more important?" Simon remained silent, looking at the floor.

Chloe took hold of Simon's chin and flipped it upward so she could see his eyes. "Idiot?" she barked. "Are you listening to me?"

"Hate," Simon said, his voice trailing off. He took a moment to consider that powerful word. Simon gave a long pause, an uncomfortable duration to the always urgent and impatient Chloe. "Seems a pretty serious word for a friend I've had most of my life, don't you think?"

Simon coped with the situation as best he could. And in the worst way in Chloe's world: He simply laughed.

Furious, Chloe spun around and spotted one of Simon's guitars sitting in front of a vast array of floral arrangements sent by radio stations, business associates and fans. She approached the three thousand dollar Gibson Les Paul, kicking it into the flowers with a violent crash. Chloe turned around victoriously, looking expectantly at Simon for a response. She hoped he would become furious enough to strike her. It would have been perfect: The judge would rule in her favor, sympathetically looking at the photograph of the red hand mark across her cheek, admonishing the unruly rock star for his violence toward his innocent and gentle wife, entitling her to nearly everything he had, except for the shirt on his back.

But Simon would not indulge her. Regardless of her cruelty to him, he could never strike a woman. However, Chloe would upset him enough that he had no choice but to take *some kind of action*. Simon reached for the night's only link to serenity, a walkie-talkie at his disposal, to be used in case he came into contact with an unruly or dangerous fan. In this case though, he would not call security about another hyper fan barging into his dressing room with pen and magazine cover in hand. Instead he would call for a security detail to escort his furious wife safely from the arena and to her limousine.

The men, with their bright yellow t-shirts with bold, black lettering identifying them as security would immediately enter the room, closing the door behind them. "Take her away" Simon commanded, his voice was defeated and sad. "See her safely to her car." The security guards approached Chloe who yanked her rail-thin arms from their grasp. She teetered angrily to the desk, snatching up her ten thousand dollar purse and making her way to the door.

She flung the door open, revealing a certain large man, who until just a moment ago had his ear pressed so firmly against the door, he nearly fell on top of her.

He stuttered an explanation. He failed miserably. "Uh, Chloe. I um…er-"

The furious Chloe shoved Valletta out of her way. The heels of her shoes could be heard clicking down the long hallway. The arena security guards struggled to keep up.

Valletta, though a kind man and gentle at heart, couldn't resist one last dig at his old nemesis. He called down the hallway to her: "Chloe!" he bellowed. "Does this mean you don't want me to setcha up a chair for the show?"

Chloe's voice could be heard, shrieking down the hallway. "Go to hell, Valletta!"

The policeman by the door tried and failed to suppress his laughter. Valletta closed the door and turned to Simon.

"You ok?"

Simon gave a sigh and shrugged his shoulders.

The very moment Chloe left the room, the walls seemed to pull themselves back several feet, air instantly found its way back into Simon's lungs. He looked at his guitar lying among the corpses of several floral arrangements. Simon pointed at the guitar while looking at Valletta who said nothing. Valletta nodded his head to Simon, when he realized how it had gotten there. "Yep. Another one bites th' dust."

Simon remained silent and slipped into the bathroom, closing the door. In the bathroom, Simon mustered the courage to look into the mirror and recited a poem. The poem, written decades earlier by Mary Brent Whiteside, held special meaning to Simon. He recalled the slip of paper his mother kept on the refrigerator. She used a magnet Simon made in grade school. The refrigerator magnet was made of macaroni, glued together in the shape of an angel and it held Whiteside's poem to the door of the fridge. Even if he were to try, Simon would never forget this poem from his past. Softly, he recited the poem to himself:

"Who has known heights and depths shall not again
Know peace-not as the calm heart knows
Low, ivied walls; a garden close;
And though he tread the humble ways of men
He shall not speak the common tongue again
Who has known heights shall bear forevermore
An incommunicable thing
That hurts his heart, as if a wing
Beat at the portal, challenging;
And yet-lured by the gleam his vision wore-
Who once has trodden stars seeks peace no more."

Simon found the courage to exit the bathroom and finish getting dressed. He found Valletta standing by Simon's wardrobe rack, laughing. "What?" he asked. "Don't like the choice of attire for this evening's performance?" He smiled and took another sip of bourbon from a sweaty tumbler.

Valletta laughed again. As always, it was loud and joyful, but usually only to Simon. "Oh, I just dunno if this shirt is," he paused, lifting the sequined shirt up between two fingers as if it was infected with the Ebola virus, "you."

Valletta put his hand on Simon's shoulder. "She ain't good to you, Sy." Simon remained silent, except for the sound of his groaning as he knelt down, pulling the rose stems from the strings of his guitar. He paused and wondered to himself if Chloe would catch the red eye back to Los Angeles or if she would stay the night in Kansas City. Chloe never cared for Kansas City. He expected her to leave on the first thing smoking.

"What does it matter, where she went?" Valletta's voice sounded exasperated. Simon was surprised that Valletta answered the question he could have swore he wondered silently to himself. Apparently he spoke aloud without realizing it.

Valletta grabbed the surprised Simon, putting him into a

headlock a gorilla would struggle to escape. Simon laughed with what little breathe he could muster. "She's a nice girl, Val," he gasped.

Valletta laughed long and hard. "Oh, if she's nice, then you must think this is adorable." He then smacked Simon on his backside, *hard*. Simon gave a yelp that gave the policeman posted outside the door reason for concern. He gave a sigh of relief when he heard laughter and leaned back against the wall. And finally, his shift replacement had arrived. He was going home to his family.

Valletta cracked the door to listen to the opening act as they roared through their set list. Together, they listened to Packmule struggle through their final songs. The crowd continued to chant Simon's name over the blare of their guitars. Simon stood up and approached the door to have a listen.

Simon watched as Valletta's face turned serious. He looked at his watch. "Let's get your cover on," he said, reaching for Simon's hooded terrycloth robe.

"It's show time."

The members of Simon's opening act finally received their loudest applause of the night as they exited the stage. The singer saluted them with a single, offensive finger. They passed by Valletta and the man he was facing. He wore a terry cloth robe with the hood over his head.

With a loud pop, the mountainous black speakers buzzed back to life and Aaron Coplan's "Fanfare for the Common Man" swelled to mind-numbing volume. The crowd exploded with anticipation.

Valletta took Simon by the shoulders.

"How ya feelin' Sy?"

"I feel ok. I'm ok."

"Are you ready?"

Simon hopped in place. "Yeah Val. I'm ready."

Valletta's voice increased in volume and intensity. "I said, are ya ready boss?"

With the roar of the crowd getting louder and louder, and with Valletta's prodding, even Simon was getting excited.

Simon yelled back, "I'm ready."

"I said, are ya ready, boss?"

"Hell yeah!" Simon screamed. "I'm freakin' ready!"

Valletta knew he now had Simon sufficiently pumped up. "Now I want ya ta go out there and show 'em *they're your daddy!*"

Simon paused, his expression went blank. He spoke the

correction slowly: "I think you mean, 'Show *them* who *their* daddy is, Val…'"

Nearby, roadies could be heard laughing while they stood in a semicircle rolling up cables.

"Yeah, that's what I meant, Sy."

Valletta handed Simon his in-ear monitor, and with a slap on the back sent him to his spot behind the curtain. Simon's ear monitor buzzed to life.

"Test, one-two-three." Valletta spoke softly into his microphone headset as not to risk blowing out his best friend's eardrum. "Can ya hear me, boss?" Simon acknowledged with a thumbs up. "Don't screw this up, Sy," Valletta laughed. *"They actually like you here."*

Simon smirked as he turned back to his microphone stand. When the intro music hit its crescendo, the stage curtain dropped on cue and the crowd exploded as Simon rushed to the front of the stage, thrilling them with another performance.

Valletta looked out into the smiles of the crowd as Simon sang his songs to them. Simon bobbed his head as the audience swayed their arms back and forth in unison to the 4/4 beat of the kick drum. Valletta was proud of his friend, though he would never tell him. Valletta looked down at the flickering lights on the mixing board that demanded his attention. As he flicked the sliders on the board and tweaked knobs, he couldn't help but laugh.

"Yea," Valletta beamed. "Simon Glenayre is back in town."

As Simon performed for the stadium of fans, someone else's smile remained in the back of his mind. In his heart, Simon longed for someone, who unknown to him was closer than he imagined. For at a nearby hospital, she had just clocked in for her shift. Her scrubs freshly pressed and a stethoscope hung at the ready around her neck.

That night, as Simon Glenayre performed before the adoring gaze of thousands of fans, she would be fighting tooth and nail to save the lives of total strangers. It was her strength and it defined her. She was beautiful and moved with a grace seen only in a painting by Degas. And she loved Simon Glenayre, still.

Her name was Bailey Eden Piper.

CHAPTER 3

The most hardcore fans remained behind, hopelessly pounding on chairs, chanting Simon's name and rallying for another encore. They would leave disappointed.

Valletta handed Simon his terrycloth robe. He put it on as instructed. But there was a disagreement brewing.

"But I don't want the belt, Val." Valletta insisted Simon use the belt anyway. That was why it was sewn to the robe in the first place. He reasoned that a belt not used was, well- a wasted belt. And that was pointless. Still, Simon refused.

"Let's not forget," Simon spat with authority, "who the boss of this operation is."

That night, as the equally headstrong Valletta tossed people from their path en route to the dressing room, Simon followed close behind, with his belt fastened tightly around his waist and complaining quite loudly about it.

They would make their way to the door that bore Simon's name without incident. Simon slogged his way to the office chair Chloe used earlier and dropped into it like a heavy load of filthy laundry. He sat and listened to the fluorescent lighting buzz, spinning in his chair and looking up to the ceiling.

There was another bang on the door. Valletta answered as he always did. By the time Valletta shooed off the record company execs and groupies, he turned just in time to see Simon slipping into the shower room and closing the door behind him.

It was time to wash the day's worries away. That is, if he could manage to get the knot undone in his belt. He cursed Valletta under his breath.

Simon managed to undo the knot and began to peel away the

layers of sweaty clothing. From outside the shower room, the clothes could be heard slapping the tile floor. Simon reached for the knobs protruding from the wall. The shower head coughed and belched at first, then built up pressure quickly. The steam crawled into Simon's lungs like a fiery wet blanket.

Simon leaned, outstretching his arms against the wall, letting the hot water course down the curvature of his back. He wondered if anyone in tonight's crowd walked away with their lives changed for the better. What was the point, he wondered, if no one walks away somehow changed? He took in a deep breath and held it as long as he could. As he expelled the air from his lungs, he gave further thought to tonight's concert and searched his soul for the source of his ongoing sense of doom, wondering aloud to himself. *"What am I gonna do?"*

He wanted to pray to God, but he felt so unworthy.

The shower room soon filled with thick blankets of steam, so thick, Simon could hardly see past the length of his arm. He reflected on a verse of Whiteside's poem.

"Who once has trodden trodden stars seeks peace no more." He shook his head, frustrated, and tried to get the poem out of his mind.

Through the steam, a clicking sound, as if two stones were being slapped together. Simon lifted a hand from the wall and turned around. "Val?" He looked through the steam but found no one. He held his hand up to gauge his range of vision. His other hand soon found its way back to the tiled shower room wall. His head hung low so the hot water would resume coursing down his back.

Someone entered his thoughts. Simon imagined her appearing to him through the steam of the shower. Her hair golden, her face, looking towards a future that would never arrive. He imagined what she would look like today, all these years later. He recalled that she seemed to smile with her eyes.

The pleasant thought was interrupted. It was the clicking sound once more. As if one were banging two rocks together. Simon found himself growing angry that someone would dare interrupt his shower. Perhaps it was Valletta, but he knew better. Most likely a fan, he thought to himself. It took a lot of guts, he imagined, to sneak through the corridors of the arena avoiding security, locate his dressing room door, get past the mountainous Valletta, and then...have the gall to interrupt his shower. Again, he scanned the haze as best he could.

"Hello?" The clacking sound continued.

"Val!" he shouted, trying to sound angry but coming across as more frightened than anything. "You know better!"

The voice came from behind him, uncomfortably close to his ear. From within the heat of its revolting breath, Simon could hear the crackle and pop of an ancient and hateful voice.

"Give us the key."

Simon raised his head, the soap burned his eyes. The ongoing clicking sound echoed through the shower room. Again, he heard the voice. *"Give us the key, Simon."* Simon spun back around and faced the wall. He grabbed a bar of soap and began to scrub his hands together, furiously. "Hold it together," he heard himself say, "nobody there."

"Val?"

The comforting tone of Valletta's voice would not arrive, and still that distant clicking sound from somewhere within the blanket of white steam. And again, the voice.

"Give us the key, Simon." Pain shot through his neck, and again he heard it. *"Give us the key."* His breathing kept pace with his galloping pulse. Simon felt his knees buckle beneath him. Falling to a knee on the floor of the shower, he covered his mouth to keep from screaming.

The alarming sensation of a claw running up his back made Simon gasp. Fighting to stand, he only fell to the floor again, as if he were unable to control the muscles in his own legs. He fought to fill his lungs with air so he could speak.

"What did I do to deserve this?

The voice in his ear answered. It's claw still running up and down his spine. *"Hell is what we make of it,"* the voice giggled. *"And oh, what fun we'll have with you there, Simon."*

Simon, still crouched on the shower room floor, looked up to see the shower head begin to bleed. He shut his eyes, tight, and wished the moment away.

Tears streaming down his face, he opened his eyes to see his nightmare hadn't ended. "Whatever I've done," Simon cried through the thick saliva in his mouth, "why can't I just fix it?"

"Why can't you fix it?" The voice giggled again. *"Why can't you catch the wind in your hand, Simon?"* Simon cried aloud but immediately found himself muted by a will that was not his own. *"Why did you run out on your grandfather and Max, Simon? When you were a child, why did you pick on the mentally retarded boy on the playground, humiliating him in front of all the other children, when all he needed was a friend?*

And Simon-

Why weren't you there for your father and mother when they needed you the most?"

The voice commanded visions to race before Simon's eyes. The visions consisted of moments of his selfishness, his pride, his failures as a son, his failures as a husband, as a Christian and his failure as a father. "I didn't know it was going to happen," he sobbed. "I thought everyone was fine. I made a mistake-"

"And what did it cost you, Simon?" The voice in Simon's ear was thrilled to dig the dagger deep into one of his most sensitive and painful memories. *"Selfish little Simon. Just had to get one more fix. Bye-bye, Lily. Bye-bye."*

"How could you!" Simon screamed. "Of all the things you could throw at me. I died that day too!"

Simon felt the scrape of the claw against his back disappear. It was replaced by the soft hands of a woman. The vile stench from the voice in his ear disappeared to be replaced by the soft tonality of a seductive feminine voice. The voice sounded as if it cared for him. As if it were about to weep on his behalf.

"Just end it, Simon" the voice pled. *"Leave the pain of this world behind for those foolish enough to endure it…"*

Simon tried to scream for Valletta, but his voice was restricted to only working when he spoke to his tormentor. His attempts were then equal to little more than a soft croak.

"Give us the key, Simon" the beautiful voice cried. *"You've been so selfish all your life. It's time to give something back."*

Simon covered his face with his hands, sobbing.

"Just end it." The hand moved around to his chest, caressing him. *"I know where there's another rope. And it's a good, strong rope, Simon. And there's a pipe to hang it from. A good pipe. Stronger than the one in Cleveland. Really close, Simon. Really close."*

The clacking sound drew nearer, Simon looked up to see a face emerging from the haze.

The face began to take shape. It was a man's face, as white as the steam. He was black around his eyes, blackness oozed from his opened mouth. It was Whiteface. Simon had come to know him well since the first time he encountered the fiend, at a bridge all those years ago.

In the dressing room, Valletta moved towards Simon's guitar case and eased open the lid. It creaked from the movement. He scanned the room for witnesses.

With a fumbling effort to extend the length of the guitar strap, Simon's guitar soon found itself strapped to Valletta's enormous body. And a few strums on the guitar was all it took to remind Valletta why Simon Glenayre was a star, and he was the man who carried the guitar cases for him. Having abandoned the foolish mission of playing Simon's guitar, he carefully unstrapped it and gently laid it back in its case, failing to remember to adjust the guitar strap to its original length. This oversight meant that the next time Simon strapped on his guitar, the Les Paul could fall to his ankles, if not all the way to the floor, smashing into shards at his feet.

The shriek from the shower room came quickly and with no less severity. Valletta raced to the locked shower room door. Backing up only two short steps, he smashed through the door reducing it to a pile of wooden splinters, absorbing the trembling water on the floor. Through the haze he could vaguely see the shape of Simon crouched against a wall. Tentatively drawing nearer, Valletta stopped and snapped his head to the side in a desperate search of fresher air. The haze had grown thick and hard to breathe. He tried to breathe through his mouth to offset the foul smell, but it had little effect. A few more steps forward and Valletta had Simon in full view. His head suddenly felt as if it was swimming. The room began to crumble away in huge chunks. Valletta could feel his heavy frame flop to a knee and his body fell against the wall. "Oh no," Valletta cried out, "what's happened to you, Simon?" Valletta wiped the needles from his lips. The heel of his boot found the seams between the tiles on the floor as he struggled to push his back against the wall.

Valletta struggled to find himself in the void. But still, he managed to pull himself together because his friend needed him, desperately.

"I'm here, buddy. Ol' Val is here." His own vision was still blurry, when he felt the sudden grip of Simon on his forearm. Valletta, still looking forward through the haze, drug his body nearer to Simon. For a moment, Valletta thought he saw a figure disappear into the steam. His vision strained, he looked again and could swear he saw two dark eyes fading into the white. But whatever it was, if it was anything at all, was gone. There was a more immediate need to be tended to.

His friend needed him, desperately. He found the round of Simon's far shoulder and wrapped his arm over his friend, pulling Simon nearer and ultimately halfway onto his lap, wailing. "It's gonna be OK, Sy. Ol' Val is here," he said. "It's gonna be ok."

Simon was still hysterical. "They want the key and I don't have the key," he rattled on and on. "They want the key, Val, and I don't have the key." Valletta scanned the room again as best he could, finding no one. "They want the key, Val…"

"I know, little man," Valletta sobbed, "it's gonna be ok. We'll fix this. It's gonna be OK."

Valletta rocked Simon in his arms as if he were his guardian angel. Rocking forward and back. Endlessly rocking. Using his hands this time not to forcefully move crowds of people, but to comfort his dearest friend. "It's gonna be OK, Sy."

"Ol' Val's here."

Simon used to love the stage. He would often remark that his time "up there" was like "Leaves drifting on a stream, beneath his bridge." Simon stopped playing music for money and success years ago. He would often remark that he played his music for the Salvation. "Yeah, man. The Salvation."

The night of the shower incident has long since been placed in a thick, leather-bound journal and flung into the dusty attic of memories best left forgotten.

CHAPTER 4

The corn flakes tumbled into the bowl, resting at the bottom atop an intricate floral pattern. The milk in the fridge sat just behind the opened bottle of Tramonto.

Bailey Eden Piper shoved the half-consumed block of cheddar cheese out of her way so she could get to the plastic container. The sun shone bright, it was a beautiful day. She unlocked the window and slid it all the way up. The chimes just outside her window were ringing clear and beautiful in the early morning chill.

It had been a good morning. The sunshine illuminated the glass of orange juice that sat upon the countertop. The juice filtered the sunlight onto the table in orange waves. The bright kitchen was small, but nice and tidy. A small basket of fresh flowers sat at the middle of the small round table by the window.

NPR was in the middle of its morning newscast, and she listened in religiously. She had been a contributor since high school. She was surprised to hear children out playing this early. An early morning it was, but already, the neighbors had started mowing their lawns before the dew even had a chance to evaporate. The harsh sound of the mowers had begun to fill the room, but so did the smell of fresh cut grass. To her, this was a fair trade-off.

She loved the smell of fresh cut grass.

Reaching into the pocket at the side of her housecoat, she found a scrunchy to pull her long, blonde hair back into a ponytail. The bagel had just popped out of the toaster when the phone rang.

The voice on the other end of the line was friendly, but overly chirpy.

"Bailey! What's going on?" the voice on the line sang.

"Oh nothing. Just having some breakfast, that's all." Her voice sounded light and feminine, pleasant to the ears.

"So what in the world are you doing up so early?"

The girl with bagel in hand laughed as she smeared butter across it. "Well gee, Cheryl. I don't know," she said. "Why are you calling me so early if you think I might be asleep?"

"Fine. You got me there. Well look, there's this guy-"

"No thanks. And you know better," Bailey laughed. "What is he this time, a car salesman? Perhaps one of your husband's buddies. Now they are really something." She smiled as she rinsed off the butter knife in the sink. "Well if you must know," Cheryl said, "he's in the car detailing business."

"Not interested, thanks."

"Well then what are you going to do tonight? We're going to The Club and wanted to know if you'd like to come along. Interested? And don't tell me you're just going to rent some movies and just stay at home all weekend."

Bailey Eden Piper laughed. "Well as a matter of fact I went to the store last night and bought-"

"Casablanca, right? Casablanca?" Bailey fidgeted with the salt on the kitchen counter. "Actually," she said, "yes. I did buy Casablanca. How did you know?"

"You watch movies every weekend, Bailey," the voice on the line sighed. "It doesn't take a rocket scientist to figure that out." Bailey spun the bagel on her plate and laughed.

"Yeah, I know. I could have flown to Casablanca for what I pay in DVD's."

"So come on, Bailey!" Cheryl urged. "Why don't you just go out with us! It would be fun you know. If you want, we could ditch the guys and just make it a girls night out! It's no biggie!" she said. "We could drop the guys in a New York minute! They'd get over it y'know. They'd just end up at Erik's house playing poker all night getting drunk or something."

Cheryl's voice turned serious.

"C'mon Bailey. We've been worried sick about you. You don't do anything anymore, don't go out anymore." There was a pause. "We miss you and we're worried about you."

"Well don't you worry. I'm fine. It's just that I've gotten tired of all the excitement," she said. "I just like to go home after work and relax. That's all."

"Bailey, you're not going to meet anyone if they don't know you exist."

"I know that."

"So why don't you just do it. C'mon! Go out with us. It would be a blast! All the girls would be thrilled to see you there!"

"Nah." Bailey eased, "I already have a date. Me and Bogey."

"Bailey, he's gone, sweetie. It's time to move on."

Bailey sat the bagel back on the plate. Her face turned a bit serious.

"I know that, Cheryl. Ok? If I don't want to go out, I don't want to go out. That's all. When the time is right, I will do it," Bailey groaned. "But until I feel comfortable with it, it just won't happen."

Bailey rapped her nails on the countertop, expecting a snappy comeback or a dial tone.

"It's like you're in mourning." The voice on the other end of the line paused, searching for the right words. "It's been years and he isn't even dead. We care about you, that's all. We want you happy."

"I am happy. And don't you worry. When I feel like it, I will meet somebody. But the bar scene isn't the place for me to do that. It just isn't my scene. You know that. When the time is right, the right guy will come along."

"The next Simon, you mean?"

"Don't go there, Cheryl. When the right guy comes along, he'll...come along," she said, her voice a little pained. "All right?"

Bailey could hear the sigh from the other end of the line. "Fine then. We just love you and miss you, y'know? We want our friend back!"

"I know. Look, I have to go, ok? My bagel is reaching arctic temperature. I'll swing by your cubicle on Monday, ok?"

"All right then sweetie. Tell Bogey I said 'Hi'."

Bailey sat back at the table, looking out the window. The neighbor stopped mowing for a moment to take a sip of his V8.

He wore polyester shorts with a plaid pattern, cut off just above the knees. His white cotton t-shirt fit too small to be worn in front of the entire neighborhood. He could have been the cover boy for "Dorks R' Us" magazine.

As he wiped the sweat off of his forehead, his children ran up to him, dancing around him as he stood there laughing. He knelt down and hugged them. He had a nightmare for a wardrobe, but she could tell he was a good father. This made him ok with Bailey.

The world needed more of those.

As she sat there and smiled, her thoughts again turned briefly to *him*.

She wondered to herself: Does he ever think of her?

CHAPTER 5

Simon pulled the blankets over his head but the voice refused to leave him alone. Its harsh pronunciations from within the thick Brooklyn accent would not be ignored. Almost as if it were created for the sole purpose of ruining wonderful dreams, *it just kept on and on.*

He recognized the sound of heavy drapes being flung open before he heard it again.

"Simon, wake up."

His name sounded as if it were being screamed from the far end of a tunnel and now this invasion voice was bearing down on him from the darkness at breakneck speed. Simon rolled onto his side, facing the door. The glaring sunlight now flooding the room prevented him from opening his eyes. This time the voice sounded abhorrently closer. "Simon, wake up…"

"Dad?"

"I ain't your dad, pal…"

Simon grabbed the nearest pillow and pulled it tight over his head. "Phil" he growled, "good morning."

"It's time to get up, you can't spend all day in bed."

The pillow swelled as Simon's grip on it tightened. "Phil, you know I don't want a darned thing to do with you until after-"

"Breakfast?" Simon heard the sound of a heavy glass clunk onto the nightstand next to his head. Phil could be heard stirring the red concoction with a piece of celery. "All right. Here's your breakfast. Now get your butt out of bed."

Simon's body jerked to the torturous rhythm of dresser drawers being opened and slammed shut. "You gotta interview in less than an hour with The Star, so you better get your tookis outta bed." Simon hatefully pulled the blankets from his sculpted body and stumbled his way to the bathroom. "Where the hell's breakfast?" Simon could hear Phil expel a loathsome sigh and listened to his polyester suit swish outside the bathroom as he grew closer. "It's right here," Phil snipped, "remember?" Phil gratingly stretched his r's to infinity. "Set it on the nightstand right next to your thick head. But here it is, now in the bathroom, thanks to me."

Phil Brueno was the road manager who had cursed Simon since leaving the "Annie" tour group for reasons unknown to most. His resume found its way to the offices of the record company, and ultimately hooked him the job of Simon's tour manager. "Phil Brueno: Simon Glenayre's Tour Manager." The thought tumbled through his head like a load of wet towels in the dryer. "Sonofa-"

Simon strangled the toothpaste tube in rhythm with Phil's unnecessary banging. He looked down to find a swirling mountain of blue twisting its way down the drain, the bristles of his toothbrush bare. Phil retrieved a small vial from his coat pocket and twisted off the cap. Simon listened from the bathroom as he tapped the vial's contents onto a mirror.

"Need a line?"

"No, Phil," Simon barked from the bathroom, "I don't need a line."

"Yet."

Simon's outburst from the bathroom drove Phil to make his retreat to the large window overlooking the Kansas City Plaza. "So what kind of trouble did the two of you get into last night?" The rustling in the bathroom came to a sudden halt. Simon was unable to ignore that for once, Phil was silent, an occasion to be marked on a calendar and never to be forgotten. "Well, Simon," Phil spoke his words as tactfully as he knew how, "I couldn't find you or Val anywhere last night, so I assumed you snuck out to the bars in disguise." In the bathroom, Simon leaned against the counter, rubbing the marble sized knots in the back of his neck.

Now he remembered last night.

The shower room.

He recalled the expression on Valletta's face upon entering. That's all Simon could remember right now. "Yeah, we snuck out for a while. Insulted that we didn't invite you along?" Phil watched the shoppers below in their Saturday best strut several stories below him. He observed them as they swung their shopping bags, doing their best to ensure their badges of social stature were obvious. "Doesn't matter to me anyhow," Phil said in the most argumentative voice he could manage. "You're the one who will probably be a father in nine months and not even know it." Simon peered around the corner and observed Phil standing by the window. The sunlight illuminated his frizzy hair as it formed a nest around his otherwise naked head. Trying to draw Phil from his timid retreat in front of the window, Simon mended fences as best he knew how.

He changed the subject.

"Who do I interview with after The Star?"

Phil felt his reply faintly ricochet off the large windowpane and brush past his face on its way to the opposite side of the room. "You interview day after tomorrow with-" Simon popped his head out of the shower with a look of curiosity on his face. "Yeah, I interview with who?" Phil's voice rose in volume. "Well, give me a minute. I don't have my planner with me. I think it's 'Rolling Somethingorother...'"

The shower curtain flung away from the wall and Simon's face again popped through the opening. "Rolling Stone, Phil?" Simon's voice this time reflected not irritation, but pure fear. "Jesus, you scheduled an interview with Rolling Stone magazine and didn't even realize it?" Phil appeared in the doorway of the bathroom, reached for Simon's untouched and watery Bloody Mary and knocked it down with rapid gulps. The celery stick gave a thud as it hit the wastebasket. "Well if you must know, they contacted us for the interview. We didn't go to them."

"What do-"

"They want to interview you about the state of your career, Simon."

Simon felt the weight of that sentence on Phil's voice. He twisted the shower dial till the water pipes died with a vulgar scream from somewhere behind the wall. Simon reached in vain for the towel rack, placed a sinister distance away. Phil came to the rescue with a thick towel embroidered with the hotel's logo. "What do they mean by *'The state of my career'*, Phil?"

Phil nervously produced a twenty dollar bill from his pants pocket and rolled it tightly. With two rocky snorts the crystalline powder found its way into his system. The red borders of his eyes soon produced tears as he rubbed his nostrils. "Well let's face it, Simon," Phil sniffed, "you don't sell 'em like you used to, y'know?" Simon growled as he toweled off his hair. "What the hell are you talking about?" he sneered, "I've sold out every show-"

"No, no, no," Phil forcefully interjected. "Don't confuse

concert sales with music sales." Simon wadded up the towel and thoughtlessly fed it to the cluttered countertop. "Yes, you do sell out your concerts. But the overwhelming majority of that money," Phil said as he rubbed his index finger with his thumb, "goes into your pocket and *not* the record company's."

"And what goes into your pocket after paying the tour expenses… well Simon," Phil laughed as he shook his head, "that ain't much to write home about. So do you know what that means?"

Simon folded his arms across his chest and gave pause, trying to decide if he wanted to know more. "What does it mean?"

Phil rambled through the tiny liquor bottles in the mini bar, "That means you're pissing off your record company, my friend. You make some money on the road, but you don't put much in their cash register." Simon raised his hands, as if he had the answer in algebra class. "But I thought that I had been getting some good reviews on the new-"

"Who cares about what the critics say, Simon? Sol could care less if you make it into the history books. The only book he cares about is his *ledger book*." Simon groaned.

"Go on…"

"So what I'm saying, dear Simon, is that you have turned out to be a respected ambassador of thoughtful, artsy rock music," Phil explained. "But you aren't expanding your fan base with this new 'Baroque n' Roll style of yours and it's costing you. Big time." Phil gave pause as he noticed the exasperated expression across Simon's face. "They don't want a respected musical ambassador of intelligent music," he said, "what they want is another 'Wizz-bang' type of artist. In other words," he said, "they would rather you sell a butt load of records-"

"Don't you mean MP3s?"

"Right. MP3's. They would prefer that you sell a ton of MP3's and be god-like on the charts for two or three years and then disappear as opposed to selling a 'respectable' amount of music over the course of fifteen to twenty years and be a drain on their resources."

"And Simon, you *are* a drain on their resources."

Simon leaned against the counter-top, staring blankly at the floor. "So they would rather I burn brightly, quickly and then fade away…"

"They make a hell of a lot more money that way," Phil said as he opened up a miniature bottle of bourbon. "And no, they don't want you to burn brightly and then *fade* away. They want you to burn brightly, then *go away*," he urged. "Quickly."

"So what does all of this mean?"

"What it means Simon, is that you haven't got many friends left in the industry."

"So it's the new CD." Simon's voice sounded surrendered and numb. Phil, who was again down on one knee and fishing through the refrigerator, shook his head. The clanging of tiny bottles ceased from within. "They're tired of your ways, Simon." The tone of Phil's voice sounded as if he were in confession. Stalled and apprehensive but forced given the circumstances, to tell the whole truth and nothing but the truth. Phil continued as gently as he could, stalling and apprehensive. "They invested a ton of money on your last couple of records, and the chance of getting the desired return on them, especially from your latest CD isn't looking so good."

Phil, now leaning against the windowpane, scratched at his arm through the polyester. "And to put it bluntly," Phil said, "you've been a pain in their neck," Phil said. He could tell Simon was getting defensive.

"I've been a pain in their neck…"

Phil's voice rose to drive home the truth.

"Simon, do you have any idea how much it costs to open up a recording studio in the middle of the night? To supply the full complement of required staff, not to mention dragging the irate producer out of bed, just because you get a sudden musical inspiration?" he barked. "Now you just sign on the dotted line and Sol picks up the tab, right?"

"That's right."

Phil's handkerchief found its way to his naked, sweaty forehead. "Well do you think that money just grows on trees, Simon?" Now, the frustrated Phil was yelling. "Do you think that Sol Glenn is going to continue paying bills on your vast musical visions without demanding a return on his investment?" Phil watched as beads of sweat gathered on Simon's forehead.

Simon stepped forward. "Phil that's what I need to do to make the music right. To touch people. What is the point of making music," he asked, "unless the people who hear it walk away somehow changed for the-"

"And Simon, it gets worse," Phil interrupted.

"Is it about Sol?" Simon asked. "I'll talk to Sol. We'll work it out. We can work it out, don't you think?" Phil's silence sent a shiver galloping up Simon's spine.

"How does it get worse, Phil?" Phil's silence was digging into

Simon's nerves deeper than his voice in the morning ever could.

"Phil, how does it get worse?"

Phil's mouth opened for a moment and then shut again without uttering so much as a grunt. Simon looked at Phil as he looked longingly at the door, possibly contemplating an escape. Simon could tell he was trying to find a way to throw him from this roller coaster somehow without killing him. "Look, Sy," Phil said, trying to tone down his voice with a deep breath. "Studios cost money, y'know?"

"Yes, I know that recording studios cost money," Simon rubbed at the base of his nose, between his clenched eyes.

"And upper tier producers, they get their cut up front. And it's a huge cut, Simon. Regardless of what the sales turn out to be." He took another swig from a freshly opened bottle. "It's called a 'Front Loaded contract that they sign."

"Sure, Phil. I knew that."

Phil began to grow visibly irritated. "Simon, the entire stringed orchestra for your last CD wasn't cheap, assembling an entire choir in the middle of the night," he barked, "does not come cheap." Phil got louder and louder as he went, Simon listened as he felt the blood drain from his face. "Simon, look," Phil said, now glaring at the floor, "the record company wants all their money back. They want a return on their investment. And your CD sales aren't giving it to them. Your sales aren't even coming close. The music industry has changed over the years, Simon. It's dangerous out there." Phil's voice sounded as if he were a general in a losing war, his troops cornered and hopeless.

Simon shifted from one foot to the other. He could feel the knots on the back of his neck swelling. "So why don't we just start to pay it back from what I make on the road?" Simon asked.

"Simon," Phil snapped, "start to pay it back?"

"Start to pay it back?" Simon watched the veins in Phil's neck grow darker.

"I don't think you could afford it if you sold out your next *three tours*." Phil watched as the color in Simon's face faded to ashen gray.

"So what does all this mean, Phil?"

Phil twisted the top from the bottle of liquor. "The last two CDs were expensive as hell, Simon. I mean, the costs incurred *broke records...*" Simon was tapping his nails on the tabletop at a furious pace.

"What are they planning, Phil?"

"The orchestra you used for a month, good grief. That was a

lot of money…"

"What are they planning, Phil?"

"The producer of your last two CDs is suing the record company for the fulfillment of the dollar amount on his contract…"

"And?" Simon asked.

"And it was a damned big contract, Simon!" Simon jerked from Phil's outburst.

Simon slowly took the bottle from his hand as he kept his eyes locked on the shag of the carpet.

"Tell me, Phil."

"There's rumors going around, and Simon," Phil said softly, "my sources are pretty good." Simon knew the answer was coming now. He pressed Phil no further and waited for the pain.

"Simon, I've received word that the record company is going to place a lien against all of your assets, including your houses, cars, instruments, guitars…" he said, "the shirt on your very back. You can just about name it and they plan on selling it off. Piece by piece."

"Can they do that?"

Phil nodded. "This is corporate America. They can do whatever they want."

The content of Phil's bottle of liquor coursed down Simon's throat. The only sound that followed was the bottle hitting the wastebasket. Suddenly the strains of pans rattling from within the hotel's far off kitchen could be heard through the silence as if they were colliding right in the next room. Phil's eyes stayed locked on the carpet. He couldn't yet bring himself to look Simon in the eye right after telling him the grim news. Simon looked out the huge window, viewing the shoppers below, hopelessly searching for options. Simon exhaled from his mouth and watched the fog form on the window. "They're also considering cancelling the remainder of your tour. And that is just out of spite." Again, Phil rubbed at his face with both hands. "You won't have a pot to piss in."

Simon choked out a laugh. "Now I know why Rolling Stone wants to interview me about the state of my career."

Phil finally found the courage to look at Simon, a worldwide celebrity and musical genius, whom he had just told was worth less than himself. "Phil," Simon whispered, "give me that vial." His voice was low, monotone and moist with doom. Phil retrieved the vial from his pocket and tossed it to Simon without a word.

He watched as Simon knelt hunch backed over the windowsill, making a succession of snorting sounds. Eventually, Phil slid out the door, leaving Simon to wonder to himself how he could escape this nightmare and return to the dream Phil had woken him from.

CHAPTER 6

The boardroom was long and thin. The walls, covered in rich, stained oak panels, kept the room dark, even with the large window at the end of the room. From the golf course outside, silhouettes could be seen milling about within the large floor to ceiling window. Running down the center of the room was a long, highly polished oak table with several leather bound chairs surrounding it.

The high backed chair at the head of the table was the largest in the room. Most people in the room tended to avert their eyes from it. To sit in that chair was unthinkable.

Two men in their early thirties stood looking through the blinds, taking in the panoramic view of the executive golf course. "Any idea what this is all about?"

The other executive, clad in a suit that most in their early thirties could only fantasize about, shook his head. "To be honest," he said, "I haven't the slightest clue."

"Do you think they're downsizing?"

Noah shrugged his shoulders confidently to the question. "No, I really don't think so. The old man would have just held a sudden meeting and made the cuts in front of God and everybody. No, he said, "I think you're safe. For now."

"Do you think he's stepping down?"

The question was like a needle popping a balloon full of laughter for Noah. "Are you kidding me?" he snorted. "He'll be running this company from his deathbed," he laughed, "and probably beyond."

If you were to spend a few minutes in the boardroom, your eyes would eventually adjust to the lack of light. It would reveal eight people all whispering in fearful tones. Much of their lives were spent here, jockeying for position and safety, in a room where careers and lives could be either advanced or ruined with the single damning wave of a fat Cuban cigar.

Everyone in the room jumped in unison with the sudden flinging open of two large doors. His smoke quickly filled the room with floating ash. The chatter immediately shut down as a large body, clad in a suit that could effortlessly swallow several above average salaries, slithered its way towards the opposite end of the table. A cane with the highly polished brass head of a lion landed on the tabletop with a loud crack. Sol Glenn, owner and GM of Magic Tree Records, stood and glared at the room's occupants in a long silence.

"Ladies and gentlemen, sit."

The majority scrambled for one of several chairs around the table. All scrambled but two, who took a seat at their own leisurely pace, confident and cocky as they snickered between themselves at the other's gutless submission to this man. Sol Glenn, ever alert to all happenings in his presence, took notice of this. He took notice, *and he would remember.* Their newness stood out like an embroidered Star of David in occupied Poland. Sol glared as the smiles on their faces fell to the ground like bricks. Their faces were fresh, well rested. Every hair thoughtfully placed in their locations, secured by copious amounts of hair gel. Sol rubbed the two hour stubble on his face as he glared at the glass jaws of his next victims.

They were new and had to be trained. Sol relished these opportunities. Another chance for him to humiliate and dehumanize. Man, he thought to himself, life is good.

One of the two Sol was sharpening his claws for flicked nervously at his pen. When he realized Sol was watching him, he immediately stopped flicking at the pen and fumbled it into his pocket with a cough.

"You," he sneered. "What's your name?"

The young man with the pen, one of the two best-groomed, well-rested and now most terrified looking people in the room, stiffened up in his chair, tugged on his collar. "Rora-" He cleared the catch in his throat. "Roranaugh. Bill Roranaugh," he timidly whispered, "Mr. Glenn."

The cigar found its way to his thick lips and cackled as he sucked the black air into his ample lungs. After a brief pause, he expelled one day's life in a thick cloud of smoke.

"Well, Mr. Rora-"

"That's Roranaugh, Mr. Glenn." Again, the smile on the young man's face begged for a tether that the owner of Magic Tree records threw nobody. Glenn smiled broadly. His teeth surprisingly, weren't filed down to sharp points. "Right. Well, Mr. Roranaugh, as you can tell, we have some business to tend to here this morning. So if you don't mind," he said as he leaned his bulk forward in his huge leather chair, "why don't the two of you do us all a favor and get the hell out."

Among those lucky enough to find a seat was Marcus. Hoping the flicking of his empty money clip pocket could not be heard.

Everyone in the room, with the exception of Sol Glenn, felt the blood drain from their faces. An emotional jolt shook most bodies in the room. Sol's two latest victims avoided eye contact and began the task of gathering up their untainted legal pads and other still unread memos. Shaken and humiliated, both made their retreat for the large dark red double doors. On his way through the door, Roranaugh dropped several papers from beneath his arm and witnessed in horror as they fanned out around him. Bending over to pick them up, the remainder of papers beneath his arm escaped to the guffaws of Sol.

Too humiliated by this show of clumsiness, he simply stood up and walked out the door, leaving his associate in humiliation to gather them up for him.

Sol watched with pleasure as the second man gathered up the mess of papers all the while never lifting his face to the others in the room. Before the morning's entertainment was done, Sol had to take one last shot:

"C'mon Stiles, hurry the hell up," Sol Glenn barked. "We don't have all damned morning!"

Stiles stood up, finally, and looked around the room. He could see the expressions of pity from most in the room. They understood what he was going through. One even tried to force a comforting smile without being seen by Sol. All she could muster in confidence was a vague upward turn of one corner of her mouth.

Stiles grabbed the doorknob, but with his sweaty hands, a tight grip eluded him. He could hear Sol rumbling in the background, purposefully just loud enough to be heard from his side of the room: "Where in the hell did you get this idiot?"

With one last desperate squeeze, he managed to twist the doorknob and make his escape, but not before hitting the door frame with his shoulder, echoing with a thud on the way out. The door shut, and then there was silence, save for the labored breathing of Sol Glenn, also known as "The Lion of The Music Industry."

"All right, ladies and gentlemen," he said as he twisted his cigar. "We have some important business to discuss."

The room remained silent. The room knew better to talk. To those in attendance, it was best to nod in agreement. It was just safer that way.

"Now I know," he said in his rumbling voice, "that you probably can't wait to get back home and crawl into bed with those expensive hookers of yours." Sol looked at the woman sitting next to him, dressed smart in her business suit, and visibly embarrassed by what she heard. Sol continued to look at her as she kept her gaze locked onto the grain of the conference table and laughed at the side of her head.

"Do we need to take a break before we even get started, you know, so you can sneak off to the bathroom and stuff your noses with that powder you people love so much?" After a long guilty silence from those around the table, Sol sat back in his chair punching the air with his cigar, laughing. "Oh, what the hell," he spat, "they say breakfast is the most important meal of the day."

After his own laughter died away, Sol gave pause then took off his massive gold framed glasses and cleaned them with a handkerchief snatched from his pocket.

After clearing his throat, Noah Glenn was the first to speak up. "So what's going on then, Dad?" While lighting a fresh cigar, Sol's eyes scanned the room. Usually, he was never guarded about who heard what. This was *his operation*. And he said whatever in the hell he wanted to, but this time the atmosphere was different. He leaned forward slowly. The other six executives gradually leaned forward in their chairs in anticipation. "I want to talk about our own, dear, Mr. Glenayre."

CHAPTER 7

A raggedy blanket, nailed disreputably to the window frame was just thick enough to keep the odor from escaping through the cracks around the window. If you were to cross the run-down house's dusty front yard, step over the broken down lawn mower and approach the darkened window, you would have picked up a scent of booze as recognizable as the stench of fish that fills the air at the City Market. You would also have heard the indecipherable rumblings of conversation punctuated by intermittent hacking.

Finally, Hix's coughing eased enough for him to speak.

"Hendricks," he laughed, "was that the last piece of pizza?"

Another beer can found itself crushed and tossed atop several album covers spread over empty milk crates. Ted Nugent grimaced from a CD case lying beneath a pile of empty beer cans.

It appeared as if they'd just awakened (well after most had returned to work from their lunch breaks), and appeared vaguely prepared to drift through the rest of their day. They'd begun this day just as they started many before it: Making pyramids out of empty beer cans, eating cold pizza, talking about rock n' roll.

And getting more stoned than The Grand Canyon.

The third and usually mute member of the trio sat listening from beneath a swirling cloud of smoke. The framed portrait of a clown with broad, sad eyes trembled from the rumbling of monstrous speakers placed at both sides of the room. The clown in the painting seemed to yearn for rescue as it hung timidly from an oversized nail among the various posters of wrestlers thrashing each other.

Hix and Hendricks found their silent friend at a party they

attended (uninvited, of course). Taking up residence beside the keg some months ago, Hendricks turned around to find What's-his-name just standing there. He followed Hendricks and Hix around for the rest of the night. In fact, he'd been following them around ever since. In his awkwardness, he usually said the stupidest things when the three of them were trying to meet girls.

He was embarrassing. He was annoying. He smelled funny.

But he could get beer.

This made him OK with Hix and Hendricks.

They never even bothered to ask his name. He'd always been referred to as "What's-his-name."

Having built up enough courage to stand, Hix rolled his backside from his beanbag chair and worked his way to the kitchen, passing What's-his-name as he fished through the CD's. On one CD cover, Stevie Nicks danced, her chiffon flowing, her enchanting beauty spied upon through the crystal ball of her admirer. "And what about the new Simon Glenayre?" Hix's stuffy voice rang from the kitchen as he searched among the empty pizza boxes for a lost soul covered in pepperoni.

Hendricks made his view clear, the clown in the painting looking down on him while he spoke. "I think the new Glenayre sucks." What's-his-name tried to share his opinion of the new CD by Simon Glenayre, but he was interrupted before he had a chance to complete a single word.

Next up for discussion, the new offering from the band Packmule. Hendricks eagerly gave his views, and stamp of approval, all the while discouraging the nameless third member of the party from sharing his own opinion. Again, What's-his-name was passed over for a beer as he pointlessly held out his hand. Yes, the new Packmule was far better than the newest collection of classically inspired songs from Simon Glenayre, according to both Hendricks and Hix. The shuffling of pizza boxes from the kitchen came to a sudden halt, followed by a long silence. Hix stood at the sink watching the brown water move on its own, an overlooked detail suddenly caught in his less than steel trap of a mind.

"Well," What's-his-name groaned as he pried himself from his bean bag chair. "That's not important" he said. "Get up. I want you to come with me. I have something I want to show you."

Hendricks and Hix both looked at one another, concerned. Neither said anything.

"Oh c'mon!" What's-his-name barked. "Get up!"

History is littered with countless unsolved mysteries.

Mysteries that have been researched, reviewed, tested, poked and prodded for explanations. These include, but are not limited to: the Lost City of Atlantis, UFOs, the identity of the alleged gunman on the grassy knoll and how three young men, stuffed into a smoke-filled Ford Pinto managed to get from one side of Kansas City to the other without being pulled over by the police. But somehow, they managed to make their way to What's-his-name's home without incident. And upon arrival, for Hix and Hendricks, the real mystery began.

They both stood wedged in the doorway of What's-his-name's bedroom, mouths agape.

"What th' hell's this?"

The tall, thin and usually quiet one of the group was amused from the bewildered sound of their voices. He finally answered in his usual shy, soft tone. "Well it's my bedroom, guys." What's-his-name observed his friends, both lodged in the doorway, silently taking in the contents of the room's four walls. Much of what they saw was foreign to them.

Later, all the questions would come, but for that moment they would only attempt to understand what they saw.

For Hendricks and Hix, this was like trying to shove a gallon of milk into two shot glasses.

Equipment nameless to Hix and Hendricks, sat at attention on a grounded electronics workbench. Cables hung on the wall above, all precisely wound and arranged, color coded. Framed portraits on another wall revealed the visages of Nicola Tesla, Albert Einstein, Benjamin Franklin and Jesus Christ.

A long wall was lined with books. Hundreds of them.

"A Brief History of Time" by Stephen Hawking, "The Physics of Immortality" by Frank J. Tipler, "A Spaniard in the Works" by John Lennon, Ray Bradbury's "Fahrenheit 451," "Quantum Physics: Details" and The Bible sat among countless others. All books sitting respectfully beside each other, temporarily resting. Their worn pages calling out to their owner to be read, over and over again.

Another wall stood hidden behind banks of computer monitors. Several screens displayed chess matches being played by the computers against themselves. Another monitor flashed computations, mathematically intricate equations working towards an ultimate answer known to none. What's-his-name often wondered if the computer's CPUs might eventually burn out before they could reach their ultimate conclusions. The room was a techie's fantasy come to life. An electronic wonderworld plugged into reality in the form of power cables and the droning hum of power supplies, its presence felt in the heat generated by several rows of computer monitors.

From the corner of his eye, What's-his-name caught Hix smearing the snot from his upper lip with his shirtsleeve. Hix's voice always sounded as if his tongue was stuck to the roof of his mouth. To be ensnared in a conversation with him was to be overwhelmed with the damning feeling that one's own head might soon explode.

The world is inhabited by a minority of outcasts who ultimately manage to find one another. Others with whom to circle their wagons together in order to fend off the rest of the world. And in this city, three outcasts who found one another at a party had been circling their wagons together ever since. And no secrets had been kept between them, or so it was thought. The truth came out that afternoon.

One of them just might be smart, at least a little.

Hendricks stood still as a marble column in a museum after one timid step into the room, trying to take in all its mysteries. Hix smeared more drizzle from his lip, caring less and less if anyone should notice. His head twisted this way and that, as if he was searching for something. "So where in the heck is your bed?" he demanded. "It's through those beads," was the easygoing reply, "in the next room over." By this time Hix had built up the courage to begin exploring this strange room, filled to the brim with its books and its strange equipment and its search for answers.

Hendricks stopped dead in his tracks. He found something of interest, his index finger stabbed the air towards a workbench.

"Whassat?"

The quietest of the three, the one who spent most of his waking time with his nose in a book in this room, stepped forward. "Oh," he beamed, "saved up for years to get that one."

Hendricks pressed him for an answer. "So what is it?" Looking at the piece of equipment with its flickering green waves across its dark screen, What's-his-name flipped a switch on the front panel and focused his attention on the printout of results from a recently performed self-calibration. Finally he pried his attention away. He was for some reason, visibly baffled.

"Yeah, it's called an 'oscilloscope,'" he mumbled. "You take readings with it. Peak to peak, frequencies," he said with a dismissive wave of his hand, "stuff like that."

Hendricks looked to the door to find Hix still standing there, a clueless expression on his face, snot still running down his nose. "Peak to wha-?"

"Peak to peak. You see, when-" the quiet one stood for a moment observing Hendricks as he twisted his finger into his ear and gauged his chances of successfully explaining this complicated piece of electronics equipment. In his mind he calculated the odds and came to a conclusion: "Oh, forget it."

"So what's that? Hix said as he stumbled further into the room, his grubby finger extended curiously ahead of him. "With the ones and zeroes?"

What's-his-name joined Hix and Hendricks peering curiously at a single computer screen with its ones and zeroes scrolling relentlessly from left to right.

What's-his-name had no immediate answer. He stood between Hix and Hendricks and shared in their bewildered expressions. The fan above their heads could be heard chopping through the hot, electronically charged air like a wobbling child with a butter knife, flinging thick wads of accumulated dust from its blades to land on a workbench behind them. A gust of air from an air vent sent a dust bunny airborne again and floating towards the opposing wall, over the three friends' backs, landing on one of several computer monitors with ones and zeroes scrolling across their CRT screens. "It's hot as heck in here." Hendricks fanned his face with his hand.

"I know," What's-his-name sputtered. "I need to get these old monitors replaced with LCD screens."

Hix pointed to the computer monitor again. "And the ones and zeroes?"

What's-his-name flicked the dirt from the glass.

"Yeah. Right," he said oddly, "that's a language that all computers talk to one another in. It's called binary language."

Hix took in the snot with his bottom lip. "What's binary language, then?"

"It's the language that computers talk to one another in."

Hendricks spoke up next, almost cutting off What's-his-name in mid-sentence. "So why are they zipping by on the screens like that?"

The tenant of the room scratched his head for a moment. He nibbled at his bottom lip half-expecting that a reasonable explanation might suddenly pop into his mind. In fact he was hoping the elementary questions from his two friends would help him to think even further outside the box.

For weeks he had wrestled with that very question: "Why the

ones and zeroes?"

Again, he flicked another dust bunny from one of the rambling screens.

"But you said those ones and zeroes were-," Hix stopped in mid-sentence. "Can you get 'Star Destroyer' on these things?"

What's-his-name sighed. "I don't play games on these computers." He stood between Hix and Hendricks and felt both of them burning inquisitive holes into both sides of his head.

"I don't know why they're there." His hands gave a slap as they landed desperately at his sides.

"I was lying in bed reading one night and watched through the beads in the doorway just as they popped up on the screen." "There's no reason for them to be up there," he said, "that just shouldn't happen." He looked to his right to find Hendricks looking at him expectantly. He looked to his left to find Hix stripping the wrapper from another Snickers bar. All three found themselves standing silent for several moments, watching the computer monitor scroll its ones and zeroes against a black background.

The only sounds in the room, created by the cooling fans and Hix picking nougat from his teeth.

"OK." Hendricks chimed in. "So you've got some numbers racing across your computer screens," he huffed, "so what's the big deal about that? Can't you just turn 'em off to reset them or something?"

"Like cheating on a video game deck when you're losing?" Hix asked.

Hix's question was indeed a logical and simple one. What's-his-name was impressed that his friends were insightful enough to think of that. He gave Hix a congratulatory pat on the shoulder then wiggled his hand away trying to separate it from the chocolate that had bonded him to his friend's grubby sweater. "That's a good idea," he said, "and I did kill the power just in the off-chance that the RAM could somehow be screwing things up because it simply needed to be cleared out. It didn't work. I fired the computers back up," he said with a broken waver to his voice, "but after a few seconds the numbers came back. Didn't even give the operating system a chance to boot up."

In this room, What's-his-name's demeanor was different. Here, he was in his environment. This was a place where a young man, reduced in title to "What's-his-name" to the rest of the world, spent his time asking vital questions about himself and the universe around him. And then through the advanced use of science and mathematics, would enthusiastically dive head first into the eternal, glorious search for answers. To him, science was art, and art was science. And to search for answers was to hold hands with God.

What's-his-name bent over to pick up Hix's candy wrapper, tossing it into the nearby wastebasket. He flopped his back against the wall, watching to see what Hix would get into next.

Trolling through the contents of the workbench drawers had lost all its appeal to Hendricks, who was now strolling to a nearby bookshelf. He read through the titles on the book spines with a vexed, vertical crease separating his eyebrows. "So," Hendricks spat as he plopped into a leather office chair, spinning, "What do you do with all these books?"

CHAPTER 8

Lorena Gonzalez had lost count of how many rooms she'd cleaned that afternoon. She reached for the soda can sitting beside the disinfectant only to find the near empty rattle of only a few drops. With a sigh that could be heard down the hall, she yanked the tab, stuffing it into her pocket and tossed the empty can into the trash bag at the front of her cart.

"I should be making a hell of a lot more than minimum wage here," she thought to herself. "It *is* the Kansas City Hyatt for Mary's sake." She snatched a brush out of her bucket and hatefully sloshed it around the toilet. Afterwards, glancing down at her cleaning cart, she again read the note left for her by a supervisor:

"Lorena-
Please don't forget to empty the wastebaskets this time.
Thanks, Maria."

Lorena gave a wearied sigh. Feeling depressed, she headed for the over-sized window and opened the curtains hoping the sunlight might lift her spirits. She peered down into the posh shopping district below, wondering to herself how she ended up cleaning up after these people, instead of paying other "Lorena's" to do it for *her.* "I deserve better than this," she moaned to herself, "and my kids deserve better than this." She flung open the windows to let the fresh air fill her half capacity lungs.

Just before she dumped the wastebasket, she glanced down out of habit and eyed a single piece of paper with something scribbled on it.

Ignoring her conscience, she reached in, pulled it out and read it.

"My life is a picture book
Its contents seldom seen
Twisted and torn
Are the pages in between"

The piece of paper had two letters scribbled at the bottom. The initials "SG."

"And I thought I had it bad." She thought.

"Well, he must not be too miserable," she said to herself with a raspy laugh, "he stayed *here* last night." Lorena threw the paper into her trash bag, and went to the next room.

CHAPTER 9

Simon could barely see the Sky Needle through the thick, monsoon-like downpour. Seattle was in the midst of a storm and its huge raindrops soaked you to the bone if you weren't properly prepared.

If you weren't emotionally prepared, the grey sky could drown your soul even faster.

"The Hyatt again?"

"Yeah. The Hyatt." Phil answered without even looking up from the floorboard.

"I think I've forgotten what it was like to make my own bed," Simon moaned to himself. Phil, keeping himself entertained by repeatedly flicking the ashtray open and shut, was about to get on Simon's last nerve.

"Phil."

"Yeah, Simon?"

"You wanna stop flicking that ashtray before I pull your arms off?" Simon snapped his gaze out the limousine's tinted window, and spotted a license plate that read "JOHN."

Turning on the radio, Simon spun through three stations, before settling on a song of his own. "Sixteen years, sixteen tears."

"Funny," Phil laughed, "I thought you didn't like to hear your own songs on the radio anymore. I thought you were sick of hearing your stuff."

Simon responded without turning his attention from the rain on the window. "Guess there's a first time for everything, Phil."

It was obvious that this was going to be another one of those days. Phil shifted his eyes out the opposite window, trying to find patterns from within the beads of storm-tossed raindrops.

The limousine driver hit the button lowering the electric window dividing the front half of the car from the passenger's half. "We're coming up on the Hyatt, gentlemen," he said, "you will find two complimentary umbrellas underneath your seat. Thanks for riding with Royal Limousine Service, and have a great evening."

The driver sounded less than sincere. It was clearly a speech he'd given numerous times. The rain started to pick up, as the limousine came to a stop in the middle of the intersection. The tires squealed as the limo turned left into the parking lot. Simon felt beneath the seats for the umbrellas, dislodging both from underneath as Phil grabbed two leather bags.

The hotel's doorman swung open the car's side door, allowing both Simon and Phil to exit the car. Approaching the large double doors to the hotel, Simon stopped to take in a breath of the moist air. While paused, Phil entered the hotel entrance.

And then Simon felt a tight grip around his ankle.

"Hey buddy, got any change for an old man?"

Simon looked down to find an old black man sitting on a folded up cardboard box. He wore an old, raggedy overcoat and the fingers were cut out of his gloves. His voice croaked. It sounded like cheap wine and broken glass. He smiled, showing Simon his grimy, yellowed teeth. "So what you say, boy?" he said, "spare any change for a poor old fart?" The old bum eyed Simon quickly from head to toe.

"Looks like you could afford it."

Simon grit his teeth, then bent halfway down to the old man. "And do you know why I can afford it?" He hissed, "because I work for a living," then jerked his leg away. Walking back toward the hotel door, he turned back around to see the old bum.

But the old man and his cardboard box were gone.

For a second or two, Simon felt guilty for not helping the stranger.

For a second or two.

CHAPTER 10

Simon tossed and turned in his bed.

The dream began with him reading reviews of his latest CD release.

It would only get worse from there.

"Simon Glenayre should stick with what he knows best: pure, grind it out rock n' roll. His vain attempt at the so-called art rock genre has blown up in his face. My only regret for not having vinyl records anymore is I can't turn "Seize the Day" into an ashtray.

1 ½ Stars out of 5."

-Marlon Heldon, Metal Magazine

"Simon O' Simon...where for art thou?

There was a time when we could put on one of your CDs and forget our problems. Now you're trying to solve them. People don't want their problems solved.

We're Americans. We love our damned problems.

What we hate is being preached to. Do us all a favor and get off your soap box."

-Kim

Sarasota, Florida

"Simon Glenayre is a modern-day Moses.

Our Sonic Messiah, he was sent to deliver us from the evils of predictable corporate pop sin: Rap/techno/comercial/screw-the-world-I-know-two-chords-and-im-playin-'em-till-doomsday-rock n' roll.

His thought-provoking music is an audio tapestry of the human spirit. Someday "Seize the Day" will be thought of as the "Sgt. Pepper" of the New

Millennium."
    4 1/2 out of 5 stars
    -Kurt Green, Rolling Stone

The pages of the magazine squeaked from within Simon's trembling grip. He realized Phil was rubber necking, rolled up the magazine and stuffed it in the velvet pouch on the back of the seat in front of him.

Phil cleared his throat and Simon knew he was about to talk. Phil always cleared his throat when he was nervous about saying something.

"One of them was a good review." Phil cracked an unconvincing smile.

"Two out of three of them sucked, Phil." Simon looked over at Phil who could only clear his throat in response.

"Excuse me," Phil said to the child in the seat in front of him. "Would you mind turning around, please?"

The plump boy in front of Phil stood defiant, leaning against the back of his seat, dangling one arm over the back of his seat and wiggling his other sticky, chocolate-smeared hand at him. His mother had long since given up prying the plastic horn from her little darling's kung-fu grip and had resigned herself to defeat. She sat embarrassed, doing her best to ignore the grumbling of her fellow tour bus passengers about her son while they tried to enjoy the "Tour of Utopia".

"And if you look out the right side of the bus, you will see 'The Great Array' in all of its glory." The tour guide at the front of the bus, dressed all in white with immaculately chiseled blonde hair, smiled through every syllable she spoke. Simon looked out the window to see the stained glass pyramids, all illuminated from within by glowing, amber light.

"So these pyramids, they just showed up one day? Like, outta the blue?" Valletta bounced back and forth.

Simon could feel the rocking motion in his own seat.

"Real stained glass pyramids!"

Simon rubbed at the base of his nose with his thumb and forefinger at Valletta's enthusiastic outburst. "Val," he said, "please, man. That was loud."

The tour bus crept slowly down the avenue, illuminated by amber streetlights. He watched couples stroll in front of a pyramid, it's colored amber glass revealing the image of Moses, his arms uplifted and the Red Sea, parting obediently.

"I have to admit, this is amazing, don't you think?" Phil took a sip from his Perrier bottle and waited for a reaction. "Maybe you could whip out a song about this place, Simon?"

"Yeah Val, I'll just whip out a song about it" Simon mumbled looking out the window. "That's all there is to it."

The tour bus crept down a giant, ornate avenue lined on both sides with brilliant amber streetlights and statues. A modern metropolis, the city had a heavenly feel to it. It looked very modern, and yet something about it felt ancient.

Eternal.

Pyramids lined the surrounding area in astrological order, all glowing with amber light from within, revealing ornate, multi colored stained glass designs. Scenes of David and Goliath. Daniel and the Lion's Den. King David. Other stained glass pyramids revealed the visages of Abraham, Moses, and Jesus Christ at the Crucifixion, The Resurrection and the destruction of Sodom and Gomorrah.

Simon pressed his hand against the glass. "Look at all those people. They're all filing into that pyramid" he said, astonished at the sea of humanity. "They're just piling into it, ten abreast." He heard another voice from another part of the bus, unfamiliar to him.

"By the thousands…"

Simon recalled seeing all the fans at his own concerts. Thousands of people there, just to see him. Suddenly, he felt so unclean. He felt guilty. He couldn't understand why.

"This would be a good photo-op for your interview with the magazine." This got Simon's attention. "Wha?"

"I said this will be good for your upcoming interview with Rolling Stone magazine. Don't you think?" Phil slapped Simon on the leg.

"I suppose." Simon thought for a moment. He watched the children playing beside the bust of Socrates. "But the positive from me being on the cover seems counterbalanced by the fact that it's a negative article." Simon kept his attention out the window. "I think it makes me look ridiculous."

Simon turned to Phil, hoping for a positive response. The reassurance wouldn't arrive. He looked back out the window.

The seats on the bus were comfortable. Other passengers chatted pleasantly amongst themselves, remarking about the beautiful surroundings in this utopian place. Children could be seen playing on golden statues of assorted animals in beautifully ornate parks decorated with finely trimmed shrubs. A little boy, pushing his younger sister on a swing smiled with delight from hearing her giggles. Elderly couples held hands as they strolled down the avenue, enjoying the cool summer breeze. Overhead, steady traffic of colossal stained glass zeppelins circled. Like the pyramids, they were illuminated from within, revealing multi-colored, detailed stained glass renderings of scenes from The Bible. The zeppelins appeared as if they weighed a ton. Yet they floated softly in the air, as if a stiff breeze could fling them away like a feather.

"Aw jeez, Simon. Now ain't that cute?" Valletta said. "Lil' kids playin' in tha park. Doesn't that make ya feel warm n' fuzzy inside?"

"Yeah Val. Warm n' fuzzy." Simon grinned when he saw the children, too.

Lush, multipart harmonies from an unknown source floated through the air. The ethereal voices were audible to those on the bus regardless of where it went.

The tour host continued. Endlessly smiling and pointing out scenic high points with the precision-like posturing of a game show spokesmodel.

"What th' heck was that?"

"What the heck was what?" Simon asked.

Valletta's massive hand pressed against the window for a moment. His breath fogged the window. "Dunno," he said a little concerned. "Probably nothin'."

Simon retrained his attention on the tour guide at the front of the bus. As always, her posture was perfect, her glassy smile, maddening. It seemed her every sentence ended with a squeak. Simon could see an old man stopping to take a drink from a golden water fountain that was shaped like a lion's head. Simon looked away for a moment. Looking back at the fountain, the old man was gone. In the blink of an eye he was *gone*.

"Moves quick for an old guy." Simon kept his thoughts of the old man to himself. Crossing his legs, he sat back in his seat and took a sip from his water bottle. The other passengers chatted pleasantly.

Simon enjoyed this reprieve from the usual. Drunken fans, clamoring to get a lock of his hair. The bikers. The drugs. All of the hangers-on. This was the most relaxation he'd had in a long time. It was a beautiful evening. It was a nice way to spend a night off. Tonight, he felt different. As if anyone could see right through him. And he didn't mind at all.

And yet, in reality as he lay in his bed dreaming, Simon feared the worst. He clenched the sheets between his sweaty fists. He winced in his sleep as the dream continued.

"That's awesome!" Valletta barked. "Giant zeppelins!" Valletta bounced in his seat. Struggling to look out of every window of the bus simultaneously.

"Val, please!" Simon pled. "Quiet down!" Simon heard a whimper coming from Phil. Looking down, Simon realized he was digging his nails into Phil's arm. "I'm so sorry," he explained to Phil. "Val got me a little wound up."

"There it is again." To Simon, the usually unshakeable Valletta sounded nervous.

"What, Val?" Simon turned his head, trying to see Valletta through the crack between the seats. He found it strange that Valletta was bothered by something. Rarely did Simon find Valletta anxious about anything, except when the safety of his friend seemed at risk, or of course when he was running late to breakfast, lunch or dinner.

"I could swear I saw somethin' again."

Phil spun around in his seat facing Valletta: "So what was it?" he barked. "The boogieman?" he laughed. "Now will you please quiet down? You're embarrassing Simon in front of everybody! He doesn't want to stand out in the crowd, remember?" Phil felt the familiar sensation of Simon's nails digging into his arm again. "Alright already, Simon. I shut him up. Now let go of my arm," he plead. "That hurts!" Looking over at Simon he noticed his face was white as a sheet. He settled back down in his chair.

"Are you ok?"

Phil leaned over Simon to get a good view out of his window. Phil saw nothing but an elderly woman stopping at another water fountain. "What was what, Simon? There isn't anything there."

"A-ha! I friggin' told you I saw somethin' out there!"

"Shut up, Val." Phil waved his had dismissively over his head at Valletta.

Valletta turned his face back to the window. He wanted no one to see him pouting.

Simon remained quiet, looking out the window. Valletta's tone of voice turned the corner of a neighborhood it was unaccustomed to: seriousness. "Dunno. It was somethin', it was-

"It was a man in black, Phil."

Phil looked over at Simon who didn't turn his attention from the window. Simon spoke, with his eyes still glued to what was going on outside of the bus. Phil continued: "So what's so crazy about a man in black?" he asked. "We live in LA, remember?

Everyone wears black in LA." Simon took in a deep breath and exhaled.

"I'm not sure, but I have to agree with Valletta," Simon whispered to the window. "Something is going on." The bus rolled to a stop at an intersection. The passengers continued to talk. The tour hostess was still posing, still smiling. Leaning over Simon again, Phil looked outside of the bus to see what struck the others as so odd. The elderly woman who had stopped at the water fountain was gone.

"Well there ain't nobody out there dressed in black now guys, just look. See Val, there's nothing there. Now, will you two please grow up?"

"Yeah? Well look at that, Phil. There's more of 'em now. See?" Valletta urged. Simon sat still in his chair. Silent and as still as a stone on the dark side of the moon. Phil refused to even look out the window again.

"I ain't looking Simon. I ain't looking cause…have you been doing coke again?"

"No! Look Phil! There are men out there running around in black! They're scaring those people."

Again, Phil felt the familiar pain of Simon's fingernails embedded in his arm.

"Simon! That hurts!" As if he had lost control of his muscles, Simon could only manage several twitchy pats upon Phil's forearm. "Shut up Phil! Look!"

Phil could tell from Simon's hiss that he was alarmed, so he leaned over him once more, attempting to see what everyone else was seeing.

The mood outside the bus was now evident to the other passengers. The couples had ceased strolling aimlessly. Some had begun walking at an accelerated, fearful pace. Others stood deathly still as a statue, wearing the hash white expressions of a medieval death mask. Expressions of shock splashed violently across their faces. "What the hell is going on Simon?" Phil looked at Simon, expecting a response, but heard nothing. Simon sat frozen, looking out his window at something. Leaning across Simon's lap, he braced his sweaty hand on the window to keep his balance, trying to get a better view outside the bus as it moved at a crawl down the avenue.

Phil felt the heat bursting from Simon's skin. Slowly, he moved his gaze towards Simon's face and found it frozen in fear. "Simon, you ok? Hey. Simon…you ok?"

Large beads of sweat surfaced on Simon's forehead as the

blood raced through his veins at breakneck speed. Phil looked around the bus to see if he was being watched, then leaned a bit closer to Simon and whispered. "Simon, are you ok?"

"Simon?"

Simon did not look at Phil. Simon did not reply.

Simon could not breathe.

Sitting up on his knees, Phil turned around to face Valletta behind him, whose eyes by this time were glued to the window as well. "Val, what's everybody freaking out about out there?"

"Phil, somethin' ain't right out there," he said concerned. "Those people are scared."

"Look at them Phil, they're really scared of something." Valletta's voice quivered.

Phil leaned over Simon trying to get closer to the window. His nose touched the glass.

The hand struck the window with a solid thud and smeared red down the glass slowly. Screams coursed through the bus as thousands of bodies draped in black now blitzkrieged the streets of this heavenly place like the Black Plague. "Oh my Lord," Valletta yelled. "Simon, people are being attacked out there. People are dyin' Simon! Look!"

Phil could hardly hear himself talk as the passengers on the bus were screaming at ear shredding levels. Phil looked at Simon again, he just sat in his seat, frozen. He was mumbling something.

"I don't have the key."

"Simon-"

"I said I don't have the key." Phil put a hand on Simon's arm. "What key, Simon?"

"Key?"

Outside of the bus, people ran for their lives. The black-draped hordes, their faces hidden behind black masks, swarmed the city like locusts. Simon could see a young couple running as fast as they could, trailed closely by a dozen of the horrible beings. While at a full sprint, the lady made the fatal error of looking over her shoulder, losing her balance. Tripping over her own feet, she struggled to stay upright. Her male companion fought to keep her up, but his own legs became entangled with hers and together they fell to the pavement. Disoriented, they struggled in vain to get to their feet.

It was too late.

The men in black swarmed them like a horde of bees to honey. Falling back to the ground, they both shuffled backwards slowly, pleading for their lives.

The evil beings flung their own bodies on top of the couple. Then as suddenly as it had begun, they were finished.

"Dear Lord."

Simon looked back towards the back of the bus to see the response of the rest of the passengers. He heard it again, but couldn't see who was saying it. The inside of the bus went dark. All he could see was the silhouettes of the others. Another voice from the back of the bus, sounded as if it was from an old man.

"I don't have the key..." Simon muttered.

"What key, Simon?" Phil didn't get an answer.

His usual ability to find reason under any circumstance had by then greatly diminished. Phil plopped back onto his knees in his seat to see Valletta. Valletta sat quietly by now, his eyes shut, whispering to himself.

More screams from outside the bus turned Phil's attention to the window.

The career tour manager in him knew it was time to take over and get them out of this. "Val, we gotta get outta here, Val? Simon, where's Val? He's gone. Simon?"

"I don't have the key..." Simon's trembling voice trailed off.

"Simon, what key?" Simon didn't notice Phil's hands on his shoulder, or that he was being violently shaken.

The bus kept moving forward down the avenue. Simon looked to the front of the bus and could see the silhouette of the driver against the light of the dashboard. Shifting his gaze back out the window, he could see another golden water fountain in the shape of a calf. Yet this calf's mouth was closed, closed with what was formerly a human being crunched tightly within its jaws, hanging lifelessly.

"Simon, where's Val? He's gone Simon."

Phil looked at Simon. "Simon!"

Yet he just sat there, with his hand pressed up against the window.

"I don't have the key."

"Simon, what key? What key?" Phil grabbed Simon's arm and again shook him violently. "Simon what are you talking about? Does it have something to do with what's going on out there? What key Simon?"

The screams and people's movement inside the bus began to take a violent turn. The noise became louder. One could hear the sounds of bodies thumping into bodies.

"What key, Simon?" Simon leapt from his seat and across Phil's lap, elbowing him in his cheek. Phil could still hear Simon saying it, over and over again.

"I don't have the key."

Simon jumped to the other side of the bus and threw a boy out of his way. The boy's screaming mother had to be pulled away next so he could see outside. The bus continued down the avenue at a crawl. Looking ahead of the bus, Simon could make out a lone figure standing by a park bench facing the avenue. As the bus moved toward the park bench, he got a better look at the man standing there. It had the dimensions of an ordinary man, dressed in black, yet he wore no hood like the others. Creeping closer to the bench, Simon realized the man had his eyes locked on the bus, as if it where the very bus he was looking for. Approaching the bus stop, Simon saw the body of a woman sitting lifelessly upright, with her head cocked to its left towards the bus. The details of the man's face became clearer to Simon as the bus drew closer. Simon came to the mortifying realization that the man was looking directly at him the entire time.

"It's him," Simon's voice quivered. "Again."

"It's who?" Phil asked.

It took two tries for Simon to say it. Finally, the words came out.

"It's Whiteface."

The man's face, white as a snow, his eyes gleamed as black as night. There was black, chalky smoke bursting from behind his head as if it were an unholy halo.

The bus passed by the bench. Simon looked at Whiteface.

Whiteface looked at Simon. Directly.

Though he couldn't hear the man's voice, his lips revealed what he was saying. The mocking words that Whiteface said pierced Simon's heart. He grabbed his chest in shame.

"Selfish little Simon," the man hissed. *"Just had to get one more fix."*

And then he smiled showing the blackness seeping from his mouth.

The body, lying lifelessly on the bench, opened its eyes. It looked directly at Simon, its voice echoed throughout the bus for all to hear: "Give us the key, Simon."

Simon felt his body shudder as this happened, falling back onto the center aisle floor. Someone stepped on his leg. He sprung back to his feet, sending another person to the floor with a thud of his shoulder.

"I don't have the key!" Simon screamed. "I don't have the key!"

Simon felt the bus slowing down for the next bus stop. And

the smiling Whiteface was already there, waiting.

Simon looked out the window and saw Whiteface crack a hideous smile. "What are you doing?" he screamed to the driver. "Don't stop!" he plead. "They want to kill us!" Simon screamed hysterically.

"But this is one of my stops. Number 6?" he laughed. "Yep! Sorry sir, but this is one of my stops. It's part of my job driving the ol' bus!"

Simon could hardly see the man's face. The driver turned around and looked at Simon. He was black under his eyes. His face, illuminated from below by the lights on the control panel. He had the smile of a simpleton smeared across his face. As though it were just another careless evening: driving innocent people to their slaughter.

"What are you doing?" Simon plead. "They're gonna kill us! Go! Go! Go!" Simon rushed forward to the front of the bus, reached down and plunged the driver's foot down onto the accelerator. The engine gave a violent roar, reacting to so much fuel while in such a low gear. "Whoa, now buddy," the driver laughed. "*I'm* the bus driver here!"

Simon looked at the driver. He was still smiling. "Don't you see what is happening?" he cried. "People are dying out there! Don't you dare stop or I'll kill you myself!"

The bus driver only turned around, shifted the bus into a higher gear and continued on his way. The screams hit a shrill high as people were flailing in the limited space of the bus, not knowing what to do. Simon could hear Phil in the back of the bus, screaming for the now-vanished Valletta. He could hardly understand what was being said through all of the mayhem.

Valletta was nowhere to be seen.

Simon moved towards the door of the bus. Looking up, Simon looked on in horror as one of the giant stained-glass zeppelins plunged slowly into one of the pyramids with a rumbling crash. Fire burst forth from the behemoth structure while it belched out hundreds of people.

The entire city was covered with dread, as if Hell had mercilessly been unleashed on this place. And still, through all of the screaming from within the bus, Simon could hear those words again and again.

"Give us the key Simon," the voice hissed. *"Give us the key."*

Outside of the bus, another stained glass zeppelin crashed to Earth, a crumbling mass of beautiful, melted glass.

"And if you look to your right, the Great Fountain of Peace

and Love can be seen…"

The tour guide stood at the front of the bus, gesturing and still smiling. Simon wiped the burning sweat from his eyes and told the tour guide to radio for help. Simon looked at the tour guide in shock. "Can't you hear me, you fool?" Simon screamed. "Call for help! We're gonna die! Call for help!" The tour guide continued on: "And here in a few moments, we will see the location of the second Great Crossing, where-"

Hysterical, Simon grabbed her by the arm and threw her to the floor, knocking her little white hat from her perfectly shaped hair. She immediately snapped right back up as if her spine were made of rubber bands.

Stumbling back a few steps, Simon kept his eyes locked on the woman in white. She had taken on a soft glow of amber light all around her, an aura of evil. As she continued her giggly dialogue, she snapped her head to face Simon. She smiled big, and then dropped her arms to her side.

Her face went blank. *"Selfish little Simon. Just had to get one more fix."* She snarled in a voice that screeched across several timeless octaves.

"Give us the key you piece of trash. It's time. Give us the key and you'll only burn for eternity.

"I, I don't have the key!"

The tour guide, in her all white double breasted business suit snarled at him. "Yes, you do! It's ours! Now give it! Give it! Give it!"

Simon fell back onto a seat that an elderly woman was sitting in. She yelped in pain as Simon fell onto her fragile body. He struggled to get to his feet as the tour guide began to spring toward him. The elderly lady continued yelping in pain. Simon regained his footing, and leapt up and away from the woman.

"Give us the key Simon. Give us the key." Her voice warbled and hissed. "We've saved a place for you in Hell. Simon, we've saved a place for you in Hell."

The tour guide came upon the old woman Simon had fallen on and struck her across the face. The guide grinned as the elderly woman yelped in pain.

"Well whaddya know? It's time for another stop! Lookie here," the driver chirped. "Good ol' bus stop number six again!" Simon heard this, stood on his toes while keeping an eye on the tour guide, and yelled over the woman's shoulder to the driver. "Don't stop! They're going to kill us! Do you hear me? Don't stop! Don't you dare stop!" The tour guide gave an evil grin, turned to look at the driver, who in turn looked back at her and smiled his simpleton smile.

She turned back around to Simon and hissed "Give it to us, Simon! Give it to us! the key," she demanded. "Give it!"

Simon could feel the bus grinding to a stop.

The bus doors flung open, and the front of the vehicle immediately filled with the men draped in black, led by Whiteface. Simon watched the thick, black smoke burst around the being as if he were a living volcano of hatred. From the back of the bus, Simon could hear Phil yelling something. He couldn't make it out.

The men in black moved towards Simon, led by the tour guide. "Give us the key Simon, give us the key."

She held out her hand to him.

"Please no. I don't know what you're talking about. I don't have a key. This key you're looking for. I just don't have it" Simon plead. From the back of the bus somebody yelled to Simon: "Just give them the key, buddy! Give it to 'em so they'll go away!" Simon screamed back without taking his eyes off the stewardess. "I don't have the key!"

"I don't have the key!" he screamed at the tour guide.

"Yes you do," she sneered. "And we're going to carve you up until you give it to us, Simon. We're going to carve you up." Simon crammed his hand deep into his pants pocket, producing a heavily populated key ring. Shaking violently, he scrambled through the jangling keys looking for something, anything that would satisfy these things. "I, I...I don't have anything you're looking for. J-just my house keys, my car keys.

Looking up from his key ring, he saw the tour guide suddenly lunge toward him, with a large knife in hand. Her eyes ablaze, she slashed at his throat.

And then there was darkness.

Simon awoke screaming on the floor beside his bed, with blood on his lip and alarmed police pounding upon his door.

CHAPTER 11

If you were to take the autobahn thirty five kilometers south of Frankfurt and then just a few more minutes down a much smaller road, you would find it there.

And at that place, the red ceramic rooftops reach up and shake hands with the heavens.

Little cobblestone streets wind between old stucco houses like string tossed in the air, and left to land where they may. It's a place where the sidewalks are swept daily by small, elderly ladies. The loudest sound is of laughter from playing children, the conversation of couples on an evening stroll or the gossip of old women dancing on the morning air. Beuern as it is called, sits tucked away in a small secluded valley in the German state of Hessen. The village seems hidden, as if God in his infinite wisdom wanted this creation of his to be sheltered from the swift winds of change. This is not a place to rush about and merely survive. It is a place where you sip the fine wine of life. And savor it to its smooth finish. Here is fertile breeding ground for Hope.

And this is why it is hated most terribly.

For in another place, one hundred and eighty degrees in another direction, a thick swirling blackness splashes in upon itself in an angry dance of eternal hatred over and over again.

Black, putrid smoke encircles all traces of hope here and strangles it to its last desperate breath. Distant rumblings can be heard as an audible backdrop to the cries of those so countless in despair as they cry aloud for an end that will never come. Those who inhabit this place stand no chance of ever walking along peaceful cobblestone streets. The occasional bright flash reveals their faces, laying frozen in an eternity of torment.

As you are pulled reluctantly and ultimately closer to this place, you will come to a giant, black iron gate. Upon this gate are words wrought of twisted black metal. The mocking phrase is illuminated from the distant fires on its other side.

They can be read as one is drawn reluctantly but ultimately closer:

"TO ALL WHO ENTER HERE, ABANDON ALL HOPE."

This is Hell. And it is here that a place has been prepared for Simon Glenayre.

CHAPTER 12

10101111100011101001111001010111110001110100111100.

What's-his-name sighed while prying himself from his computer chair. It was time for another soda. He could always think better with a drink in his hand. Stepping over cables and books, he emerged from the bedroom into a long hallway. The light at the end of the hallway shone in from a large window in the foyer. The window looked out onto a large, well-manicured lawn, bordered by a stone garden wall. Passing through the living room, he walked by several oil paintings set in their bulky gold leaf frames.

The tables were made of green marble. They had bruised his knees more than once over the years.

At the center of the kitchen sat a breakfast island. Above it hung a heavy wrought iron ring with several stainless steel pots and pans. What's-his-name opened and closed several of the upper cabinets until he found the one containing glasses. Grabbing the nearest glass, he slammed the cabinet shut and shuffled over to the stainless steel refrigerator set into the wall. The fridge spat crushed ice into his glass from a hole in the door. He opened one of the side doors and grabbed a cola.

"What in the heck is going on?"

He rubbed his eyes, and sat on a stool at the island, staring blankly at the marble pattern set into its top. He was tired as could be, and his greasy unwashed hair hung over his stale two day old t-shirt. All his efforts the night before had proved fruitless. He sat and yawned occasionally and never lost the puzzled look on his face. No matter what he did, he couldn't get the ones and zeroes off of his computer screens. He searched furiously for virus updates on the internet, only to come up empty handed.

Berkley, he thought to himself. This had to come from somebody really good at Berkley. What's-his-name hopped off the stool and began another search around the kitchen cabinets. Soon he found the cabinet with bread in it, as well as a jar of peanut butter. On the inside of a cabinet door, he found a marker board with the family maid's schedule scribbled on it.

"Mon-Fri: Cathy/7am-7pm

Sat: Cathy/Off

Sun: Cathy/Off

What's-his-name looked down at his watch, pressed the button on the side to switch the readout from the calculator to the calendar. Today was Sunday. What's-his-name realized he'd been working on this thing for days.

His 'Twin Towers' weren't even playing chess against one another anymore. They were stand alone computers for that matter. How could two stand alone computers, constructed of new parts and having never even *sniffed* the internet, be infected with a virus? The only answer available was that it simply wasn't a virus at all. Between those two computers and his other four that had also started flashing ones and zeroes, What's-his-name was left with only one working computer: a laptop. He opened up the jar of peanut butter then took out two slices of bread and tore the thick brown paste across the bread as he thought to himself.

"No virus updates and it isn't a joke program."

He stuffed the bread back into the wrong cabinet without the twist tie, and flopped down on the stool again.

The computers sat there in the room at the end of the hall mocking him with their ones and zeroes.

1010111110001110100111100101011110001110100111100.

"That shouldn't happen."

In a desperate attempt at fixing the problem, he built a new computer out of new parts. He loaded the operating system, ultimately booting to the main screen. He held his breath. He wanted to get to bed. But he couldn't let this beat him. The hard drive made faint grinding noises. The screen flickered.

The tower beeped.

Beautiful. It worked.

When he sat back in his computer chair with his hands clasped triumphantly behind his head, it happened.

1010111110001110100111100101011110001110100111100.

"No!"

As he sat there on the stool in the kitchen and thought about it, he couldn't help but to shake his head and laugh. The fix he worked for all night long lasted a whopping fifteen seconds. And now for all his efforts the night before, he was left with little more than one peanut butter sandwich, and still no automated chess.

And to make matters worse, he discovered they were unplugged. And they still worked.

They still worked. Somehow, even though they had no source of power, they continued to run the binary ones and zeroes across the screen.

He slapped the sandwich onto the countertop then picked it up, forcing himself to finish it.

All the years he'd spent in pursuit of knowledge did What's-his-name no good. All that was left on the plate were a few crumbs. He was tired. At this point, he almost didn't care anymore. Moving back down the dark hall, he slipped back into his bedroom and shut the door with his foot. As he leaned back against a wall, the ones and zeroes from the computer screens flashed across his face in the dark room.

CHAPTER 13

Simon's voice crept across the living room, through the doorway and into the kitchen.

Bailey Eden Piper sat on a bar stool, spinning a stainless steel bowl on the counter top, whipping its contents together with a wooden spoon.

Her stirring soon lost its pleasant, buoyant rhythm when she heard his voice.

Bailey recognized his distinct syntax and melodic tonality and in a moment of hopeful insanity found herself believing he was with her in the house. The wooden spoon smacked the floor, sending brownie mix splattering across the tile. She leapt off the stool and to the window connecting the kitchen to the living room.

The living room was dark now, save for the blue light from the television. In the flickering screen she saw a face she knew and loved from years past.

The flash bulbs made Simon wince and he snapped his head away from the flash of the cameras over and over again. She heard his name being called out while he made his way down the red carpet in the footage broadcast on the cable show, Star Gazer.

"Simon," a photographer yelled, "what do you think of your chances tonight?"

Simon smirked from the corner of his mouth, the best he could muster under the uncomfortable circumstances, thought Bailey. He never liked being in the center of a crowd and Bailey knew it. She observed the woman with wavy red hair clinging to his arm and whispering into his ear. Simon glared down to her and groaned an answer. "You can never tell…I think I have a chance."

"And how about all these people, all the excitement?" another reporter yelled. "How does it feel, Simon?"

Bailey watched. The woman with red hair tugged again at Simon's collar, yanking him down to her. She whispered something into his ear and this time he jerked away, visibly irritated. Simon glared at the horde of paparazzi for a moment and looked up to the stars, almost as if the stars above were an escape route.

"How does it feel?" Simon asked. "How does it feel? It feels like the end of the world," he said.

She'd seen Simon unhappy before. But not like this. He not only looked unhappy, he looked hopeless.

Bailey never held any hatred in her heart for Simon. Yes, as far as she understood, he'd sacrificed their love upon the altar of fame and addiction. But for Bailey forgiveness came with every breath. She couldn't help it.

It was just her nature.

By now she lost her sweet tooth. She found herself worried sick about this man who years ago had broken her heart. And still, forgiveness with every breath. Simon needed her. Quite simply, Simon had never reached out to her because it was never in his nature to do so. His passive, always face inward mentality kept him from reaching out for Bailey. It kept him from reaching out for help of any kind.

The stainless steel bowl and its contents found itself tossed into the sink. Bailey snatched her purse from the breakfast table. Her hand scrambled the contents of the bag in a mad search for a cell phone. Held in the cell phone's memory, an old number. It was a way to reach Simon in case of emergencies, given to her years ago during his first tour.

It was a long shot: Bailey suspected his number had changed hands numerous times over the years. But maybe this one phone number could lead to someone who knew of another phone number who might know of another phone number…

A silly thing to try, she thought to herself. It would take a hundred phone calls to a hundred different managers, publicists, record company people and personal assistants before she even had a *chance* of reaching him. And yet, as she leaned against the counter-top looking at the small cell phone in the palm of her hand, Bailey thought of something Simon said to her years ago.

Rocky Mountain National Park, Colorado.

They snuck off together that week, on a whim. Together, two fingers stopping a spinning globe determined their destination. Bailey laughed, thinking of Simon and herself laughing together.

The globe could have stopped on Siberia. Lucky for them, their fingers landed on Colorado.

And it was there they walked along a stream against a mountain backdrop. She recalled the sound of bees buzzing in the near distance. She remembered watching dragon flies dancing around the nearby flowers. They held hands and talked. Bailey and Simon discussed life's possibilities. They shared their hopes and dreams. She talked about her lifelong fascination with Native American history. Simon talked about his music. His voice still rang in her ears like the drone string of a mountain dulcimer. He told her he could do anything if he put his mind to it, including getting her to fall in love with him.

She laughed when she thought about what he did next: Simon pointed to a mountain off in the distance. Next, from the running stream he plucked a small stone, polished smooth from years of water rushing across its surface. Rubbing the stone with his thumb, he stated the impossible. He told Bailey he could throw the stone over the mountain.

Bailey laughed at him and he stood laughing right along with her, tossing the stone from one hand to the other, smiling. "Oh yeah?" giggled Bailey. "And just how do you think you can toss *that* stone all the way over *that* mountain?" She walked her fingers up his chest and flicked his chin flirtatiously with her finger.

"Simple" Simon smiled. "I'll throw it as hard as I can. And sure, it'll land far short of that mountain. But I'll just keep picking it up. And I'll just keep throwing it" he said. "And I'll get this stone over that mountain."

"...*No matter how many throws it takes*."

Bailey recalled Simon looking down at the stone in his hand, watching him smear the last of the creek mud from it and smiling.

"But I don't think we should throw this one anywhere." Simon took Bailey by the hand, placed the stone in her palm and gently folded her fingers over it.

"Some things" he whispered, "just aren't meant to be thrown away." Bailey opened her hand to find an arrowhead.

And at that moment she fell hopelessly in love with him.

Yes, Bailey knew she had a long journey ahead to locate Simon. There would be many slammed doors. There would be many unreturned messages. He might not even want to see her at all. But she had to try.

Tonight, she would pick up the stone and make her first throw.

CHAPTER 14

The figure sat in a shadowy corner of the conference room. The room occupied a corner of the building owned by Simon Glenayre's record company.

The figure sitting in that dark corner kept so silent, no one noticed she was there. The figure absorbed every spoken syllable. Whenever the man at the far end of the long conference table leaned forward, he would stab the air with his cigar to drive home an important point. It was when he did that, her pulse increased at an insane, lusty pace. Her heart leapt into her throat.

And then she would smile.

And those two fumbling idiots.

She knew they wouldn't last long here. Their type never did. They lacked the vital ingredients to survive in the company. Pride, envy, gluttony, lust, wrath, sloth.

And greed.

She looked over to her right, towards the door. The doorknob still glistened from their sweaty hands. She thought about how pathetic they looked as they fumbled around for their dropped papers. The ridiculous expressions on their faces. The chair incident meant that they were out of "The Loop" for good. And she knew it. She would end up being the one to fire them on Sol's orders. How Sol enjoyed his little torments.

She flicked her fingernails and smirked, "The losers."

Earlier, when the meeting began to take on a quieter, but more intense tone, Sol ordered the track lighting dimmed and the blinds on the windows completely closed. The faint glow from the lights illuminated Sol's cigar smoke, which spread around the room like the Black Plague. She knew he wanted the room darker just to add to his already sinister image. No one dared to cough from his cigar smoke and several struggled to suppress the urge. They did not want to bring attention to themselves. They did not want to appear weak. Like Stalin, Sol ruled his world with fear. And he had to keep up his image. There he sat, leaning back in his chair. He never looked at his employees. He glared at them. She half expected him to don a pair of plastic fangs and a black cape, perhaps even fly around the room.

The talk continued, as the evil spoken monotones slithered down the table, and along the carpeted floor towards her ever attentive ears. He stabbed the air with his cigar again. And again, her pulse raced. Again, she smiled. She knew when Sol did that he was talking about something dear to her heart. Something she would ultimately gain. And no one was going to take it away from her. The shadowy figure watched all the people at the long table lean forward whenever he did. Then, when he sat back in his chair, they all sat back in their chairs. She was set. What did she have to worry about? Someday she would end up owning this company. She just knew it. Who could stand in her way? Certainly not Noah. Sol hated his own son. He was just another little "yes" man. Just like the rest of them. And what had he accomplished lately?

The little jerk wasn't even a factor anymore.

She quietly shifted in her seat, uncrossed her long legs, and crossed them the other way. Her leg bounced lightly over the other as she hung her stiletto-heeled shoe off the tip of her toes. Watching it bounce around, she could not help but to smile again. The occasional flash from a crystal glass glistened off her painted, red lips.

She continued watching the nobody's jockey for attention. Some would tentatively raise their hand with a question or a meek little comment. And then they would sit there in their sweaty chairs and scan Sol's face for a reaction. And if it went well, they wouldn't lose their jobs.

Could it possibly get any easier?

It wasn't always like this. She didn't always have control. If she only knew back then what she knows now. All the sex on uncomfortable office desks. She remembers how she hated the way the leather of the sofas stuck to her backside. But it all changed for her when she met *him*. As his success increased, so did her status at the company. And so did her power. And now here she was. Sitting in the mighty "War Room" with *the* Sol

Glenn. Listening to every word as if it were her God-given right to do so. She was the J. Edgar Hoover of the company. She did whatever in the hell she wanted. Nobody said anything without her knowing about it. She had more recorded phone calls than Nixon. She spent her life grabbing the jugular of this industry and squeezing it for all she was worth. And there was no way she was going to let go of it. And to think that she was just a delivery girl.

And for that delivery, she had power.

The underlings leaned forward and then back into their seats again…

She knew she had Sol all zipped up in her leather Gucci bag. She could do whatever she wanted. She had power. She had looks. She had the hunger.

"Track 'em, bag 'em, hand 'em over to Sol…"

A man sitting at the corner of the conference table closest to the woman turned his head, his eyes wandering back in her general direction. He then noticed her sitting there silently in the shadowy corner of the room and smiled to her. His left eyebrow rose in a flirtatious gesture to the woman whom he could hardly see. All that his eyes could make out were the edge of a short, black skirt with two long shapely legs emerging crossed. He could make out the very faint outline of a woman's business suit top, half unbuttoned to reveal ample cleavage. Yet, he could not see her face. The man at the corner of the table watched as a slender hand slowly emerged from within the shadows, revealing bright red fingernail polish. The hand slid in a slow, caressing fashion down the thigh, towards the knee. The man smiled at her again. As the hand reached the knee, it clenched into a fist, the index finger slowly began to rise. He watched as the finger began twirling, gesturing at him to turn back around.

The man shuddered in his chair and averted his eyes.

He then immediately turned back around in his chair and never looked back again.

The figure continued with her thoughts. Watching constantly. Listening.

Learning.

She knew Sol was saying something heavy. He leaned forward again in his big, leather chair. All of the underlings leaned forward again, too.

He stabbed the air with his cigar.

Again, she smiled. She breathed in deeply. So deeply, it further opened her blouse. She did not care. She knew what worked on men. Except this time, she knew how to use it to her advantage. By now she was far more selective of her targets.

She wondered, what would be the compensation for her services? For doing Sol's "Deed." A percentage? A huge lump sum? Part ownership in the company?

Screw that, I'll be my own millionaire someday, *regardless* she thought to herself.

I'm giving them *Simon.*

CHAPTER 15

Again, the phone rang.

Simon was lying on top of the blankets of the bed looking up at the ceiling. As the phone rang again, Simon rolled over and knocked the phone off the hook bouncing onto the floor. Now lying there on his stomach, his arms were folded across his chest. Not a single thing worthwhile was on television, just more reality shows.

Simon rolled again onto his side and swung his legs over the edge of the bed. Leaning back on his elbows, he scanned the room. It looked the same as the other one hundred sixty three rooms he had stayed in so far this year. Before he got up off of the bed, he leaned down to pick up the phone and put it back on the hook. As he looked out the window, he could see that the rain was still pouring down. Gazing down to the street, Simon could see the main doors to the hotel below. He caught himself looking for the old bum that grabbed his leg earlier. There was a collection of homeless men milling around aimlessly out there, but not a sign of the old black man. He was gone so suddenly. If Simon had some change, maybe he would have given it to the old man. It was a bad time for anyone to grab Simon's leg, and a bad time to be making demands at him. Phil was working his old magic again, needling Simon to the point of a furious outburst. Yeah, that old man, Simon thought. He was gone so suddenly.

The fridge was located beneath the ornately carved wooden cabinet that also housed the television set. Simon opened it to see if his demands were met. At each hotel, there was always a list of food and drink specific to Simon's needs. If this list was not met by the time he arrived at any given hotel, there would be hell to pay. Phil always saw to that. He scanned the shelves of the fridge. A bottle of merlot, a bottle of vodka, box of snack cakes.

Perfect.

Few hotels failed to meet his requirements.

Simon grabbed the bottle of vodka and made for the couch by the large window. Beside the table sat another phone. Simon eyed the label on the bottle, looking at the year it was made. Good week he thought to himself as he began to unwrap the foil around the top, unscrewed the lid and took a drink from the bottle. The phone began to ring suddenly. "Damnit! Isn't there ever any quiet?" The cord became separated from the wall with a sudden jerk, giving Simon a few seconds of peace. The phone by the bed picked up where the phone by the couch had left off. Ringing endlessly.

Jumping off of the couch, Simon sprang on the phone like a demon possessed. The phone was ripped from the wall and sent crashing through the hotel room window. It could be heard hitting the street below; as could the screeches of the car it narrowly missed. Simon found himself lying on the floor in a fetal position, trying not to let anyone in the surrounding rooms hear him cry. How had he come this far? Why was it that no matter which way he turned, it was the wrong way? Why was it that regardless of what changes he tried to make in his life, no positive results were seen? Why did he feel guilty all the time?

Simon lay there on the floor, the phone next to him, quiet.

Simon could smell the carpet, his face buried in its shag. "Is all of this worth it? Would anybody notice if I was even gone? Would anyone care?" There was always a gun, but he would not want to be found like that, that was too messy. He could surely find enough downers in Chloe's purse to drop an elephant, but she was back in L.A. Suddenly a voice whispered through the room.

"A rope, Simon!" the voice urged. "That should do it! Get a rope!"

Simon sprung up, looking around the room. A body to put to the voice could not be found. Again, the voice sounded. "The rope Simon! You can find one in the janitor's closet, just down the hall!" The voice sounded kind, yet excited like the voice of an old childhood friend. "Anything is better than this Simon. They don't really care about you! Now's the time to get them good! Get the rope! They wouldn't know what to do with themselves. Get the rope! That will show them! Get the rope! It's in the janitor's closet!"

Simon got up from the floor and made his way to the door. Wiping the tears from his red face, he grabbed a Kleenex from his nightstand and blew his nose. He looked down at the Kleenex and saw his hand shaking violently. Still the voice persisted. "It's in the closet!"

"Yeah, that's right. They don't love me anyway. I'm just a meal ticket. They would just move on to the next big thing. I'll show them. They'll be in fricking shock for the rest of their lives." Simon thought about how he was too tired to be awake, and too tired to be asleep. He thought about how he never fit in his whole life, and how if it had not been for his songs, nobody would have ever given him the time of day anyway. At his core, Simon felt like a bum himself. Surrounded by wealth and possessions, he still felt empty and alone. If this wasn't the good life, then there was no such thing to begin with.

"Yeah, Simon. It's in the janitor's closet," the voice laughed. "Just down the hall."

The maid down the hall was whistling an old rhythm and blues tune to herself as she pushed the towel cart down the hallway. The middle aged woman in her mid-fifties whistled as though she had not a care in the world. "Two thirty-six, two thirty-eight...all done on this side." She stopped whistling briefly to break out a clipboard from her cart and check her next assignments. "Shoot!" she wailed. "The Governor's Suite! That'll take me forever!" The maid dug out a pack of Juicy Fruit from her apron pocket, and proceeded to unwrap it.

A creak sounded from behind her, over by the janitor's closet, a couple of doors down. She spun around to find the janitor's closet door just closing. She walked over to see who was on duty that night. "Jimmy!" She knocked again. "Yo, Jimmy! You in there?" She grabbed the warm doorknob and gave it a twist. Opening it slowly, she peeked around the corner. There was a mop in a mop bucket and cleaning supplies tossed in an open box. A girly calendar hung on the wall, next to an empty hook that just moments ago, held a rope. But there was no Jimmy. She dragged out a large key ring and locked the door after she closed it and went on her way. She wondered why the usually dependable Jimmy left the janitor's closet unlocked this time.

In his room, Simon looked through the peephole in his door, and across the hall he saw the maid walk through the two large double doors and into the Governor's Suite. The two doors closed.

Again, he could hear the voice. It sounded like it cared for him so much. Like suicide was the best thing for him. The voice just wanted his suffering to end. He deserved a break from this hell. He had given his love to the world. And how had it repaid him? The voice sounded so kind, as though it really wanted what was best for Simon. It loved him. It gave him warmth. It was just time to go now. Give himself, and everybody else, a badly needed permanent break. Maybe it wasn't Them. This voice cared. Maybe it was his own inner voice, showing him the truth that he could not see through the haze of his own suffering. He wondered to himself if it was God. He looked out the window, it was raining still. What would they write about him? Would his death picture be all over the Internet? He figured his songs would receive a great deal of airplay afterwards. At least Chloe would get a steady income for the rest of her life. He never trusted her, but perhaps he was wrong about her lately. Perhaps he owed her an apology. The thought of his parents flashed through his mind. He thought about his father, and how larger than life he was. He thought about his mother, and the poem she always had taped to the fridge. Valletta would be so hard on himself for not being there to stop him.

Simon thought about how he'd felt so alone all these years, and how it had all come to a head these last few months. How wonderful it would have been to have a daughter of his very own. And the girl, from years past. She had the prettiest voice, silky blonde hair. They used to look in each other's eyes all night long. They would sit up forever, just to watch the sun rise together. "I'm so alone..." he thought.

Simon looked around the room; it looked so gray and so desolate. The room, covered in a thick blanket of hopelessness.

With a couple of good, solid tugs, the pole in the closet proved to be strong enough to hold his weight. Simon tied the rope in a double-knot to ensure that it did not come loose. The glass of merlot sat a couple of feet off; he reached around the corner of the closet for it. He took a sip and then dropped the glass. The fine lead crystal shattered upon the carpet. The light red wine stain spread slowly through the carpet fibers.

He took off his shirt and threw it on the bed. He took off his watch and put it on the nightstand where the wineglass previously sat. His wedding ring was placed next to it.

Simon dropped to one knee and for a moment, almost prayed for help, but rose speechless. No prayers escaped his lips.

Rising up, he slipped into the closet and closed the door. "Sometimes I wonder/ If my tomorrow will ever come/ Show me where to look/ Show me where to look…"

"Now damn! That song has been goin' through my head all day!" The maid several doors down the hall agreed. "Yeah, you got that right. You been singin' that song all day!"

"Shut up, Cheryl. Don't you like it?"

"Well not after hearin' you sing it since seven this mornin'!"

Glenda had just finished The Governor's Suite, when she had popped out between the two large doors and closed them with a solid thud, when she heard a second immediate thud from the room across the hall. "Well, what in th' world was that?" She wiped her hands on a clean towel, and then stuffed the feather duster into her belt. Her large pink house slippers swished as they moved across the carpet fibers to Simon's door. Still curious of the source of the unexplained thud, she kept singing the old song as she knocked on the door.

"Sometimes I wonder/ If my tomorrow will ever come/ Show me where to look/ Show me where to look…"

She knocked on the door again.

Still nothing.

Then from inside, another thump. And yet, for reasons she did not understand, she kept singing that old song to herself.

"Show me where to look…"

She knocked again.

Silence.

"Humph." She interpreted the silence as the symptoms of a rude guest. She stood there at the door, hand at her hip, tapping her house slipper on the rug.

Glenda spun around towards her cart, and digging around in the drawer, she pulled out her master key ring. Making her way back towards the door, she knocked just one more time.

Silence.

"Well, ok then. You wanna be that way about it…" Glenda fully expected to find somebody fallen in the bathtub or passed out on the floor.

She stuck the key into the door.

She turned the knob.

"Hello?" she said aloud.

Silence.

"Hello?" She was louder.

Nothing.

Glenda jumped back and out of her slippers as the door jerked open, its door knob flying out of her hands. The man at the door was shirtless, his face beet red. It was obvious to her that he had been crying. And yet, there he stood, now laughing. It looked like he was laughing at her. In her sudden shock, Glenda had jumped back and landed in a Kung Fu-like fighting stance, feather duster held in the stab position ready to attack at the slightest sign of aggressive behavior from the stranger.

Sensing the man meant her no harm, she eased her grip, and her fighting stance.

"You think it's funny scaring an old woman like that?" she yelled. "You could have given me a heart attack!" She stood there patting at her more than ample chest, showing Simon where her heart was. Her other hand was still holding the feather duster up, as if at any moment she would dust him to death with it.

The man at the door continued to laugh. "So what's so funny, man? You got drugs in there? Cause if you do," she commanded, "we gonna kick you out. And it don' matter who you are! Now don't you have drugs in there!"

The man at the door finally managed to say something. "You know that song?" Glenda took a step back. "Well hell yeah I know that song! Sam Cooke, Greatest Hits album!"

"Yeah, Sam Cooke, Greatest Hits…" The man wiped the drizzle from his nose, and snapped Glenda into a monster bear hug and a huge kiss.

"Hey now! Hey now! What do you think you're doin'? Just what do you think you're doin'?" Simon continued to laugh. "You hear me? I'm old enough to be your mother!" she waved her feather duster at Simon. "Don't you think we do that around here!" She doubled up her fist and struck Simon across the face with a solid crack, and then turned on her heels and whizzed down the hall with her cart.

Simon could hear her, still yelling at him from down the hall.

"I'm old enough to be your momma, boy!"

Simon laughed again and shut the door.

He soon found himself back at the window, looking out towards the city skyline and the clouds just as they were beginning to surrender to the sun.

In the last moments of that morning, the clouds finally decided to break, revealing dancing colors filtered through a silver lining. The lush shades of gold and purple flooded into the room, splashing bright colors across the walls and reflecting in Simon's eyes. He could have sworn he saw that old bum looking directly up at him as he glanced down from the sky.

But just a blink later, he was gone. Maybe he was not there in the first place.

And maybe he was.

Simon made his way to a duffle bag. Rummaging through its contents, he produced a single bottle, saved for just this special occasion: another day of survival.

He's smuggled the alcohol illegally across several state lines, it being his favorite wine, it was worth the risk.

After allowing only a few moments for the opened bottle to breathe, Simon poured Montserrat Winery's Tramonto into a plastic cup and sat looking out the window, humming old folk songs till he fell asleep.

And in Seattle, there is a hotel where it is said, Simon Glenayre once slept. And outside of this hotel by the employee's entrance, an old homeless man was heard singing.

CHAPTER 16

The sun finally decided to make its grand reappearance. Valletta sat there at the counter of the diner, his back turned to the cook, looking at the people shuffle by on the sidewalk. He saw the bright colors filtering through the clouds, falling down to Earth. The usual clatter of silverware, as well as the constant chatter of customers, came to an abrupt halt as the colors from the sky filtered in through the large plate glass windows. Looking around the diner Valletta watched as everyone around him stopped in their tracks to take in the beauty shining down from the sky. This made him think about his own father. It had seemed like years since they had spoken, and yet in reality it had only been this morning. He loved him very much, but his father *was* a little intimidating in person. Valletta fixed his gaze yet again towards the east. That was Simon's direction. The direction of the Hyatt. As Simon flashed through his mind, he closed his eyes and hoped for the best. He had boundaries set for him he had to observe. Valletta spun back around on his barstool and took another bite out of his fried egg sandwich. The grease drizzled between his bratwurst sized fingers.

The scent of fresh brewed coffee found its way to Valletta's cavernous nostrils. Having downed the second half of his sandwich he raised his hand to get the waitress' attention. The waitress was at the tail end of one hell of a long day. Her pink top was stained by twelve hour's worth of grease: Bacon grease, grease from double cheeseburgers, and coffee stains. Her little white hat sat skewed atop her long stringy hair. A pencil poked out from behind her right ear. As she sprinted along the counter, a large hand thrust itself within her centrifugal vision. Valletta had her attention.

As she spun around, the bags under her eyes made themselves evident to Valletta. "What can I get you, sweetheart?"

Valletta grinned. "Well how about a cup uh' that coffee what smells so good?"

The waitress smiled then spun around on her heels and grabbed the fresh pot of coffee. "So where are you from?" she asked. "I don't think I've seen you around here before, honey."

The large Italian at the other side of the counter gave a broad smile and popped open a creamer. "I'm from everywhere" Valletta muttered. "I travel around most of the time."

Smiling, the waitress leaned against the counter top on her elbows. "Well the reason I asked was that you look pretty darned familiar." Valletta didn't say anything. He just smiled and took a sip of his coffee.

"Jenny! Get your butt over here! "The old man's loud drawl turned heads, Valletta's included.

The waitress' expression plunged south of irate as she turned around. Upon fixing her sights on the source of the outburst, she laughed. "Well I'll be darned," she laughed. Valletta hardly acknowledged the outburst. "What are you doin' here, daddy?" she sang out. "I thought you'd be somewhere between L.A. and Phoenix?"

The old man from the booth laughed and hopped up to greet his daughter. The stainless steel panel on the wall gave off the reflection of the father and daughter embracing. Valletta heard what the man said to his daughter, sincere comment of affection, shared by a rough man as best as he could communicate: "Goodness child, you look just like your mother."

Valletta did not turn around. The waitress' father took the stool right next to Valletta, who by this time had pulled the collar up on his jacket in an effort to disappear. The man tried to start up a conversation, of which Valletta hardly seemed open to.

"So c'mon!" he urged. "What's yer name? I think I have the right to know who is talkin' to my daughter!" The stranger's breath reeked of fast food and booze, he had a red snakeskin neck. The man's tone of voice was playful, anxious to make a new friend. Valletta reluctantly gave him a reply. The man smelled of oil and sweat.

"Just not too talkative, that's all."

The waitress leaned against the tall countertop, chin resting on her palm. The veteran waitress constantly monitored the cups of coffee between the two men.

The waitress' father continued on with his questioning of Valletta. "I travel around a lot. No, not a salesman, you could kinda call me a bodyguard. Valletta kept his eyes from view of the stranger.

The old truck driver's eyes looked at Valletta expectantly. Then with a sudden sniff he turned his total attention to his daughter. Valletta noticed the man's present conversation played a distant second to what was really on his mind. The man knew he recognized Valletta from somewhere, but he could not recall from where, no matter how hard he tried. Valletta meekly rapped his coffee cup on the countertop at the waitress without saying a word. The waitress abruptly stopped in mid sentence to answer the summons.

"So, does that mean you want another cup of coffee, honey?" The waitress put a hand on her hip and cocked her head to the side.

"Yeah, please" Valletta mumbled. "Sorry about that."

The waitress twisted on one heel and grabbed the coffee pot. The metal lip of the coffee pot gently clanked against the glass of his cup. Though he did not look directly at her, he could still see the gleam of her large white toothy smile. He returned with a grin, still unable to look at her in the face. Valletta also noticed the smile disappear from her face due to his suddenly rude inward behavior.

He could still feel her father sitting there. Staring at the side of his head.

"Y'know, I just know I know you. You drive a truck?"

"No, I don't drive no truck." The Brooklyn accent was more pronounced more now than ever. "You wouldn't happen to be from Kansas City would you? You just look so darned familiar to me." Valletta's voice took on a faint tinge of irritability. "No," Valletta lied, "I ain't ever been to Kansas City."

"Y'know, I ran loads of beef out of Kansas City years ago and met a guy that looked just like you." He rubbed the deep wrinkles of his old, weathered forehead with his filthy hand. His voice softened: "But hell son, that must've been nearly forty years ago." The man sat there as his daughter scanned the diner for someone in need of a refill or perhaps another plate of greasy fries or a slice of day old apple pie. And still, her father sat there looking at the side of Valletta's head. Puzzled. It seems he ran into him in the late sixties or early seventies.

He just knew it.

He knew Valletta from somewhere, and he never forgot a

face. Never. But this man was too young to be the same trucker from so many years back. Didn't look no older than the kid he had riding shotgun on this trip. And the kid he gave the lift to was no older than thirty-five years old, max. He saw the Italian glance at him out of the corner of his eye. The old man slowly shifted his gaze forward, trying not to look too obvious in doing so. But he could still see their reflections in the grease smudged stainless steel wall behind the counter.

"Well you just wait a minute! I'm on my way!" The old trucker looked up at his daughter and watched her grab the coffee pot and slip around the counter top, sprinting with a laugh towards the laughs and the four coffee cups outstretched from a distant booth. The colors coming in through the large plate glass windows were too much for the old trucker to ignore. He had seen plenty of beautiful sunsets in his long lifetime on the highways. Nevada, Arizona, California. Quite a few nice ones back East. But none of them could hold a candle to this one. As a crumpled pack of cigarettes found their way out of his dirty flannel jacket, he spun around to make one last attempt at friendly conversation.

But the large man, and his secrets, were gone.

CHAPTER 17

He woke seeing only white.

Sitting up in bed, his eyes were matted nearly shut. Shaking his head, he heard a rattle and tried to look around the room. Again, all he could see was white. As his eyes focused, he was able to see a single word written on the paper sticking to his head:

"Loser."

What's-his-name slid to the edge of his bed and pulled the piece of college ruled notebook paper from his sweaty forehead and read what it had to say:

"...While we are indeed awestruck by your determination to raise the bar of mediocrity to its highest possible level, your mother and I just have to ask the question: Will our only son be a loser for the rest of his life?"

What's-his-name let his hand drop to his knee and threw his head back and groaned. "Not again." Somehow, he built up the nerve to raise the note back within view and continued reading: "You have been accepted to some of the finest schools in the nation. Harvard, Yale, Berkley..." again, he dropped his hand to his knee, threw is head back, groaning.

"...MIT among others has offered you a full scholarship!" the words barked at him. "Do you know how many people would kill for that opportunity? And you just sit on it! You have driven your mother and I to the breaking point. Of course we don't mind you being here. It's just that you are not accomplishing anything!"

Looking away from the note, he eyed a collection of old diet cola soda cans on his nightstand. He continued to read the note as he jiggled the cans, one by one, listening for any trace of fizzle.

"…So son, as hard as this is for your mother and me, we have mutually decided that you should have some deadlines in your life. Some goals.

And here is a fine first example: Get enrolled for this coming semester, or you're out on your ass.

Love,

Mom and Dad."

"Ps: We will be *very disappointed* if you do not have an impressive stack of applications filled out by the time we get home late this afternoon."

He knew what "very disappointed" meant.

"Pss: What are all of those ones and zeroes flashing on your computer screens?"

"Great. Just great"

Finding a soda can that seemed to have a little life left in it, he took a sip. He immediately spat it right back into the can.

Looking up, the curious numbers continued to race across the screen.

"What the heck is that?" Half expecting the maid to pound on his door any minute, he remembered that Sunday was her day off. His outburst went unheard.

He stood there at the foot of his bed, scowling at the computer screens. This was getting stupid. It was leading nowhere. Maybe this was fate telling him to go in another direction. Maybe his parents were right after all. They hadn't started complaining until the problems with the computer started up. Then it became his life. The scowl turned to a chuckle, upon a realization he just had. "Is it any wonder they're so pissed?"

He had, after all, been sequestered in his room for weeks, slaving over these computers, obsessed. Is it any wonder that his parents were so concerned? He began to feel angry with himself. He probably scared the hell out of them.

"Screw it."

He snatched the nearest computer monitor and set it in the least cluttered corner of his bedroom. Then he grabbed the computer tower. It went into the corner with the monitor. Everything but the laptop went into that corner of his room till ultimately, it was a mountain of gadgetry. He fell, emotionally spent, into his computer chair. Leaning back in as far as it would go, he looked up at the ceiling, as if it would give him all the answers. His hand found its own way to "The Drawer." He hardly had to look down to find it. He grabbed the heavy wooden handle and gave it a tug. Reaching in, he grasped several letters and pulled them out, spilling them onto his desk. In the pile were letters from MIT, Berkley…

All were practically begging him to go to their school. And he hated them for it.

"Lightweights." He sat there, filling out the applications for college, finally convinced this was the right thing for him to do. He had enough. This would, after all, get his parents off his back. That alone made it worthwhile. But school was so boring. Sweaty rooms filled with imbeciles who thought themselves as brilliant. And none were worse than the morons occupying center stage with chalk in hand. The subject matter, the books, bored the hell out of him. He laughed as he thought aloud to himself. "They call college a challenge?"

Having an eidetic memory and intelligence that proved beyond accurate measure, What's-his-name knew his lifespan in any given classroom would be short lived. He knew he would be unable to refrain from laughing at his professors, proving them wrong in front of the class and demonstrating it at the chalkboard, further infuriating his professor. It had gotten him in trouble during high school and would most certainly earn him a speed of light ticket out of college. And ultimately deliver him into the furious hands of his parents.

An eternity seemed to pass as he filled out form after form, question after question. Fill in the blanks, check this box, don't check that box, and "fill out this section *only* if…" When What's-his-name looked up at his laptop, his face went blank.

It was his laptop.

The last of the working computers. The only computer screen that did not flash binary code…

Was now flashing the ones and zeroes.

His pencil snapped, he snatched the laptop up from his desk, and with a Frisbee-throwing motion sent it whizzing into the trashcan. All of the college applications found themselves torn to shreds, spread out across the room. Leaning against the wall, he looked towards the trashcan, and saw a glow coming up from within. With still enough adrenalin for one last surge of anger, he took the laptop out of the trashcan and doubled up his fist to send it through the screen. But instead, he found himself just looking at it. He still could not get it out of his mind. A problem he could not tackle. Something broken that he could not fix.

Something broken he could not fix…

As he stood there, tears began to roll down his cheek. For someone who loved to search for answers to questions, his inability to tackle this, combined with the pressure of his family to find a path in life, became too much for him to bear. And still they were there. The numbers scrolling across the screen. For some reason, his eyes winced.

The numbers picked up their pace.

He stood there and then the craziest thought popped into his head.

Again, the numbers seemed to be scrolling at an accelerated pace.

He wondered: "Maybe I can't fix it-"

"Because it isn't broken."

CHAPTER 18

The home screen on Bailey's computer displayed a meadow. In the photo a lone horse stood magnificently on a hilltop beneath a tree. In the photo the horse appeared as if it were standing guard over the world below.

Bailey interrupted this scene to pull up the browser. She typed "Simon Glenayre" into the search field. There were over twenty five million hits for his name.

The gossip sites featured pictures of Simon's wife with other men. They stated her name was Chloe. It was the woman she saw clinging to him on television. She certainly was a beautiful woman. More and more websites tagged with Simon's name were ultimately linked to another gossip page placing Chloe with other men. Bailey wondered if Simon ever used the internet. How else could he miss all of this? Bailey envisioned Simon as she knew him: wrapped up in his own thoughts and, as usual, being desperately ignorant of bad news. It was not out of the realm of possibility. He either had his nose in a book or his eyes shut with a guitar in his hand. If it wasn't Herman Melville or Ray Bradbury it was a Gibson or a Fender guitar. It seemed the only time his mind could function clearly was when he was involved with one or the other.

There were plenty of pictures of Simon from early in his career. He looked so much younger then. His face was fresh and he still had color in his cheeks. In one photo he even smiled a little. Still, Bailey could tell there was much on the mind of the man in these pictures. Only Bailey understood the expressions on Simon's face. It was as if something sad boiled beneath the fragile fiber of his existence. Fan sites for Simon Glenayre showed timeline photos of him throughout his career. Clicking through the photos in sequential order by date, it was as if Bailey could see him disintegrate before her very eyes. It nearly brought her to tears.

Bailey clicked on the link displaying photos from his live shows. Judging by the pictures of him on stage, she could tell one thing hadn't changed about Simon: On stage was when he felt his best.

Simon's live clips through the years were a sight to behold. In the footage, Simon was clearly in control of the crowd. He held them all in the palm of his hands. In the clips he was just as Bailey remembered him from his years playing in Westport. He was still the ultimate rock star and entertainer. Simon Glenayre has that glow about him, an aura of greatness one only sees in old photographs of Buddy Holly, Elvis Presley and Jim Morrison. He was one of them, but a little too much for her heart to handle. Bailey theorized that Simon Glenayre was made of the same timeless matter as the falling stars that dash across our night sky. They dazzle so briefly, but for only a few spectacular moments before they wither away and die in the black ink of night. Bailey prayed Simon didn't share the same fate as the falling stars. She watched the footage of him on stage, shining so bright and dazzling like the falling stars in the night sky. He was in control on stage. And yet she knew that after every show Simon was most likely bundled up in a thick robe by Valletta and could probably be found huddled in a corner of a dressing room or in his bus with a notepad and pen.

One story quoted an anonymous source, obviously a nurse. Breaking the HIPAA laws, the source revealed Simon's condition during his last stay on the mental ward of the hospital she worked at. She used the words "exhaustion" and "dehydration." She also said he had little scars across his wrists and arms and needed to be sedated upon his last arrival. After a couple days he would check himself out against the doctor's wishes, and into the care of a mountainous, frustrated Italian who pled with Simon to stay and get the help he desperately needed.

"Valletta," Bailey said aloud after a sip of hot tea.

Bailey swore she would thank him someday for being there for Simon. She imagined Simon without Valletta. It was hard to do. She suspected, and rightfully so, that Simon probably would not have lasted this long if not for his friend and protector.

Further searching revealed the odds makers in Las Vegas had Simon in the "Death Pool." His odds were 1-3 he would commit suicide or overdose within the next five years. Bailey fought back her tears.

Why was she holding out for this mess of a man? Of all the suitors who called on her, knocking on her door with flowers in hand, promising their lifelong devotion and love, it was Simon for whom she still held out for. It wasn't as if she hadn't *tried* to open her heart. There were times of loneliness when she felt the need to just give up. To give someone else a chance. And once she did. The results in her eyes were disastrous. There was one occasion of weakness and poor judgment, when she tried to open her heart, and in a desperate reach for long forgotten tenderness shared her temple with someone else. Never had she felt so filthy. Bailey viewed her body as something precious, and to let another touch her was just plain wrong. She imagined her father's disappointment in her. It was a mistake she would never make again. Bailey Eden Piper knew where her heart was. And it was out there, somewhere, searching.

CHAPTER 19

The thumping outside the door seemed to go on day and night.

The pornographic strains of moaning could be heard seeping in from the hallway. Again, another thump. The low secretive rumble of voices could be heard if one's ear were pressed against the door.

And again, another thump. This one could not be ignored.

That time, it shook the velvet painting of Martin Luther King Jr. on the wall. It was a cheap recreation of the minister standing at the podium in Washington D.C. giving his "I Have a Dream" speech. But now Martin Luther King Jr. hung at an awkward angle. The boy sat there in the ratty old recliner, staring blankly at the hole on the left armrest. It had dirty, old filler that had been pulled out by the family cat. The hole in the ceiling was dripping again. He could see that the big brown spot above had enlarged since just this morning. He knew he'd have to move the recliner again.

Another mushy ceiling tile would soon fall.

The rustling from one of the bedrooms produced a crash, and a drunken cry for help. The teenage boy rolled his eyes. He planted his face in the palm of his two hands. Samantha would start crying again if she were awoken. He had to quiet his mother down, or he would never be able to get his baby sister back to sleep. The young man pried himself up from the recliner, standing up; he turned and looked at the seat cushion. It had springs poking through the material that jabbed him in his backside.

His mother had fallen out of bed again, drunk as she usually was at this time of the evening. He could smell the stale odor from the recliner, even though he was no longer sitting in it. Another cry from the back bedroom.

By now Samantha was yanked into consciousness by the rude crash of a lamp falling onto a pile of empty whiskey bottles. The little girl cried, standing up in her crib, clutching the bars with much more fear than any toddler should ever have. It was almost as if she were in prison. In many ways, they all were in a prison. Seemingly forever incarcerated in this place by the bars of poverty, drugs, chance.

Hopelessness.

The boy suppressed the urge to cry along with his little sister. He simply walked up to the dingy off-white crib, leaned down, and softly kissed his baby sister on her forehead. Her lonely cries for nourishment pierced his eardrums. His sadness at being unable to fill her hunger at this moment crushed his soul. Despite his gallant effort to suppress it, a tear slid down his cheek, off of his chin and landed upon her tiny forehead.

"I love you, Sam."

The voice he used with her was low and soft.

Again, he heard his name cried out from the dark bedroom at the end of the long hallway with its creaking floors. "Izzy," the voice slurred, "get your butt in here, boy."

He went into the back bedroom. His nostrils would quiver at the stench as he walked down the short hallway. It was a dark hallway. The light bulb had burned out months ago and was never replaced. The money just wasn't there.

"Get in here! You gon' let me laaaay here on th' floor all day? What th' hell's your problem!" The boy stood leaning against the doorframe in the manner of a forty five year old just off a twelve hour shift. His mother's room, a darkened pit. He hated going in there. It always stunk to hell. But prison was never meant to be pleasant. And that is how Izzy viewed this place. Under what authority was his family put here? His baby sister and himself both sentenced to this putrid hell by fate, or by God, or by the selfish habits of his mother. He often wondered who handed down this sentence.

In his heart, he accused his mother of the crime. He still found God innocent. Izzy knew this place, down to its brick and its mortar, down to its crime and its drugs was the result of people and their poor decisions.

Regardless, life still had to be endured even after he handed down his pointless sentence to his mother. Izzy could see the faint glimmer off the needles, which had worked their way deep into the stained, green shag carpet. He made a mental note to himself of the locations of the syringes. They seemed to multiply every time he poked his head into her bedroom. The mattress had no sheets, just an old raggedy quilt, sewn years ago by his grandmother. He often thought about how sad his grandmother would be if she could see what had become of her youngest daughter.

The alcoholic. The addict.

The mother of him and his baby sister.

And there she lay, at the side of the bed, head awkwardly propped against the nightstand. Her eyes as red as a tomato. Her speech eternally slurred. To hear her speak was an abomination unto the ears. Her condition had plummeted so far that no more money was to be made from prostitution. He was relieved of this, though he wondered to himself how he would get the money for formula that his sister was so badly in need of. She was hungry again, and big brother had long since picked up every penny from beneath every seat cushion, from every corner of every kitchen drawer. They were broke. He could smell his mother's flesh burning against the naked light bulb on the floor. He leapt to yank the power chord from the wall but the cord could not safely be found without the risk of a prick from an undetected needle.

He reached down for his mother.

The flesh from her arm strung from the light bulb like melted cheese and the stench of burning flesh made him gag. His mother, in her drugged stupor, felt nothing.

And now he could hear his hungry sister crying from the living room.

CHAPTER 20

The sensation of infinite expanse crawled up the back of his neck, delivering him into consciousness.

Simon lifted his head and fought to open his eyes only to find the kind of haze created by peering through vast empty distances. It was as if he were experiencing the thick fog or the English countryside early in the morning. And yet, Simon knew he was "indoors."

There was much for Simon to realize at that waking moment, the least of which was the brilliance of his own skin. With slightest motion, the iridescent silver dust lifted from his skin, dancing into the air before finally coming to rest at his feet. Simon's first reluctant step left behind a footprint within the sparkling crystals. This place, with its luminescent silence and its breathtaking space was alien to him. Yet he found this terrifying paradise absorbing. Simon stood alone with only his inner voice whispering questions but no answers into his ears. Simon awaited the waves of demands to come splashing down upon him that would never come. He waited for the voices that still hadn't roared and the scream of telephones that had yet to shake him and the bad news that was sure to arrive with a pounding at his door. But this time the pounding was noticeably absent. The explanation for this was simple.

Here, there was no door. Here, there wasn't anything.

Silver footprints easily numbered led to Simon as he trickled forward.

Soon the passing moments found more tracks less easily counted, pursuing him at full sprint in pointless directions. The adrenaline slap of feet and anxious breathing were the only sounds echoing off distant walls not visible. Simon soon found himself battling for precious breath, each contested breath stirring up another silver cloud. The sparkling dust trailing him slowly came to rest again upon the marble floor. Simon ran a finger upon the surface of that floor, as one would scrutinize a fireplace mantle with a white glove. He found to his fascination that his fingertip now shimmered with the stars. But Simon had to pull his attention away from that finger and its tiny occupant universe. Something had caught his eye.

He knelt over, wheezing downward.

It was the floor. It moved.

Another step forward and another wheezing downward gaze.

Again, the floor. Simon observed as the veins and clouds of its marble swirled beneath his feet like the wind as it twists the layers of gray during a furious storm. Simon lost his balance and nearly fell as he watched in wonder and terror as the floor swirled violently beneath his feet. Simon did not fall to the floor though, fighting himself back to sleep, as much as he desired to. He considered the colossal walls, which he could now barely see off in the distance, certainly they would be unable to sustain their own weight and would fall down upon him from above. Would his life now come to an end, here, wherever "here" was? Perhaps it had come to an end already, leaving him in this Heaven or Hell. Here on the swirling marble floor that seemed to come alive beneath his very feet, here with the silver dust that held countless worlds resting serenely upon his very flesh. And now, a humbling, rumbling noise. Simon looked to the floor to find it now moving at a blur.

With a gust of wind and a foreboding growl, the surrounding haze began to take the form of colossal pillars as if a celestial architect was molding it like clay. The pillars formed upward with low, belly twisting rumbles as Simon looked on in astonishment. Before his disbelieving eyes the mammoth pillars crawled further and further upward completing the Pier Arches, working its way with otherworldly efficiency up into the Triforium and finally completing the Clerestory, high above his head. The fearful rumble had eased, finally, but Simon could not convince the muscles in his body to unclench. He watched as silver light broke through the windows residing high up in the Clerestory, beaming down into the nave. The windows on both sides of the room soon followed with white and silver light of their own. With much less violence, the remainder of The Cathedral formed swiftly. The fan vaulting raced from above the lancet windows, coming joined together by intricate fleurs-de-lis hundreds of feet above his head, leading to a majestic dome. Angels peered down upon Simon from that dome, their faces painted more than four hundred years ago by Michelangelo on his back in the Sistine Chapel, terrifyingly high above the floor. The Saints lined the walls, more than one hundred in all, having dual occupancy here as well as their usual places in Westminster Abbey.

Simon said nothing. His breathing so shallow, he couldn't speak even if he desired to.

The enormity of this place had not diminished, Simon realized, *it only revealed its shape to him.*

Another gush of silver light pressed at his back, and he looked down to find his own lonely shadow looking back up at him eagerly. Spinning around, the source of light was revealed to be a giant rose window in the far off distance. Its size was incredible, he held up his hand to try and give it scale. His one hand alone or even two would not cover it. Simon theorized if he were to find and throw a good sized rock, find it and throw it again many times over, the intricate glass of that rose window would still be safe from the crashing ruin of the stone. This realization made him feel infinitely smaller at a moment in time when he already felt so tiny. Peering off into the opposite distance, he could see the semi-domed apse, forming above the altar. There was no Crucifix.

Simon began his journey towards the front of The Cathedral, bypassing the invitingly covered loggia, opting instead to remain nervously exposed in the wide open space of this nearly infinite sanctuary. If someone were to find him, as he maddeningly desired, maybe he would get an explanation of this strange and cosmic cathedral he'd found himself in.

Simon looked up to the vaulted ceiling and almost fell over backwards.

Suddenly a thought leapt into his mind. The creases of his forehead deepened as he wondered aloud. "Color," he said to himself, "why isn't there any color?" He looked at his hand realizing it was not pink with the hues of life, but like the rest of this place was colorless, save for the different shades of gray and silver. It was as if he was dropped into a Fredrick Evans photograph.

Simon looked at his hand again, then at the rose window at the back of The Cathedral, wishing for color. "Now that's a shame," he sighed, "that would've been beautiful."

Simon turned again, starting his journey forward when he felt a gust of wind run its fingers through his shoulder length hair. The rose window seemed to call out to Simon, pulling at him from behind, jerking him to a standstill. He turned just as the silvers and grays of its fine glass and intricate construction began to break up as color seeped through, splashing blues and greens and gold upon the marble floor below. Colorful light pierced the lancet windows at both sides, bringing them to life. Simon found himself spinning in all directions, frightfully trying to take in all the wonderment without missing the arrival of a single hue. The floor with its writhing storms was now still, as if it had fallen into a calm sleep. Its colorful veins and crystalline composition softly illuminated Simon from below.

The pleasant buoyancy of the voice did little to curtail the shock Simon felt upon its sudden intrusion from behind. He spun toward the voice and almost fell into the Archangel Michael as he stood, a painted holograph projected from a stained glass window, full figured and to Simon's shock seemingly alive. Silently, Michael motioned with a sword of otherworldly glow towards a man dressed in coveralls, standing framed perfectly by the golden apse behind him off in the distance. The stranger seemed real enough, his face was dirty, his coveralls smeared with grease. His cap read "CAT" in grubby white and gold letters. It sat crooked atop his unkempt hair, strands flopping out rudely this way and that.

"I said, don't you think that's better?"

The stranger walked cheerfully towards Simon, his hands in his pockets. He crossed through a multi colored blanket of light beaming in from the windows. Simon looked at the man's leather work boots; they looked worn enough to appear that a toe could pop through at any moment. His hands still in his pockets, the expression on his service station face said that this stranger had nowhere to go for quite a while, and really couldn't care less about it.

He seemed delighted to have a visitor for a change. He spoke again.

"Finally, you know, a visitor for a change."

The stranger walked past the stained glass projection of the Archangel Michael, who bowed his head as the stranger passed by.

When the man held out his greasy hand for a shake, Simon took a jittery step back, like a hummingbird that wants the sugar water but for some reason is too flighty to partake in its offerings. The stranger laughed at himself. "Oh," he chuckled as he wiped his hand on a dirty rag accomplishing nothing. "Sorry, man. Not everyone wants to get dirty like me, I guess."

He held out his hand again.

"Name's Al."

Simon kept one hand firmly locked in the other. His fingers twisting around themselves.

"Hi, Al."

Al smiled a mischievous smile. His eyes sparkled more than it seemed they should. He popped his tongue on the roof of his mouth and slapped the palm of his hand with a wrench as he waited for Simon to speak. Taking a subtler step forward, he patted Simon on the back, nudging him forward. "Why don't you come with me. I feel kinda stupid just standing here like a *doofus.*"

They walked. Simon listened to the soles of the stranger's work shoes shuffle upon the floor. "Where are we-" Simon paused.

The man laughed. "Name's Al."

"Where are we, Al?" The man laughed again from his belly as he scratched the back of his head. He pulled the hat tightly back into place, tugging the bill to his hairline. "You're in God's Museum, man." The tone of his voice was almost one of surprise that this unexpected visitor knew nothing of his whereabouts.

"God's Museum." Simon stopped in his tracks as the stranger in his greasy coveralls and crooked cap continued walking. He stopped when he realized Simon had fallen behind. "Hey, c'mon man." He said, with vague seriousness in his voice, "I got work to do. And I'm almost finished." Simon stood still as the pillars surrounding him. Al turned back, and again put his hand on Simon's shoulder, pushing him gently forward. Simon's eyes glazed over. "God's Museum…"

The greasy coverall man laughed. "That's right," he said, "God's Museum." Simon looked around, seeing nothing but the interior of a massive, dream-like cathedral. "A-" Simon exhaled long held air from the very bottom of his lungs and rethought his words. He tried a different angle: "A museum is for collections of things, right?" The stranger named Al continued on, forcing Simon to do the like. "Right. Museums are for collections of things."

Simon stopped again, dead in his tracks. Al tossed his hands up into the air, landing at the grease on his hips. "So what's the big deal?

"What in the world would God want to collect?"

Al snapped the hat from his head and gave a scratch right

above the back of his neck. "Well," he said, slightly put off, "haven't you ever collected *anything*? You know, like football cards or stamps or stuff like that?" He snapped his fingers: "Hey, I got a collection of Elvis plates you just would not *believe*." Simon found his easy smile somehow comforting. He walked slowly towards Al, who again pushed him anxiously forward.

"But what in the heck would God collect?" Simon said as he walked reluctantly on. "And what kind of museum is this?" He said, his dismay morphing slowly into irritation. "I mean, there's nothing here. Look around!" Simon turned in a semicircle, his hands held out in front of him. His shoulders creeping up towards his ears. "There's nothing here!"

"Oh," Al said as he looked over each of his shoulders and then directly upward. "Oh…I guess I forgot."

Al took an awkward half step forward and with a grunt shoved the wrench into his back pocket. He leaned in Simon's direction with his ever present grin still on display. "Check this out man," he whispered, "it'll knock your socks off." Al held his hands up to the dome, gave a quick look around and then clapped his hands together twice. The sound slowly diminished into forever, disappearing into the distance. Al looked over to Simon who was still looking around. Al squeaked from heel to toe and then back again. Still nothing happened. He looked around to find that Simon appeared a bit more confused. "Let's just try that again, shall we?" He laughed under his breath. "Ahem." The second time he clapped with more authority and things began to happen. What materialized made Simon's heart leap into his throat.

They were not in an empty cathedral anymore.

"My God." Simon's voice quivered. He grabbed Al's coverall sleeve, trying to keep his balance as his eyes raced in all directions. Again he gulped, "I can't believe it."

"Yeah," Al said as he leaned over. "When He collects 'em," he said softly, "He really collects 'em."

CHAPTER 21

What's-his-name leaned against his desk for hours on end, writing out the possibilities.

He knew his parents would be back soon. He had to fill out those college applications. If he didn't have them done, he knew it would be his fanny. But he couldn't stop this. Not now. Though he could not put his finger on the "how" or the "why," he knew he was onto something. It was a problem, it toyed with him, as if it were challenging him to a duel. What's-his-name loved to duel with problems. However this particular problem parried his every move.

The two wires in his head were trying like mad to make the connection. He knew he had to approach this from a different angle. But how? All other frequently travelled avenues had gotten him nowhere. Instead of looking for the answer to a problem, he tried to examine this particular problem as if it weren't even a problem at all. Perhaps the ones and zeroes weren't the symptom of a problem, but instead the symptom of something altogether different. And this opened up a world of possibilities to him. A light went off in his head and he was working like mad to keep it lit.

"It just has to be something else." With his long, stringy hair pulled back in a ponytail, the light from the ones and zeroes were still flashing across his forehead. Scribbling furiously, the veins began to pop out of his neck. The sweat, so thick in his palm, began to smear the page. His pencil pushed nearly to its breaking point. The ones and zeroes filled the sheets of paper by the hundreds. He ripped out the page from his notebook, wadded it up tossed it towards the trash can in the corner. It fell well short of its target, landing on the pile of wadded up papers on the floor. He yanked another sheet of paper and began scribbling like mad. The endless array of numbers stacked atop one another in an insane equation that would boggle most upper caliber minds. Another try. Advanced calculus.

Nothing. Simplify.

Boolean Logic.

Nothing.

"Maybe it's just an IP address or something to a web site."

"Two, four, eight, sixteen..."

"Darnit."

The ones and zeroes, as used in electronics, are known as Binary language. Ones, denoting "on" and zeroes denoting "off." Unknown to the casual user surfing the internet, these powerful ones and zeroes are the language that fly through electronics connections faster than the mind can imagine. And from within these ones and zeroes What's-his-name searched furiously for an explanation. He continued writing.

Nothing. The numbers had no sequence that was recognizable to him. There were no octets that stood out. No rational numerical sequences, anyway. Nothing.

There was something in these numbers, an answer. He just knew it. But where was it? He stood up from the desk, and stretched his back. What's-his-name stood there rubbing his neck and glaring at the laptop. Spinning around, he made for the door and bolted down the hall. Time for another soda.

"It has to be there somewhere." He stood frozen at the refrigerator, with his hand gripping the handle to the door. What's-his-name stood there for several moments looking blankly at the handle on the fridge. After a long pause the door was opened and a can of soda snatched from within.

He shut the door and stood there for a moment just looking at the can in his hand.

He popped open the can and took a sip, and held it still to his lips as he looked at the ceiling. He brought the can down slowly.

"Maybe I'm making this way too complicated."

He spun on his heels and made for the bedroom. As he flung open the door, he noticed the numbers scrolling across the screen at a furious pace. He settled into his chair. He hit the "Print Screen" button of the keyboard. He wondered if the printer would print. Nothing else seemed to work, why in the world should the printer? He sat there for a moment looking at the monitor. He heard nothing from the printer. "Crap, it ain't gonna print if it ain't plugged into the laptop." He leaned to his right in the chair and grabbed the cable that was attached to the back of the printer. Flinging the cable out of the tangled mass of other cables, he brought it towards the laptop when the printer began to work. What's-his-name remained in the awkward leaning position with the printer cable still in his hand. The printer continued printing. He dropped the cable.

"That shouldn't happen," he said aloud. "Printers don't print if they aren't plugged in." Still, the printer continued spitting out the papers one by one as What's-his-name sat and watched. He grabbed the bottom piece of paper and compared it to what was on the screen. It matched. He jumped up out of his chair and stood there looking at the desk, as the objects that laid on it vibrated from the violent pace the printer was working at. He could see his can of diet cola dancing towards the edge of the desk and moved his hand to catch it before it fell. He missed, the can landing on the floor spewing cola all over the carpet. He knelt down to pick up the can, eyes still on the printer. Looking down, he could see the soda soaking into the carpet fibers. He pulled his hair behind an ear as he looked around to see if there were any computer parts that could be ruined by the soda *when he saw it.*

He jumped up, eyes flashing, his fingertips tingling.

The printer was unplugged from the wall outlet.

What's-his-name paced around the small circular clearing on his bedroom floor. Wiping the beads of sweat from his upper lip. He stopped, looked at the outlet for a moment, and continued his pacing. His attention turned once again to the laptop sitting on his desk. He paced some more, chewing on a fingernail. He leapt over a pile of books and boxes of computer parts towards the desk. He yanked the power cord from the laptop.

Still on.

Flipping it over, he pulled the battery from the back. He flipped it back over.

The numbers continued to race across the screen, almost too fast to be recognized as numbers. He laid the computer on the desk and took two steps back and stared at it. The light from the numbers reflecting in his bloodshot eyes. "Ok. What's going on? Who are you?" He bellowed, "What do you want?"

The numbers immediately ceased scrolling, and sat there.
10101111100011101001110010101111110001110100111100
10101111100011101001110010101111110001110100111100
10101111100011101001110010101111110001110100111100

Kneeling down, he grabbed another pencil and eased slowly into his chair. What's-his-name slid another piece of paper in front of him. He was on to it. Suddenly, he had a grip on this, though he couldn't understand why.

He began to write the numbers on the screen down. If what he was witnessing was in his mind, or actually on the paper, will never be known. The numbers on the white sheet revealed their alignments to him, as if he were staring at a 3D Stereogram. Gradually, the ones and zeroes began to explain themselves to him. He sat and watched.

1010111110001110 100111100101011111000110100111100
1010111110001110100111100101011111000110100111100
1010111110001110100111100101011111000110100111100

His eyes remained locked on the piece of paper before him.

He realized what was before him was simply a few sets of repeating numbers. They just repeated over and over, much like the keys that repeat themselves across the octaves of a piano. "Why didn't I see it before?" He continued writing. It was difficult to see because it was so simple. "There *is* a pattern."

It wasn't until his hand glanced over where his pencil wrote that he realized his hand had smeared black ink and not pencil lead.

He sat there scribbling. As he continued to write, the more he sweat. What's-his-name ransacked another drawer for his calculator. He wanted to double check his binary to decimal conversions. They were all correct. He could hear the sound of his parent's Bentley pulling into the driveway.

He ignored it.

What's-his-name knew they were going to be furious about the incomplete college applications he didn't care.

With a gazelle leap he landed on the other side of his overturned chair and made for the bookshelf. Within seconds a book of Latin translation was flung open. He began furiously scribbling the translations into English.

He heard the double chirp of a car alarm.

He ignored it.

He read from the book and wrote the translations down, racing to quench the flame of his curiosity. It was all falling together. And then, there it was.

It was a name, a number and a paragraph. All were familiar to him. He dropped the pencil, and from it, black ink splattered upon the paper.

He heard their keys jangling in the front door.

What's-his-name stood up with the thick book. Below he could hear the responsible shuffle of his parent's feet on the stairs and his name being called in that familiar, judgmental tone of voice.

The book of Latin translation dropped to the floor with a solid thud.

The window was left open as he scurried across the roof and down a tree. He would spend the night with friends. Tomorrow, he would be off to a place where he could always clear his mind and better think things through. His parents opened his bedroom door to find it trashed, the corner window left open. The stack of unfinished applications lying shredded on his bed.

The computer screens now playing chess with themselves.

CHAPTER 22

"Now don't call 'em a 'pack rat', whatever you do," Al urged. "He's kind of sensitive about that."

"Simon?" Al turned to find Simon still frozen in place. He wondered if he was paralyzed or just too terrified to speak. "Simon?" He looked around at the usual and then again at Simon. *"Why don't we just try to walk?"* Al took Simon by an arm and began to walk him slowly, as if he were a parent steering a child through the narrow aisles of a shop teeming with fine, breakable everything. Simon walked slightly, his mind too entangled with his surroundings to make the minimum computations required for left foot, right foot.

Simon spoke. Or at least he tried to. "Al," he said, "that's-"

"It's just another flying machine, man. That's all."

"But look at all of them," Simon stuttered, "there's hundreds, no. Thousands of them." Simon's head nearly twisted off as they walked along an airplane so large, his mind could barely wrap around it. "I know that airplane..." Simon continued to point. "That's the Spruce Goose."

Al pulled him along without even looking at it. "Yeah, I know. I see it every day." Finally, they made their way past the lumbering airship conceived in the mind of a reclusive billionaire. Simon pointed this way and that as they continued past a row of fully assembled Gemini and Saturn rockets. Al kept walking, repeating the same words over and over again, "Yeah, I know. I know..." Several Graf Zeppelins rested overhead. Amelia Earhart's Lockheed Vega sat resting on the marble floor next to a glass case. Within the glass case hung a large set of wings. Hand crafted of string and wax by Daedalus for his only son, the wings now lacked a deadly amount of feathers. Finally, they stopped walking.

"Here we are."

The airplane before them was orange and shaped like a rocket. Simon looked at the aircraft and then again at his surroundings, as if he was putting together a puzzle in his mind. Al looked at him expectantly. "Well? What do you think, man?" He climbed a stepladder and took the greasy rag from his pocket and tried to rub a shine on the words painted upon the aircraft's nose. The name "Glamorous Glennis" shone less than when he'd begun. Al saw the oily streak and pulled his shirtsleeve over his hand trying unsuccessfully to rub it away. "Uh, you wouldn't happen to have a clean rag on you, by any chance?"

Simon swallowed and finally spoke. "This can't be here. This very plane is in an aviation museum," Simon said pointing at it, "I saw it when I was a kid."

Al balanced on Simon's shoulder as he hopped down from the stepladder. "Well, sure kid. It *is* in a museum," he laughed. "But this aircraft is here *in spirit*." Simon walked around the craft, taking notice of tools resting upon a workbench beneath one of its wings. "Wasn't this…" Al interrupted Simon. He wanted to be the one to say it. "It was the first manned vehicle to break the sound barrier." Simon picked up on the pride in his voice. "That's Mach One to you and me, baby."

Simon motioned to the tools on the workbench. Al smiled. "Yeah, that's just for a little fine tuning."

"So why would God want to collect airplanes, of all things? I mean, why not collect something that man couldn't possibly possess," he said. "You know. Like, 'I have this thing that you can't ever have…'"

Al laughed aloud and shook his head as he cleaned one of his wrenches, tossing it upon the workbench, picking up another. He stopped and looked at Simon who was still waiting for an answer. Al held up the dirty wrench and waved it in the air. "And just what do you think all of this is? One day you're struggling to make fire and then before you know it, you're breaking the sound barrier, man." He said smiling. "And then traveling through space." Al couldn't contain his awe. "Man in Space, *now that's heavy*. That's about the only way I can explain it. What can I say," he said, "I guess He's impressed."

"Impressed? How did mankind impress God?"

"I think it was your vision. Maybe it was expected of you, or maybe, just maybe, *you surprised Him*. Maybe in all of His omnipotence and wisdom, even He didn't foresee this. I mean the heights you've reached. And the speed that you attained them in is really… incredible."

Al looked overhead with admiration as a French Concorde floated upside down past the Montgolfier Balloon. "I think it showed Him your potential, Simon," he said. "The wonderful things you could achieve if you put your minds to it." Simon looked into Al's eyes, they seemed bluer still. He realized none of the airships were machines of war. No guns protruded from their noses. No missiles hung from beneath their wings. Simon leaned against the workbench, arms crossed, watching as Al continued to clean his tools. He looked at Simon from the corner of his eye. "I like to keep a clean shop," he said, rubbing a wrench to an otherworldly shine. Simon looked up at him. "So cleanliness really is next to-"

"No, no, no," Al's body jerked and Simon could feel the air shiver around him. "God loves you," Al laid his oily hand on Simon's shoulder. "And it doesn't matter how dirty you think you are." When he lifted his hand from Simon's shoulder the sensation of infinite love remained for a brief, enlightening moment. "What matters most is where your heart is at."

"Al," Simon asked, "*Who are you?*" Without looking up Al asked what was meant by such a question. The mechanic in greasy coveralls dropped a handful of tools into a toolbox. The clang echoed off distant walls as the mosaics of angels looked silently on.

"Look, man. I'm just a mechanic." The nearby painted projection of the Archangel Gabriel turned its head to Al, listening intently to his every word. "So how did you become a mechanic," Simon stopped and looked around again at his surroundings, "*here?*" Al arranged the tools in the toolbox without looking up. "Well I guess nobody else cared enough to take the job."

Al had an answer to the next question before the words had a chance to escape Simon's lips. "The voices you hear…"

Simon felt the tremors in his knees as he grabbed the edge of the workbench sending a caliper clanging to the floor. "What do you know about the voices, Al?"

Al sat on the workbench. He motioned with his hands, to illustrate as he spoke. "Maybe you hear those voices Simon, because those are the only voices you have opened your heart to." He pointed to his own ears and eyes. "You hear and you see only the things that you have *learned* to hear and see. But maybe,"

Al paused to soak in the warmth of the light from the rose window as it crept over his smiling face, "maybe there are other voices trying to communicate with you. But you just don't know how to listen to them. It's almost as if," Al lifted up a screwdriver, twisting it mischievously in his hand, "you could use a bit of a tune up yourself, man."

Al stood up from the bench and motioned Simon to walk with him. "You can't do it all yourself. It's like quicksand, y'know? The more you fight it, the faster you sink." Simon pointed off to the left towards a large silver disk with a dome on its top.

"And what do you have to say about that?"

"Ah," Al said as he pulled Simon onward, "mankind isn't ready to know about that flying machine yet."

He inhaled and continued.

"What you need, Simon, is to learn how to talk to God."

Simon smirked. "Who's to say all of this isn't just another dream and doesn't mean a thing? What if I don't believe there is a God-" Al interrupted.

"Do you really believe God doesn't really exist?"

Simon continued, the lines of his forehead deepening. "...And if there is a God, considering all that I've been through, why would I even want His love anyway?"

Al's smile reached from one side of his face to the other . *"The thing about God-"* Al said as he stopped walking and put his hand on Simon's shoulder, *"is that He loves you whether you like it or not."*

The now familiar sensation of movement swept over Simon. He noticed Al calmly observing the changes in their surroundings. The Cathedral now resembled The Sainte Chapelle Cathedral of Paris, France.

Legend says that Sainte Chapelle once housed The Crown of Thorns worn by Christ at The Crucifixion. Legend also states it housed a piece of the cross from which He hung. Emperor Baldwin II of Constantinople would sell The Crown of Thorns and the sacred shard of wood to King Louis IX, who as legend states, would carry the sacred relics to Paris bare footed and wearing only a peasant's robe to Sainte Chapelle. The precious relics disappeared during The French Revolution and haven't been seen since.

Simon continued: "So how do I talk to God?"

"Well, you open the doors of your heart to him," Al said. "And then invite him in for a conversation."

Simon knew this place was not his reality, but still, he knew that it was *a* reality, nonetheless.

The Gossamer Albatross passed delicately overhead. Al slapped Simon on the arm. "Hey, let's go."

The Wright Brothers' biplane eased quietly into its landing nearby as they walked on. Simon wondered aloud. "So, now what?"

"Well, I guess you have a decision to make."

Simon feared they were coming to the part he dreaded most. He knew Al's answer would lead to the determination that a change in his life was in order. The struggle for Simon was whether or not to make the change he knew he needed.

"And what decision is that?" he moaned. Simon felt Al's timeless grip on his elbow. He jerked away, turning towards a far-off flying buttress. Nearby, the Archangel Gabriel continued to observe with respect and admiration of the man in coveralls. "You have to decide whether or not you are going to be a voice for God, Simon, or if you will continue to be a resounding gong or clanging cymbal."

Simon's hands found themselves crossed over his chest. He felt himself hiss. "Resounding gong or clanging cymbal." He rolled his eyes. This did not escape Al's attention. "You know, you never did tell me who you are. You just can't spend eternity here, fixing airplanes and patching hot air balloons," he laughed. "So tell me who you *really* are."

Simon's words dissipated in the mist as he realized he was again standing alone in a limitless empty room made up of nothing more than four massive walls in the distance and loneliness once again at his side. The man in greasy coveralls and old leather shoes and eyes that sparkled more than they should, was gone.

He spun around several times looking for Al. Again, he yelled aloud towards the distant walls. "Who are you?" Tears streamed down his cheeks. Simon was again left alone by a stranger who for some reason made him feel safe and unconditionally loved, even though the word "love" was never spoken. It was something Simon *felt*.

Again he yelled.

"Who are you?"

A mist swept past the side of his face. Simon felt the words *"Agnus Dei"* whispered into his ear. He snapped his head in the direction of the voice hoping to find the playful Al standing there smiling, but Al was gone.

A feeling of exhaustion poured upon his shoulders like a ton of lead, pulling him to a knee upon the floor. Fighting to keep his eyes opened, he could see the last of the rose window slowly diminishing. Sleep forced Simon to all fours.

The words "Ego sum vobis" breezed past his head, almost as if he could feel someone breathing in his ear.

As Simon struggled to lift his head up for one last look around, he could barely see what was left of the rose window.

His surroundings continued to blur, and with the disappearance of the rose window, Simon fell into a deep sleep.

CHAPTER 23

Tonight he left them wanting more. Simon pushed his way past the Sharpies held out for autographs, past the screaming girls, past the leather. Last night's dream still hung heavy in his heart.

The red and blue and green lights from above the stage dissolved behind the hellish silhouettes of bodies jostling around aimlessly in the darkness. Simon and Valletta made their way deeper into the bowels of the auditorium. No matter how hard Simon tried he still couldn't get the knot undone that Valletta tied on the belt of his terrycloth bathrobe.

"Val!"

The stomping of the crowd shook the floors and walls of the mammoth structure. Simon caught himself wishing for the concrete of the arena to open up, sending them all spiraling down into the bowels of the Earth. He imagined the fluttering orange from their outstretched lighters fading as they fell down into the darkness.

He also caught himself asking the same question he asked himself following every performance: wondering if anybody was going to walk away from this night changed. What was the point, he asked himself, if nobody walks away somehow changed for the better?

Another anonymous body thumped Simon's side. He couldn't see the man's face in the darkness of the tunnel. He felt Valletta reach over his shoulder and grab the youth by his jacket to yank him from their path. The person in Valletta's grip said something and then said it again. "Give me the key…"

"Val," Simon barked, "wait a minute."

Valletta placed the body back in front of Simon.

"What did you say?" The youth was speechless when he saw Simon's face, now illuminated from the warm glow of a nearby Zippo. Simon repeated himself. "What did you just say to me?"

The youth stuttered for a moment. "I said, have you seen my keys?"

Simon sighed. "Your keys?"

"My keys," the disembodied voice said, "I dropped 'em somewhere around here. Can't see nothin'. Just the darkness." The phrase echoed through Simon's head.

"Can't see nothin', just the darkness..."

"Yeah, I know how you feel, kid. Good luck finding your keys." Simon gave Valletta the look. Valletta promptly grabbed the young man by his leather jacket and flung him aside.

CHAPTER 24

Tonight the pull towards home was strong.

Everyone would be furious for his disappearing like this. Tonight he didn't care. Simon had to get to a place where his bare feet could touch good solid ground. It wasn't Beuern, but it would do. Seattle to Kansas City. Most likely a full night's flight due to the likely layover in a hub city. Three or four days drive straight through, or a risky eternity thumbing it incognito.

Simon fell asleep behind the wheel far too easily to make the drive straight through, it couldn't be risked. Hitchhiking it was unrealistic and dangerous.

Simon settled on taking to the air, it was far quicker and much safer. The risk of being recognized was always a possibility at an airport. Fans were everywhere. But maybe for a change, the throngs of holiday travelers just might work to his advantage and help him to blend in. Maybe no one would recognize him among the usually tired suit-clad business warriors and weary vacationers who usually troll the dreary midnight halls of a hub city airport.

The good news was that Phil was careless enough to leave Simon's credit cards on the table. A mistake he would regret come Simon's next show. Phil would have no star for the forty-five thousand plus fans that showed up, tickets in hand. He would have to be the one to walk out on that stage and explain it to them.

And now he found himself hoping for a seat in first class. It would save him the potential indignity of getting caught trying to sneak a bottle onto the plane. The top shelf liquor was always served in first class. The remnants of Simon's liver expected no less.

A decision as simple as taking time out for himself became a foreign concept to Simon. For years, so many people depended on him and he'd always watched out for their well-being. He played when he was deathly ill. He played when he was crushed beneath the weight of his own depression.

Simon now played music not because he wanted to, *but because he had to.*

And for the longest time, there had been a tension, firing within the cauldron of his soul. All the booze poured for him could not drown it out, all the crystals chopped upon a mirror couldn't cover it up. And there was no more solace to be found from the prick of a needle upon his flesh. It was his last escape from the guilt of the loss of his parents, the guilt of running out angry on his beloved grandfather and cousin, the guilt of Bailey Eden Piper and their shared passion for each other. And now the high was getting harder to find. Simon only wanted peace. He'd frequently fantasized about getting peace at any cost.

A nauseating sensation twisted his gut from day to day, a result of playing his music the night before. It was the guilt of playing his music when he no longer wanted to. It now made his songs feel so... unclean.

But to miss a show affected so many. His band, the roadies, there was the union to deal with as well. They'd be sure to get paid, and it would be out of his pocket, too. All of this raced through his mind, as he pulled his baseball cap tight over his head. A voice in the back of his mind begged him to make for the door. To get his bare feet on good, solid ground. "Get away," it said. "Life is all about choices." Simon recognized this voice as being different from the one that urged him to that broom closet and the rope. This was the voice of reason. It was the voice of his father and mother, it was the voice of Bailey. It urged him not only to survive, but to *live*.

Simon wondered if it was a ridiculous idea to "Go for the Smile" with his music. It was costing him his career. Still, it was a chance he had to take. He had to try to reach somebody, anybody. What was the point to all of this, if no one walked away somehow changed for the better?

The hallway was long and thin. As he walked slowly along its length, he hoped no one would pop out of one of the side doors. The long carpeted hallway felt safe to him. It's silent, echoless walls draped around him like a warm blanket. Midnight. Almost. The very last door at the end of the hallway and to his right had a "Do Not Disturb" sign hanging from its shiny brass knob. An empty bottle of Champaign rested between two empty wineglasses and a half-eaten plate of strawberries. Simon couldn't help but notice the strains of heavy breathing seeping out from beneath the door of the Honeymoon Suite. Suddenly, he found his thoughts turning back to *her*. Yes, she had the most delightful voice and shimmering blond hair. And as usual, when she visited his thoughts, the smoothness of her memory was soon drowned out by a chaser of bitter regret. More doubts about the choices he had made. And again he wondered to himself which side of the fence had his soul fallen on.

Simon stopped at the brass buttons for the elevator. Should he turn back? Where was the redemption in running away from his troubles? What was he expecting to find after his escape? This wasn't going to be the beginning of a new life and he knew it. This was merely going to be a short vacation from the gallows of his mind. His troubles would still be here when he returned. If he decided not to return he knew they would find him. "Oh hell."

The bell gave a ding, the door opened. After a jerk and a pause, Simon stepped in.

CHAPTER 25

It had been a good day for Bailey. She had the previous night off and even managed to pull a few z's that evening, a rare occurrence for an E.R. vampire such as herself. The day was spent at the city market though, enjoying the street performers and musicians. She had lunch at an outside diner beneath the shade of an umbrella. Her sandwich was going down slow; most of her time was spent watching people mill about and visiting. On the other side of the market, a stage was being set up for the evening's entertainment. Bailey enjoyed watching the organization and structure exhibited by the men assembling the stage, p.a. and lighting trusses. The large burly men operated like an intelligent and well organized machine. They were testing the lights before she got half way through her sandwich. Ten minutes later a drum tech was banging on the snare drum to get a good volume level. The sound man told him "again," and again the roadie cracked the snare. Bailey smiled when the soundman started to EQ the guitar and bass. Whoever this guy was, he was good. And Bailey herself knew how to get good sound out of a PA. Simon had taught her well.

One of the last times she saw him play was a night she worked sound for Simon and his band. The club was old, the ceiling, low. It was in a basement. The place was a nightmare to get a good mix in, but if anyone could it was Bailey.

Bailey leaned back in her chair lifting her face to the sun and stretched her arms behind her head. She ignored the looks from men as they passed by. The cup of ice cream sent to her table anonymously sat melted by now. Whoever sent it never introduced himself, probably because he saw she didn't eat it and took that as an outward sign she wasn't interested in being joined. How right he was. Bailey preferred to be alone with her thoughts, and at this time her thoughts were of particular enjoyment.

Bailey recalled that night. It was down in the Westport area of Kansas City. A good place to party. It was a great place to get a nice meal too, or if you were the wrong person in the wrong place at the wrong time, it could also be a place where you could get dragged into one of the meanest brawls ever imagined. She suspected she remembered it more ideally than what it really was like, however, she enjoyed thinking of it through the rose colored mists of time. It had been years since she'd been down there. She sat back and smiled.

It was three a.m. outside the bar. They had just loaded up all the equipment. She recalled how dark Simon was under his eyes. They were both exhausted, and Simon was struggling. It was as obvious to Bailey in that dark alley as it would have been at high noon. He wanted a drink, or at least he thought he did. Simon had resisted Bailey's pleas to change his performance venues. Get away from all the temptation in those bars. Find new places to play. Maybe find a church he could attend. She remembered Simon rolling his eyes.

She also recalled Simon's performance that night. It was magic. Simon swayed to the music. That night, in that tiny basement on that corner stage, Simon Glenayre showed what he was capable of. He lifted those people up that night. They would have crawled on the ceiling for him if he asked them to. Simon Glenayre had a gift, she knew that much even then. The question was, what would he do with it? She was aware of the suffering brought on by genius, too. How self-destructive artistic visionaries could be. Bailey shuddered when she thought of how well he fit into that mold. How incredibly talented he was and how terribly troubled he always seemed to be. By then she had heard him talking in his sleep. She had heard him talk about "The Key." How many nights did she wake up to the sounds of Simon rustling through the closet, half asleep looking for that key? All the following mornings she woke to him sitting at the window, reciting that poem, half asleep. "Who has known heights shall bear forevermore..." How she dreaded the course he might take. Simon was a "path of least resistance" kind of man. And to many, the path of least resistance was a self inflicted hell on Earth with an even worse end. And everyone else would be left behind to endure life with that horrible empty space previously occupied by him.

She kept a close eye on Simon as they loaded the equipment that night. Simon was having a hard time, there was so much on his mind. He was a recovering alcoholic, living in a world filled with people, places and things to trigger his urge. And there was the fear he felt over something he himself could hardly wrap his mind around. His voice always trembled when he mentioned "The Key." But that was the tip of the iceberg for Simon, *and* for Bailey. They had plans to make for themselves, important plans. And he had to do it all through the fog of addiction to boot. He fought bravely, as best he could. He couldn't have gotten this far without Bailey. She watched, listened to the nuances of his voice. It was time, she thought. That night she unlocked the back of the trailer and was lucky that Simon's acoustic guitar was by the door. She wouldn't have gotten it if it were any further towards the front of the trailer. Without a word she unlocked the case, took out the guitar and handed it to him. Simon smiled as best he could. "But Bail," he said, his tired voice trailing off, "I just got done playing all night for a room full of people."

Bailey handed him a blue tortoise shell guitar pick. "Yes, I know, Simon," she said. "But now it's time to play for *us*."

"You and me."

Simon sat on the hood of the car, with Bailey sitting next to him. There was one lonely light in the alley that for a little while was a safe place. Anyone with thoughts of evil deeds remained in the shadows during that time. Like Bailey, they only wanted the music. To get away for a while. Unknown to Simon and Bailey, that alley was also occupied that night by a knife and by a gun. The people to whom these tools of destruction belonged, put them away. Like Bailey, they only wanted to listen to the music. They faded back into the shadows, one behind a dumpster, the other in a dark doorway. As she listened to Simon play, and listened to him sing, Bailey reflected on why Simon *needed* to play. It wasn't just for the attention. It was for the salvation he got from it. She remembered him saying something about how it was "water under his bridge." Once he even said he felt the presence of God when he played. Once she tried to get him to say that again, but he refused. How nice it would be, she thought, if he would attend church with her.

Maybe someday.

She suspected that though the bars were hard on him and the temptations were many, the drink and drugs offered at every turn, she theorized, it was a hardship Simon chose to expose himself to. It was where his music flowed, she thought: In the places that needed Simon's music the most is where he got the most out of the performance. Right here in this alley. The world needed Simon Glenayre, she imagined. But what would be the cost? She shuddered to think about it.

After playing, Simon placed the pick in her hand, much like he had with the arrowhead during their trip to Colorado. He gently placed it in her hand and folded her fingers over it with an "I love you." He always knew how to make her melt.

The sound of the bass drum invaded Bailey's thoughts and pounded her attention back to her current reality. She looked down at her sweaty tea glass and half-eaten sandwich. The ice in her glass was melted and it was about time to go. It would be time to place some more calls and home would be the place for that. Too many distractions here, too many memories. Yes, she would start making calls. She knew he had family here still, in Kansas City, but would they know his whereabouts? She doubted it. Far too much petty bickering had been allowed to tear his family apart at the seams. They would be of no use to her. They were all as hard-headed as Simon. They locked up when they were pissed. Getting through to his family would be harder than walking into the White House wearing a ski mask and a dynamite vest.

When or if she did manage to find Simon, would she even be able to help him? And, she had grown since they had been apart. Would she even want him again when she saw him face to face? Most certainly yes, she thought. She loved him dearly. But she would not be blinded by her love this time. Sure, her heart beat straight and true, but bubbling just below her fantasy of having his presence in her life again, was the acknowledgement that there would be a much required effort for Simon to make. He would have to get into a program again. She would have to contact his AA sponsor.

No, she thought. That was Simon's job. He had to want it for himself. And that's where Bailey figured she went wrong the last time. She policed Simon and his addictions. She wanted sobriety for Simon more than he wanted it for himself. And such is the life for the family of loved ones who are slaves to booze and chemicals. But still she felt no hatred for what he had put her through. She had educated herself on recovery much since then.

She opened her hand to find the blue tortoise shell pick from that night in the alley.

CHAPTER 26

The inside of the elevator reeked of polish and stout cologne. Simon hummed along with a few bars of the Muzak version of "Yesterday" from an overhead speaker.

After a few floors, the doors of the elevator flung open with a brassy ding to reveal an elderly couple, dressed to the nines for an evening out together. They slipped onto the elevator with a pleasantness exhibited only by those old enough to appreciate the value of each and every passing moment. It seemed their feet never touched the floor.

Simon self-consciously pulled his long hair behind his right ear. Straightened the front of his leather jacket. He tried to smile to them as he looked down at the floor.

Not too much eye contact. Simon feared he might scare them with too much eye contact.

He was aware of what he looked like and what they surely must be thinking of him, and how could he blame them? He knew he looked like horrible. He could feel the vessels throbbing in his bloodshot eyes. The elderly couple talked softly between themselves. Simon caught himself wanting to lean forward and listen to every sweet syllable that passed between them. He wanted to ask them, "How did you get this far? How did you manage to stay together? What do you have to be so happy, relaxed and in love about?" The man's voice, while in casual conversation with his wife, spoke volumes to Simon of survival and of endurance. Of enduring the Great Depression, of surviving his tour of duty island hopping with Macarthur during the war. Without speaking directly to him, the old man's voice spoke of coming home and starting a family. He looked Simon in the eye and told him of the birth of his first child, then of the birth of his second and of his third. He spoke of the thrill of pacing in the waiting room as he was about to become a grandfather for the first time. Simon looked to the man's wife and then snapped his gaze back down again. The woman's voice was soft. Much softer than most a third her age. He saw her hand reach for that of her husband's. Simon looked up at the man again. He looked into her eyes as he spoke. She looked into his as she listened. And then she spoke back. The old man smiled because he liked not only what she had to say, but because he simply enjoyed the beauty of her company and the sound of her voice that was as soft and as young as the day they met. They looked at Simon, who again looked back down, embarrassed. With his head still tilted towards the floor, he glanced up to find they were looking directly at him.

"Got a big evening planned?" the elderly man inquired.

Simon found himself reaching for the jumbled mess of words in his mind. Grab something in there, anything. String them together. Yes. There. Make a sentence. They're nice people. Don't scare them. Don't embarrass yourself. Pull your hair behind your ears. Hide it. Don't let them see into your blackness. Make your sentence complete. "I'm going back home for a few days."

The lady smiled. "Ah. Isn't that nice. Going home is always nice. Has it been a while," she asked, "since you've been home?"

Simon looked down at the carpet and then back up. He forced a smile. He could tell he already lost the conversation. "Since I've been where?"

The lady smiled at Simon again. "Where?" she said. "Home, dear. Since you've been home."

"Yes, ma'am. It's been a long time," Simon whispered. "A really long time."

The man wove his arm within that of his wife's. "And where *is* home, son?" he asked.

Simon thought, which town, which city to name. Stick with what's familiar to them. "Kansas City." Again, as he had already done so often in only the past few moments, the man smiled yet again.

"Ah. Kansas City. We've been there," he said looking at his wife, "haven't we?" She only smiled with a nod, her eyes never leaving his. "She took me there to see me off to the Pacific during the war. She came as far as the Union Station. Beautiful building if you ask me. Is it still there?" he asked.

"Yes sir. It's still there," Simon mumbled, "they refurbished it."

"Well I bet it looks real nice. Hope they did it right." The elderly man said. "There's no use in doing something if you don't do it good" replied his wife. "Kansas City' she said, "the best kept secret in the country."

The bell gave an unwelcome ding. The doors of the elevator slid open on the restaurant floor. Simon felt himself wishing for a few hundred more floors with this couple, with their soft voices and their history together and the way they made him feel in their company. The old man patted the hand of his wife. "Well, I guess this is where we get off, son."

Simon wanted to grab them both. He wanted to ask them, to plead with them. "Don't leave me." He thought, "stay in the elevator and talk while I listen. Please, stay and talk about anything. Hold hands so I can see you together, being happy and in love and at peace with your lives."

The man curled his arm in that of his wife's and led her fragile body through the elevator doors. Simon opened his mouth to say something to the couple as they stepped away. Hardly half a whispered word managed to escape his lips.

Before the two sliding elevator doors closed completely, four boney fingers brought them to a stuttering halt, forcing the elevator's sensors to open them again. The old woman and the man stood arm in arm in the doorway. "You have a safe journey to where it is you're going, son." The old man grinned.

"You know," said the old woman as she pried her gaze away from her husband, "the destination isn't the only important thing when you're on a journey." She smiled. Her husband smiled too. "Yes, you have the potential to make some new, wonderful and important friends along the way."

"That's right," said the elderly man, "sometimes making new friends is the entire point of our travels, even though we may not even know it." The man's voice sounded as if he were trying to suppress his excitement over a wonderful secret he wanted to scream to the world. "And then, maybe you will be able to look people in the eye and not feel the need to hide your smile."

The man held up his long boney finger to Simon. "Yes! She's right!" he said firmly. "You do that my friend, and you have found the key!" For a moment Simon lost his breath.

"That's where I met my Sarah. Not at my destination, but during my journey."

The elevator bell gave a ding. Simon looked up at the red

light. The couple stepped away from the door and smiled again as it closed.

CHAPTER 27

In the parking lot, the throngs of Seattleites began filtering their way across the acreage of cars, busses and rain-soaked flesh and were packing against the still secured arena doors like the undead looking for a meal.

Deep within the bowels of the arena and at the end of a dark sweaty hallway, two familiar hands chopped a concoction of different crystalline powders on a small mirror. The razor's deadly symphony sparkled on the ceiling like midnight stars from the bathroom countertop. After tonight's show the mysterious powder was to find its way into Simon's drink. But to the surprise of those hands, with its razor and its deadly intentions, Simon would not be there to drink it. In the next dressing room over, the echo of drumsticks could again be heard smacking against tabletops. The chirping of groupies flitted above the hum of amplifiers and the twang of guitars not yet tuned up.

For the audience, the evening was destined to get ugly. Tonight, they expected Simon Glenayre to perform right before their very eyes. After the opening act left the stage, Simon's signature theatre curtain would be raised. His band would take the stage. His gold plated microphone would be put into place. His guitar sat tuned and rested on its stand at the side of the stage. Valletta lifted the mixing board faders to soul-numbing volumes. As the prerecorded vamp began to swell in the PA system, the crowd would leap to their feet, screaming.

Phil would race through the endless halls of the arena screaming Simon's name.

CHAPTER 28

On the flight back to Kansas City, Simon managed to fall asleep, somehow without the aid of a drink.

As the metal tube flung itself through the skies, Simon dreamt of a voice beneath the constant hum of jet engines. The voice soon gave way to light. The surrounding colors of green and gold took on a familiar shape to Simon. The squirrels made their usual noise as they scurried about in the leaves. Their chase took to the trees. The voice continued.

"Simon," his father said and sounding a bit concerned about it, "are you listening to me?" The clean German air filled Simon's nostrils. He looked down to see his hiking boots. Again, his father reached out to him. "This is it."

Simon felt a splinter from the bridge rail dig into the palm of his hand. "What?" he stuttered, pulling out the splinter and sucking on the wound. "Oh, yeah. You were saying..." as if he was caught passing a note during class instead of immersing himself in his lessons.

"You were talking about the bridge."

Simon's father, one eyebrow still shifted upward approximating the acute angle of concern, turned and leaned against the bridge's wooden rail. The stream below could be heard trickling, carrying the water from the winter's fall from the surrounding German hills.

"...What I was saying," his father said "is everybody goes through this." The man, dressed in Army fatigues turned toward his son. His left hand coming to rest atop Simon's hand on the bridge. "Don't think for a moment that your own father didn't find himself in nasty situations," he said. "Sure. I stood out in the crowd too. And I caught hell for it. Everybody is different, Simon," his father said. "The important thing is what you are going to do with this experience." Turning away from the field to face the trees on the opposite side of the bridge, Simon looked at the playing squirrels and sighed. He could hear his father's knuckles rap on the stone bridge. The stone groaned as if it would crack beneath the man's enormous fist.

His father's hand found its way to his shoulder.

"This is it, Simon."

Simon looked up at his father to find him smiling. He looked at his father's enormous hand on the stone bridge. "This is what?"

"This, my son," his father beamed, "is where you go." Simon mockingly laughed and looked around, hoping no hikers were nearby listening in. "If ever you need to get away from it all, Simon, find your way back to this bridge. This is where you will make your stand" his father smiled. "This is where your difference will be made. And your new path will begin. Your new path for the rest of your life."

Simon rolled his eyes.

"It will never be too late, Simon," his father smiled, "to start again."

Simon looked at his father, the look on his face curious. His father looked back at him, his expression saying "someday you'll understand."

Through the trees and way off in a distant field, Simon could make out a tractor tilling the soil around a pill box, one of the many remnants from the war. Simon often wondered why that wart, along with all the others left standing across this great nation, were not destroyed years ago. Perhaps some scars were best left alone, he thought to himself. One of many reminders left to stand purposefully in this nation. Like the still standing Camp Dachau: A way to remember the past in order to prevent its recurrence. Like recovery from drugs or alcohol, this nation moved forward gripping its token of recovery, sixty-plus years later.

The voice of his father repeated in his ear "This is where the difference will be made." Simon turned to the voice, but found himself alone on this tiny bridge over a tiny stream, next to a great forest bordering a field in a nation he once called home.

"Find your way here, Simon."

It repeated over and over in his head. Grudgingly, the roar of the jet engines invaded his sleep.

When Simon awoke, he eyed the blonde stewardess with her perfectly coiffed hair and endless smile with great trepidation. He found himself leaning forward to confirm that the seat ahead of him was not occupied by a small boy with chocolate stained fingers and a plastic trumpet. To his relief, he found a large, sweaty man with a walrus mustache snoring. The passenger next to him, tired and miserable, sat squashed up against the side of the airplane. Simon sat back in his seat and exhaled sharply. Several hours had passed since he skipped out of Seattle. He could feel the tension from Phil at thirty thousand feet. He knew at that very moment Phil was sprinting through the arena screaming Simon's name and listening through the cold echoing blackness for a response. Would Valletta ever forgive him for leaving without taking his bodyguard and closest friend? The big Italian would let him know if he was forgiven within the very first moments of his reemergence. Either he would be embraced by two hulking arms, or he would wake up on the floor with a broken nose.

Over the intercom, the voice of the pilot. "Coming up on Kansas City International Airport. Thanks for flying..." Out of habit, Simon lifted his hand to the stewardess signaling for a drink, but then without much inner deliberation, waved her and the drink away. She spun with a glare halfway down the aisle and slogged back to her station to resume practicing her smile in her tiny hand held mirror. Simon just cleared a hurdle, and it went nearly unrealized, until he arrived on the other side. With hardly a thought, he had leapt off the side of a towering black cliff and landed light as a feather in new, exciting territory. He refused a drink.

All he could do was smile.

Simon peered out the window and saw the lights of the Kansas City Plaza as the plane made its final approach to KCI. He found himself thinking of the old couple from the elevator. "All journeys need a place to begin." Simon could still hear the gentle allegrezza of the woman's voice singing in his ears. The way a pleasant aroma hangs in one's sense of smell, the old woman's voice hung musically in his mind. As he looked out the small window and down into the lights of the airport, Simon decided where his journey would begin.

Not at the end of a glass straw, but at an old Kansas City landmark.

CHAPTER 29

Again, he pounded on the door.

What's-his-name looked down the street for police as he heard Hix hissing at Hendricks to "pour it out!" More pounding on the door produced increased shuffling from within the old house, with its peeling paint, its sagging roof and its inhabitants hidden from the world behind ratty blankets and faded flag. How lucky they were, he thought to himself, that he was not a cop. The odor of marijuana easily found its way through the ample cracks around the door and to the waiting nostrils of whoever waited at the doorstep. Slowly, the door cracked open.

The eye peering through the crack in the door suddenly relaxed. "Oh," the voice groaned, relieved. "It's *you*." The door slammed shut to the clanging of locks unlocking and chains being undone. The door then flung open, and the smell smacked What's-his-name in the face. The painting of the clown with the large, sad eyes pled to What's-his-name to be rescued from this place. What's-his-name, for reasons that even he could not explain, had cleaned this house from top to bottom. Maybe he hoped it would make the right impression on its inhabitants. Perhaps he did it to make the place inhabitable so he would not feel so dirty when he came to visit. Either way, this room did not resemble the living room he left behind the last time he walked out the door. Hix and Hendricks lie in bean bag chairs amongst empty beer cans, album covers and grit. Hendricks coughed. "So what's up?"

What's-his-name waved the twisting, purple smoke away from his burning eyes. "Get up," he coughed, "we have to go."

CHAPTER 30

The airplane's landing gear chirped on the runway.

The shudder of the flying machine was barely noticeable to Simon as he caught himself drifting into sleep. In the years past, sleep would only come from the end of a needle, or with the swallowing of a pill, or at the end of a full night of sobbing. Waking up often required the use of a needle, or a pill, or the sound of his own screams. Tonight, Simon would sleep. And sleep well.

At the end of his brief nap, he woke not to the familiar screech of Phil's voice, but to the pleasant chatter of strangers around him. This was the equivalent of switching from the banging of pots and pans to the soft whisper of a loved one saying softly in his ear, "Wake up, honey. Let's start our day together." Starting tonight, Simon would try to hold hands with the world again and search for answers. He would walk out of this airport, wave down a taxi and go to the only place in the world where he felt he might find them. Why he felt drawn to that place, he had no idea. Maybe it was the architecture that pulled at him. The age of that old building, with its rich history of love and pain and its greetings and its farewells, it called to him. The automatic doors slid open with a swish and the rich sounds of life once again greeted Simon. The armada of yellow cabs sat in a long line, their drivers playing cards, smoking, eating sack lunches. He watched a cabbie toss a cigarette into a stream of water and observed silently as it cut through the waves on its journey to a dark grave in the waiting gutter. Another cabbie cursed at his radio as his football team coughed up the football on the five yard line. Another flipped aimlessly through a newspaper. He did not immediately approach them. He only stood and watched for the longest time. He turned to the sound of a child singing and found a couple with their daughter as they summoned the attention of a cabbie. Simon watched as the driver carelessly tossed their bags into the trunk. The mother winced at the thought of a scuff on the expensive leather bags, her shoulders creeping up to her ears. The father frowning. The little girl giggled with her doll dangling at her knees as the cabbie took notice of her smile and began to make silly faces at her. The man in the worn flannel shirt jammed his bulky thumb in his mouth and popped his cheek for the child who squealed with delight. Mother watched with a smile, father observed sternly at first. His almost frown finally surrendered to a bit of smile from the farthest corner of his mouth. Then they all got in the car and with a hiss of the tires on the wet pavement, shot off towards the waiting highway and its swift current of speeding cars. Simon wished them safely to their destination.

It was now after midnight and with precious few minutes of real sleep, Simon leaned back and enjoyed the sights and sounds around him with one foot propped up against the wall. Tonight he felt more alive than he had in years. For once he was in no hurry.

Simon would not darken Union Station's doors tonight. At this hour the building was closed. Its doors chained shut forcing Simon and the rest of the world to wait until opening hours. Simon stood wondering what ghosts roamed through its massive halls at that very moment. Eternally saying goodbye to loved ones, the mothers, wives and girlfriends forever wiping ancient tears away with handkerchiefs so ethereal you could gently blow them into nothingness. He imagined the now absent sounds of the locomotives steaming off to the East or West coast. Sending men off to war like so many cattle cars off to the slaughterhouse. And then Simon thought of the old man and his wife from the elevator. The sound of their voices still hung sweetly in his ears like a Shakespearean sonnet. They too had said goodbye to each other many years before in that very place, with its high frescoed ceiling, its arches and it's still echoing voices saying softly, sadly, "goodbye." Most of the farewells drenched in fear and yet sprinkled with hope for a safe return. Simon took in a deep breath and exhaled slowly. "My God, how did they do it?"

Simon finally pried his back from the wall of the airport and scanned the collection of cab drivers to decide which one to summon. There was the cabbie reading the newspaper. There was the cabbie smoking a cigarette and cursing at the football game on the radio. There was also the cabbie sitting on the hood of his chariot eating a bologna sandwich.

Simon looked to his left and settled for the cabbie sitting on the hood of his car smoking a cigarette, eating a bologna sandwich over an open newspaper all the while cursing at the football game on the radio. It seemed he had all the bases covered.

Simon waved to him. The large man with the ratty stocking cap and cratered face rubbed the stubble of his massive jaw as he looked at Simon's feet. "That the only bag you got, buddy?" Simon smiled at him as the thought of Phil bitching while he signed a cash release to the hardly used and still fresh union workers as he cursed his name. "Yeah," he laughed. "That's all the baggage I got *tonight*."

The cab driver raised one eyebrow, his bottom lip always sticking out farther than the top, cracked and smeared with chunks of mayonnaise. "Well, all right then. Just hop in and I'll put your bag in th' trunk." The entire car shrugged as the overweight man stuffed his frame into the front seat and with a belch, strapped on his seat belt. He answered the call over his CB, groaned aloud, then spun around in his seat to face Simon. "So where you wanna go?" Simon gripped the credit card in his pocket. "Let's get downtown."

"Ah," the cabbie smiled, looking Simon over. Over the years, the stranger in the front seat had developed a sixth sense of which hotels different people would want to go to. He rarely got it wrong. "I bet I know where you wanna go. The Hyatt, right?"

"Yeah, I guess so," Simon frowned. He drummed his fingers on his knee. "No. Not the Hyatt tonight," he then whispered. "Let's hit the nearest Holiday Inn."

And with a hiss of the car's four tires on the wet pavement, they sped off towards the highway, its glaring red taillights accelerating into the flow of traffic racing downtown. Simon laughed aloud as he held on for dear life.

CHAPTER 31

Two o'clock in the morning in downtown Kansas City.

The sounds of a car horn echoed in the distance. A fine mist floated in the air, giving the street lights an otherworldly amber halo. The dampness on the city streets set an industrial perfume to the air. A large and rough looking cat crept across General John Pershing Boulevard. Not moving too quickly, the cat was well aware it could fight fiercely for its life if needed, against any predator foolish enough to pick a fight. But it would not tempt fate by racing across the street as if it were weak and scared. Slowly, menacingly, the large cat with its dusty matted hair growled its way across the road. The animal would eventually make its way safely from the World War I Memorial, across the street and into Union Station's parking garage where it would begin hunting for a meal and eventually settle into a safe place to sleep for the rest of the night. From outside one could hear the sound of the evening's first unlucky meal squeal through the chilly night air.

Looking down on Union Station from the plaza of the nation's World War I Memorial, one could see three figures standing hopelessly, irritably at the main doors of that massive structure. The World War I Memorial Tower, with its four statues stood nearby. Two of the memorial tower's four statues faced the Union Station. Honor and Sacrifice, one wearing a wreath of honor, the other wearing a star. They both seemed to move their gaze. The stone of their visages shifted, looking down from the Kansas City skyline to the figures grumbling and complaining amongst themselves. The sounds of the night, the hiss of distant tires on wet pavement filled in the silent holes left between Hendricks' bitching.

"Well, sheee-it."

Hix, Hendricks and What's-his-name stood three abreast in front of the sealed-tight Union Station. Its doors lashed impossibly tight with heavy chains. A siren wailed in the distant night ripping their attention from the doors and towards the direction of the sound. When the whine of the far-off siren disappeared into the night air, all three spun around without a word and began flailing at the doors. With a final burst of angry rattling, Hendricks jerked away, kicking his feet, full force at absolutely nothing.

What's-his-name groaned and rubbed at his face. Hendricks continued to yank at the doors, wishing to himself that they would somehow open just because he willed it. Hix unwrapped another candy bar and crammed it deep into his ever waiting beak. Hendricks would be the evening's first voice of dissention.

"Well, what in the world were you thinking?" he hissed. "It's two o'clock in the morning! Did you think Union Station would be open twenty four hours a day?" What's-his-name said nothing. He only looked at the chains through the glass of the doors. From deep within the shadows of the parking garage, the glow of the amber streetlights reflected off of two slit-like corneas. The last remnants of blood, savored from sharpened claws. And with a purr that sounded more like the final rasp of an old tractor, the cat curled up at the side of the entry way and watched the threesome bitch.

A cat's senses, like its claws, are sharp. Hearing, that picks up on the faintest of distant sounds, such as the tiniest of steps from the smallest mouse creeping for its very life. Eyes created for even better sight in almost pitch black conditions.

Cats also have a sensitivity to *presence*. Nothing of this world gets near them without their being totally aware. It is also said in many old superstitions and ancient religions that cats are sensitive beings that are very aware of excursions into this world from visitors outside our realms of understanding. Look into the eyes of a cat too long, they say, and you just might get a glimpse into Hell and never be the same again.

This large black leather boot caught our cat by total surprise, catching it directly in the ribs and sending it spiraling several feet away and finally rolling to a stop beneath a rusty construction truck. Shocked at the stealth of the attack, the animal crept behind a tire as it struggled for breath, glaring at the hulking dark figure in the shadows and planning it's revenge. The animal hoped beyond all hope that this stranger in black might look in its eyes far too long. It continued watching the silhouette, observing the three in front of the large glass and brass doors argue.

"So why are we here in the first place?" Hendricks' shoulders crept up towards his earlobes as he gestured outward with his hands.

What's-his-name stood facing the twin doors, his back to the others. "It's just kind of hard to explain…" Hendricks rocked back and forth heel to toe glaring at the back of What's-his-name's head, watching as he stood staring at the door lost in his own thoughts, nearly oblivious to the rage building up in everybody else.

Almost everybody else.

Hix was satisfied as long as there was another candy wrapper he could conquer. He could have cared less and McDonald's would be serving breakfast soon enough. In the meantime, Hendricks was *furious*.

"It's almost three o'clock in the morning!" What's-his-name's silence only enraged Hendricks further. He jerked forward and grabbed What's-his-name's arm to jerk him backward. It was as if What's-his-name was now as heavy and solid as the largest stone carving. He budged not an inch. Hendricks caught himself from falling forward only by clinging to What's-his-name's arm. Hix continued spinning himself around an art deco light pole as Hendricks crept up beside What's-his-name and looked into his eyes. The hair on the back of his neck stood on end as he observed his friend and irritant. His eyes, it seemed, sparkled more than what they should in this dim night air. He was looking somewhere beyond the glass of the large brass double doors. At that very moment, What's-his-name was somewhere else. Hendricks could hear Hix's hand squeak on the light pole as he continued spinning around and around.

Hix's chocolate-stained mouth grinned wide as he watched the world spin by: Hendricks and What's-his-name, the WWI Memorial, the parking garage entrance, Hendricks and What's-his-name, the WWI Memorial, the parking garage entrance, Hendricks and What's-his-name, the WWI Memorial, and then the parking garage entrance with the large, dark figure standing in its shadows. Hix nearly tripped as he slowed the momentum of his flabby frame going round and round in pointless circles before finally letting loose of the light pole.

He stopped to face the darkness of the parking garage

entrance.

The figure in the darkness was gone and now Hix found himself wondering if he had really seen anyone there in the first place. He stepped off the cobble sidewalk away from the others and towards the dark parking lot entry way. What's-his-name and Hendricks were oblivious to his creeping absence. Hix could swear he could see someone in the entry way if he looked deep enough. The voice that swam around his head told him to come just a little bit nearer. There was something urgent the voice wanted to share and he needed to go to the voice in the shadows immediately. Hix stopped for a moment and turned to look at the others as What's-his-name stood still as a marble statue and Hendricks stood by his side, looking silently into his lost, otherworldly gaze. Again, that voice in his head called for his attention. He moved slowly towards the parking garage entrance. In the background he could faintly hear What's-his-name and Hendricks, now talking. "I always come here when I need to think. When I'm looking for ideas or answers."

Hendricks winced and pulled his chin back towards his Adam's apple. "So, the reason you dragged us all down here," he groaned, "is so you can get answers? Give me a break," he hissed.

The voice, it demanded Hix's attention. It drew at him and controlled him like a puppet master displays his control over a marionette. Faintly, he heard the low growl of an old cat from somewhere. He could still, though very faintly, hear What's-his-name and Hendricks talking.

"It's hard to explain," he stuttered, "but do you remember that thing that was happening with all my computers at home?"

Hendricks stuck his hands in his pocket and turned around, vaguely wondering to himself where Hix was wandering off to. "Yeah," he said, watching as Hix continued slowly towards the entryway. He turned back towards What's-his-name without saying anything to him. "Yeah, the computers with all the ones and zeroes." He kicked at the kick plate at the bottom of the brass door, listening to the thick chains jangle from the other side of the doors. Their metallic sound echoing off distant walls, waking the ghosts for another sad farewell.

"So what. Did you figure out what it meant?"

What's-his-name replied. "Yeah," he grinned. "I guess you could say I did." He pried his attention from the doors. For a moment he thought he saw a woman bidding farewell to a man wearing a fedora and a well-cut suit. Tears streaming down her

142

face. Uncertainty and bravery in the man's eyes. And in the instant he saw them, they were gone.

He turned towards Hendricks. "I gave simple numerical equivalents to those ones and zeroes."

Hendricks interrupted as he watched Hix move further away. "But wait a minute, how many numerical equivalents' can you possibly give only two numbers?"

What's-his-name appreciated that Hendricks was using his mind enough to think up the question. "The numerical value I assigned them was not really for the ones and zeroes themselves, but rather to their positions in *relationship* to one another." He took an excited step towards Hendricks who in turn took a cautious step back.

The voice in his head called Hix closer still towards the deep blackness of the parking garage. The vengeful, scruffy cat continued to rumble and growl at the large figure as it stood framed by the garage entryway. Intelligent beings think in the language they speak and understand. The cat could only imagine this thing looking deep into its eyes for too long, perhaps earning a one-way ticket to fire and brimstone. The feline could also see another person making his way towards the darkness of the parking garage, and his new sworn enemy.

The cat let out another low, raspy growl.

What's-his-name continued explaining to Hendricks. "What I found out, when I put all these numbers and letters together on paper, was that it made sentences."

Hix, now very near the entry way to the garage and the source of the voice in his head now felt the damning feeling of helplessness. For some reason he knew that he was going to die. And yet all he could do was move forward. All he could do was what he was commanded by the puppet master voice that tugged at the marionette strings in his feeble mind. Again, also from within the darkness, he heard that raspy low grumbling.

Hendricks continued to push What's-his-name for an answer. "So what in the heck did you find? What did all the numbers say when you did your thing? When you changed them into sentences?"

The smile leapt off and on What's-his-name's face several times before speaking. Finally, he managed to speak. "What it said was…" Hendricks leaned forward.

"What it said was, *For God so loved the world that he gave his only begotten Son, that whosoever believeth in him should not perish, but have everlasting life.*'"

Hendricks took a step backwards. "It said that John 3:16 thing?" What's-his-name smiled. "Yes, it did. What do you think of that?"

Hendricks looked over his shoulder towards the rapidly disappearing existence of Hix off in the distance. "Well, to be honest, I kinda think you may be full of-" he looked towards Hix again. "Hey, bonehead," he yelled, "Get back over here. We're leaving soon!" The cat in the garage could be heard now. The old scrapper hated the figure in the doorway and observed as it led the smaller chubby figure from the outside toward itself in the darkness, a familiar method to the cat who had captured many a meal that very way.

"So now what?" asked Hendricks as his curiosity for Hix's destination grew. Hix, unbeknownst to him, would soon become a fading memory. Hix drew nearer and nearer, the cat watched as the gleam from an ancient Babylonian blade flashed across its corneas. Hix reached the doorway, mindless, pointless and ready to be slaughtered in the name of a faceless evil.

"Hix!" The only voice that Hix was able to hear came from the figure in the garage. Again, Hendricks yelled his name. Hix, silent, and now standing still in front of the entry way, said nothing. Suddenly, a figure, very large for a cat, burst from the darkness, its teeth ablaze, eyes on fire. The large cat sprung on Hix's leg striking at his pants and reducing a large section of his pant leg to shreds. The pain of the cat's sharp claws snapped Hix back into reality. And as soon as it had started, the animal was gone.

"Hix!" The startled Hix jerked and spun back around. The dark figure, at home within the darkness of the garage entryway would put way the gleaming blade and under his breath, curse the day cats were created. It was always harder to get the job done with cats around.

The cat had his revenge on the one who had harmed him. The large figure in the shadows would not feed on the soul of that person as was planned. The flash of its blade put back in the darkness of the long black leather coat to be used at some other time. Hix was not his main target anyway, but merely a target of opportunity. A good place to start.

There would be other nights.

Other chances.

There was still time.

Time was the one thing he had on his side. Like the Grim Reaper making his rounds, he would finish. Ultimately.

The cat coughed a rough and satisfied purr as he settled into a new and somewhat warmer place to sleep for the night and observed with satisfaction as the three strangers pulled back onto the main road and disappeared into the distant streetlights and far off siren wails.

CHAPTER 32

The hiss of Interstate 70 echoed off the sliding glass doors of the posh hotel.

It wasn't a Holiday Inn as he requested but only a place like the luxurious hotels that Phil regularly booked him in. The cabbie insisted this would be a good place to stay, sensing from years of experience that Simon could afford better than a Holiday Inn, which of course meant a better tip. Simon agreed to stay there, he was tired and only wanted to get some sleep. The gruff driver popped open the trunk with the aid of a screwdriver and a few mumbled words, playfully tossed Simon his bag with a smile. Simon stuffed a wad of bills into the man's giant hand who smiled his best smile and then spit on the pavement.

"Anything else I can getcha?" he smiled. "Maybe a girl for the night?" The smile fell from the man's face when Simon gave no reaction. "Or" he said more discretely, "maybe a guy?"

Simon assured him he was fine on his own and would soon be down for the night. Simon watched as the cab turned right on red and spun off for the highway. He turned on his heel facing the hotel, grabbed his bag and made for the sliding doors. The too-firm grip around his ankle felt familiar to Simon, who for a second before he looked down, wondered why in the world someone was now grabbing him by the leg.

"Hey boy!" The old black man belched at Simon from between his yellowed grimy teeth. "You got some change to help an old fart?" The old man with his fingerless gloves and pitted face looked familiar. Simon ignored his déjà vu. Of course, thought Simon, it couldn't be the same man. An old bum with the resources to beat a rock star to any given point on the map?

Surely not, he thought.

"Well, you gonna dish something out to help your fellow man," the bum growled, "or are you gonna just stand there like a big lump of doody with that stupid look on your face?" Simon tried to jerk his leg out of the man's grip, but the stranger was deceptively stronger than he appeared.

He jerked his leg again with no success. "I got a few bucks on me. Ok?" Simon dug in his bag of belongings, jerking out a wad of bills and threw it in the bum's lap. "Now, will you please let go of my leg?"

The old man released his leg without even looking at the crumpled mess of bills on his lap. It was as if he really couldn't care less about the money. His voice softened as he watched Simon stomp on the activator pad for the automatic sliding doors. "You know, the funny thing is, you th' one with all the money and I'm the one without," he said. "And do you know why that's funny about that?" He kept his eyes on Simon who was still stomping in vain on the rubber mat trying to open the doors.

"No," Simon grunted. "Why is that so funny?"

The old bum shifted on the wet pavement, and bracing one hand against the brick wall labored to pull himself to his feet. Simon expected to see an empty whiskey bottle tumble out of his grimy layered clothing and smack the sidewalk with a shatter. "What's so funny," he said, "is that you got all that money you throwin' around, nice clothing, a mouth full of expensive teeth and-"

"And what?" Simon sneered, still glaring at the unattended counter on the other side of the sliding doors that wouldn't open.

The old man continued. "It seems I'm a hell of a lot happier than you are. Why do you think that is, boy?" Simon turned around and flung his bag onto the rubber mat hoping in vain it would open the sliding doors. It did not. He spun back around to the old bum.

"Findin' happiness boy, is easy, if you know which door to knock on."

"Oh God," said Simon. "You're not going to preach at me, are you?"

The old man laughed aloud and scratched at his ruddy black beard. "No, boy. No," he shook his head. "But you got problems and you ain't gonna find it at the end of a needle or at the bottom of some bottle!" He wagged his crusty huge finger at Simon. "You need to get right with God, boy! Get right with God!" He waved his finger again at Simon who did not care too much for having a finger waved at him. This brought back memories of his grandfather setting him straight after catching hay on fire behind the barn many, many years before.

"You tryin' to open doors with keys that don't fit, boy!"

The word "key" hung in Simon's ears longer than he would have preferred. "And just how do you get right with God?" he said, a hint of sarcasm in his voice.

"It's simple. I can tell you don't wanna really know right now, but when you are ready to talk to God, he gonna listen to you. You just gotta know how to get in His house."

"How do you get in His house?"

"You knock at the door, baby!" The man belched his reply aloud. Simon jerked at his volume.

Simon gave an exhausted stomp on the pad again, hoping for the doors to finally open. They sat silent, budging not an inch. Again, Simon groaned and rubbed at his face. "It's friggin' four in the morning," he said, looking at his watch. "At least I'll be able to get breakfast soon." He looked through the glass doors, hoping to see an attendant pass behind the desk. The counter was abandoned. The clerk most likely asleep on the floor.

"You understand me, boy?"

"Yeah, right. I understand," Simon said absentmindedly, still wishing through the glass.

The bum smiled again and sat back down on the damp pavement. "Ask and it shall be given to you, seek and ye shall find, knock and the door shall be opened unto you." And with that, the familiar stranger leaned over to the rubber doormat and touched it with his crusty, cracked finger. The door, so stubborn and impossible to open, obediently slid open with a speedy "hiss" of its electric motor.

Speechless, Simon bent over grabbed his bag and backed through the door before it closed. The old man watched as Simon rang the bell on the counter, the receptionist rising from below. Money being exchanged for a key. Simon disappearing into an elevator.

"Yeah. It's just like the song, ain't it?" the bum said to the twisting, rumbling skies above, as if he were being listened to. "Yeah, just like that old tune."

"Sometimes I wonder/ If my tomorrow will ever come/ Show me where to look/ Show me where to look…"

He sang to the clouds, "Show me where to look."

CHAPTER 33

The hand shook as it scraped signatures across one check after another. A drop of sweat landed on the final signature and absorbed into the paper, spreading darkness across it like the black plague. Amid the nervous silence of the packed room of Union leaders, stage managers and record company suits, Phil groaned again.

"I'm gonna kill him."

Phil slapped the pen on the tabletop and fell back in his chair with an exhausted sigh. He rubbed at his temple. "I can't believe he did this to me."

The door at the back of the room opened and an anonymous unimportant face peered through the crowd towards Phil, obviously nervous. He leaned over the chair and whispered. "It's Sol. He heard about what happened" the voice shook. "He wants you to call him back, A.S.A.F.P." Phil tried to think up an excuse. He knew at that very moment, Sol's people were calling more runners to contact Phil about calling him back. He also knew that it was their direct orders to immediately confirm with Sol's people that they had found Phil and passed on the message. There was no getting out of this and he knew it. His high-back chair spun around towards the privacy of the wall and a loud snorting sound bounced from the wall. Phil spun back around towards the table and reached for his glass, spun the ice around his glass with the celery stick and downed the red concoction with one damning gulp, slamming the thick tumbler with a whack onto the table top.

"I'll kill him."

Phil rubbed the top of his frizzy balding head, wiped away the remaining crystals dangling from his nose and rocked slightly from right to left while staring at absolutely nothing. "Alright," he spat, "better get this over with." And with a snap of his fingers an anonymous hand reached around the chair with a satellite phone. Phil took hold of it as if it were a hand grenade. Without looking up, Phil felt the room empty without a sound. He knew he was alone. Suddenly his voice echoed off the distant cinderblock walls. The voice on the other end of the line was low. The sound of thick cigar embers could be heard burning through the receiver. Phil nodded his head. "Yes sir," he shuddered, "I understand." Phil rolled the chair slowly from left to right, eyeing his now empty glass, wishing for another. The voice coming through the phone from Los Angeles growled another command. Phil answered. "Yes sir, but-"

Phil regretted using that word in this conversation. He wished to hell he could take it back. But now it was too late. To trudge forward was all he could do. He could hear the voice growl over the receiver. "All I'm saying, sir, is will he really go through with it? I mean-"

Phil bit nervously at dead skin of his bottom lip. He knew he had again overstepped his bounds. With a loud pop of the cigar from his lips, Sol Glenn interrupted him.

"You leave that up to me, Phil. You just do what you're told." Phil said nothing, he only nodded his head as if Sol could see. Perhaps in his own way, Sol could see.

Within the hour, the teams were let loose. They wore matching dark suits and sunglasses and walked briskly with a deadly determination out of a castle-like warehouse in the darkest most forbidding corner of a warehouse district. Their black bags clutched firmly at their sides, nearly bursting at the seams with the tools of destruction.

CHAPTER 34

Before leaving the apartment he could have chosen a different pair of shoes had he thought about it. However nothing would have been gained from rummaging around the apartment in the near darkness. All of Izzy's shoes had holes in their soles anyway.

He could feel water squish between his toes with the splash of each undetected pot hole within this seeping, filthy alley. The bang of trashcans and the rustle of garbage told him he was not alone in this place. Izzy could hear the silhouettes whispering amongst themselves hunched over, against the sweating bricks of a Chinese restaurant. Izzy jerked to his right when the back door slammed open, a Chinese cook leaping out, cursing at the figures in the darkness and waving a ladle in a threatening manner. The men, emerging from the anonymity of the shadows, wore shabby clothes and had not yet fully hidden the tools of their self destruction. A bent spoon with residue still steaming upon its surface flipped out of the stranger's hand, landing at Izzy's feet with a suicidal "clink." Izzy stopped in his tracks, nearly picking up the spoon for the man out of sheer habit. He spent his days picking up Sam's spoon at the dinner table. He caught himself just in time.

The addict, with his raggedy coat and fingers cut out of his gloves growled at Izzy while stumbling over his own feet to get to the spoon. The man snatched the spoon and disappeared back into the shadows. Izzy exhaled.

For now, Izzy's baby sister Sam, was fast asleep. A positive sign. This meant for the moment she was not hungry. However Izzy knew it wouldn't last and before long she would be awake, gripping the bars of her cradle and crying out for the warm embrace of her brother and hopefully something to eat.

He knew he had to make this quick. He did not trust their mother to handle Sam. And she was terrifying when she was forced awake.

Izzy would not approach these strangers. One can never deduce the true intentions from the faces of these flimsy addicts and hardened killers. And who would be there for Sam if something happened to him? Grimm would reveal himself in due time. Izzy marched on, the tears welling up in his eyes. He promised himself he was above this. He promised himself that he would set a good example for his sister. Izzy hoped that someday Sam would forgive him. But this would help him to procure dinner for his sister, tonight and on many nights as well.

Izzy kept telling himself his baby sister was worth chipping off this corner of his soul. A tear landed on the sweaty alley floor, his reflection shone upon the damp brick beneath his feet. He kept walking.

The middle of the alleyway. Two dumpsters sat beneath a rusty, decrepit fire escape. This was the place. He was told to be here no later than one a.m. The police would be by at two o'clock to once again chase off the users. The deal would have to be done quickly. And it had to go off without a hitch. Any other way meant disaster. Though Izzy had isolated himself from the others of his neighborhood, he still heard the stories. He understood how these things went down. One misunderstood phrase or the wrong facial expression could be construed as having something to hide. Having something to hide meant he could be an informer for the police. Being an informer for the police would land a bullet from a .38 into his chest cavity, forever separating him from his beloved Sam. He knew how to play it cool. He learned from his mother. Finally, the voice from an earlier phone call rang from the shadows behind him. A voice Izzy both loathed and needed at this desperate point in his life. The voice oozed from the shadows again.

"You're Iz, aint'cha?" Izzy opened his mouth, nothing came out. He watched a hand extend from the shadows, placing a cigarette to thin, cracked lips. The man struggled to light a match against the wet brick of the wall behind him. "Yeah" the man gurgled, "I'd know you anywhere."

"You look just like your mother."

Izzy bit his lip. Still, he could control his terror as long as this filth remained ignorant to the existence of his baby sister. To hear her name across his lips would make him physically ill. He scratched the side of his neck. It itched, just like it always did when he was nervous. Pulling himself together, he took a step forward and spoke with authority.

"Yeah" he said, "I hear that all the time." Ten yards behind him, the Chinese cook again lunged through his alley door, threatening the users who had found their way back to his dumpsters. Izzy hoped this man did not see him jerk. It would be perceived` as a sign of weakness. The stranger yanked the cigarette from his lips with a "pop" and smiled. His coffee stained teeth seemed to glow through the darkness. "What's wrong, Iz?" He gurgled a laugh. "Nervous?"

The face of a fourteen year old boy is hardly worn enough to put on a convincing poker face. No matter how tough he talked, no matter how hard he walked, or stuck out his chest in scary situations like this, his youthful face would always give him away. He was nervous. And he couldn't hide it. Still, he tried. "Hell no I ain't scared" he spat. "This is *my* neighborhood." The man laughed hard and loud. He burst from the shadows and grabbed Izzy at the back of his neck with hard, weathered hands. "So," he laughed, "you wanna gun, eh?"

"Yeah, sure." Izzy stuttered.

"I- I got work to do."

The large thug, his sandpaper hands still wrapped around Izzy's slender neck laughed again. "Oh" he snickered, "you got work to do." Izzy looked up to see all the gold teeth fill the huge hole in the man's face. "Look," the stranger said, "you're just a kid. If you wanna get high I'll set you up." He then looked up and down the alley. "Hell, I'll even get you there for free. The first time."

"After that it'll cost ya, of course"

Izzy refused with the strongest yet most considerate voice he could muster.

An agreement was reached. Izzy would get the gun. But not at the self deprecating price he was expecting. The gun would be his, but the full cost would be determined at a later date. The man explained to Izzy that when the time came, he would be called upon to use the gun on somebody. Upon completion of the as of yet undisclosed task, the gun would officially be his. Until then, it was strictly a loaner. He would not be allowed to return the gun to avoid the pending task. An attempt to do so would be disastrous.

Grimm gave Izzy a most basic rundown of how to shoot a gun. Hold it with two hands, point. Pull the trigger. He also gave

Izzy the gun's story. Where it had been, what it had seen. It had a sad and murderous history. Its serial number long since filed off. The man with pale skin and rough hands and the voice drenched in booze, reached into his leather coat and pulled out the .38 snub-nose revolver. He slapped the cheap, nickel plated gun into Izzy's hand. It felt harder and colder than he expected. Looking around quickly, he hissed at the boy. "Don't just stand there! Put the damned thing in your pocket!"

Another trash can knocked over, and Izzy could again hear the Chinese cook yelling. More rustling in the dumpster behind him. He wanted to turn around and look, but to turn his back on this man in the middle of a deal might be seen as disrespectful. In the streets of this city, "disrespect" could be interpreted from many things, but most usually from the simplest and most innocent of actions. He felt the cold steel of the gun in his hand and wondered if there were bullets in it.

"Now look, the serial numbers on it are rubbed off. No prints on it. It's clean and can't be traced back to me." Izzy could feel the sudden tension in his voice. "So you better be careful with this thing," he said. "Cause if you get caught they gonna try to figure out where you got this thing." Izzy could feel the man's grip tighten on his neck. The coarseness of his hand irritated his young skin. "Yeah, sure Grimm" Izzy jittered. I won't get caught. I won't do anything stupid."

"Good." Grimm smiled showing his glowing yellowed teeth. "Cause if you do get busted and start singing my name…well that would be bad. Wouldn't it?"

"And you wouldn't want anything to happen to your mother, would you?"

Izzy shook his head. Now he was truly scared but had to fight out a convincing and toughened answer. "No, I don't want anything to happen to my mother."

"And how about that baby sister of yours?" he said.

Izzy's legs went numb. He nearly fell to the ground in shock.

"Yeah. I hear she's a cute one and relies on her older brother. Yep," he gurgled. "You gotta be careful for her sake too, dont'cha?"

Izzy stood thunderstruck. If he was certain the gun in his pocket had bullets, he would have pumped two into Grimm's head and flew out of that alley like a bat out of hell. Again, the man laughed his twisted laugh.

"Oh don't be so shocked, Iz" the man said. "Ain't much that gets by me. After all," he said, glaring at the boy,

"This is *my* neighborhood."

The two observed a police car pass by one end of the alley. It was almost time for another alley sweep. The man shoved Izzy towards the other end of the alley and disintegrated into the darkness of an alley door.

Izzy emerged from the alley, blending into the anonymity of the pedestrians. With each convenience store, every liquor store the boy assessed his chances of success. Liquor stores tended to have thick, bullet proof glass between the cash register and the customers. It seemed everybody had video surveillance. He had the ski mask in his hip pocket. His identity would be protected. He knew his size and build would certainly give away his age. Izzy prayed for forgiveness for what he was going to do this evening. He convinced himself this had to be done. An evil task to accomplish a greater good. Sam was hungry, and he was sick of it. He was sick of feeling helpless. She deserved better and he would give it to her. The boy settled on a convenience store. If he was lucky he could dip in, and if the store had baby formula, could grab it and make a dash for the door. Wouldn't have to show the gun to get cash. Any heroes would be thwarted when he exposed the .38. But if he was lucky, he could just get the formula and wouldn't have to show the gun. He knew this was a long shot. He had always heard in the neighborhood that for every robber, there was a good Samaritan hero wannabe. He feared accidentally shooting someone out of sheer nervousness.

He dipped into an alley beside the convenience store. Tugged the ski mask onto his head. He twisted the mask around so the eyes were in place. Just so. A quick prayer. Izzy spun on his heels and quickly emerged from the alley and dipped into the store. A single gunshot rang out.

CHAPTER 35

The red numbers where blurry.

As Simon squinted, the more they came into focus. He lifted his head for a view over the pillow. 11:59. The clock. It said "11:59."

A voice in his head said the time on the clock had an immediate significance. But the importance of that number proved beyond his fuzzy grasp. After having the best night of sleep he'd had in years, Simon was still too groggy to grasp much of anything. The full night's sleep did his scarred mind and abused body good. He slept like a baby, and without the aid of booze or downers he found it to be a much more rewarding rest. But still, 11:59. Something about that time. Its significance would soon reveal itself.

The pounding at his door was rapid, intrusive. "Housekeeping...hello." Simon listened as a key ring jangled, the master key being crammed into the door knob. The door cracked, again the voice. It was in the room. "Hello? Housekeeping..."

Simon pulled the blanket halfway up his chiseled torso. The housekeeper popped around the corner, and her mouth dropped open. "Oh honey," she cooed, "I think my morning is startin' off just fine."

Simon groaned and tugged the covers up to his chest. "I'm sorry. Overslept" he said, fumbling items off the nightstand in a sloppy search for a cigarette.

"Here," the maid said, slowly, and with the most seductive tone she could muster, "let me get that for you." She watched, a dreamy expression on her face as Simon popped a match and lit his French cigarette. "You know the checkout time is noon, right?"

Simon took a long drag from the expensive cigarette, its embers popping and flaring in his eyes. The maid gave a sigh. "Yeah" Simon groaned. "Guess I'm paying for another night."

"Thank goodness" the maid mumbled to herself as she dusted off the dresser on the other side of the room. Simon laughed. Without turning around the maid froze. "I can't believe I just said that out loud." Simon laughed agian. The maid laughed with him. Together they surrendered to the blissful awkwardness of the moment.

"I'll tell the front desk you are staying another night, if you like." Simon smashed the cigarette in an ashtray and spun his shirtless body over the edge of the bed. He could hear the middle aged house keeper surrender a groan. "Sorry. I guess I could get dressed."

The maid spun around. "Oh, don't rush yourself on my account." Simon grinned, pulled the blankets around himself and worked his way to the shower. "So you want me to tell the desk you're here for another night?"

"Please?" she said.

"No," Simon said from the bathroom. "I'll do it myself."

"I think I'm going to stay around for a while."

The maid exited the room with a loud thud of the door. The shower. Hot water. Just so. A little cold. Perfect. The shower ran so hot it steamed the mirror in the bedroom.

Simon rushed through his shower and as he toweled himself off he realized he hands were shaking. Unlike other fits of jitters he often endured, these jitters were of a different source. Simon was excited just to get out on his own for a little while. He smiled in the mirror, tugging a baseball cap down over his face. Sunglasses completed the disguise. The mini fridge, right beneath the television cracked open, Simon's right hand found its way to the bottled water, sitting right next to the small bottles of whiskey and vodka. The hotel room door slammed with an optimistic "thud" and Simon worked his way down the hallway towards the elevators.

With a "ding" the elevator door opened, revealing a young couple caught in embrace. Embarrassed, they separated. Simon nodded and entered. Astrud Gilberto's voice swelled inside the elevator as "The Girl from Ipanema" piped in from the overhead speaker. This made Simon laugh. Seeing the couple at the opposite side of the elevator staring at him, he cleared his throat and tried to lose his smile. "The Girl from Impanema" he said. "I love this song." The couple exited the elevator at the next opportunity without saying a word and kept their eyes on him as they backed out.

To many, the beginning is the most exciting part of a journey. The anticipation discovering something new and exciting fires our imaginations. Yearn for something exotic? A new location fueled by unfamiliar sights, new tastes and new smells usually does the trick. However, for Simon Glenayre, the opposite held true. To our musician and poet, the exotic became a familiar sight and the new and unfamiliar became old hat. What he yearned for, with every fiber of his existence, was what most of us take for granted every single day.

Simon wanted the ordinary.

No more strange, new locations whizzing by the windows of a tour bus, unfamiliar cities of which only the clean, most polished sides he was allowed to see. Simon wanted to be "normal," in every sense of the word. Simon's thoughts, in their usual mad whirlwind, turned to a friend from years past. An old friend, a recovering alcoholic, used the term "my triggers." This man, a person he trusted, spoke to Simon from his distant past. He reminded Simon of the lessons he learned and tried to share with our musician, our tortured poet. In order to cease dying, Simon had to admit he had a problem, and control the "triggers" of his own self destructive behavior. And at that moment, Simon realized the reason he disappeared. The reason he made his escape from the foolish clutches of his own life. Everything about his lifestyle was a trigger for self destructive behavior. From his manager to his roadies, his band and the fans milling around in the dark corners of stadiums, the promotional people…they all shared a common thread. All, in their attempts to befriend the superstar had at some point offered chopped powder on a mirror, or a glass of something mixed. If Simon played his cards right, on this day nobody would know him. Nobody would want to talk to him or curry his favor. It had been several hours since he had used. Simon had thought earlier his trembling hands were nervous jitters caused by running away from his obligations, or perhaps it was because he hadn't had a drink or a snort of anything. Most likely, he thought, a combination of both. Still, as frightening as his current condition was to him, with the trembles and his racing thoughts, he was glad to feel it. Simon knew the reasons. And he knew the reasons were good. Today would be his Lazarus Day. The day Simon

Glenayre came back from the dead and reentered the land of the living.

Simon cracked the door of the cab before the cabbie even had a chance to fold his newspaper and slide off the hood of his car. The old man's cigar growled upon the wet pavement beneath the man's boot. The front door slammed shut. A pause. Simon laughed and the man spoke.

"In a hurry, buddy?"

Simon laughed again. "Yeah," he said, "I got places to go and people to see." The cab driver paused for more information. It never came. He looked into his rearview mirror at the stranger who sat smiling and looking out the window.

"So you wanna go-"

"Hell," Simon laughed, "I dunno!" Simon leaned forward, his cheery, trembling voice uncomfortably close the driver's ear. He leaned against his door. "How about where there's just...people," said Simon. "Someplace to shop? Maybe?"

"Well there's a lot of shoppin' to be done at th' mall, you know" the man suggested. "Crown Center?" Simon plopped back into his seat, seemingly disappointed. "Sure." With relief the cabbie tugged the shifter into drive when Simon's voice burst from the back seat. "No" Simon said. "Wait." The tires came to a screeching halt. Everyone in the car fell forward.

"I don't want to go to the mall. Take me to the nearest...superstore." The cab driver spun around, flinging his beefy forearm over the back of his seat. To Simon his face looked irritated. This was because he *was* irritated. "Sorry" said the cabbie, eyeing Simon suspiciously, "but you look like a guy who can afford better than a superstore."

"A superstore is so...typical."

Simon slapped the man on his forearm. "Typical! That's what I'm looking for!"

The cab driver stared vacantly at Simon for a moment. And without saying a word he turned slowly to the wheel, tugged the shifter into drive and merged into traffic.

"All right then," he mumbled. "Destination: Typical."

CHAPTER 36

The allegro tapping of the pencil would tell most people this person just might be a little frustrated.

However, Bailey Eden Piper was not frustrated at the lack of help from those she contacted. She wasn't frustrated with the rudeness of the record company receptionists she'd endured. She wasn't frustrated with the moist squishing of chewing gum in her telephone's receiver. No, she wasn't frustrated at all.

She was pissed.

The warbly soprano of the receptionist's voice gave her away as being in her early twenties. The girl's penchant for rudely smacking her gum into the telephone as well as her limited vocabulary, limited to trendy phrases, also gave away her age. Bailey bit her bottom lip. The pencil cracked in her fist as the receptionist continued. "I know, right" the girl chirped. "It's so hard to get through to people."

Bailey squeezed her cell phone. She could hear the plastic crack. "Oh, right you are," Bailey lightly hissed. "And it's probably hard to comprehend when you can hardly speak your own language."

A long pause followed by the squish of chewing gum. "Uh," the voice on the other side of the phone stumbled, "I don't get it."

Bailey dropped the pieces of pencil and rubbed her temples. "Of course don't honey. Do you know anything that *can* help me?"

The receptionist giggled. "Oh! That was funny!" "What was funny?" Bailey asked. She felt the crease between her eyebrows deepen. The receptionist giggled again. Bailey could hear the laugh of a male in the background. "Oh, sorry," the girl smacked her gum. "Somebody just made a funny right next to me."

"I see..." Bailey said. "Someone made a funny. So, is there anything you *can* tell me? I'm an old friend of Simon's and it's really important that I reach him." A long silence followed. Bailey could swear she could hear the teeth of rusty gears jamming up in the mind of the receptionist.

"Ok" said the girl. "Look, I get phone calls all day long from people looking for Simon Glenayre. And really, I don't know much of anything." This comment made Bailey smile. Finally, she thought, this person made a factual statement. The receptionist continued, her gum still squishing into Bailey's ear.

"But you've been so nice to me. And I can tell you're so, you know-" she gushed, "smart."

"So here's what I am hearing."

Bailey stopped pouring her orange juice. "Yes? What are you hearing?"

"Simon Glenayre has disappeared."

"Disappeared?" Bailey slapped the pitcher of orange juice onto the table top. Juice splashed on her hand. "What the hell do you mean he disappeared?"

The smacking of gum ceased oozing from the cell phone's receiver. "Hold on a moment." A few seconds later the girl was back on the line, but this time with no gum chewing and she spoke with a whisper. "I know, right?"

Bailey rolled her eyes. "Ok. So Simon disappeared?" she said, now rubbing at the back of her neck.

"Yes! The phones have been firing off the past day and a half," the girl whispered from Los Angeles. "Everybody in the industry is asking about him. Press doesn't know- yet."

Bailey leaned forward in her chair. "So have you heard where he *might* be?" A long pause, and another whisper.

"No. I haven't heard anything," the girl whispered. "But what I do know is Sol Glenn has hired every P.I. he could get his hands on." "And," she whispered, "all of 'em have been checking in twice a day. The messages are all coming through me."

"I've been taking like, forty to fifty messages a day" she groaned. "It's been horrible."

Bailey made her way to a kitchen towel hanging from a cabinet. "Aaaw," Bailey mockingly sobbed. Bailey averaged the number of messages per hour in an eight hour shift and grabbed another pencil to strangle. "They've really been working you hard, haven't they?"

"I know, right?" said the girl.

"Right," said Bailey.

"Well," Bailey sighed, "you've been a great help. What's your name?" The smacking of gum cheerfully resumed. Bailey could swear the girl was smiling by the timbre of her gum chewing.

"My name is Kierra. But really, I want to be called 'Konstanze', and with two dots over the 'O'. That's what I told my agent. Two dots over the 'O'. Always. And a smiley face at the end. Do they make a laptop key with a smiley face?"

Bailey fought back her laughter. "Well, Ki- Konstanze, I can't really say for sure. But here is what I do know: You've been such a great help! You are...awesome?"

"I know, right?" the girl on the line Sang out.

"Right!" Bailey mockingly gushed. "So can I call you again sometime? You've been a great big help."

"Sure!" the girl beamed. "You're so awesome. Remember," she said, "make sure you're talking to me, Konstanze. With two dots over the 'O'."

"And a smiley face at the end?" said Bailey.

"Awesome! You remembered the smiley face!"

Bailey laughed. "I know, right?"

"Awesome! I'll talk to you later!" The line clicked. The chewing had disappeared.

Bailey sat down the cell phone and sighed.

"Awesome."

CHAPTER 37

The shoplifter watched Simon's cab ease to the store's entrance as the cold reality of handcuffs tightened around his wrists. The driver whipped the lever to "Park," glanced absently at the youth in handcuffs as he flung his tattooed forearm over the back of his seat. He looked at Simon. "Well, here we are" he said with a hint of bewilderment. "An everyday superstore."

Simon smiled. "Yes, I know."

"They can be found in any city in the continental United States" groaned the cabbie, with a hint of frustration.

Again, Simon smiled while looking at the entrance. "Yes, I know."

Something about his latest fare told this veteran cabbie that this man, with his long but well kempt hair and easy but dark demeanor was not usually one for box stores or fast food. Though unacquainted with Simon Glenayre or his music, the driver felt that something about this stranger was different. And this man was excited to visit a superstore. To the cabbie, it just wasn't normal.

A wad of cash found its way into the eager hand of the driver. Too embarrassed to look Simon in the eye upon seeing the denominations, the driver muttered "thanks pal" and quickly spun off. Simon turned to see the policeman's hand on the shoplifter's head as he shoved the youth into the back of the cruiser.

The door slid open and Simon went in. He found his idealistic memory of a shopping center shattered the moment he walked inside. After only a dozen steps, he nearly sprinted back the way he came. Simon Glenayre, our showman and poet, our shaman and orator, our rock star who had spent the nearly two decades lifting stadiums of fans up in the palm of his hand, found himself rattled by the endless beeping of electronic registers and crying children. After a few stuttered steps he ultimately found his rhythm and soldiered on. Simon passed by the cauliflower and felt the front wheel of a shopping cart yank the shoe from his heel. Simon winced in pain and lowered his sunglasses to see the woman pushing the cart. With a smirk and nothing more the woman turned on two wheels down the next aisle cursing under her breath. He pulled the bill of his ball cap lower and made his way past canned goods.

Simon found himself browsing through the different children's cereal. Colorful cereal, hot cereal and ultimately cereal that had the appearance of chocolate chip cookies. He rolled his eyes when he thought of the dental bills. Simon felt surprised at the practical and responsible thoughts he was having and moved further on. Two carts blocked the aisle, an elderly woman on one side, and a young man with his pants hanging below his backside, bobbing his head to music on his mp3 player.

A couple from behind blocked Simon's escape from this sugary aisle. Their attempt at concealing their heated disagreement failing miserably, the intensity of their voices, regardless of how low they managed to speak was not lost upon Simon. Over the years he had become adept at being aware of the moods of those nearby, and hardly a whispered word escaped him. Again. The ongoing cries of a toddler soon followed the brief but intense outburst from the mother. The couple behind him arguing. Off in the distance, another crying child. Simon slid around the arguing couple and leapt over the broken jar of pickles, past the barking mother and screaming child. He could feel his legs getting weaker by the second. Gripping his chest he burst from aisle 9 and leaned against the first display strong enough to hold him up. Sweat burned Simon's eyes and the room spun around him. How ridiculous, Simon thought to himself, that he didn't take the cab driver's offer to go to a more reserved shopping environment. His stomach turned, his thoughts tied up in knots. Another arguing couple passed him by. A stage, he thought to himself, if only I were on stage. Yes, with music, Simon could calm things down. He knew he could unite these fussing couples, calm their crying children. If only he had a stage. This could be fixed from a stage.

The guitar player's opening guitar riff in the key of C played from a speaker directly over Simon's head. The familiar pentatonic scale felt like a blanket, soft and warm to his soul. Feeling a smile surface on his face and his spirits lifting, he once again found his legs when the vocalist's smooth tenor sang the intro to one of his favorite Motor City love songs. The voice of The Temptations' "My Girl" filled the air.

And at that moment, the five part harmonies of the song became the soundtrack to the lives of everyone in that store. The sounds of fussing children fell silent. The arguing couples found themselves holding hands and gazing longingly into one-another's eyes once again. The stock boy sang along with a smile on his face while he cleaned up the broken jar of pickles. For two minutes and fifty nine seconds, every person within earshot of that song, be they in electronics, sporting goods or cold cereal, walked on air that day. For two minutes and fifty nine seconds everything in the world was right. Simon strolled lightly, observing those around him. It seemed like everybody existed, walked, floated even, on an ethereal wavelength where hope reigned. They all walked, sashayed and danced on a higher plane where peace was just around the corner and true love was only a whisper away. The electronic beeps of the registers could not be heard. Simon turned a corner onto a small isle of obscure discounted items to find an elderly couple kissing passionately, unaware they had been caught acting in a way they would never have dreamed in public, except when one of the world's most famous love songs was being played. Simon covered the smile on his blushed face and dipped off the aisle before he was seen.

It was always the case in magical and sadly rare moments like these that Simon's thoughts turned once again to her.

Bailey Eden Piper. Their trip to Colorado. Her spirit and sense of good, so strong. Her unwavering commitment to kindness, truth and honor could not be beat out of her with a lead pipe. And God help anyone who tried. They wouldn't have stood a chance against her. In Bailey Eden Piper, her commitment to the care of others was equaled only by her commitment to keeping her body in peak condition. And put simply, any man who had the guts to attempt physically harming her would be lucky to get off with only being broken in half. Bailey represented what was best in mankind, she was pure. She was strong. And he broke her. He broke her with his ego. He broke it with his sense of entitlement. So many women, so many selfish conquests. He rolled in sheets with women whose names he never knew. And simply because they paid attention to him. All because for a little while they made the pain go away. Many drinks were shared, many blankets ruffled. The thought of it all made Simon feel like trash. When the thrill of sexual conquest was gone, Simon was only left with himself and his thoughts of her. He hated himself for the waste. Simon knew he was not worthy of Bailey's forgiveness. He wouldn't dare to ask for it. He had no right. And he thought of the last time he ever saw someone smile with their eyes. She was so beautiful, if only for a while.

The memory of Bailey's voice and the scent of her hair made Simon smile. She had the most joyous laugh, and the most beautiful hands. From an overhead view, from perhaps an upstairs office, one would see down onto the sales floor as well as the final notes of "My Girl" draw to a close. As soon as it had begun, the song ended. People ceased holding hands. Children resumed their fussing. And in the middle of it all stood Simon Glenayre, alone again in the world and wishing for another two minutes and fifty nine seconds of a silly love song. If only he could once gaze upon someone's beautiful face. She smiled with her eyes.

CHAPTER 38

Men drove around the block just so they could see her again. Bailey Eden Piper, jogging in the cool, early morning air turned heads like she always did. With her long and slender frame, she ran with the grace of a gazelle and the control of a cheetah. One could not tell where the gold of her silken hair ended and the rays of the morning sun began.

Out in the morning sunshine, she could be herself. It was a good time to process what she experienced the night before in the ER. "Think about it now, Bailey" she thought to herself, "the gunshot wounds, traffic fatalities and victims of spousal abuse" Now was the time, to get it all out of her head, before she went to bed. Otherwise she wouldn't get a single moment of shut eye.

Acutely aware of her surroundings, she knew she was being watched. Her finely tuned hearing noted the slowing of tires on pavement as men crept past her on their way to work. She ignored them, but like the sonar of a shark, she was keenly aware of their proximity to her.

Bailey found herself thinking of the last time she jogged at night. It was the reason she now jogged in the morning.

It was two years ago. 10 pm. She was off that night. She didn't feel like watching t.v., so she went out.

The Waldo area of Kansas City. Quaint and trendy, the neighborhood sits nestled in the heart of the city, surrounded by rustic restaurants and coffee shops. She felt safe there. How embarrassing, she thought, to allow herself to get so comfortable in her surroundings, exposing herself to attack. The late night air had the same calm as the early morning air. The night was quieter though and with less traffic. The darkness of night blocked out unwanted visual distractions too. It helped her to think clearly.

The darkness of the night also hid a man. A man six foot two, two hundred thirty five pounds. A serial rapist released early for good behavior due to overcrowding. He sobbed at his parole hearing and swore he was a changed man. The parole board didn't buy his performance, but ten men had to be released regardless due to overcrowding. He was the lesser of many evils they encountered that day. The scum's laugh could be heard through the corridors of the prison. The guards glared at him as he strolled out a free man, extending his middle finger all the while planning his next attack. He emerged from prison that day a more powerful rapist, eager to use his newly toned, fast body on a soon to be chosen rape victim. Years of weightlifting had made him stronger. It made him leaner and vastly quicker too. Once outside the prison, he spun around and lifted his t-shirt revealing his chiseled abdomen to the tower guards. He yelled "you wish" at them as they shook their heads. The guards hoped they would greet him at their doors again someday soon.

On that very night he sat in the darkness, scratching at his stubbly head, the flakes of dead skin caking like thick paste beneath his fingernails. The predator rubbed at the stubble on his chin, smiling. His mouth foamed at its corners as if he were a mad dog. Bailey's silhouette and bouncing ponytail danced against the backdrop of the streetlight. He could tell her frame was slender, her muscles tight. Very low body fat. He would snap her like a twig, he thought to himself. Tonight would be one of his easiest "hits," and he would brag to his jealous father of it in the morning.

It was his intention to tackle the jogger, using his weight against her. And with a quick, fierce blow to her skull he would render her unconscious and take her any way he pleased. Her lifeless and mangled body would be smuggled easily out of the Waldo area and disposed of in the nearest creek or alley dumpster. It would be so easy. Just like it always was.

Or so he thought.

He slithered around a car and crouched down. As Bailey approached he prepared to spring on her. He would slam his body into hers and with his momentum fling her into a gathering of tall dark bushes. He could hear the sound of her light, effortless footsteps drawing near. He listened to her rhythmic breathes. Closer. Closer. His timing would have to be perfect. Closer.

He timed his leap on the approach of her shadow. The animal

flung his large frame against Bailey, knocking her into the bushes as planned. This is where the beast's plan, so well thought out and perfectly executed many times before, went straight to hell.

Bailey leapt to her fighting stance before he even made his way behind the bushes. And behind those bushes, *she waited for him.*

Bursting through the branches, his club like hand immediately shot towards Bailey's head but glanced off her forearm, a perfectly timed block performed thousands of times in martial arts classes. He lunged at her immediately with his other meaty fist, throwing all his body weight behind it. His momentum and the overextension of his arm resulted in throwing himself off balance. This gave Bailey the upper hand and she knew it.

Bailey latched onto his fat, sausage like thumb, breaking it effortlessly. She could feel the bones crack as she thrashed it backwards towards his wrist. Six of his ten fingers would be broken that night. For several weeks afterward, he would have to eat with a plastic fork taped to his hand.

From the outside of the dark bushes, a passerby would hear endless thrashing. Knuckles striking against flesh. They would also hear the sounds made when a large man is tossed this way and that, much like a rag doll because he underestimated his opponent's acute understanding of angles, tempo and how to control a fight. Bailey knew how to use every weapon at her disposal. Her knees, her elbows, fists and her speed. She used her weapons effortlessly and with humbling precision. He chirped and farted when her perfectly placed elbow cracked two of his ribs, one of them puncturing a lung.

The man sobbed as he was wheeled into the ER that night. The doctors tried to reset the bones in his hands and discussed how to best approach his half bitten off tongue, the injury fearfully self inflicted during the beating given him by his intended victim. He also sustained ruptures of several fibrous tissues in his body due to the severe twisting motions subjected to him by Bailey. He would cough up blood for days. The large man shrieked when Bailey, escorted by the police, entered his room for positive identification. Being a nurse, the damage she did to him was immediately evident. Bailey could tell she punctured a lung from her blow to his ribs because the scum wore an oxygen mask. And a tube protruded from his body, a sign of the pnuemothrax he received in the beating. His face was bruised black and purple. He was fearful of her and in a great deal of pain.

Bailey drew no satisfaction from this.

She told the police she recognized him, not only from his face but also by the squeaking sound his nose made as he cried. The police laughed as they led her out of the room. One officer offered her his personal cell number and asked her to dinner. She politely refused, saying she was in a relationship, though she was not. She would refuse a ride home and jog there, shower, and have a cup of tea to calm down.

Bailey needed to snap out of the past and back to the here and now. She was jogging. Yes. And the sun shone hotter on her face.

She ran around a corner and now the sun was in her eyes. Without losing her steady rhythm, she lowered her sunglasses to ease the glare. Bailey knew it was time to change her train of thought. The attack was two years ago. Again, it was time to focus on the here and now. The sun rose in the sky. The birds were singing and she had planning to do. Simon Glenayre. The girl at his record company said she was giving Sol Glenn updates twice a day. She planned on calling Konstanze for an update. As she showered she would try her best to prepare mentally for the sounds of gum being chewed into her receiver. There was much she already knew about Simon that nobody else could tell her, however. Perhaps it would be good to start with what she *already knew* of Simon, instead of the deductions and educated guesses by those who hardly knew him at all. Where would Simon disappear to? What would make him want to disappear at all? An understanding of what Simon was running from would tell her where he was running *to*.

She listened as the tires of another vehicle slowed behind her. She could tell it was a pickup truck without even looking up. She winced at the thumping of the youth's stereo and spun into her next turn and lost the pickup, the driver yelling at her as he sped away. Simon would want to get away from the crowds, she thought.

She glanced at the mp3 player strapped to her forearm. Simon ran away because he needed to charge his batteries. And he was threatened by somebody, or the perception of a threat from somebody. Or something. Where would Simon feel safe? Where would he go? The synapses of her mind fired off like the cylinders of a Formula One race car. The ultimate conclusion exploded in her thoughts. "Sonofabitch" she said aloud, skidding to a stop and panting. "He's right here in Kansas City."

CHAPTER 39

Kansas City. Commonly thought of as a cow town, it remains the Midwest's best-kept secret.

Upon passing through the city, travelers come expecting juke joints, cattle being rustled down Main Street and shootouts like the OK Corral. However they are often surprised at its fine boulevards, excellent restaurants, shopping and the kindness of its people. Frequently, travelers are taken aback by the extended hand and warm greetings of this city's natives, and leave with their understanding of the city forever changed.

Kansas City also enjoys numerous fountains, second only to Rome, and boasts nearly as many boulevards as Paris. Destinations include the Union Station, the Jazz District, and The Nelson-Atkins Museum of Art. And it's at that very museum where our Simon Glenayre feels most comfortable. Artists such as Van Gogh, Rembrandt and Monet call to him. But one painting in particular pulls at Simon the strongest.

As we walk across the South lawn of the museum, past the famous shuttlecocks, games of Frisbee and picnicking lovers, we approach Rodin's "Thinker," framed from behind by the magnificent stone columns of the Nelson-Atkins. The 45 steps to the entrance are soon conquered. Together we shuffle through the giant revolving door and into the atrium of the museum. Magnificent Corinthian columns made of the finest marble wait ahead and whispering voices echo from distant walls. We continue ahead and turn to our right. We see the Greek Pentelic marble lion guarding the entrance to one of Simon's favorite places. And it is in front of Caravaggio's "St. John the Baptist in The Woods" that we find Simon Glenayre standing silent.

Thinking. Silent.

The painting of St. John the Baptist, hanging upon the wine colored wall of the Nelson-Atkins Museum of Art dominates the room. Caravaggio's dramatic use of light and dark adds to the mystery of the painting. Over the years, Simon made many trips to see the painting. To Simon, St. John sat in the shadows, reflecting on his life and likely fearing for the safety of his cousin Jesus Christ. Perhaps he even pondered his own coming violent death. Simon Glenayre related to the painting. In its dark and brooding Baroque style, Caravaggio broke from the rules of how to portray a religious figure. For the first time, an artist portrayed St. John, not according to the standard perceptions and expectations of Christian lore, but as he really was: only a man. Yes, an important figure with a hand upon the head of Christian history, but still, only a man. And it is for that reason that Simon identified with the painting: the real St. John, in the shadows. Brooding. Vulnerable. His future in doubt. Pondering his next move, as well as the possible impact of his decisions on others. Simon knew these feelings all too well.

A children's tour group entered the room. Their chattering broke the silence as they made their way to the Caravaggio. This sent Simon retreating through an exit at the other side of the room. Simon did not hear the equally immature voices of Hendricks, Hix and What's-his-name, arguing as they entered at the opposite side of the room.

"What's with all these paintings?" spat Hendricks.

What's-his-name moved toward the Caravaggio without answering. He stood in the spot previously occupied by the elementary tour group. He glanced down to find the discarded candy wrappers left in their wake. What's-his-name picked up the wrappers and stuffed them into his pocket. Approaching the painting from a sharp angle, What's-his-name knelt down a few degrees, observing the cut line in St. John's left calf, a mark cut into the canvas by the artist to use as a guide. After a few sighs from Hendricks and Hix, he answered. "This is the Caravaggio" he said as if in a dream state. "Yeah, see I read an interview with Simon Glenayre a while back," What's-his-name said as he moved to a different angle, looking for new details in the painting's brushstrokes. "He said he loves this painting." What's-his-name whispered to himself, "he said he related to it."

What's-his-name moved back from the painting, taking it in from a distance, its aura further enhanced by its surroundings. "It makes sense to me," whispered What's-his-name. "The thing is mesmerizing."

Hix dropped a candy wrapper on the floor, shoved the chocolate into his mouth. What's-his-name picked up the wrapper, shoving it into his last empty pocket. For a moment, all three were quiet, looking at the figure in the painting of St. John, Jim Morrisonesque, with his shoulder length dark curly hair. It looked as if Caravaggio was influenced by carvings of the Greek god Apollo.

"Yeah," What's-his-name sighed, "I guess he isn't here."

The three friends exited the room and made their way to the main entrance. From behind, their silhouettes stood against the outside scenery of the South lawn, with its shuttlecocks, games of Frisbee and its lovers. "So what now?" said Hix in his usually frustrated tone.

What's-his-name sighed. "I dunno. I was told he would be here."

Hendricks scratched a place usually not scratched in a place like an art museum, grumbling. "Yes! So who told you Simon Glenayre would be here?"

What's-his-name's mouth opened, but not a word passed his lips. The school children passed in front of them in the atrium. Their young voices were energetic.

The three friends watched as men on the front lawn played fotball. One miscalculated throw struck the intended receiver in the head. They watched as the man fell to the ground, laughing. "I was told to give Simon Glenayre a message," he said. "I was told I could find him here. Down to the very spot. In front of the Caravaggio."

Behind them, Simon Glenayre passed in search of Monet's "Boulevard de Capucines."

"I just don't understand," What's-his-name said. "I was told by a very good source he would be here."

"Right," spat Hix. "And who was your source?" Hendricks kicked the base of a marble column, and immediately wished he hadn't kicked it quite so hard. "I think you're making all this up," he said glaring.

What's-his-name pushed his way through the building's massive revolving door. The sun was setting, and to the left, the Steven Holl-designed Bloch buildings began to glow white in the cooling air. The air was shivering. The season was changing. Fall was approaching. The last of the South lawn's inhabitants were leaving. The forty five steps down to the lawn passed less enthusiastically than their ascent.

Back inside the museum, Simon wandered into an unfamiliar room and without knowing why, spun to his left. Hanging on the wall he found the daguerreotype of Gustav Le Gray's "Brig upon the Water." In the photograph, a ship disappears off in the distance, appearing as if its destination is uncertain. Simon took a step closer. The line between his eyes deepened. The waves look troubled; the future of the ship feels unknown. The photograph brought to mind Bailey Eden Piper. She was the love of his life. And in a fit of confusion, stupidity and selfishness, he cast her adrift upon the waves of heartbreak. He recalled the cold detachment he felt as she wept. And just like the ship in the photograph, her mast disappeared over the horizon, never to be seen again.

Simon tried to remove himself from the guilt. He preferred to think of better times. There was the night they drove out into the country with a CD player, a telescope, and a bottle of wine. He recalled Bailey dancing to Duke Ellington's "Solitude." Slow and sensuously she swayed and turned in the night air. He could see her figure through her sheer dress and thanked the universe for the moonlight that illuminated her from behind. She danced carelessly in the cool air. She danced with slow and easy abandon. She danced to show him her sincerity. She danced to show him her vulnerability. That night Bailey gave herself to him. She trusted him with her body, heart and soul.

And then like a fool he set her adrift, like the ship in Gustav Le Gray's photograph. Simon felt his stomach twist into knots. He backed out of the room looking at the photograph and hating himself.

Simon made his way through the South exit and moved slowly down the forty-five steps toward Oak Street. Hopefully he would catch a cab before he was recognized. Off in the distance he spied three figures. Though their conversation could not be heard, he could tell it was tense and argumentative. Two people appeared to be giving hell to the figure in the center. They stuffed themselves into a rusty compact and sped off, its muffler rattling as it twisted the corner on two wheels. Simon pulled the bill of his cap lower and thumbed a cab which he hopped in.

The cab passed a speeding blue Honda Civic as it slashed to the curb and a tall, lean blonde woman leap from the car. She sprinted across the lawn and conquered the forty-five steps to the museum entrance in an effortless and gazelle-like nine leaps. The door was locked. Bailey dug her nails into the palm of her hand. She knew she was close to finding Simon. She could feel him.

She'd experienced this sensation before. Like every time he would enter a room. Like then, the air still felt electrified by his presence.

Bailey's eyes darted around the surrounding area. Ever the romantic, she hoped to see his silhouette against the otherworldly glow of the Bloch buildings to her left. She imagined running into his arms, their silhouettes embracing for all the traffic on Emanuel Cleaver II Boulevard to see. But Simon was nowhere to be found. She plucked her nails from the palm of her hands. Opening them, Bailey looked down to see the resulting blood pooling in her palms. It looked as if she was touched by stigmata, but stigmata had nothing to do with this. It was once again time to inhale deeply, exhale and just think. The sad walk to her car oozed by. She knew she was so close to him, if for only a moment.

It was time to go home and get cleaned up. Her second love called. Work would begin before long, and she would need time to meditate before going in. It was going to be a full moon. All hell broke loose on a full moon, and everyone in the ER knew to be prepared for it. More gunshots, more rape victims, more abuse. And through it all, Simon Glenayre would be in the back of her mind. Always there, desperate for her help but never reaching out to her.

Just around the corner from the museum, Simon told the cab driver to stop. A wad of crumpled bills found its way into the cabbie's hand and just as quickly the cab spat Simon out onto the JC Nichols Plaza sidewalk. He made his way through the strolling crowd towards the nearest bookstore. Simon could see it through the misty evening air. A man played bagpipes on a nearby corner while across the street another beggar scraped a bow across violin strings. Simon could see the sign of the bookstore up ahead. He turned to the side to slip between two slow walking shoppers. Simon could hear the jangle of change in a cup nearby. He barely made out the man through the crowd. He could see the man was sitting on an old bucket. The man continued jangling the change cup, barking at passersby for change. Simon drew closer and he could make out the man's fingers sticking through his fingerless gloves. It was the bum from his hotel. And the same bum from his hotel in Seattle as well. Simon froze when he saw the man and hoped he hadn't been spotted. Without looking in Simon's direction, the man spoke. "So," slurred the old man, "still wandering your problems away?"

Simon froze. "What?"

"Yeah," the old man turned and smiled. "My father calls it 'chasin' rabbits'."

"Your father," Simon smirked at the old man, "is still alive?" He chuckled as he looked around. "You bet he's alive." A passerby thoughtlessly tossed a couple coins in the direction of the cup and missed. The old man yelled towards the shopper. "He's the Alpha and the Omega, baby!"

"So" the old man grumbled through his cracked lips. "You think any about what we last talked about?" Simon remembered. He also was aware of the surrounding shoppers, with their glossy bags and expensive clothes. They watched Simon talk to this man, sitting on the bucket, jangling a cup of loose change. Simon was getting embarrassed about it. The old man on the bucket let out a bellow, loud and booming. People nearby stopped in their tracks. Others stared as they went past. "You didn't think about it at all, did you?"

Simon cringed. "All right" Simon said softly. "I didn't give it much thought."

Pennies missed the man's paper cup and landed at his feet. He looked down at the money and sighed. "Good Lord, forgive them. They just don't feel much like givin' today."

"Your music is changing, Simon." The old man stabbed the air with his finger again. "Just like you."

Simon knew this man was right. This old man, jangling his change cup and harassing shoppers as they passed by knew so much about him. He wondered if he was from the record company. But he couldn't be. If he was from the record company he would not be pushing him to maintain his new course. Simon could feel the evening mist cover his face when he looked up.

"That feels good, doesn't it? Simple joys." Simon opened his eyes, turning his face from the sky and looked down at the old man.

"Simple joys?"

"Sure" the man laughed. "The simple joy of holding someone's hand again. The joy of knowin' you really are loved unconditionally. The joy of choosin' your own destiny, instead of someone else choosin' it for you."

Simon laughed at this. "I don't know what you are talking about. I chose to come to Kansas City, didn't I?" Simon paused for a moment considering that he asked this man that very question, even though he already knew that this upwardly mobile beggar already knew he was going to be there, probably before he himself did.

"Oh, you hardly decided for yourself." He laughed aloud. "Boy you just kinda floated here like a balloon with no direction."

"And what you doing with it boy?" the old man pled. "A balloon that don't know where the heck it's floatin' off to."

Simon scratched at the back of his neck, like he always did when cornered. "To be frank, I've never given it any thought."

The old man jerked his cup to the right, catching loose change before it hit the ground. His eyes never left Simon. "Gotcha! You see boy?" the old man said, "if you want something worthwhile, you gotta reach for it, 'stead of waiting for it to just jump into your cup." This made Simon think of Bailey Eden Piper. He looked longingly at the entrance to the bookstore and turned his attention back to the old man.

Two pennies landed at the beggar's feet. The man scowled at the sight of the change laying there. "Oh yeah! Thank you sir!"

"You're already on your mission, Simon," he said. "You know your music- it's changing. And your music is changing you right back. But they don't like it, do they?"

"Who?" Simon asked. The old man nearly fell off his bucket.

"Well who the heck you think? The same folks who are pulling your strings trying to shove you in a different direction than what you know to go in." The old man sighed. "And you wonder why you have those bad dreams," he said rubbing again at his beard. "You don't even know who you are anymore."

"Be not afraid, have I not commanded you?" The old man paused looking for a reaction. He received only a blank stare. "You ever heard that before, Simon? You know where it comes from? You remember your momma and daddy tellin' you that verse when you were a kid?" The man picked up the change and tossed it into his cup. "And your music has a message" he barked. "Use it!"

Embarrassed by the beggar's volume, Simon spun on his heels and made for the book store's entrance. But still, he could hear the man yelling at him. "Stop tryin' to do it all yourself, Simon! Put it in his hands, and keep your path straight and true!"

Inside the store, Simon turned to look out the window, but the man with his paper cup and plastic bucket were gone.

CHAPTER 40

The line moved too slowly for Valletta. He knew if he had too much time to think about it he wouldn't even get on that plane. Rolling sweat tickled his cheek. He could see the Boeing 747 through the window and noticed its wings sagging from the jet fuel. This was no way for an Italian to go down, he thought to himself, in a raging inferno of jet fuel and provolone. The voice was faint. He felt a tug at his airline ticket.

"May I have your ticket, sir?" the stewardess pled. "Please?"

Valletta looked at the stewardess and let go of the ticket without saying a word. Putting more thought into the simple movements than he normally would, he put one foot in front of the other. Hardly moving at first, then finally working up to a snail's pace. He felt a hand upon his shoulder. And a familiar but unwelcome voice.

"Slow in the mind *and* slow on your feet, aren't you?" Valletta was surprised he didn't pick up the all too familiar scent of Hermes' 24 Faubourg, the perfume Chloe always wore. He could swear she bathed in it, even at fifteen hundred dollars an ounce. He turned to find her in an Armani Collezioni jacket, heels and shockingly, denim jeans.

"Hi, Chloe," Valletta said. "You got friends in KC too, huh?"

This made Chloe laugh. "Oh Val" she sighed. "You know why I'm going to Kansas City. The same reason you are. I'm looking for him too." Chloe coughed and motioned Valletta forward towards the jet bridge. Valletta spun about, took a deep breath and forced himself forward. He continued on, hardly taking his eyes off the sagging wings of the plane. Once inside he felt the claustrophobic hum of the plane, the air stale and still filled with the stink of previous passengers.

Making his way down the aisle he found someone sitting in his seat and nodded at the stewardess. "I'm sorry, sir," the woman said. "I'm afraid they double-booked your seat."

"Your new seat, sir," she smiled, "is right down there." Valletta moved forward to find his seat stuffed between two other passengers, next to the plane's jet engines. For the next three and a half hours, he'd hardly be able to think clearly.

He grumbled as he squeezed his way through the kneecaps and plopped down into the too thin seat, sandwiched between a spherical old man and a twenty-something who sat nodding his head to the thumping of his mp3 player. Valletta looked to see where Chloe sat, he spotted her just as she took her seat in first class and heard her bark demands for mineral water and a hot towel.

Valletta understood why Simon flew the coop without him. He knew it would have been next to impossible for his friend to disappear and blend into anonymity with a hulking six-four Italian stuck to his side, tossing fans, thugs or cars out of his path. He knew what Simon was thinking. He also understood that by looking for his friend he could very well be putting him in danger. Valletta knew whoever it was, or whatever the reason might be that made his friend want to disappear, he was going to be there for his Simon. And God help anyone who got in his way. Valletta waved down a stewardess and asked for a drink. He knew to keep it simple and requested a screwdriver. She returned with his drink, made no eye contact and handed it to him with an absent smile. He held up the mixed drink, viewing the orange tinted water with a sigh. The watery concoction went down in one gulp with rolling eyes.

The thought of the hulking Valletta suffering, his huge frame squeezed along with the rest of the cattle way back in coach, brought a smile to Chloe's lips. The crisp one hundred dollar bill was well spent, carefully folded and discreetly handed to the primary stewardess with whispered instructions: "Stuff the gorilla way in the back." It ensured Valletta would suffer even worse stuck between two fellow passengers instead of the aisle seat she knew he would prefer. He pissed like a race horse too. She knew he would need to make several trips to the bathroom. His back would be aching ten minutes into the flight. Though she was faced with no other choice than to make the trip to KC to deal with this Simon situation *personally*, still she thought, life was good. She giggled when the stewardess told her he ordered a screwdriver. The cruel irony was perfect. Once again, a chance to put the screws to Val. The stewardess mixed the drink to Chloe's exact specifications. It only cost her a twenty this time. It was money well spent. Again, she smiled. She took out a leather bound folder and tapped a pen at her ruby lips.

She began scribbling notes.

The Nelson-Atkins Museum of Art. She knew he would go there. He dragged her to the place every time they went to Kansas City, either during an overnight stay in the city or just passing through. And she knew he would be found in front of that silly painting. If not by her, by Val or perhaps one of the many that Sol dispatched to kill him. She was fine with anyone other than Val getting to him first. But she had to be there to be sure the job was completed. If Val got to him first she would have to be the one to do the act. Only she could view herself with pride as being the modern version of Empress Dowager Cixi. The Empress, who initially acted as the Chinese Emperor Xianfeng's favorite prostitute, would maneuver herself into power over the Chinese empire upon his death. During what is considered by many to be the weakest period of the Qing Dynasty, many of her people starved, but she surrounded herself with the fruits of comfort and status. She possessed hundreds of thousands of pieces of jewelry, a stationary ship constructed entirely of the finest marble for her to dine upon. Her avarice was only matched by her murderous ruthlessness. She died in 1908 of arsenic poisoning.

Chloe admired Cixi for her determination as well as the chess-like mastery of manipulation she used to put herself into the seat of power. This empress to be, however, would not fall. She put those very words to paper in quotes, though she knew not whom she was quoting. She hoped she made it up herself. From her wide, comfortable seat in first class, she imagined Simon's movements around Kansas City.

The City Market. She recalled Simon talking about the place, and the stars in his eyes as he spoke of it. The pleasure he took from walking anonymously among such a diverse and fascinating group of people. The shoppers and fresh produce. The musicians playing just a stone's throw away from every corner of the place. He might work his way to Westport and its collection of shops. It had bookstores galore, and numerous eclectic clothing nooks. She might find him at The recordBar. She would do her best to make her mission a quick one. Not only for the fortune and power she was certain to snatch upon Simon's death, but also because she wanted to get the hell out of Kansas City. The people there looked you straight in the eye. They spoke calmer and with a warmth that she viewed as being fake and two faced. She hated the place. New York and LA were far more to her liking. And the waiters on the coasts knew they were below you and understood not to look her so directly in the eye... or at least they acted like it.

Valletta was sleeping. It wasn't hard to tell. She could practically feel the seats of the plane vibrate from his snoring. That slob. Somehow he still managed to fall asleep! She slapped her leather folder shut and pulled the stewardess to her with a hooked finger.

"Mimosa" she hissed. And make it quick."

CHAPTER 41

Upon returning to his hotel room, Simon felt sleep pull at his eyelids. He collapsed on his bed, an arm across his forehead as he looked at the sunbeams shining through his hotel room blinds. It had been far too long since he enjoyed the simple pleasure of a nap. It would have been an uphill battle, fighting this urge to sleep, but he surrendered and shut his eyes.

In moments, Simon found himself walking along familiar cobblestone streets. The streets wound carelessly through old stucco houses with red ceramic rooftops. He could hear the rattle of a weather vane from atop a distant barn and off in the distance a church steeple could be seen. He could also hear a faint swishing sound. Curiosity pulled him towards the sound. After he turned a corner, he came upon another person. A young woman, her hair protected from the wind by a blue scarf, stood sweeping the sidewalk. She wore a smock with a floral pattern, a faded dress and her shoes made of new black leather. Simon approached the woman and she looked up at him as he drew closer. Her face was heart shaped, her cheeks were rosy from the chill in the air. She spoke to him. Simon fought the urge to look too long into her alluring eyes.

"Guten tag, mien Herr."

Simon smiled far and wide upon hearing an authentic German accent for the first time in years. He was certain this was Beuern, and if he indeed was correct, he knew he was not far from The Bridge. He thought about what his father told him, when they both stood together on that bridge all those years ago. He inquired.

"Wo ist die Brücke?" he said in his nervous, rusty German.

A blank expression blanketed the woman's face. Without saying a word she raised her hand and pointed towards a small road. Simon turned and made his way down that road, between a house and a watch shop. Realizing how rude he was being, he poked his head around the corner.

"Wie heißen Sie?"

After an awkward pause, the woman replied. "Ich heisse Kruppa," she smiled. "Frau Charlotte Kruppa."

"Vielen dank." Simon smiled. The young woman smiled back. Before Simon disappeared between the house and the watch shop, he heard the young woman's voice once more.

"Mien Herr" she said just loud enough for him to hear, "Gott ist mit Ihnen."

Simon drew great comfort from this. Surely if this were a place where he would be accosted by his demons there wouldn't be a woman telling him that God was with him. Reinforced by this, he moved forward at an intrepid pace.

Coming upon the village square, he approached an unfamiliar sight in this place he knew so well. A fountain, exceedingly large and ornate for a small German village such as Beuern, and yet for some reason it just fit in here. Simon took a step back at the realization that the figures making up a large portion of the fountain, ballerinas…they moved. No, he realized. They were not only moving.

They were *dancing*.

He took a nervous step back as he observed a dancer execute a brise', so flawless and graceful in its execution the most seasoned and acute eye might be reduced to tears. Again he heard the weather vane clang in the wind. Simon knew this would not last. The pleasant dreams never did. Working his way further around the fountain he came upon a bench and without taking his eyes off the fountain he sat down.

Directly in front of Simon a ballerina executed a Grande' Cabriole, and leapt out of sight. He leaned back, his arms stretched out across the back of the bench. Simon could feel his face stretching from smiling. He looked up to the sky and continued looking around the village, waiting for the next bronze ballerina to dance his way. From across the fountain, Simon saw something blown into his view by the wind. Strands of gold. And just as quickly it was gone. Valletta entered his thoughts. He knew his friend would be looking for him. And he knew Valletta would find him. He laughed to himself as he imagined Val invading even this place, this private dream state, as if it were his right to do so. He imagined Val putting him in a head lock and cursing him for disappearing without any notice. He hoped his old friend would understand. Once more the wind blew something up into the air on the other side of the fountain. Simon stood up. Whatever it was, the wind blew it into the air again. While not quite a light breeze, the wind in this place was hardly a strong gust. Whatever was being moved by it must be very light, very fine and very soft. He worked his way around the fountain, following the strands of gold, and discovered it was the hair of a woman. She was vaguely familiar to him, and yet difficult to recognize. Her face, while not distorted and ugly, was difficult for Simon to focus on. She was beautiful, he could tell that much. Somehow, though in this place he was denied the full details of her face, he could still tell she was smiling. The details of her eyes were unclear. It was as if he were looking at this person through a window of ethereal fog. He spoke to her.

"Do you live here?" The woman turned her face to him.

A nervous step back, but still, she did not run from him. She answered, but he could not understand every word she said. He could tell she was not German. "What was that?" he smiled. The woman reached out and placed a hand on the fountain.

She laughed as a ballerina leapt over her hand. "No," she said. "I don't live here." Though he was denied the pleasure of this stranger's face, he still felt comfortable being here with her, at this fountain with its dancers in this village with its red ceramic rooftops and its far off clanging weather vane. "And you?" she said.

Simon struggled to understand her. He could have sworn she said "Do you love here." The voice was flirty and playful.

Simon twitched. "You're asking me if I live here or if I love here?" He smiled. "I don't understand the question…" He could vaguely make out a smile on the woman's face.

Again she spoke, this time with a giggle. "What I asked was "do you love here?"

Simon moved closer to the woman, hoping the details of her face would become clearer. The stranger took a precautionary step back. Though pleasant, this dream also proved to be one of the most irritating he had ever experienced. What stood before him was what he believed to be a beautiful vision. A companion to enjoy this dream with. And yet he was denied even knowing what she looked like. This was so unfair. After all, this was his dream, damnit. He remembered to answer the question. He looked up to the woman, but she was gone. He looked over the fountain and caught a glimpse of the familiar long strands of hair being blown about by the wind. He walked in the opposite direction hoping to intercept her halfway around the fountain. And there she was.

"I guess I never answered your question" he smiled. "As weird as it was."

Simon could tell she was having difficulty understanding him as well.

"I used to love here," he said. "I mean, I love this place" he stuttered. Simon turned and looked around as he spoke. "Many years ago I lived here," he said with longing in his voice. "I have returned here from time to time, but only in my dreams." He took another step forward. "But I must say I have never had a dream as pleasant as this."

Simon lost his smile when the woman only replied "oh." He leaned against the fountain himself, hoping not to come across as brutish.

Between two houses and past a barn, a dark forest could be seen. Leading into the thickness of that forest was a path, used over the years by countless inhabitants of the village. The tree line so dark, one could hardly see past the first layer of trees. He recalled walking down that very path years ago with his father. Of all the return visits he had made over the years to this place in his dreams, there were many firsts in this particular visit. The fountain, the girl and seeing that tree line and the path into it, for the first time in years. Simon found it puzzling that these three things had come to play during this particular visit. Why now? Why was it so different this time? The figure of the woman remained, leaning forward against the fountain, watching the ballerinas dance. Though he could not see her face clearly, he could swear she was smiling. He cleared his throat and spoke.

"And you? Where do you come from?" he asked. "Are you from this place?"

The woman sighed, as if she was on the last day of a long vacation and knew she would have to leave it behind and go back home again. "No," he thought she said. "I am not from here" she sighed. "I don't even know how I got here."

Simon had so many questions, but did not know where to start. He could swear he recognized this person. If only her voice was clearer. If only he could see her face. Simon felt a low rumble from behind him. He turned and looked at the pathway into the forest. He felt scared, though he did not know why. He had walked that very path with his father many years ago. He knew he had nothing to fear in this place. And yet he could feel the rumble emanating from down that path, and deep inside that forest. Simon felt time drawing to a close, much like his encounter in God's museum. The pleasant dreams, he thought, went by so fast. The bad dreams, well they just went on forever. He thoughtlessly moved towards the woman at an urgent pace. She leapt away from him. Though her back was turned, she was aware of his proximity to her. It was almost as if she had radar. Simon apologized.

"It's ok," he thought she said. Though Simon could only make out small pieces of her sentences, he could make out "ok" and breathed a sigh of relief that he did not scare her off. He held out his hand to her.

"I feel this is all going to end shortly, though I don't want it to." He could barely hear her reply. Though only a few feet away, her voice was so hard to make out. It was as if the wind blew away many of her syllables, replacing them with the gust of a melodic breeze. "I know," she said, sadly. She did not take Simon's hand.

"I would like-" he stuttered. "May I have your name?" The woman turned to him and pointed towards the forest, Simon turned around to see. Another rumbling. From behind she spoke to him. Or she tried. He was beginning to think that she was having trouble hearing him as well. "May I have your name?" he asked again. Simon heard her say something. Her tone, once one filled with hope and yearning, did not answer his question. He turned to find her still pointing towards the forest and the path that led to it.

He heard her ask a question. "What is that place?"

Simon felt his heart go up into his throat. He knew what that place was. He struggled to say it. From within that forest came another rumble, this time louder than before. He turned to see the woman take a step back. He could barely make out what she said next. It was the question she asked. "What is that place?"

Simon could feel his time here drawing to a close. "I'll answer your question if you answer mine." The vision turned her head sideways, as if she were trying to better understand him. Frustrated at their difficulty communicating, he decided to be the first to give in. "Down that path, and somewhere in that forest," whispered Simon, "is my bridge."

The woman tried once again to speak, but what was once hard to understand was now nearly impossible. The woman flung her arms in exasperation. He could make out that much. From within the forest came a thunderous 'bang'. Both people jumped. Simon realized the distant weather vane had stopped clanging. The wind had stopped blowing. And the girl, with her long hair, and strange questions had gone. Another thunderous 'bang' from the tree line and with a heavy jerk Simon awoke, on his bed, his muscles so tight he could hardly move.

In another place across town, in her bed with the blankets pulled over her head, Bailey Eden Piper wept. Before long she would have to get ready for work.

And once more, she felt so close to Simon and she ached because of it. Now awake, it was clear who that distorted vision of a man probably was. If only she could more clearly understand what he was trying to say to her. If only she could see his face clearly. Never had she felt so close and yet so far away from Simon. She hoped her dream would someday become reality. The rest of the night while she was at work, stopping the bleeding of bullet wounds, counseling victims of attack and trying to stay awake, in the back of her mind she would contemplate that path into the woods. And what lay beyond.

CHAPTER 42

Lincoln Cemetery. Kansas City, Missouri. The air feels colder than it did the day before.

The sound of flapping wings draws our attention to the incoming "V" of wild geese off in the distance. The trees have changed color and the grass is fading to brown. Nothing in particular stands out about this place of rest today, and with the exception of a lone figure standing off in the distance, there doesn't seem to be another living soul within miles.

The first thing that stands out about the grave marker isn't the legendary name on it, but what is engraved above the name of the musician who rests below.

A saxophone and a bird stand at the ready above the name "Charles Parker." It is here that What's-his-name stands, listening to the geese honk as they fly over his head going south for the winter. He looks back down to the grave of saxophonist Charlie "Bird" Parker. Charlie Parker, legendary saxophonist. The brilliant Parker also suffered from drug and alcohol abuse. What's-his-name reflected on the life of this man and musical trailblazer. He admired Charlie for his intelligence and commitment to the theoretical side of music. It was Charlie Parker who discovered how the chromatic scale can lead into any other key with its twelve tones. What's-his-name also reflected on the sad demise of this brilliant man, his body wrecked by years of alcoholism and drug abuse. Another brilliant musician who fell victim, not as much to his demons, as to the ways he coped with them. Charlie had a great deal in common with another musician of these difficult times. A sadness swept over What's-his-name, thinking of Simon Glenayre. He was given a task. Seemingly a simple one, and the instructions were so clear: Go to the Nelson-Atkins Museum of Art on a particular day, go to the room with the Caravaggio painting of Saint John The Baptist, and you will find Simon Glenayre standing there. He believed in the source of the message. Not his computer, but of the true source. And he knew better than to question it. A divine message should not be ignored or questioned he thought, only obeyed.

So with his two friends at his side, he did as he was told. He went to that museum, entered that room and came up empty handed. It occurred to him that he should have stayed longer. Surely a difficult task with both Hix and Hendricks there, his dear but very impatient friends. He probably should have gone there alone. He could have waited for hours. Instead he left. "I just gave up too early" he mumbled to himself. "I'm so sorry."

What's-his-name felt puzzled as to why he came to this place. He had never felt drawn here before. Perhaps by coming to this cemetery and reflecting at the grave of who he viewed as Simon Glenayre's musical forefather, he might somehow come to grips with his failure. Maybe even forgive himself. There would be much more to deal with too. He still had to go home and face his parents and what was sure to be their anger for never sending off those college applications. He had not been home in several days because of it. Still, as had been the case since he deciphered the message, his thoughts again turned back to Simon Glenayre. He prayed that his failure did not rob the man of what was left of his hope or his very life. The messages had ceased, and Simon Glenayre was nowhere to be found. The news of his disappearance had already hit the airwaves and a pundit on a cable news station even proclaimed him dead, his body simply not yet found. He recalled his disgust when the man on television said this with a smile on his face. The man on television did make a good point. Hollywood has a history of famous actors, actresses and musicians being found dead from overdoses. A sad exit from this world, he thought: To die alone and sad in a strange hotel room, with only your drugs to cling to. Everyone had more worth than that, even the worst of us, he imagined. He feared that any day the reports would hit the internet. Simon Glenayre found dead. In a hotel room on Hollywood Boulevard, or at the far, deserted corner of a park.

"Damnit," he cursed himself, "I should have tried harder."

Another flock of geese passed overhead, and What's-his-name watched as they passed. He shut his eyes tight and turned his face downward. His fists swelled with frustration and failure.

"A long time ago I saw a documentary on Charlie Parker."

What's-his-name jerked at the stealthy intrusion. He said nothing at first and didn't look at the stranger standing beside him. He didn't want the redness of his eyes to be seen. The voice continued.

"I remember he said something about people always insisting on boundaries in music, and how those boundaries are forced on musicians, artists..." What's-his-name noticed the reflective but relaxed tone of the man's voice. "Yeah, he said there can't be any boundaries to art, or else it isn't art anymore."

What's-his-name finally pulled himself together enough to speak. "I don't even know why the heck I'm here today," he mumbled. "It's just a silly, wasted journey."

The man next to him laughed. "That's so funny you said that." What's-his-name could almost hear the smile in this man's voice. The stranger continued. "Not long ago I was in a hotel elevator, it was in Seattle," he said. "And this old couple came in and talked to me."

Curious, What's-his-name listened. He needed something to cling to and hoped this man would throw him a tether.

"Sure," the man said. "Well I was having a terrible time. And this happy elderly couple, obviously still in love, came in and said some things to me. Some things that just stuck with me."

"They said life wasn't about the destination, but about the journey." The man laughed. "You know, I have heard that silly saying all my life, but when it came from them, it suddenly made all the sense in the world." The stranger put his hand lightly on What's-his-name's shoulder. "I don't even know why I came here today, but it felt like the place to be." What's-his-name looked to the man, he wore a zip up sweatshirt and its hood hid his face. The man noticed him looking and removed his hood to introduce himself.

"Nice to meet you," the stranger smiled.

"My name is Simon."

CHAPTER 43

Simon Glenayre: known as a musician and poet. But on this day, he was a bewildered and sad excuse for a medic.

He leaned over What's-his-name as he lay passed out on the ground. His head bled impressively, having struck a tombstone on the way down, proving that marble is indeed much harder than human flesh. He shook his new acquaintance. There was no response. He wished Bailey was here. She would know what the hell to do in a situation like this. He stood up and frantically looked around, hoping an ambulance would just happen to be passing by. He shook What's-his-name again. This time he heard a groan from the young man. In all his experiences with fans over the years, not once could he recall anyone fainting and hitting their head on a tombstone. He shook him again. "Oh for the love of Pete," he barked, "will you please wake the hell up!"

From behind a distant tombstone, a large man watched them. He watched and he waited. His fists were clenched, his eyes red with flame. He hunched over, dressed all in black, a leather coat shielded him from the chill. The man was so large he could only conceal himself behind the largest of tombstones. He observed the men and plotted out their movements ahead of time. How they might try to defend themselves, and what direction they might run if they somehow managed to escape his grip. Still, he knew he would overcome them before they knew what hit them. And hit them he would. Though more convenient to simply strike their heads against the tombstones, he knew he possessed more than enough strength to unearth a small tombstone and hurl it if he chose. His blood pressure rose, and the man could feel his cheeks getting flush with blood. It would soon become impossible to watch anymore without springing. The mere existence of these two men felt like flies buzzing about his head. They had no place on this Earth and he just might see them off it accordingly.

Finally, what he expected to happen, happened.

One of the men pulled from his jacket a knife, just the right length to dispatch a man quickly. He watched as the other man produced a Glock 9mm from a holster beneath his arm. They continued to slither towards Simon and What's-his-name. The large man saw Simon with his back turned to them and slipped behind the assassins, just as they positioned themselves within striking distance. The men with their knives and their murderous intentions had no idea someone was behind them, and within moments they would be out cold.

The flapping of wings drawing near drew Simon's attention back towards the sky. A flock of geese, having spotted the nearby pond began landing to take in some rest. The flapping wings and honking filled the sound spectrum, covering the chirp of a man gasping as he was taken by the neck by a cinder block sized hand and slammed against a mausoleum wall. In a fraction of a second he was out cold. His pants darkened with urine before he even hit the ground. The second would-be assassin hardly had a chance to apply pressure to the trigger of his handgun before the hand with the weapon was crushed within a vise-like grip. He had a second to yelp out in pain before his neck was broken. The geese honked and flapped their wings as a warning to the others of the occurring violence.

Simon Glenayre stood up, his heart bounced into his throat. He hardly noticed the two men, laying on the ground or their weapons still laying within plain view. But he looked at the man who stood above them, and felt as if he had been caught by his parents sneaking back into the house after a night of drinking. He gave a nervous laugh. He tried to smile. Finally, he spoke.

"Hi Val," he stammered. "I bet you're *pissed.*"

"No, you wouldn't say," Valletta mocked in his thick Brooklyn accent. "Why would I be upset with you?" He stepped over the two men and embraced Simon before he had a chance to escape. There were many times during Simon's friendship with Valletta when he feared he would be smothered within the joyful embrace of his friend. This was one of them.

"Ok, ok," he gasped. "I'm ok!"

"Ok?"

Valletta released Simon and growled at the semiconscious

men as he yanked them up and tossed them between a mausoleum and pine trees. Simon could hear their groans. Valletta emerged from behind the mausoleum to find Simon knelt down over the now groaning What's-his-name. Valletta laughed. "So what the hell happened to him?"

Simon rubbed at his face. "I told him who I was, Val." Again, Valletta laughed, kneeling down with his hand on Simon's shoulder. "Well you knew better than to do that, dummy."

A cream colored luxury SUV could be seen through the wrought iron fence. Simon followed behind Valletta but stopped cold after only a few steps. He turned back and looked beyond What's-his-name and walked back in the opposite direction. The now upright but wobbly What's-his-name followed Simon back to Charlie "Bird" Parker's grave and watched as he dug in his coat pocket, producing a cell phone.

Simon tossed the phone to What's-his-name. "Get my picture, will ya?" The phone bleeped and blurped in response to What's-his-name's frantic button pushing. He smiled when the screen flickered to life revealing the camera application.

Valletta could be heard yelling for them to pick up the pace. His voice, loud. His footsteps, equally as loud. "What the heck?" he bellowed. "You just had an attempt on your life and you stop to take pictures?" Simon hardly gave this any thought. Valletta stopped and did a doubletake.

Simon was smiling.

"C'mon, man," Simon groaned as he lay on the ground, his head leaning against the tombstone. He looked to his side to be sure Parker's name and the bird and saxophone would be in the shot as well. "Let'r rip."

What's his name found the conversation in the SUV lighter than what he expected, considering two men had nearly killed Simon Glenayre and himself, he and the star only being saved by the watchful eye of the loud Italian. The two old friends visited and caught up on what had transpired during the past few days of Simon's disappearance. Valletta found himself too relieved to be angry at Simon. He was well, somehow in one piece, and right next to him. Where he belonged. Nothing was going to happen to him now, and he would see to that. What's-his-name sat in the back and took in the intimate details of the rock star's life. He listened as they talked about Phil, whoever he was. And how indescribably angry he was with Simon for disappearing right before a show. They discussed the dollar amount which had to be paid to the union out of Simon's pocket. This cost a small fortune, and Simon had no money coming in that night to offset that debt. Valletta told Simon that Phil has formally offered to reschedule the concert date, but the feedback from the promoter, as well as the fans, was not favorable. He heard Simon groan. They also talked about a girl. Her name was "Chloe." Nothing too negative was said, but it was clear to What's-his-name that neither one of them were anxious to share a room with her again anytime soon. Valletta told Simon he shared a flight with her to Kansas City. She was here. And she would find him if he didn't get out of town, and quickly. Valletta explained to Simon who most likely sent the hit men, and why. He watched from behind as Simon rubbed at his face. He heard Simon groan in disbeleif.

"Hit men," he whispered. "I just can't believe it."

Valletta shrugged. "Well believe it, pal," he said. "Cause you were just seconds away from joining Jimi Hendrix, Janis Joplin and Joe Cocker in the history books."

"Joe Cocker isn't dead" Simon snickered.

"Shut up," Valletta said right back.

Further down the road, What's-his-name heard another name spoken between Simon and Valletta. But this time in a much softer tone, and with an air of yearning. The name was "Bailey." In a few seconds the conversation diminished. The only sound was of the rolling palace's heater. What's-his-name sat in the back and tried to find a way to tell his friends, Hix and Hendricks, that he had finally found Simon. Of course they wouldn't believe him. He recalled their frustration with him for the wasted trip to the Nelson-Atkins Museum of Art. He thought of how he had failed to do his job. How he failed to simply relay a message to Simon.

It also hit him like a load of bricks that he was actually in the very car that had Simon Glenayre right in its front passenger seat. Only one and a half feet away.

And upon this realization, he fainted again, hitting his head on the armrest of the seat next to him.

CHAPTER 44

It sounded as if the voice was a million miles away. And the voice was pissed.

"For cryin' out loud, Sy" Valletta wailed. "He's frickin' bleeding all over the place!" Through the blur he could see two figures leaning over him. One silhouette large, the other small. He felt his face being smacked. He heard Valletta grumbling again. "C'mon, man. Wake up, will ya?"

Simon and Valletta dragged the wobbly What's-his-name out of the SUV, propping him up against the vehicle. The details of Simon's face came into focus. His facial expression, equal parts concern and frustration. He heard the horn of an eighteen wheeler as it swerved around them, the wind from the trailer blew everyone's hair to the east. Valletta fidgeted in his pocket for a comb. "So," Simon said as he nervously lit a cigarette, "do you have a medical condition we should know about?" Simon tried to smile as he said this, perhaps trying to make it a joke, but his eyes gave him away as being serious. "I mean, this is the second time you've done this to me and I've hardly known you for an hour.

"Simon Glenayre knows me" What's-his-name thought to himself. "*The* Simon Glenayre knows me."

What's-his-name's hand lunged at Simon, yanking him near. "And you're right here!" Valletta's club-like hands yanked the young man off Simon, protecting his friend like he always did. "No!" What's-his-name pled. "You don't understand!"

"Sure I understand," Valletta replied as he locked the youth in the headlock Simon knew all too well. "You're a frickin' looney."

"A looney who likes to pass out a lot." Valletta felt Simon's

195

hand on his shoulder. "Let 'em go, Val." Valletta felt Simon tugging at his elbow. "Really, let 'em go. Either he is a really sick guy who needs help or he has something important to say."

"Or at least he thinks he does. C'mon, Val," Simon said, "let him go."

Another semi trailer blew past, its horn blaring followed by the lesser horns of smaller vehicles. Valletta shook his head.

"Either way I want to know his story before we drop him off somewhere." "Anywhere," Valletta barked. Valletta released the coughing and gasping What's-his-name tumbling into Simon's arms. Simon held on to him for a moment, then pulled the youth upright, and walked him to the back of the car. "So," he asked, "What's this news you want to tell me?"

What's-his-name straightened himself up as best he could, cleared his throat and looked around. His big moment had arrived. He knew the message, and Simon Glenayre stood right before him. And now everything seemed almost *too* simple. He feared Simon would think him crazy, just another person perceived as being a religious nut. In but a few moments so much passed through his memory: Sitting in his bedroom, watching as multiple computer screens flickered the ones and zeroes across their faces. All the time he spent trying to fix what he thought was a problem, only to come up empty handed. And how in the world did he come to realize it even was a message to begin with? It seemed like ages since he first saw them. He also considered for the first time perhaps anything could be interpreted from those numbers. For a terrifying and soul wrecking moment he considered not giving Simon the message at all. He looked up at Simon, and behind him the ever present Valletta, whom he could tell was aching for the chance to pull his arms off. No, he thought. Simon had to know. "This means something," he thought. He took a step towards Simon but a powerful blow to his chest knocked him back against the car. "Easy, fella..." Valletta warned.

"You're going to think I'm crazy."

Simon shrugged. He knew crazy when he saw it. This kid wasn't crazy. "So?"

What's-his-name straightened himself up and did his best to come across as a sane person. "Simon," he said, "there was a reason we ran into each other at the cemetery." Valletta groaned. With his eyes darting between Simon and Valletta, What's-his-name continued. "I've spent days combing the city looking for you." Simon interjected that nobody, and he meant nobody, in

Kansas City or beyond knew he was in town. There was no way some local kid could possibly know he was here. And this kid spent days looking for him? Simon had only been in town for a couple of days, and for someone to know he was coming to town even before he did, well, that bordered on precognition. It was only by chance, he explained, that the two of them met. Sure, the boy wasn't crazy, Simon thought to himself, but he obviously wasn't beyond letting his imagination run wild either. "No," he said as gently as he could, "we weren't supposed to find each other."

"We both just like Charlie Parker." What's-his-name watched over Simon's shoulder as Valletta waved down a passing cab. "And that's only by coincidence." Impatient after only a few moments, the cabbie spoke up. "So you need a ride or what?" Valletta walked over, and snatching his wallet from his leather coat ripped several bills, tossing them into the driver's window. "Shut up and wait." Valletta glared at the cabbie, watching for a moment as he looked at the bills in his lap. As he walked away, he heard the cabbie. "Oh!" he laughed. "Take all the time you need."

Valletta moved towards the boy, taking him by the arm, in a gentler way this time, and walked him towards the cab and opened the door for him. "C'mon, kid. He'll drop ya off wherever ya wanna go." What's-his-name resisted. Valletta's grip became stronger, his handling of What's-his-name became more aggressive. Simon watched as the strange kid from the cemetery was stuffed into the back seat of the cab against his will. "But you don't understand…"

For most of his life, Simon Glenayre felt as if the wolves were always at his door. He played music for many reasons, among them it was his way of keeping those wolves at bay. Simply put, music made him feel safer. On this day, as he watched this kid from the cemetery being shoved into the back of the cab, he felt the wolves were being locked out. And he was locked outside with them.

A voice inside told him the safe place was wherever this kid was. Simon was guilty of many things, among them never acting on something when his heart told him it was the right thing to do. Usually, the first move had to be made by someone else. He hated himself for it. He chose to stay outside the cab, and watch the cab drive off with this stranger. He seemed so sincere. Of course his fans always did. They all did, and then something crazy or dangerous always happened when he let his guard down.

Simon didn't need any of that right now. He was here to find himself, somehow. Maybe find a little peace before he had to split town, and maybe, just maybe, a break from the terrible visions and depression. With a bit of struggle and a grunt, Valletta got the door of the cab closed. The kid inside screaming.

Valletta held the door shut as the cab began to roll. What's-his name rolled down the window. Simon watched the kid's hair blow in the wind as another semi trailer blew past. Simon heard familiar words. His knees weakened. He heard the words again. What's-his-name screamed as the cab pulled away. Simon grabbed Valletta's arm and pulled. There was an urgency in his voice. "Val" he said, "stop that cab."

"Now!"

The sight of Valletta, six foot four and weighing in at over three hundred pounds running down the side of the highway had to be shocking to anyone passing by. Equally shocking to Valletta was his rented white SUV zipping past, leaving him abandoned on the side of the highway. Simon's foot had the gas pedal shoved to the floorboard.

Valletta tossed his hands to the air and shrugged. "Crap!" He nearly flung his body into traffic, trying to stop a cab, but it was no use. Again he tried, nothing. Valletta looked around and sighed.

"And not a burger joint in sight."

The cabbie kept a close eye on his fare in the rearview mirror. He could tell the kid in the back seat was crying. "I blew it," the he said. "They didn't even give me a chance." The cabbie asked where he wanted to go. What's-his-name didn't want to go home. That was the last place on Earth for him now. He looked out the window without saying a word. The cabbie lit a cigarette. The smoke burned his eyes. "It's ok kid. The big Italian gave me twenty bucks. So you got twenty to get anywhere ya wanna go."

He lied. Valletta tossed him five twenties.

Failure buzzed around What's-his-name's head like flies. He felt robbed of the chance to do what he was called upon to do, and now he felt as if his life had no direction. The cab sped towards a bridge and What's-his-name saw standing ahead an old man, a member of the encampment of homeless people living beneath the overpass. It looked like he was waving at him, his lone figure standing at the side of the highway looking directly at him through the rapidly closing distance. He was waving. No, he was not waving.

He was pointing.

He was pointing at something behind the cab. What's-his-name's eyes remained glued on the bum, he wore gloves with the fingers cut off. In the split second it took to pass him as he stood there, What's-his-name could tell something about the homeless man appeared to be out of place. Standing at the side of that highway. In that split second, they made eye contact. And at that moment, he was still pointing at something. What's-his-name looked behind the cab. Gaining ground at a violent speed, the white SUV. Still off in the distance, but he could tell it was gaining on them, and quickly. He feared Simon's Italian friend had decided to chase him down and harm him. "Hey" he stuttered. "Step on it. I think that big guy from the SUV wants to kick my butt."

"He's coming up behind us."

The cabbie hardly seemed concerned. "Everybody drives like a bat outta hell here cause you hardly see cops on this stretch of road," he snorted. "Probably nothin'." Once more the cab driver glanced in his rearview mirror but this time, there was concern in his voice. "Oh," he said. "You may be right kid."

"He's really gainin'. And it *is* him…"

The SUV overtook the cab, cutting across its lane of traffic and nearly sending it into a ditch. The cabbie said things he hadn't even heard Hendricks and Hix say at their worst. What's-his-name was thrown against the back of the driver's seat, and his head began to bleed again. He thought it might even be better to just go home, even if his parents were crouched in their attack position, ready to pounce on him over those unfinished college apps. He looked over the shoulder of the cab driver to see an arm slamming the door of the SUV shut. He prepared for the worst. He knew that Valletta character wanted a piece of him. And he was going to get it. Self defense was not one of What's-his-name's strong suits. His door flung open. But the hand…it was smaller.

"Get out here." What's-his-name did as he was told. And before him stood Simon Glenayre. Sweaty and urgent. He grabbed the youth by his arm. "You said something back there," his voice trembled. "What was it?"

Simon snatched a bandana from his pocket and pressed it against What's-his-name's head. "You said something. I know what it meant. And I want you to tell me how you know what it means," he plead. What's-his-name took over the bandana from Simon. "Simon," he said, "I was given a message to give directly to you." What's-his-name shared the tale of the ones and zeroes flashing across his computer monitors. He shared with Simon what binary code was, and its function in modern technology. He lost himself in the explanation until Simon lost his patience. "Yeah, yeah, yeah," he coughed from the cab's exhaust. "Just explain how you knew."

The cab driver lost his patience as well and demanded payment. "Hey!" he barked. "That Italian guy only gave me twenty bucks to get this kid home and now its way past due." Without looking into his wallet, Simon snatched a stack of bills from it. Money once again found its way onto the lap of the gleeful cab driver. He spun off, laughing with his radio blaring. Valletta arrived in another cab seconds later. He squeezed out of the back cursing and made his way to Simon. Another semitrailer nearly blew him over. "Simon" he said, "it's dangerous just standing on the side of this road like this."

"And by the way, you may not have noticed, but you deserted me back there." Simon kept Valletta in his peripheral vision, fearing another headlock. "Go ahead."

"Let 'em get it out so we can get the heck outta here." Simon looked back at What's-his-name.

He continued. "So what I am saying is, I could not for the life of me figure out why my computers were doing this. Simon," he said softly, "I even built a new computer, I didn't even get a chance to plug it in and these ones and zeroes came up." What's-his-name now had Valletta's attention. "One of those computer things, with the ones and zeroes...not even plugged in?" Simon could feel the rusty gears in Valletta's mind try to grasp what was being said. What's-his-name went on. "Simon, out of sheer desperation, I tried to think differently. Tried to solve this from a different angle. So I treated it as if it were a code."

"A code?" Simon said.

"A code." What's-his-name replied. Valletta put his hand gently on his shoulder, and amazingly, did not pull his arm off. "Go on kid," Valletta said.

Relieved and feeling safer, What's-his-name continued. "So I broke these digits down, and I simply assigned them a numerical value." Simon asked what he meant by that, What's-his-name shared his idea to give each of the letters of the alphabet a numerical value, and from there he let the ones and zeroes dictate the order of the alphabet, repeats and all.

"And what I got was something in Latin." Valletta, now excited, shook him, hard. "Well what th' hell did it say, man?"

What's-his-name stalled. His mouth opened but at first

nothing came out. Then he spoke.

"It said- *Sic enim dilexit Deus mundum ut Filium suum unigenitum daret ut omnis qui credit in eum non pereat sed habeat vitam aeternam.*"

He watched as both men took a step back. He feared they would think him crazy. Simon did think he was crazy. What a waste of time this probably was. Strangely enough, he did not get that feeling from Valletta. Simon barked at the boy. "What is that about? I raced here and you give me that?" he yelled over the boom of another passing semitrailer. "Mumbo-jumbo?"

"No, Sy." Valletta urged. "It does mean something."

They both looked at What's-his-name, whose mouth opened, but at first nothing came out. Then he could feel the words leave his mouth though for some reason he could not hear them. He said it again to keep his sanity. It said,

"For God so loved the world, that he gave his only begotten Son, that whosoever believeth in him should not perish, but have everlasting life."

There. It was done.

Simon's expression was one of bewilderment, and it was on the fast track towards all-out anger. "The John 3:16 thing?" he hissed. "I chased you down for the John 3:16 thing?" His voice rose, Valletta now had his hand on *Simon's* shoulder, just in case he sprung at the kid. "I could have seen that on a televised football game, you moron!" Simon felt Valletta's grip tighten in vise-like proportions. He was flung against the SUV. Valletta had never handled him in anger like that before. Perhaps, it was his sense of urgency. He knelt down to eye level with Simon and growled.

"Listen, you whiney little jerk. I've spent the last twenty years looking out for you. Protecting you from people who want to harm you, the women who hate themselves so much they throw their only bodies at you like they were cheap candy at the fair, and men tried to kill you today, Simon. But the hardest of all Simon, the hardest of all... has been trying to protect you from yourself!"

Simon remained silent, shocked. He dared not interrupt.

"And now...now there is someone who really has something to say. *This is important, Simon.* Someone who truly is here to help you, and you talk to him like that? Don't you see what's going on? Do you even know who this kid *really* is?"

Simon could not recall the last time he had been so scared. His dear friend, the one he knew he could count on, feel safe with, his friend and protector just scared him so bad he might wet himself. The urgency and the gravity of the moment landed on Simon like a ton of bricks. He heard the words What's-his-name spoke but it took Valletta's sheer volume to open his mind. He had been such a fool. "So you are saying that this message, the one that you got from all those numbers on your screen…"

"Came from God." What's-his-name smiled and slapped Simon joyfully on the arm. "It's a message from God!" Simon laughed. "Yeah," he beamed. "I guess it is."

"But Simon," What's-his-name said- "there's more…"

CHAPTER 45

The interstate was four lanes, but to the man behind the wheel it looked more like eight. His pickup truck wove and rumbled down the road, belching noise and smoke in equal parts. On any other highway, there would have been a squad car nearby to recognize all the warning signs of this fool behind the wheel. A prime reason this road was frequented by those seeking an alternate route was to avoid drunk driving check points. And he used it frequently.

Duane lived in this city all his life and knew the location of every liquor store within range of his house. Anyone with an ounce of common sense pulled to the side of the road when they saw him in their review mirror. The rolling and clanging of empty bottles on the floorboard rang their alarm to oblivious ears.

His cell phone rang.

"Yo," he belched into the gadget, pressed against his wiry beard. "No luck? And you're a liar!" he screamed. He jerked the phone from his ear as the voice in the receiver barked loud and long back at him. Duane stuttered an explanation for his outburst. He'd forgotten who he was talking to. "It's just hard to believe there isn't an eight ball in this whole town, ok?" Curses spewed from his lips as he snapped the greasy cell phone shut and tossed it onto a nest of empty hamburger bags on the seat next to him. The horn of a car sounded right next to his truck. Had it not been for the other driver's reflexes, the car's occupants would have been struck by Duane's truck and sent spiraling down a deep concrete embankment to their deaths. Watching the truck weave past them, the passenger caught a glimpse of Duane's extended middle finger.

The phone buzzed and rattled the trash in the seat again. He fumbled around with one hand as the other hand perilously fidgeted with a three quarters burned cigarette. The cigarette burned his finger, falling between his knees onto the floorboard. Garbage ignited. He stomped it out.

Keeping his buzz going would take more than beer. He had to find something to smoke. He preferred meth, as he loved the way it hit him so quick. His hand emerged from the rattle of crumpled paper bags with the cell phone. Flipping it open, the phone slipped out of his fingers and down into the dark of the passenger's floorboard. He took a quick glance ahead and hunched down to retrieve his phone.

The thump felt like he hit a deer with his truck and for a moment he could have swore he saw a rag doll flying across his windshield. The impact sent Duane's truck spiraling down the highway. In a fit of over steering, he jerked the wheel hard to the right and his truck flipped side over side several times before coming to rest against the median wall.

Through the blur he could see engine coolant rolling past his head. The smell of oil and gasoline filled the air and he could hear his wheels grinding to a halt. The engine coughed and sputtered as if it were being strangled. Off in the distance he could hear sobs and a woman screaming.

Duane tried to shove whiskey bottles behind his seat, a feeble drunken attempt: They fell out and clobbered him in the head. Feet approaching. Fast. He could hear the gravel grinding beneath the soles of their shoes. Still in a haze, he shuffled around the fast food bags looking for the baggie of soap-like chunks he had smoked through the previous week. Did he have a warrant? Or was it in Kansas? He could not remember a thing. The baggie, where was the baggie? How many did he drink before he left? He practiced his A, B S's backwards in his head as best he could. No use. He tried and struggled to practice them forward. A knife blade entered his vision. It cut through the seatbelt. A set of powerful hands grabbed him by the armpits, snapping him through the half crushed door. He was slapped effortlessly against the bed of the overturned truck. He hadn't felt that type of power since he was a little boy. He recalled being thrown over the kitchen table by his father. His head landed on the stove and bled like hell. But his father had been dead for over a decade. And his father wasn't a sobbing Italian.

Duane's knees gave way and he landed on all fours. He could feel gravel digging into his palms. Blood fled his cut lip like poured syrup. The man grabbed Duane by his neck, pulling him off the ground, slamming him back against the truck bed.

"You sonofabitch" the man wailed, tears streaming down his face. "Do you know who you just killed?"

CHAPTER 46

He was slipping fast. The person holding him pled for everyone to stand back to give this poor soul the air he was desperately fighting for. He watched as his tear landed on the boy's cheek. When he coughed, blood splattered on Simon's chest. "Shhh" Simon whispered. "It's going to be ok. You've just taken a hit. It was a truck." He looked saw Valletta with the driver of the overturned truck. "It just came out of nowhere." He tried not to look directly at his leg. He feared his repulsion would be seen by What's-his-name. "You're gonna be ok." Simon lied as best he could. "You're gonna be ok."

What's-his-name summoned his strength. He touched Simon's hand. "Listen, Simon. There was more" he coughed. "So much more." What's-his-name's efforts to speak made him cringe from the pain.

"Yes" Simon whispered to him. "Go on." He looked frantically for an ambulance. He listened to the young man while hoping for the wail of a siren.

What's-his-name coughed and sputtered. He was losing feeling in his hands and fingers, his lips were numb. It was getting hard to speak. "He is real, Simon. And He loves you. He loves us all…" What's-his-name continued as Simon cradled his head. As he was slipping, he told Simon that like all of us, God had been trying for the longest time to get through to him. To let him know that he is worth something. That like all of us, to God, he was worth *everything*. God gave his only son for him. The boy cried. He asked Simon to apologize to his parents for failing them. He worried about his friends, Hix and Hendricks. Who would watch out for them, save them from their own devices?

"Simon" his voice withered. "There was one more thing." He summoned the last of his strength, tugging Simon lower. "He said there was a bridge, Simon."

"He said you had to get to that bridge…"

Simon prayed for Bailey to materialize. He heard she still lived in KC. She would know what to do. He asked What's-his-name for his name. The boy smiled. "Nobody ever wants to know my name." He sputtered when he laughed. "Why you wanna know my name?" Simon got lower and smiled, he cared not if his tears were obvious anymore.

"I ask, because you matter, my friend. Because you matter." The boy hacked up blood again. His mouth opened but he was short of breathe. "My name," he sputtered, "is Sascha."

Looking up, Simon saw the old bum he had met in front of the hotel in Seattle, the same man he ran into at his hotel in Kansas City and at the Plaza. He watched as he looked to the sky and cried. He was not surprised to see him.

On that sad and terrible day, Simon Glenayre cradled that boy, listening to him as he used the last of his strength to weep and pray. And he continued to hold him, and rocked him gently after he fell silent.

CHAPTER 47

Izzy sat on the curb. Air hissed from an air hose above his head. New York City, Hell's Kitchen. Not a good place for any kid after midnight. The voice of his grandmother passed through his thoughts. He recalled something she said. Something about how nothing good ever happened after midnight. And there he was. He fretted over Sam. He hoped she would stay asleep while he was gone. His mother was passed out, she wouldn't be up till noon. Her pusher saw to that.

The message arrived on a note, shoved unceremoniously under his apartment door. Not a bill stuffed in an envelope with a window, as usual was the case, but a demand for payment nonetheless. He flicked at the recliner's torn material with his nail. He did not want to get up. But Sam was asleep, and if he was being summoned, now was his chance to meet. He hated leaving his sister alone. He hated that gun too. He was thankful he was not forced to pull it out. He managed to steal formula for his sister, sure. But the only time the gun was seen was when it plopped out of his pocket in the convenience store. The woman screamed and he screamed right along with her. Nobody else in that store knew what Izzy knew: The gun was unloaded. He couldn't bring himself to load the weapon. The bullets, only five of them in total, sat stuffed in a sock at the bottom of a laundry basket in his closet. In his first fumbled attempt at stealing, he dropped the gun, made women and himself scream and yet he managed to snatch the container of formula as well as his gun off the floor before the police arrived.

He leapt from the chair and walked to the door. It was a piece of paper. The foil lining from the inside of a pack of cigarettes.

He turned it over to the side made of white paper. There was a message. His hand trembled as he read it. He slipped into Sam's room and confirmed her slumber. He slid on his denim jacket and walked out the door.

And there he sat, at the assigned meeting place. It was just another convenience store with just another air hose that hissed like a black snake. He watched a hand off between a dealer and a customer at the corner. At the other street corner he observed two girls, both hardly eighteen, work the Johns as they pulled over to negotiate price. Izzy did not want that for his Sam. He loved her so, she deserved better than that. The girls on that corner deserved better than that. If only they had been loved and appreciated when they were younger. He imagined how their life may have taken a better turn, if only they were told how special they really were, if they felt valued in ways beyond their appearance . He worried night and day about Sam.

He had to get them out of this place. Daily he walked a line between the agony of his mother's self destruction and the love of his beloved Sam. One wrong move, one phone call from a good Samaritan meant he and Sam would be split up forever. The thought of it nearly sucked the air right out of his lungs. He hoped this task, the payback owed to the soulless and threatening Grimm, and hopefully what would follow would be enough to set Sam up in formula, milk, anything… for a long time. He was tired of stealing. He prayed for forgiveness nightly. Sure, he could go to the food pantry or to the local church to ask for help. But the risk of his family's situation being brought to light meant a visit from Family Services. And that meant losing Sam. No, he thought. He could do this. One big job, one big hunk of money and everything would be ok for a while, it would buy him some time. He had to get them out of this place. He wanted his mother away from the pushers. And he wanted Sam to go to college some day.

Izzy could smell Grimm's stench before he could see him. His voice occupied the same frequency as the hiss of the black air hose. Izzy stood up and turned around. As usual, Grimm was in the shadows. "I hear you've been busy, haven't ya?" Izzy only nodded. "I hear you've made quite a few bucks thanks to me and our arrangement…" Izzy shared the fact that he hadn't even pulled the gun on anyone. And yes, he did have it with him, but as always it was unloaded. Grimm's rough and meaty hand burst from the shadows and snatched Izzy out of the light. He found himself yanked into the darkness and thrown to the ooze and

grime of the convenience store ground. His head hit the
dumpster, his hand stuck to the sticky combination of soda
fountain syrup and broken glass. Grimm lifted Izzy off the
ground, pulling his face into his own. He was so close that even
in the darkness he could see the pits in Grimm's bulbous nose.

"What?" he said. "Did you think you were gonna get out of
our arrangement just cause you didn't put bullets in *my* gun?"
Izzy shook his head. He knew not why, but the vision of a
country church barged into his thoughts. For a second he saw the
ivory of a piano's keys, they were drenched in colorful light. He
felt his breathing ease. Perhaps it was his way of coping with
what he was enduring at that very moment. Grimm shook him.
Hard.

"You!" he growled. "You listening to me? You gotta debt to
pay." Izzy shook his head fearfully. He fantasized of bullets in the
gun. Grimm noticed. He had seen that look on the faces of
others. Izzy's hand rested on the gun in his pocket. He felt the
grip of Grimm's powerful hands engulf both his hand and the
gun through his jacket. Izzy yelped as he felt Grimm crush his
hand against the cold steel. He spoke up. "What do you want?"

Grimm smiled. He smiled far and wide. Izzy could tell he was
going to enjoy dropping this on him. "I gotta name" he hissed.
"And I gotta picture." From within his shirt pocket came a
photograph, printed on copy paper. He released Izzy and took
great joy in handing it to him. Slowly, Izzy unfolded the paper. It
was a man. He had long, shoulder-length hair. He had a guitar
strapped around his neck. Izzy found him to be beautiful. It was
obvious this person was a star. He'd seen him before, though he
couldn't recall where. He recalled a rare trip to the mall with a
friend. It was a music store. Yes. He saw this face on the cover of
a CD. A magazine too. Grimm saw the look of recognition on
Izzy's face. "You know this guy, don'tcha?"

"Sure," Izzy said. "I think he's someone famous, right?"
Grimm released his hand. Izzy felt the curves of the gun in his
flesh. He felt them with his fingers.

"Yeah," Grimm said. "And I want you to take care of him."

Izzy shook his head. "No, no, no…I can't kill another
person." Grimm laughed long and hard. And then he struck Izzy,
open handed, sending him down to the ooze and broken glass.
"Oh yes you can," he barked. "And you will." Grimm, a veteran
of many hits, many threats and with a black belt in intimidation,
knew how to apply pressure. And he knew right where Izzys'
pressure points were. "Well let me plant a vision in that thick

little head of yours." Izzy closed his eyes and wished he was somewhere else. He opened his eyes to find Grimm still standing there.

"Oh yeah. Sure" he said. "Would be terrible for your mother to take a fall out of an open window, wouldn't it? Your mother has been used up, she's of no use anymore. She'd be just be another ex-hooker and druggie found in a dumpster." Izzy tried not to cry. He failed. Grimm knew he had him. Never one to let up the pressure, he enjoyed digging in further.

"Or" he grinned, "envision my hand resting on your sister's head" he smiled far and filthy. "And squeeeezing."

"Hard."

"Stop it!" Izzy pled. "I get it. Ok?" From Izzy's hand Grimm snatched the paper with the face on it. He pushed it hard into Izzy's face, just to drive home his dominance. "Kill him, Izzy" he said. "That's your job. Do that, and you are free. I promise. You will never see my face again, your mother can spend the rest of her days dying away in that dump of an apartment, and your sister?" he smiled, "she can just keep on living." He motioned to the working girls standing on the street corner. "She has so much to look forward to, doesn't she?" He dropped the paper at Izzy's feet. "Do it." Grimm disappeared into the darkness. Izzy found himself alone with the paper and the hiss of the air hose. He turned the paper over, there was a name on it. "Simon Glenayre." He knew the name. Also on the back was his tour itinerary. He would be hitting New York soon. Immediately Izzy tried to think of how he would get all the way to Manhattan and Madison Square Garden. No. There would be no need. At the bottom a phone number, a cell phone number to be exact. Untraceable. Evil. The message next to the number stated they would take him to the spot. Izzy noticed the word. "We." Now he knew there would be more than one. He feared he would be disposed of after he killed the musician. He had a plan of his own: Shoot him and get out. Before anybody could get hold of him.

He cracked the door slowly. It still creaked. A little more. There. He heard nothing. Izzy slid through the doorway and eased it shut.

Sam cried out from her crib. Izzy ran as quietly as he could to their room. He eased her into his loving arms and kissed her on her cheek. She was hungry again. They both found their way down the hallway without waking their mother. The bulb hung from the ceiling. Izzy flipped the switch. Nothing. The refrigerator door still worked though. Izzy shook the opened can of formula. He shook it. He smiled. Sam chirped her approval in his ear and again, Izzy smiled. Her little hands reached out for the bottle, and she gave a soft groan of satisfaction as she put it to her lips. "I love you, Sam." From the corners of her mouth, Sam smiled to her brother, as if she were old enough to understand what he said. She blinked slow and patient at him too, as if she knew the world would be there upon her return.

In the California hills, Sol considered the plan to kill Simon Glenayre. Though a typical plan of murder, it was well thought out and if executed well, meant Glenayre would be dead, music sales and all paraphernalia related to him would go through the roof and he would be, well, richer. That's what the industry needed: Another death. Like an Elvis, John Lennon or Jim Morrison, Simon Glenayre would take his place in the pantheon of fallen stars. A mythical hero for the masses, his face and name on buttons, t-shirts, movies and it would all make his pockets fat, fat, fat.

The idea was so simple it was ridiculous. The fools he hired and spread across the country came up empty-handed. Well, empty handed save for the critical news of the two men who actually did manage to locate him. One would spend the rest of his life in a wheel-chair, and the other expected to be in therapy for the for a while. Still, some good did come of it. He knew for sure where Simon Glenayre was. Kansas City. He had seen it once, from the air on his flight from LA to New York City. He heard the people there were nice. He couldn't care less. And now one of his soldiers, the ever dependable Grimm, as disgusting and harsh as ever, had a plan ready to hatch. And he loved it. Loved it, loved it, loved it. Sol recalled how out of place the beefy and caked in filth Grimm looked, sitting there in his boardroom. As disgusting as he was, Sol recalled how his heart leapt up in his throat as Grimm shared *his* plan. *The* plan. Those other oafs were amateurs compared to Grimm. Hell, why didn't he just call him to begin with? Grimm had someone in line. Some black kid from the ghetto. If the kid managed to kill Glenayre, Sol wins. If the kid managed to kill Glenayre and get caught, Sol still wins. The kid Grimm found would just be another inner city punk caught with a gun. What did he care? Nobody would believe his story. And as long as Glenayre was dead in his cash register, he was happy. To put Sol's mind at ease, Grimm promised he would be watching from afar. If he saw even the slightest hesitation on the face of the kid, he would be there to see the hit through *personally*. Grimm's reasoning was twofold: Sure, he would be paid well, very well if the hit went off without a hitch. But if there was a snag and Simon Glenayre somehow survived, his *reputation* would be what died a horrible death. No matter the consequences, Grimm would see Glenayre killed.

Sol reviewed the scheme in his mind. The kid Sol suspected, had nothing to live for except the love of his next eight ball, or the primal lust of pulling a trigger. He was expendable. No one would even care if the punk went to jail anyway. In a few days Sol would put the word out. It would certainly find its way to Glenayre. He had always been such a softy, such a fool. He would lure him from KC to New York City with an olive branch and the promise of more creative leeway, and a forgiveness of his debt. Glenayre would be done in, not so much by the boy who would pull the trigger, but by his own foolish, wishful thinking. Once in New York, he would have his men tail the musician, and when a pattern was established, put the kid in place with the gun.

Sol Glenn's study was dark. The fireplace crackled.

Sol sat back in his house coat and sighed long and hard. He stirred his drink with his finger, and admired the rich amber color of the scotch as it spun in his glass. From behind his chair a long, smooth arm curved around him. She lit his cigar and ran her nails along his jaw line. Her long, wavy red hair fell over his shoulders as she moved in front of his chair. "Yes," Sol said to the smiling woman, "life is good."

He twisted the cigar in his mouth and fell back into his leather chair, watching as Chloe's robe fell to the floor.

CHAPTER 48

Valletta took the key from the girl behind the counter. Pretty and attentive, she worked the desk at one of the nicest hotels in the city and became a seasoned star gazer, recognizing Simon Glenayre immediately. But he did not look at all like the Simon Glenayre pictured on the cover of his CD. But still, it was *him*. She watched his friend put his arm over his shoulder. He lifted Simon Glenayre up, it seemed. He looked fragile, as if he might fall to pieces. Walking past the service desk she called out his name. "Mister Glenayre, I just want to welcome…" He did not acknowledge her at all. Valletta moved him quickly past.

"You've had this room prepared for you for quite a while," Valletta said softly. "Ever since your tour itinerary was finalized they put this room on reserve. Phil had his people set it up for ya weeks ago." Valletta wished him a good sleep, he would be near. He promised. Their rooms were adjoined.

Simon lay in bed, considering his already prepared room. He knew Phil's people stocked it with plenty of his favorite brand of orange juice. His tea. Candy bars. His heroin.

His heroin. His rooms were always stocked with heroin. Sometimes coke, but he hoped for heroin.

Phil's people always knew to stuff a "love package" between the mattress and box springs. And now that he remembered the standard operating procedure, he could feel the package pulsating beneath the mattress. He leapt to his knees at the side of the bed and jammed his arm under the mattress. There. The package. He felt the string wrapped around it and slid his fingers through. Good. He pulled it out. A trip to the bathroom produced a plastic knife, just sharp enough cut through the twine. His hands

214

shook so bad he could hardly hold the plastic utensil. A maid walked by his door and heard the sound of tearing. She paused and continued on her way. Within moments the package was opened and Simon had laid out on the bed, the vial, a spoon and a lighter. He bent the spoon around his index finger then unscrewed the cap from the vial. Ready to go. No, he thought, better to do it in the bathroom. He didn't want to catch his mattress on fire. Simon avoided looking at his reflection in the mirror. He was ashamed. He felt he had come so far. There was so much riding on his well being. He could get clean. He could have a life. Perhaps he could even face Bailey again. Tell her how he really felt about her, even after all these years. That boy, on the side of the highway. "God," he thought. He will remember looking in his eyes for the rest of his own life. The EMTs had to pry his body from Simon's grip. Again, he cried. The message from God. That's right. He said God gave him a message. Get to The Bridge. Something good would happen there. "Something good is about to happen here." He wished he hadn't looked up. The sight was frightful. A sweaty Simon, his hair disheveled and matted with blood. Sascha's blood still speckled his face. That poor kid. That poor, poor kid. Simon rubbed his eyes and laughed in the mirror.

If the needle pierced his flesh, once again his demons had him. And everything that kid died for on the side of the road will have been for nothing. Again, The Bridge. And Valletta...he was so proud of his friend. He had begged Simon for years to get help. Valletta worried about his lack of sleep. He worried Simon would be found dead in a bathtub someday.

This was Simon's chance to back away from the edge. He had never seen Valletta cry before today. If he lit it up in this bathroom, everything he fought for these past several day were for nothing. He enjoyed his journey. He was sleeping again. He had found his smile. Perhaps he would be able to call Bailey and for the first time to apologize. And those eyes, he could not get them out of his mind. She smiled with her eyes. Simon dropped the chunk onto the spoon and rendered it to liquid. He wept as he shoved the poison into his arm. The angels in the room wept with him.

Edgar Allan Poe once said he took no pleasure from his use of drugs. Poe described drugs as a desperate attempt to escape "the dread of some strange impending doom." From the moment his eyes opened, he knew he was somewhere else. This place, it was different. There were wooden panels of deep red grain on the walls. A large fireplace as well. He saw Chloe there. He could not smile at the sight of her. He drew no pleasure from seeing his wife. "Good Lord"' he thought to himself. That sounded so strange. Chloe, his wife. It just struck him as so bizarre. He saw a large fire. A large leather chair in front of the fireplace. Though curious, he did not make his way to the other side. Why didn't Chloe see him? He didn't ask any more questions. He moved out of the room and down a long hallway. It came to a staircase. It was long and dark. He knew not to proceed. But still, he moved forward. The staircase came to a landing, and with a turn went further down. Another landing. More steps down. Simon knew not to proceed, and still he proceeded.

A few more steps down and Simon slipped and fell, landing in a well lit room with a great deal of sunlight. The windows reached from the floor to the ceiling. It felt safer here. Simon rubbed at the lump in his arm. He looked down to see blood pooling beneath the skin. The dope must have hit him hard and he fell over, bumping the needle on the way down while it remained in his arm. Simon felt a sensation in his head, as if cotton was being stuffed in his ears. He jammed his finger in an ear, trying to pop it. Nothing. The sound around him was diminishing. He tried speaking, but his own voice was muffled. The room was so bright it was surreal. The hearing in his other ear was now being affected. Simon could hear a rumble, but was unsure if it was the environment or a problem with his ears. He spun around and froze.

It was a man.

It was Whiteface. He wore a white suit this time but his tie was black. His skin was white as a sheet of paper. Simon took a step back. His heart ascended. The man was black around his eyes. He looked directly at Simon and smiled. His mouth was black on the inside. His tongue, and teeth, black. The rumble became louder. Simon took another step back. The man in the corner took a step forward, Simon interpreted the man's movements as being predatory. He smiled again. The rumbling in Simon's ears became louder. Black smoke began to form behind him, filling that side of the room. He took another step toward Simon. Simon tried to move away from the man. He could not move his feet. He struggled as he watched the top of the man's head burst into flames. The smoke had an ethereal appearance to it, almost as if it were charcoal smeared across the face of roughly textured paper. The smoke began to spread around the room.

Simon struggled to get away. He could feel the approach of imminent danger from this stranger, with his white suit, black mouth and eyes and his hair of fire. Frantically he tried to pry his feet from the floor. The man moved closer. Simon rolled a leather conference desk chair between them. The man smiled and move it out of his way. Black liquid oozed from his mouth. Rumbling. Louder. Simon looked around for something to defend himself with. And like the predator Simon feared this man was, he was on him, taking him by the shoulders and crunching his teeth into Simon's skull.

Simon woke up screaming. He could hear Valletta's familiar footsteps rushing into the room. Valletta froze in the doorway. "Oh, Simon" he pained. "Please tell me you didn't."
"Please tell me you didn't."

CHAPTER 49

The alarm sounded harsher than usual. Bailey rolled over and pulled the covers over her head. That dream was horrible. Just horrible. That poor boy, dying on the side of the highway. Never had she been traumatized by a dream. It was so real. Again the alarm sounded. Her fingers found the off button without much of a struggle. She rolled out of bed, slower than her usual self. Usually bright and energized when she awoke, today was different. She felt a tremendous sense of loss and sadness that she couldn't understand.

She tried to call Konstanze earlier that day again, but according to the new girl on the line, she had been replaced. Bailey suspected this was because their conversations had been monitored and Konstanze was cut loose when their wire tapped conversations produced no information of use to the record company. She knew not to share what she had with Konstanze over the phone. She wished her well, that silly but sweet girl with her gum smacking and hopeless dreams of fame. Over time she grew on Bailey. She stood up and made her way to her bathroom and emerged shortly after. For reasons unknown to her, Bailey went directly, almost urgently to her phone. She felt the need to pick up the phone, though she knew not why. No reason in particular came to mind, and yet her hand hovered over the phone.

It rang. The realization of precognition shocked and frightened Bailey. She feared who could be on the other end of the line. She picked it up. The number was local, she could tell that much, but she did not recognize it. She hit the answer button. "Hello?"

Silence.

She could hear someone. There *was* breathing. She was sure of that. She spoke again.

"Hello?" she said. "Who is this?" A voice came through her receiver and she nearly fainted. The familiar tonality, instantly recognizable. She grabbed the counter for support.

"Bailey?" the familiar voice said. "Is this Bailey Eden Piper...nurse?"

"Yes it is, Simon Glenayre, rock star."

Simon could hear her smile through the phone. A long pause. Bailey still had her hand clutched over her chest. "I can't believe it's you." Bailey said. Simon laughed.

"I can't believe it's me either." He continued. "Well, I was in town," he stuttered. "I was in town and I just thought I would give you a call. Is that ok? Is it?"

"Ok?"

Bailey laughed. Of course it was ok that he called, she said. After all, she had only spent the last couple days combing the city for him. Simon laughed at this and shared that it was something he had frequently heard during this, his brief time back in his home town. They both laughed when he told her he'd snuck off, run away really, back to Kansas City to get away from it all. And as crazy as it sounded, other people seemed to know he was going to be there even before he did. "How did *you* know I would be here?" Bailey paused. She was embarrassed. Too embarrassed to answer. "Hello?" Simon said. "How did you know I was going to be here?"

Bailey laughed. Nervously, she laughed. "I was jogging the other day. Just jogging."

The pause was long and ridiculous. Bailey fidgeted with a salt shaker on the kitchen countertop. Simon listened as she knocked it over. "That's bad luck" he said.

Bailey paused as she brushed the salt into the sink. "How the heck did you know I spilled the salt?"

Again, Simon laughed. "C'mon, Bail. I know you" he chuckled. "Right now you are in the kitchen. And just like you always did, that was the place you go when you talk on the phone."

"Continue?" Bailey said. "And you always fidgeted with stuff on your countertop. Kind of an absent-minded habit of yours. And Bailey," he said, "knocking over the salt is bad luck!"

Bailey laughed. "Well," she said, "I feel very lucky today."

"So," Simon continued. "You were jogging and realized I was

in KC?" he asked. "How?"

Bailey laughed again at herself and shoved the salt shaker away. "Look, I glanced down at my MP3 player. It was strapped to my arm. And the battery was getting low…"

Simon asked. He couldn't help it. He had to. "You are telling me that your MP3 player told you I was going to be here?"

"Hello?" he thought she hung up.

"Yes!" She burst out laughing. "My MP3 player told me." She sighed and confessed her moment of enlightenment. "I looked at my player and it needed to be charged. At that moment I realized where you would be."

"I knew you would come home to charge your own batteries." She was embarrassed. "…So to speak."

Bailey felt a sudden change in the mood. Even if it was over the phone, Bailey could tell Simon was thinking, and thinking hard. "Bail?"

She knew where this was going. She leaned on the counter. She knew what was coming, and if not for the kitchen counter, she would have hit the floor. "Bail I've spent a lot of time thinking about Lily." Bailey leaned against the countertop as if she were in physical pain. "I miss her so much. I know I held her for only a little while, but I've never been able to get her out of my mind." Bailey wiped her eyes and let him get it out. "How long has it been?" Simon asked.

Bailey responded it had been nearly twenty years. Twenty long years.

"This month…" For a moment Bailey lost her breath. "This month would have been her twentieth birthday."

Hardly any of that water had passed under the bridge since then. Both their hearts remained broken. Bailey listened as Simon broke down over the phone. She sobbed with him. "She smiled at me," he cried. "I know she did. She smiled at me with her eyes, Bail. My little baby girl smiled at me with her eyes."

Bailey tried to contain herself. "I know she did, baby. I believe you."

Simon "she said, "it wasn't your fault. It just happened" she urged. Sometimes, and for reasons nobody can ever explain or understand, those things just happen." She could feel his pain through the receiver. "It happened to our daughter, Bail. It happened to our Lily." They had picked the name out together, the two of them. Similar to their method of picking a vacation destination, to a certain degree, they left the name to chance. Several names, thoughtfully chosen, and all of them contenders by both Simon and Bailey were written on paper, and the paper cut into little strips. The names were then put into a bowl. Together they placed their clasped hands into the bowl and laughed at themselves as they fumbled about trying to retrieve a single name. After a few moments their hands managed to pinch a single piece of paper between their fingers and a single name emerged. Secretly, Bailey hoped they would draw out the name "Lily." It was gentle. It was sweet and fragile. She absolutely loved it. And secretly, Simon hoped for "Lily" as well.

Together they drew out a name. Bailey opened the slip of paper and smiled. She showed it to Simon who laughed aloud as he poured orange juice into a cup. "Well," he beamed. "I guess it's Lily." That night he held her even tighter than usual. Crawling down the bed to her tummy, he kissed her wedding ring on the way. Simon spoke to their child, and felt her move beneath his cheek. He laughed aloud and told Lily that he loved her. He promised her he would remain clean. Bailey had helped him through so much. There was no way he could have gotten this far without her steadfast love and support. She introduced him to his sponsor at AA. He looked up to see her smiling face. "I love you Bail, and I love our baby."

"You both are the crown jewels of my life"

"Aaaw," Bailey cooed. "I have to go pee."

Simon chuckled and helped her off the bed and to the bathroom door.

Upon her return, Bailey found the blankets of their bed pulled back, her man waiting for her with open arms. That night they loved one another, as only a couple truly in love can. Later that night, Simon laid in bed with Bailey in his arms, listening to her breathe as she slept. It would be the last night the three of them would ever spend together.

"She smiled at me with her eyes, Bail."

Bailey pulled herself together, ever the strong one, she knew she had to be. "Simon, sweetie. I want to see you, ok? Will you let me see you?"

"Please?"

The silence was far too long for comfort. For a moment Bailey feared he would hang up on her. Disappear to never be found again. She feared she had blown her chance to see Simon again by being too pushy. Perhaps she asked way too soon. The silence was deafening and lasted far too long. Thankfully, Bailey heard his voice instead of a dial tone. "Yes" he said. "I would like that very much."

The meeting couldn't take place in KC. He was flying out shortly, overseas. And now that he was sobered up, he knew he had much to prove to Valletta after his slip up the day before. Once back from his trip to Europe, Simon would come back and face the music. Sol, Phil, everyone. That stop would be New York. Bailey agreed to fly there and meet him. Bailey would be his oasis during that awkward time with his employers. Inside, Bailey was giddy. "Yes!" She found herself excited for a few good reasons. She had never been to New York of course, and once her plane landed, it was determined that Simon would be only a short cab ride away. She was thrilled. But she tried not to sound too excited over the phone. She didn't want to scare Simon away. This amazing man, so brilliant and thoughtful as well as physically breathtaking, was also very fragile and afraid. One wrong turn of phrase and he would turn and leap over the nearest fence like a deer, disappearing back into the thick darkness of the forest never to be seen again. Yes, this required kid gloves. She knew there were plenty of men who would have been easier to love. After all, she had spent years spurning their romantic overtures. They would be much easier to love, if she could actually love one of them. But it mattered not. She still loved Simon Glenayre. And love was never cast aside easily with Bailey Eden Piper. Maybe it was how she was raised. But she still cared. She still loved sincerely. And if she played her cards right, she could get to Simon, have a good look at him and see how he was *really* doing. She hoped he would want to hold her hand. But if at that time she could tell he was ok, she would just go away if he so desired. At least she would know he was ok. And if that was how it would turn out, she would have no choice but to move on. She would accept a dinner invitation with another man, a thought as appealing to Bailey as busting rocks on a chain gang. She yearned to look across the dinner table and see the face of her beloved Simon. He interrupted her inner dialogue.

"So it's New York then?"

Bailey laughed. She tried so hard not to, but she just couldn't help it. "New York. And what are you going to do in the meantime?" she said. "Just curious."

"I'm going back to Germany, Bail." He said. "I have some business I have to take care of there. Bailey tapped her nails on the counter and thought.

She knew why he was going. "You're going to go to that bridge, aren't you?"

"Yes."

"The one by that village, right?"

"Beuern?" Simon was impressed that she remembered the name. She had a mind like a vise.

Simon answered that she was indeed correct. He had forgotten that she knew about The Bridge. "It's just time, Bail. It's way overdue." They discussed the amount of time passed since he last walked along those cobblestone streets. He expected so much to be different about the place. Time has its own way of grinding away the safe, wearing away the comfort of the familiar. He hoped Beuern had remained unchanged though, he wanted it to be as he ideally remembered it: a jewel set deep in the German countryside beside a forest. Bailey interrupted his thoughts. "Simon, I had the craziest dream about Beuern, by the way."

"Just two nights ago. And there was a fountain" she said. "Hello?"

"Simon?" She listened for the worst. A dial tone. She tried again. "Simon, are you there? Did I say something wrong?" Once again she was relieved to hear his voice. These pauses of his were driving her mad. "Bailey I had the same dream that very night." "Please," he urged. "Tell me more."

Bailey continued with her tale. There was a fountain, she said. Simon interjected. "And there were dancers, right?"

Bailey's heart leapt to her throat. "Yes" she whispered. "Ballerinas." She could hear his breathing over the phone. It became heavier. "It was you there, wasn't it, Bail?" And now Bailey left Simon hanging. The silence made him nervous. "Bailey? You there?"

"I am here" she said. "And I was there." In the silence that followed, Simon considered how this could be.

For a few brief and glorious moments, both Simon Glenayre and Bailey Eden Piper shared the same ground. At one point only a couple steps away from one another. *They shared a dream!* Surely that meant something. Maybe, Simon thought, just maybe there really was such a thing as true love. That somehow, it still existed in this world, somehow two people *could* still be in love. Be in love the way it was truly meant to be, not as a mere flight of fancy. Not as two lonely ships passing in the night, but as the result of a union between a man and a woman. Yes, he thought, it was still there. It had never left him. It had never left her. "All the wasted years," he thought.

"All the wasted years."

CHAPTER 50

This time Simon went about it the right way. Sure, it was tough on Valletta, but it seemed only fair to him as well.

He would not disappear as he had the last time. The conversation with Valletta went as expected. There was a tremendous amount of frustration let loose from his friend, and Simon certainly expected that. Valletta had endured so much over the years for Simon. To ask him to stay was an insult. The way Simon saw it, Valletta had the right to vent. And with the exception of his outburst on the side of the highway, Valletta always managed to bite his tongue. Simon did not sneak away from Valletta, nor did he storm out of the room on him either. He only asked his friend for the space he needed to do what it was that he needed to do. Valletta understood as best he could. He loathed the idea, but he did as he was asked and watched his friend walk out the door. Out of his sphere of protection and on to an unknown future.

He wouldn't even let Valletta go with him. On the way to the airport, Simon ordered the limo driver to stop at the nearest mailbox. When the limousine eased to the curb, Simon leaned out of his window and slipped a package into the mail. The package was his personal journal. Covered in leather, it was a gift from his parents years ago. He'd written something in it regularly for the longest time. And now all his thoughts, hopes, dreams and nightmares were slid into the darkness of that metal box. An address and name written on the brown paper wrapper. The name: Bailey Eden Piper.

Sitting in the waiting area, Simon watched the 747 being fueled. He found the clattering of nearby conversations somehow comforting, the normalcy of their chatter fed a hunger that ate at him daily. They talked about simple, everyday things. Their jobs, their children. He thought about Lily. He thought about Bailey, and how it felt to finally hear her voice again. Bailey was shocked to hear his voice on the other end of the line, sure. But her surprise paled in comparison to that of Simon's. After all, he is the one who dialed the number. He recalled the thrill as he did it. A simple act to most, but to Simon Glenayre, he might as well have been jumping the Grand Canyon in a little red wagon.

He considered Valletta further. And a realization hit Simon and hit him *hard*. He asked a question that had never occurred to him before. Ever. Valletta Angelo. His friend who committed his life to him, it seemed. And now he wondered. What had Valletta given up for *him* through the years?

Valletta never married, he never had a girlfriend. Hell, Simon couldn't even recall his going out on a date. It was something Simon would discuss with him upon his return. Valletta needed to meet somebody. It was time. Maybe if he had a woman in his life, he would not feel so intertwined in Simon's. Yes, he thought. It was sure to do him good. Additionally, Simon decided he was sending the big lug on a vacation, with a capital "V," whether he liked it or not. Valletta didn't know it yet, but at the end of the tour he was doing the Cayman Islands run. And if he didn't like it, he could bitch at the umbrella in his little foo-foo drink. Simon pictured the hulking Valletta in Bermuda shorts and laughed aloud.

Before yesterday, it had been nearly twenty years since he attended a funeral. He and Valletta stood across from Sascha's family. Simon watched as Sascha's father held his wife upright. He recalled something his own father said, something about how parents should never have to bury their own children. He recalled the sunken expression on his father's face as he spoke those words. That was not how it was supposed to be. And there they stood, kneeling down to grab soil. Sascha's mother threw her handful of soil in first, followed by his father. The dirt stuck to their moist hands. The priest spoke.

"Sascha Tremaine," he said louder than usual to overcome the sound of raindrops hitting the fallen leaves. "He has been described as a gentle soul, giving to his community." Valletta groaned. The priest continued. "He wanted to be a scientist, he loved art, and he was a brilliant student."

"He was a messenger," Valletta yelled out. Everybody's attention snapped to Valletta. Simon's included. "He was a messenger for God. And he saved a life that day."

"He saved mine," Simon whispered to himself. "And I didn't even thank him."

It was beginning to drizzle when Simon spotted something else. Two young men, both about Sascha's age. No one there that day cried harder than the two of them. The two youths stood out like sore thumbs, and it seemed to Simon that their presence at the funeral was not appreciated. And then something unexpected happened. Sascha's father reached into his wife's bag and began pulling out books. He walked over to Hix and Hendricks and handed them the books. Over the rainfall Simon could hear what he said. "He wanted you to have these." Sascha's father said softly. He hardly looked up from the books. "I figured it was you two."

Hendricks was first to reach out for the outstretched books. Hix was next. Hendricks looked at the cover of the book handed him. "How do you know he wanted us to have *these* books?" Without a word, Sascha's father opened the cover of the book in Hendricks' hand. There was something inscribed in it. Sascha's father tapped at the words with his finger. And without another word he turned with his wife and walked off in the falling rain. Both Hendricks and Hix looked into their books, reading the message written for them. "I've learned from a very good source that my time is growing short." Sascha wrote. There was a Bible verse shared by both books.

It was from the book of Proverbs. "The heart of the prudent getteth knowledge; and the ear of the wise seeketh knowledge."

Hix read aloud the last words from Sascha.

"Pray. Love. Learn. Pray."

Hendricks sniffled and laughed. "He wrote 'Pray' twice."

"I guess he was trying to get the point across" Hix said.

Hix closed his book, Hendricks did the same. Together they stood, listening to the rain drops hit the fallen leaves. A few moments later, on the walk back to the car, Hendricks took Hix by the arm and pulled him to a stop. "He knew, Hix" Hendricks nodded. "He knew. There's just no other way." Hix nodded. When they got home, they found themselves in their familiar bean bag chairs looking at one sad, empty bean bag chair across from them.

Hix was left a book called "Introduction to Mathematics"; Hendricks opened his book, titled "The Complete Shakespeare." Each also received a Bible.

Together, they discussed the changes they would make in their lives, and read together till dawn.

CHAPTER 51

It was the chirp of the plane's wheels on the Cologne/Bonn airport runway that shook Simon awake. Out of habit, he looked over to see if Valletta was still asleep. He wasn't there. Valletta was still back in The States. He hoped he was ok. However at the same time, as much as he feared he had hurt Valletta's feelings, he was equally fearful that his friend would hop the nearest pond jumper and catch up with him.

Soon another face invaded his thoughts. The face was as white as a moon-bleached tombstone. Simon shuddered as he thought of the thick, black smoke bursting around him. His black eyes. The black ooze seeping from his mouth onto his white suit. The words the man said haunted him still: "Give us The Key." Simon shook his head, this time from angry frustration more than fear. As he slept Simon screamed and drew the alarm of everyone on the plane, including that of one very frightened flight attendant who had the unenviable job of shaking him awake. Later, he watched from the corner of his eye as the attendant passed fearfully by him with the drink cart. The dreams were becoming fewer and farther between now that he was trying to get clean, and sleeping better at that. He even managed to get back to sleep.

Somehow.

"Excuse me" the man standing by the window said. "Are you gonna just sit there all day?" Surprised, Simon realized he was the only person sitting. Everyone else was standing, and all were staring at him.

"Oh" he said. "I'm so sorry." Simon dragged his bag through the air ramp, and the familiar rhythm of the German language filled his ears like music. The crowd of travelers was thick. A woman bumped into him as she rushed past. Another bump from a man coming from the other direction. Joyfully, Simon dropped his bags and he yelled aloud.

"Ich liebe Deutschland!"

From a distant point in the crowd, a voice bellowed back. "Und Deutschland liebt Sie auch!"

Smiling, Simon picked up his bags and moved forward, wherever "forward" was. At that moment he cared little where he was going. All he knew was that in many ways, he was home again. He felt it. It just felt like home. Much the same way he felt when he made his way back to Kansas City, once again he felt safe, though he knew the feeling would diminish once his taxi hit the autobahn at breakneck speed.

After a few minutes on the autobahn, the taxi swung toward an exit. Simon exhaled in relief when the Mercedes came to a sudden halt in the parking lot of the bus depot. Simon exited the cab, and as quick as the cab arrived, it spun off to its next fare, leaving Simon standing at the entrance with his bags, his hopes and dreams, and the vision of Bailey and Lily in his thoughts.

He approached the entrance to the bus depot, and as expected, the automatic doors did not slide open. He looked to his right and saw a familiar face. A face he had seen many times before. He had run into the shabby, penniless man at his hotel in Seattle, at the Kansas City Plaza, and on the side of the highway the day Sascha was killed. Why wouldn't he run into him in Frankfurt, Germany? For once, Simon wasn't surprised. In fact, for the first time, he greeted the old man as if he were greeting an old acquaintance.

"So," Simon muttered, "not going to grab my leg today? Yell at me, perhaps?" The old man laughed. And he laughed loud.

"Oh," the man said, "I don't think I need to do much more to get your attention. After all," he belched, you don' need me to tell you why you're here, boy." Simon jokingly asked him what airline he took to get to Germany, as expected both men had a good laugh at the question. "Oh, I got frequent flier mileage," the man chuckled. Abruptly, Simon stopped laughing. "Take care. Ok?"

"Oh, don't you worry yourself about that" he said, scratching his patchy, gray beard. "I been taking care for years now."

"More than you can imagine."

Simon wished the man well, turned towards the sliding door and said "Well, you going to do your thing?" he asked. "The slidey door trick?" Simon waved his finger at the electronic mat.

The bum smiled up at Simon. "Not everything's a trick, boy" he said. "Some things are just the way they are." As Simon expected, he then tapped the electronic mat with his finger and as Simon had witnessed before, the door slid open with a "whoosh." Walking into the building, he could hear the old man singing from outside.

"Sometimes I wonder/ If my tomorrow will ever come/ Show me where to look/ Show me where to look…"

When Simon emerged from the building with his bus ticket, the man was gone as expected, but the song he sang still rang in his head.

Simon followed the numerical sequence of the buses.

Dreiunddreißig.

Vierunddreißig.

Fünfunddreißig.

"There she be."

Simon tapped on the door of the bus to get the driver's attention.

The bus driver opened the bus door with a smile. He accepted Simon's ticket, ripping the bottom portion of it and returning the other section back to Simon with a smile and a "Vielen Dank." Simon looked at the driver's tidy arrangement of notes and documentation and enjoyed being back around the classic German sense of order and structure. He took his seat with that smile still on his face.

Soon the bus was pulling out from the depot with the full complement of passengers. Simon relaxed and enjoyed listening to them talk. He had no fear of being recognized here, though he did not know why. He had toured here yearly for quite a while, and his CD sales had been brisk in Germany. The German fans appreciated his sophisticated take on rock music. He suspected he had already been recognized by some of the passing glances. But he knew his anonymity would be safe. He had no fear of the German people. Passing the time was easy for Simon. He enjoyed watching the scenery as it whizzed past the tour bus. Hours passed as his bus made its way through the state of North Rhine/Westphalia, cutting across the Northern-most tip of the state of Rhineland-Palatinate and on into the familiar state of Hesse. The drone of the bus's diesel engine hummed through the night. Simon watched the German Polizei in their souped up Porsches pull over several speeders, all of whom knew better than to try and outrun them. The bus passed north of Frankfurt. Simon recalled his visit there fondly. The crowds in Frankfurt were always receptive. He turned his attention back to the whispered conversations of the surrounding bus passengers. He made a game of trying to pick out words he knew. The sun was ascending into the morning sky and Simon spied a blue autobahn sign whizzing past the bus. His heart started beating and his legs went numb. "Good grief," he thought to himself. "This feels like my first time on stage." A few miles later another sign whizzed by, but village and the distance to the village had become closer. Simon gulped as he looked at it.

"Beuern: 10 km."

Simon thought about his last conversation with Bailey before he got on the plane. Conducted in the most private place he could find in the crowded terminal, a dark corner behind what had to be one of the last remaining pay phones in the country. He thought about how firm her voice was this time. It was clear she had some time to think after their first conversation in years. Yes, she did still love him. And that love was unconditional, proven after all these years of her devotion to him as he barnstormed across the country having his selfish way. Sure, Bailey Eden Piper was devoted to him, but she also made one thing clear: She would no longer be a blind wishful fool. She would take him back. After all, with Bailey Eden Piper, forgiveness came with every breath. But there would be conditions: He had to forgive himself for his past transgressions; he had to get in touch with Daniel, his AA sponsor again. And she wanted him to surround himself with new people, people who would be a better influence on him. The best place to do this was at a church. A gathering place where he could better find the path he sought for himself. These were not requests. They were demands. Either he took them, or *she* would be the one to cut ties and flee.

"Fair enough" he thought to himself. He decided to make it so.

Approaching from the surrounding hills, the first thing Simon saw was a church steeple darting up into the sky from the center of the town. The roofs were still red ceramic. And after all these years, they still looked to Simon as if they were reaching up to shake hands with the heavens. Simon was up and gathering his things before the bus ground to a stop. The driver noticed Simon's eagerness and spoke to him.

"Aufgeregt?" Simon could only read the expression on the man's face as he spoke.

Later, the internet would refresh his rusty German, explaining to him that "aufgeregt?" translated to "excited?"

The sign on the building translated easily. After all, the German word for "motel" is "motel". Simon paid for his room, and walked down the short, dimly lit hallway to his door. Simon found it to be clean and orderly. Unlike many hotels in the United States, he would feel comfortable slipping between these sheets. The mattress of the bed was flipped onto the floor in a fearful search for a package. Simon knew there would be no package of self-destruction waiting for him there, but still, he had to check. Nobody except Bailey knew he was here. Simon watched in admiration as an elderly couple strolled along the cobblestone street below his window holding hands and once more, Simon imagined how nice it would be to hold hands once more on a stroll with Bailey. After freshening up in his room, Simon emerged from the motel out onto the streets of Beuern. He took in a deep breath and the air smelled the same as it had all those years ago. He had decided not to go directly to The Bridge. Instead, he simply went on a walk and imagined the possibilities of what or whom he might find when he *did* go there.

Would he find his father? After all, it was he who told Simon to go to that bridge if ever he needed answers. He hardly understood what his father was saying back then, and his reasoning was no clearer today. His father's tone sounded so serious. It was as if he really understood something. It was as if his father had a glimpse into his son's future. Simon recalled the caring urgency to his voice. He wanted to make himself perfectly clear. He wanted to be absolutely certain that Simon knew to come back to this village. Back to that bridge. Simon wandered through the streets of this place in a fresh downpour. Yes, another German rain was falling, but this was a wetter than usual rainy season for this area. Simon heard two people discussing it as they stood beneath the cover of a store awning. The rain let up and Simon continued on his way.

Approaching a corner, Simon heard a swishing sound. The sound grew louder as he drew nearer to the corner. Simon peeked around the corner to find an elderly woman. She was doing her best trying to sweep the wet leaves from the sidewalk. She was in her eighties. She wore a smock, and her dress was faded blue with a floral pattern. Her shoes were of old black leather.

She looked familiar to Simon. He approached her smiling. She looked up and smiled back, but her pleasant expression disappeared and disappeared quickly. Simon felt shock from what she said. The lines between her eyes deepened. She was obviously taken aback with the sight of him. She looked like she knew him from somewhere.

"Mein Gott."

Respectfully, Simon asked to speak with the old woman. He took a step forward, she took two steps back. Simon asked why she was alarmed. The woman, gripping her broom with her boney hand stood weary at the sight of Simon. But after a few moments of awkwardness, she spoke to him. "Mein Herr," she said, "many, many years ago you passed through my dreams. I was much younger then." Her voice trailed off. "This was many years before your parents ever met."

She shook her head. "But that couldn't have been you. But please, Mein Herr," she asked "would you please tell me where it is that you are going? Why are you here?" The woman said nothing further. She wished to hear what Simon had to say. "Dear lady," he spoke in broken German, "I need to get to a certain place."

The woman paused. "To a bridge, if I remember correctly."

"Mein Herr," she said in her trembling voice, "your bridge is still there. As it has always been. I hope you find what it is you seek." She lifted her thin arm and pointed towards a small road that made its way between a house and a bookshop. Simon nodded and thanked her as he walked away. Before he disappeared into the shadows of the small street, Simon turned to the woman who was still watching him.

"Wie heißen Sie?"

The old woman smiled and replied that he most certainly already knew who she was.

They had already met, she explained. Still, she smiled at Simon and gave her name.

"Mein Herr, ich heisse Kruppa," she smiled. "Frau Charlotte Kruppa."

"Vielen dank." Simon smiled. He disappeared down the shaded street between the house and the bookshop, but not too far before he heard the woman's voice calling out to him.

"Mein Herr" she called out to him. "Gott ist mit Ihnen noch." He raised his hand to her. She raised her hand to him. At that moment they both knew they shared that dream. Simon turned and went on his way. Her voice, echoing through his mind. "God is with you…still."

The sound of the rushing waters, loud even through a good distance of trees, was telling of how high the stream had risen.

And to Tuomas and Klaus, that sound called to them. The brothers had been warned by their parents not to wander too close to the water's edge when it was running high. Both mother and father knew of the dangers of that stream from their own childhoods. But to Tuomas and Klaus, the thrill of digging bullets left over from the war from the sides of old barns and houses had long lost its thrill. They had worked their way deeper and deeper into the forest in search of war artifacts, perhaps some even left by relatives of their very own. Once Tuomas found and dug up the rotten remnants of an old wooden handle, likely a part of an officer's pistol. The handle, displayed proudly on the headboard of his bed. He also knew his father detested the artifact being in the house, a rotten remnant of a hateful time in their country's history. Still, their father allowed the pistol handle to remain in the house in hopes it would spark their curiosity for history. The German people lived with their history every day. And they work hard to learn from their past. So the artifact stayed. To the father, it would serve as a sad beacon, pulling his sons towards the calling and exploration of truth and justice. The handle, with its engraved emblem, would stay.

Tuomas and Klaus also had a new friend, a visiting American boy whose parents had befriended their own, and he shared exciting tales of his excursions into the Appalachian Mountains with his grandfather. On one of the boy's visits, Tuomas and Klaus excitedly looked through Leo's collection of arrowheads, listening to the tale of how each was found and where. The German boys were thrilled to hear tales of the hunt for authentic Indian arrowheads. From real Indians! That night, Leo agreed to be the cowboy so the German brothers could play the role of rampaging Indians. They played until they passed out from exhaustion. Both sets of parents, when done with their game of bridge, split their sleeping boys up. Tuomas and Klaus, up to their beds and Leo, out to the car for the ride home.

Leo, ever the accomplished actor, faked being asleep so his father would carry him. He loved it when his father carried him. Unknown to Leo was the fact that his father knew he was faking. And he appreciated it, for he knew his time to carry his son in his arms diminished daily. Some day he would have to tackle him for a hug. Moments like this were to be savored. So it was with great joy that he carried his son to the car.

That morning, Tuomas and Klaus awoke with a headstrong agenda. Leo's pattern to successful artifact hunting was well established and obvious. In fact, it was as plain as the nose on his American face.

The place to look was at that stream. The stream their parents warned them about. Yes, the waters were high, but they would be careful.

Nearby there was a bridge.

CHAPTER 52

Sascha's father found his room just as he left it.

He'd spent the evening there, among his son's books, papers and his computers. He'd hardly paid attention to them, the monitors with their words rolling against a black background. Through his numbness he hadn't realized the computers were unplugged.

Again, he aimlessly flipped open a book and again he slapped it shut. Clenched in his fist, the last communication he ever made to his son. He regretted reading the next to last line of the note as he now viewed it as the most despicable thing he had ever communicated to anyone, but especially his own flesh and blood. Equal to his hatred of his own handwritten words was the pain he felt for having read it again. He was only worried about his son's future. He laughed out of sheer hatred of himself. As if anything less than a tenured position at Harvard would be considered a failure, worse than death. From his suit pocket Sascha's father produced an embroidered handkerchief. He wiped his eyes and blew his nose. Did Sascha really know that his father loved him? Had he ever communicated his feelings to his son from the heart, free of caveats and conditions? Again the line from his note to his very son invaded his thoughts.

"Get enrolled for this coming semester, or you're out on your ass..."

If only he could have that note back. If only he could have a mere five minutes with his boy again to tell him he was loved. Really loved, no matter what.

Now that his only child was gone, so much about his son became clearer. And it broke his heart in two. And for one simple reason: No matter what it was that Sascha would have done as an adult, he now understood that it would have been by *his* own choice and by no one else. The more he thought about it, the more his leg bounced in frustration. How true it was. If Sascha would have gone on to cure a horrible disease, or moved on to flip burgers, his son would have done it with honor, and with intrepid courage. He would have been the best at whatever profession he chose.

Whatever path he chose.

It was his choice all along.

Sitting in his son's chair, Sascha's father realized for the first time in his life, that success was not what you did for a living, but if you made a difference in the world with the life you led.

He wondered if Sascha, only in his late teens, even had a chance to make a difference in the world. Damnit! He was so young!

He and his wife had hardly spoken since they returned home from the funeral. At that moment she lied on their bed, sobbing and clutching pictures of their only child. Their Sascha. He was gone. Forever.

Charles leaned forward when the words on a computer monitor caught his attention. The words gave him the strength to tear up the note he left for his son. Perhaps those words would be the foundation for forgiving himself someday. He fell back in the chair, watching the words of the computer monitors repeat over and over again.

For the rest of his life, he never thought of Sascha without recalling that verse.

"Precious in the sight of The Lord is the death of his saints…"

Charles Alexander Tremaine, father of Sascha Alexander Tremaine, spent the night sleeping in his son's chair.

And dreaming of what could have been.

CHAPTER 53

It was as if Simon had walked into a Brothers Grimm fairy tale. With every step he took, he could swear the forest moaned.

The path from years past still remained. Simon hoped a landmark would look familiar to him, but all he saw were trees. And more trees. And beyond the nearest of trees, shadows, too many to count and so many to fear. So many sounds he could not recall here. *Now* he wished Valletta was with him.

He pulled his hands out of his pockets and crossed his arms and soldiered on. Slowly.

The forest canopy blocked out much of the sun that day.

In his adult years, Simon visited many places he had been to as a child. Many of the villages, shops, town squares, even cathedrals seemed so much smaller to him as an adult compared to their scope through the eyes of a child. Yes, as is the case with most adults, the world around you shrinks. And with the advent of the internet, the constant intrusions of cell phones and the presence of video conferencing, it seems you could cast a stone from continent to continent with hardly lifting a finger. But this place he was in, in this forest and on this path he walked with his father as a child...to this day it still seemed so *big*. To this very day, while in this dark and beautiful place, where the sun shines through the canopy of leaves like a laser and the trees seem to frown at you as you walk past, Simon felt so small. He might as well have been nine years old all over again, because that is exactly how he felt. It had been many years since he felt fear from something other than the unwelcome visitors of his dreams.

Feeling desperate for something, anything of comfort, Simon knelt down. He grabbed a fist full of wet leaves and soil from the forest floor. Lifting it up to his nose he took in its fragrance. The cinnamon scent of the wet leaves and the wet soil anchored Simon to the reality of this place. It had a scent. He could touch it. Yes. It was real. He felt the soil crumble within his very fingers. He held it in the palm of his hand. This place was real all right. It was not a dream. He was safe. He understood that. Finally. Thankfully. He moved forward. The trees didn't seem to glare so much now. And the sound of the water. It called to him.

The path wound its way through the forest. And as he usually did, Simon thought. In this particular case, at this time and place, he knew he was spot-on in his self assessment. Everything he reached for disintegrated in his hand like the blackened cinders of burnt paper. And like the remnants of those ashes, his hands would be left smudged and blackened. He found that some things just can't be washed away with soap and water. Though raised by a good family, Simon still chose the devices of his own destruction. The devices of avarice and instant gratification. Simon willingly threw himself into the pit of giant stones. And like Sisyphus, he would struggle and fight to roll the giant stone up the hill and when nearly to the top, the weight of the stone would roll over him on its way back down the hill. And there he would be sentenced, alongside Sisyphus, for eternity. Suffering from his own greed and apathy. Rolling the giant stone up the hill, only to have it roll back down again leaving Simon to the task over and over again. For eternity.

Simon recalled the Fourth Circle of Dante's Inferno, and it spoke of many of its inhabitants being those of corrupt popes and clergymen. Those charged with, and accepting the responsibility that comes with great power when communicating with masses of people in the name of God. They were charged with doing good, but in spite of their potential to do good, many wandered down a far different path.

The thought struck Simon like lightning. He'd been charged with a responsibility, a stewardship over music while he occupied this body. Maybe music wasn't even his gift at all. Maybe music was a message meant to be passed *through* him. And what had he done with that stewardship initially? He allowed his music to degenerate into a selfish, self-indulgent pile of garbage. Not for the good of the people or for the glory of God, but for his own glory instead. And it was then that Simon realized why he was so headstrong in the new direction his music was taking. A decision not derived from conscious thought, but of an inner calling to do what it was he was truly meant to do: To lift people up. It was just time.

And Simon thought of the stranger from years ago who's image to this day remained deep inside him. He was the strange man with the worn out blue jeans and denim jacket who many years before, let himself into the gate of the garden Simon's family kept. Simon recalled sitting in the family garden, vaguely alarmed at the gentle intrusion of the stranger. The man asked to play Simon's guitar for a few glorious moments before he handed Simon's guitar back. Simon fed the man, who said he was very hungry. The stranger shared a few tips on guitar playing as well as words of encouragement before he made his way into the forest, towards Simon's bridge. He remembered the stranger's face as if it were yesterday. He had long hair and a beard, his eyes were timeless. Simon never saw him again.

Simon recalled writing of that man in his leather journal, many, many years ago. Before his flight, he put that very journal into the mail to someone. If he were never to return, he wanted to help her understand why he was the way he was.

Simon reflected upon much of what the man from years back said to him, it echoed what the old bum had been telling him.

Simon's music and message was indeed changing. No wonder the record company hated him so terribly. No wonder he hated himself for so many years. And once again clarity struck him.

It might as well have been a giant sequoia falling on him, smashing him into the moist soil of the forest. Everything Simon had sought, everything he had reached for had left his hands blackened with ash. He looked into his own hand and saw two faces. The faces of Bailey Eden Piper and his beloved Lily.

Simon ran away from her. He ran away from Bailey. Sure, he set her adrift, but it was he who was running away. He just couldn't face her. Not after losing Lily. Every time he looked into Bailey's eyes, he saw his Lily. So instead of standing steadfast at Bailey's side (as he was certain she would have done for him if roles were reversed), he quit. Having chosen his career and self destructive lifestyle over the love of his life. He chose to hide the pain by rolling in strange beds with nameless women. Their sheets crashed down on him like waves upon the rocks. He hated it. It was only a way of running away from the thought of his child. Of course. It was so obvious to him now. Nothing lasted for Simon. And no one felt sincere to him. This was because he forged an existence of reaching out for all the wrong things. He reached out for all the wrong people. So many different faces, so many ships passing in the night. Strange, nameless women blew through his life like the wind through so many blades of grass. They never made him feel any better.

He should have never left her. They could have tried for another baby. But the risk was too frightening. It felt as though it would be like casting aside the memory of Lily. They gave her a name. She was a person. She had a heartbeat. He couldn't bear the thought or risk of forgetting her. And yet that is exactly what he feared would happen. But still, he did that very thing, but in a different and very self destructive way. Every time he looked at Bailey, he saw Lily's face. Her sweetheart little face as he held her in his hands, allowed only a few moments with her before the nurses took her away. He recalled sobbing and falling to his knees upon the floor. It was his fault.

The thought of holding her became ashes in his hand. Of course the things Simon reached out for always burned him. They burned him because for many years he never reached out with his heart for what really mattered. And now the ashes in his hand had a profound significance to him. Now he understood.

Ashes indeed.

Simon looked up to find he was sitting beneath a tree. Through the darkness something caught his eye. The reflection of light from the corneas of an animal, and a large one at that. Simon's eyes adjusted to the darkness. The buck, with a magnificent rack of too many points to count, stood observing Simon. Neither moved. Simon could tell the deer had no fear of him. The beast stepped out of the shadows. He stood tall and magnificent, as if to let Simon know this was *his* forest and it was well kept and under his protection, thank you very much.

Simon understood and nodded to the animal. The beautiful beast snorted and without fear or malice, slowly turned and walked back into the darkness without a backwards glance. Simon wanted to laugh, but felt it would be a sign of disrespect to the magnificent animal and his home. Simon eased to his feet. The water, it was louder now. He knew he was close. Would his father be there waiting for him? Would he find answers to his questions? What was The Key? And why did They, whomever They were, even want it? And why would they want it from him for that matter? There would be a break in the trees. Still, far down the path, it was there. He could see it. And the canopy of trees allowed the sun through. It was as if the forest wanted The Bridge to be lit for Simon. He paused and looked around. He could feel eyes watching him, but from where, he had no idea. Perhaps it was the deer.

Now the water was louder. As Simon drew closer, he saw a vision of a man in Army fatigues, his hand upon the shoulder of a young boy. He spoke to the boy, whom he could tell was hardly interested in what was being said. Though still quite a distance away from The Bridge and the vision of the man and his son, the soundtrack of their discussion played in his ears loud and clear. "This is where your difference will be made. Where your new path will begin." It was as if his father had a looking glass into his son's future. Perhaps he knew more at the time than what he shared with his son. Perhaps he knew what was going to happen, but Simon was just too young to understand. Perhaps he had gone through this too?

Perhaps.

The water was much higher due to the rainy season, and it was running fast. The sound it made was intimidating but beautiful. Hardly a stream now, it was powerful. The water rushed by, determined to work its way to the sea. Though he stood by The Bridge, Simon couldn't touch it. He reached out for the stone of the bridge, and his hand nearly made contact. But he held himself far short of touching it. He looked up to the sky through the break in the trees.

Upstream, Tuomas and the far more responsible and safety minded Klaus, searched for artifacts at the water's edge. Klaus warned Tuomas to stay out of the water. The rocks gathered algae resting on the bottom of the stream and this made them as slippery as a freshly waxed linoleum floor. He called out to Tuomas the warning their parents gave them. Of course, Tuomas would have no part in logic and reason. He wanted another trophy. And he just knew he could see something of interest, barely, through the turbulent waters. But Tuomas refused to take hold of the rope his brother threw him. He would not need it, certain that his keen sense of balance would be all that was required, he waded into the rapidly rolling waters of the stream with an aghast Klaus screaming at him to get back to land. Tuomas would have none of it. Farther through the waters he waded, struggling to stay upright in the waist high current. And with another step he dropped deeper into a hole in the stream bed. Klaus froze as he observed Tuomas standing in the current up to his chest, laughing.

And then he was gone.

Klaus screamed for Tuomas. The only sound he could hear was that of the rushing water. He spotted Tuomas' shoe floating past.

Downstream and still standing at The Bridge with his hand frozen inches above its railing, Simon experienced a shudder.

It felt as if the canary in the coal mine of his heart had just died. A terrible feeling of doom overcame him and he felt the urge to flee, though he knew not why. But Simon would stay. He *knew* this was where he was supposed to be at this moment, and whatever was to happen to him was also meant to be. He stood firm at that bridge, fully expecting something significant, and perhaps even terrible to happen to him. And whatever it was, Simon understood that he most likely deserved it. Karma, he figured, would ultimately work its way around to him for better or worse. And yet in the back of his mind he could not help but wonder why his own father, all those years ago, would tell him to come back to this place if it was to face his own destruction. Surely not, he thought.

And then he heard a shriek. And a desperate scream. The rustling through the leaves grew closer by the second. Simon turned, looking for the source. He saw a boy. Perhaps eleven or twelve, running along the stream. Even across the distance he looked scared. No. He looked terrified. He was screaming. It was a name. The name was "Tuomas."

He screamed it again.

Simon realized the boy was screaming towards the stream. He saw what the boy was looking at. It was another child. And his face was grey like the moon. Simon looked ahead of the floating boy's path. The stream made a sharp turn around a bend, and the thought of what lay beyond made Simon's heart jump to his throat. For around the bend that the stream would follow, a remnant of the war sat. It was a bunker, built so close to the stream that during the war, the Germans had to abandon it in the midst of the rainy season due to dangerous flooding. Simon recalled playing in it during the summer as a boy. When he was young, he heard stories of adventurous boys and girls being swept up by the high, rushing waters of the stream and swept down into the bowels of that bunker never to be seen alive again. He recalled chalking it up to Germanic urban legend, but now the reality of this danger came screaming at him in the form of a child chasing after his friend. Perhaps it was his brother. The boy was floating nearer to him, and now his face was turning blue.

Again, Simon wished Valletta was here. He recalled his friend on several occasions, yanking him from the path of oncoming danger. How helpful it would have been to have him here now. Valletta would have known what to do. But the cold, wet reality of the moment was that Valletta was not here. It was only Simon, a screaming boy and his friend, rushing downstream to his death. And now, precious seconds were racing by as Simon wished for an easier situation. This was the day Simon couldn't turn his back and run. He would have to handle it himself.

The blast of cold water exploded in Simon's ears. The boy was fast approaching, and if Simon timed it just right he would be able to intercept him in time and maneuver back to land. He reached out for the boy at just the right moment, snagging him by his collar with his index finger. A quick tug brought the child right up next to him, and Simon flipped him over immediately hoping that Tuomas would breathe.

Simon's plan to use his feet to shove off from the creek bed toward land proved horribly flawed. The rocks, with years of algae and sediment proved too slippery for his feet to catch. Together they passed beneath The Bridge, and the forest shook from a sonic boom of otherworldly origin. The sound echoed through the trees and as Simon fought for the life of Tuomas. Simon glanced wishfully toward land and spotted the deer, observing him as he did earlier when Simon sat at the base of the tree.

The animal watched them, agitated, as they raced hopelessly toward the bunker. As Simon and the boy passed, the deer followed.

Together, Simon and Tuomas rushed toward the bend in the river. Simon knew if he didn't manage to snag a root or anything tied to land, they both would soon drown. He looked ahead and saw the deer, visibly irritated at what was happening. As they turned the corner Simon hoped the old concrete bunker would have been long since razed, but it was wishful thinking. At the side of the structure, the top of a door and a window could be seen and the water was being sucked down into the structure with a roar.

Together they smacked the side of the concrete structure, the current pulling them ever closer to the window's edge. Once inside, there would be no finding them until hours later when their bodies were retrieved at the mournful hands of a scuba team.

The screams of hikers were barely audible over the water. Of the two couples, one raced around trying to find a stick long enough to reach them, the other couple standing at the river's edge screamed words of encouragement. Simon fought the current for all he was worth, but his fingers were slipping. The long branch held out for them was close, but still beyond his reach. One brave man from the group ventured into the water, grasping a thick root from the ground and reaching out for all he was worth. The stranger grimaced, fighting the cold current as it tried to pull him to the bunker as well. Simon's fingers were slipping. He was quickly losing his grasp on his last lifeline: a small, jagged piece of rusted metal protruding from the bunker wall.

"Lord," he prayed aloud, "don't let this boy die."

Simon braced a foot against the wall, and with one final burst of remaining strength, and a scream, he threw Tuomas to the outstretched arm of the hiker.

Simon held on, just long enough to see the boy pulled out of the water before he was sucked down into the flooded darkness of the bunker.

In a small room within a large hospital and eleven hours away as the crow flies, Bailey Eden Piper dropped her stethoscope on the floor at her patient's feet. The patient, a burly man who made his living throwing combative drunks from the bars at closing time, caught her before she hit the floor. He felt the tight musculature of her arms, and how incredibly soft her skin was. He relished the chance to help such a lovely woman. Gently and as a gentleman should, he lifted her upright and sat her on the patient table which until just a moment ago, he had occupied. "Lady," he whispered, "you ok?"

Bailey's eyes darted around the room, as if she was witnessing events as they happened far beyond the room she occupied. She clutched at her heart just as she had when she heard Simon's voice over the phone for the first time in years.

"Something terrible has happened," she gasped. "Something terrible."

More nurses burst into the room to find the patient rubbing Bailey's back as she wept.

In the flooded bunker the water's current swirled violently. But still, a little light managed to shine in. And the darkness could not overcome it.

Simon released air in tiny bursts to relieve the pressure on his lungs. He knew only a few seconds could be bought by doing this. The light from outside was still visible, and for a moment the silhouette of the great deer from the banks of the stream flashed before his eyes.

The last moments of Simon Glenayre's life were passing quickly, but his thoughts of Bailey, his thoughts of Lily, the boy named Tuomas, an unfinished middle eight of a song he thought of on the plane ride over…they all occupied his thoughts. He was so close to finally seeing Bailey again. Simon felt himself ready to go. It was time, and he would surely see his Lily soon. And together, they would both greet Bailey someday. Someday, they would all be together again like the last night he and Bailey lay in bed together. In what would be the last few moments of his life, Simon still took the time to blame himself. He thought of the night he laid his head softly on Bailey's tummy and spoke to their child. After Bailey fell asleep he would sneak into their bathroom. And in the moments that followed, he would fling himself from the lifeboat of sobriety, a silly fantasy or excuse to use again: He had done so well, Bailey was doing good and Lily was healthy in her mother's womb. Why not? He had been a good boy, he'd earned a little recreation. Simon recalled tapping the needle, shooting the bubbles out of the syringe. He shoved the poison into his arm, a smile slashed across his face and a tear rolled down his cheek. His plan, to only be in the bathroom for a few moments, shoot, and go to bed on a nice high.

To be safe, he locked the bathroom door.

Simon overdosed that night. In a cruel twist of fate, it was also the night that Lily's placenta tore. Bailey, too knotted in pain to get up, tried anyway. Her body suffered all the way to the bathroom door. Behind the door, her husband lay passed out. Bailey passed out from the pain. Their child in her womb dying.

Bailey never blamed Simon. But Simon knew better. If he wouldn't have been so selfish, he would have stayed in that bed. He would have heard Bailey's cries for help. Perhaps he could have gotten Bailey and Lily the help they so desperately needed. Maybe the doctors could have saved Lily's life. Maybe.

It was time. The light from outside the bunker had to be released. Simon could hold on no longer. The current was about to pull him down a staircase to his certain end. He could still see the horns of the deer running back and forth on the edge of land. Simon shut his eyes and let go. Someone else however, would have nothing of surrender.

Simon felt a grip on his collar. There was a jerk. And there was a tug.

As the singing of the birds was music to Simon's ears, the sensation of fresh air in his lungs was that of a choir of angels. The music stopped quickly though, interrupted by Valletta's baritone Brooklyn accent. "Oh yeah, don't come wit'cha, huh?" Valletta barked, one part angry, one part relieved. Simon coughed and sputtered, looking for the boy, his name was Tuomas, he remembered that much. He spotted him, he was laying against his brother who had wrapped his own coat around him. The hikers that helped to save the boy's life remained still, and a cautious distance from Valletta. Valletta hardly acknowledged their presence; however they were keenly aware of his. To Simon, they seemed alarmed by him. Together, they worked their way back down the path toward Beuern. Simon assumed they were taken aback by the large man's stupidity in leaping down into a flooded bunker that no one had ever survived before. But Valletta did. Valletta survived. He was a big man, sure. Hell, he was huge. But even a man that strong, fighting against that current...

The deer was nowhere to be seen. He must have finally been scared off by all of the commotion.

Valletta held Simon upright, as they, along with the boys Klaus and Tuomas, worked their way back up the path towards the village of Beuern. "God is with you...still."
Frau Kruppa's voice hung in his ears like music sliding on a silky breeze.

Simon turned back towards the bridge for one last look and for a brief moment, he saw something he couldn't understand.

Three figures, a man, a woman and a boy. The man was large with a thick beard and a long, furry overcoat. A woman clung to his arm and on his other side stood a boy. There was something different about it. And in an instant, they were all gone.

CHAPTER 54

Manhattan's heartbeat was pounding out its typical high-octane rhythm.

Horns blare at horns and pigeons swoop down from above when they spot food. The old man tore off another piece of bread, crumbling the shreds in his hand. He tossed a handful onto the sidewalk when he heard the sound he was expecting.

The 19th century wooden door shoved open and Simon emerged from the brownstone hotel to find a familiar face sitting on the stoop. The man on the steps spoke without turning around.

"How was your flight?"

Simon took a few steps down and sat next to him. He watched as a lady in a fur coat passed by. She tossed change toward the man's cup, missing miserably. The old man looked to the sky for a moment. "Thanks, ma'am," he said bending over for the change and groaning about it.

"My flight was good" Simon shared. "And how was your...flight?"

The old man laughed. He shook his coat, untwisting it. Simon watched as dust floated into the air. "Oh, my flight was good. Quick, always is, if you use the right airline."

Simon shared that he went from JFK International Airport straight to his hotel and "passed out."

"I know" the old man said, "you been asleep all night and all day."

Simon rubbed at his ruined nose. "You never told me your name."

The old man kept his eyes on the rolling traffic.

"You never *asked* for my name. Why you wanna know it now?"

Simon kicked a rock down the steps and watched it bounce across the sidewalk and into the gutter. "I dunno" he said. "Seems like we've kinda become friends these past few weeks."

They watched as a cab driver nearly rear ended a Mercedes. Both drivers stuck their heads out the car windows, shaking their fists at one another and cursing. Simon and the old man sat there. Both shook their heads. "You think mankind will ever learn?" Simon asked.

"I always felt that if there's one good person on Earth, there's always a chance" the man said as he patted Simon's leg.

"So, what's your name?" Simon asked again. "You know mine. So it seems only fair."

The old man slapped his thigh, laughing long and hard. "What?" Simon asked.

"Boy, nobody ever asked me for my name before." Simon grinned, embarrassed that the question never occurred to him before.

"But if you must know," he said, "the name's 'Ager'."

"Hello, Ager" spoke Simon, holding out his hand. "My name is Simon."

The man laughed long and hard. "I knew that, boy!" The two men shook hands. The old man's hands were far softer than Simon expected. He felt several millennia pass between them. He looked Ager in the eye. Simon shuddered. The old man's eyes, they went on forever.

Simon pulled himself together and asked his new friend where his name came from. After a pause, Ager answered. "My Father gave me that name. It's Hebrew" Ager said. "It means 'Gatherer'."

"Gatherer," Simon smiled. "I like it."

"So now what?" Ager asked.

"I've been given a second chance in so many different ways." Children skipped by with their parents who followed behind. The children were singing. Simon looked down at the steps. His words came out slow. "I need to go see my grandfather and my cousin Max." Ager could tell it was a painful subject. "I really hurt them, the way I left." Simon looked up to the sky.

"Simon," Ager said putting his hand on Simon's back, "just go to them" he said. "And someday you won't look at New Year's Day as a terrible, sad day. It'll be a day of remembrance and only the start of a new year."

Simon knew better than to wonder how Ager knew about the pain of New Year's Day. He hadn't broached the subject of New Year's Day with anyone since his discussions with his grandfather and Max at the kitchen table on the farm, all those years ago.

"Yeah," Ager said. "But you never gonna get forgiveness unless you ask for it, right? And that includes Miss Bailey Eden Piper."

Simon laughed. "Man," he said, "you are definitely in the loop." Both men observed the pigeons fidget about the sidewalk in their nervous search for more bread. They watched as more people passed by at a determined pace.

The people here were different from those in Kansas City. They kept on their way. It's like they all wore blinders you just couldn't see. And they never seemed to look each other in the eye. This wasn't a bad place, and these weren't bad people at all. They were good people. They were just different from the people of Kansas City. "It's funny," Simon reflected. "I was only home for a few days and already I feel like a farmboy when I'm away." Ager laughed. "And what do you think is so funny?" asked Simon.

Ager crushed more bread in his hand, and the pigeons swarmed their way. "Well, I think you feel that way because we are all just children, you know. *His* children. And we all just want to feel safe and warm," he said. "In Kansas City, you felt that. And when you were on your grandfather's farm, you *really* felt it there."

Simon said nothing in response. He thought those words, he didn't speak them. Or so he thought.

After a long pause, Ager broke the silence. "You wanna know what all that 'Key' business was about, don't you?"

Simon shivered from hearing the word. He was afraid to even answer. Like a person cornered by a mad dog, he was afraid to incite *them* into springing on him by merely uttering that word. Yet still, he thought: it was only a word. "Key." One vowel, two consonants.

So what.

"Sure, I guess you could say I've been left wondering where it tied in to all of this."

Ager threw more bread. "The key is a reference to your soul," he said. "Your well-being." Ager nudged Simon with his shoulder. "Look" he said, "it's a battle we all fight every day of our lives. Evil fights for your soul. You fight for your soul. Satan wanted you to give up. To kill yourself. He would have most certainly had you then." Simon remained silent. Ager continued. "We all fight our souls every day. Who knows why the evil spirits, whoever they were, called it 'The Key'. Evil doesn't need a reason to be evil. They just wanted you to give up. These spirits, whatever name they go by, knew of the source of your guilt and pain, and that is the place they applied pressure" Ager said. "They knew that if you were dead, then the threat of your service to The Lord here on Earth would be gone" he said. "Maybe that was it."

"But," he said, "I can only speculate on the intentions of evil."

"Well", Simon grunted as he stood up, "I have to be on my way. I'm meeting Bailey down the street."

"Yeah," Ager said. "Down at the 'Manhattan Fuel Mart'." Simon didn't ask Ager how he knew where he was going. He was getting used to the old man being a bit of an ethereal know-it-all. "You know, a cab ride would get you there a lot quicker, boy." Simon shared his plan to walk the several blocks to the agreed meeting place. The time to think and reflect would do him good. Hopefully, it would be a chance to calm down before he met up with Bailey. It had been years since he'd seen her, and as the moments passed, his knees got weaker and weaker at the thought of seeing her again face to face. No, he said, the walk would do him good.

"Well then, Simon," Ager said as he slapped his thigh and stood up, "I guess this is 'Goodbye' Simon paused. He didn't want to hear those words. But he understood. In a way he was expecting it. In the movies that's how these things usually ended. "Ager, I want to thank you" Simon whispered. Ager smiled.

"Aw, I'm just a gatherer, boy" he said. "No need to thank me."

Simon held out his hand to Ager who took it. "Do me a favor, will you?"

"And what is that?" said Ager.

"Please, tell your boss I said 'Hello'."

Ager agreed with a smile but added: "But if you wanna get a message to him, all you gotta do boy, is talk to him yourself."

Simon took in a deep breath and looked to the skies. People stared at him as they passed by. He didn't care.

"Well if He is listening, I want Him to know I want to be a better person for Him and I want to help other people find Him too, not because I want a reward for doing a good deed." Ager shot a curious look at Simon as he continued looking up at the purple and pink evening sky.

"I wanna do it because I love Him and I want Him to be pleased with me."

Ager wiped the tear from his cheek. "Well, "Ager sniffed. "Better be on your way, boy. You gotta pretty lady waitin' on you."

Simon took a few steps down the sidewalk when he heard Ager's voice. "And Simon" he yelled out, "don't you worry, when it's time, I'm sure we'll see each other again."

Simon found the serious expression on his face a little out of place. He waved at the old man and turned on his way.

Simon didn't bother to cover his head as the evening raindrops began to fall. He lifted his face up to the sky and took in the moist air. His face reacquainted itself with a smile while he stood with his eyes shut. He noticed the children sitting on the steps of the brownstone beneath an umbrella had stopped playing.

He opened his eyes and looked to find they were staring at him: The strange man with long hair, standing in the rain with his eyes shut, smiling like a weirdo on the evening news their parents warned them about. "Hi!" he said, trying to appear harmless in their eyes. He didn't want to walk away with those children and their parents thinking he was just another wandering danger. He looked at the father. He nodded. The mother remained still. The little girl pulled away from the arms of her alarmed mother and ran up to Simon. "My name is Janina" the girl sang in her soft Puerto Rican accent. "It means 'gift from God'."

Simon knelt down and laughed. "Well then that's the perfect name for you." The girl's father sprung from the steps toward them. Simon looked up to the girl's father and smiled. He stood up, not wanting to alarm her parents any more than he already had. "La paz sea con ustedes." The little girl's father was shocked at Simon's perfect pronunciation. Simon was shocked too. He had no idea he could speak Spanish. It seemed there was much he had gotten from the handshake with Ager than a simple farewell. He hadn't even tried to speak Spanish since he failed the required class in junior high.

The father of the child loosened his facial expression and exhaled. "La paz sea contigo también." He then smiled to Simon and took his child, rejoining the rest of his family on the steps. They watched as Simon walked away. The mother could have sworn she had seen Simon somewhere before. Perhaps it was on television, she thought to herself.

The pace of the rainfall increased, Simon enjoyed its rhythm as it struck the parked cars. He enjoyed the hiss of the tires on the pavement as well as the halos it put around the streetlights.

Soon, Simon's thoughts turned to his friend, Valletta. He was shocked that Valletta put up so little resistance to letting him go alone. He looked sad as Simon walked out the door. He would be ok when Simon returned. He'd promise him a big breakfast at the nearest diner. That would make the big guy smile. Always did. Simon stopped again and turned his face up to the sky. "I'm alive," he thought to himself.

He said it once more, screaming it loud and far.

A strong, chilly wind struck Simon on his left side, prompting him to turn to his right and continue on towards the convenience store. "Isn't it crazy?" Simon thought about how it had been years since he had done something as simple as walking to a convenience store for a simple cup of coffee. He just knew that Valletta would be pacing the floor non-stop until he had safely returned. But this was the beginning of a new time. The genesis of a new life. A life of restful sleep. No more fake music. No more business. No more Chloe.

And no more *Them*.

From now on he would get his own coffee.

Two creams, no sugar.

Walking down the sidewalk, Simon could see inside some of the apartments. Fireplaces crackling. Children playing with toys. Families sitting at the dinner table together. A couple of blocks later, Simon's thoughts wandered to those who had helped him through this. Sascha. The quiet, nervous kid who knew more about Simon than he should have. He thought about how kind Sascha was, and laughed to himself thinking about the young man's fainting spells. The boy's name, Sascha would be saved in his heart for use someday. It was a promise he made to himself. He thought about Ager, who shadowed him wherever he went, and always knew what to say when he needed it most.

Simon also considered the headlines about the record company and Sol Glenn. He thought about Chloe's involvement in all of it. They were all most likely going to jail over their conspiracy to have him killed. The government had been investigating the company for fraud and now were specifically calling on Sol and Chloe as well. The call to the police was made anonymously, but Simon suspected it was Bailey's friend, Konstanze.

It didn't matter. Justice would be served, and that's what mattered.

Simon knew that through all of this, there was one person who was there for him and whom he knew he could count on his whole life. That big fricking Italian.

"I'm alive" he thought to himself again.

He came to a stop at a crosswalk. A small crowd of people had gathered at the curb, waiting for the flashing red hand to turn green. He saw the convenience store not too far off in the distance. "Just a couple of more blocks" he thought to himself. As they stood idly beside one another, everyone in the crowd watched each other out of the corner of their eyes. Something about the young man standing off to Simon's left caught his attention. Simon had noticed he wasn't wearing a coat or hat, even in this chilly rainfall. He made eye contact with the young man, who was around the age of fifteen or sixteen. The young man looked back at Simon and a shocked expression splashed across his face. He looked so alarmed when he saw Simon. Perhaps he was a fan. He looked so cold. Simon considered offering to take him to a store to buy him a coat. The boy without the coat, obviously uncomfortable with being stared at by Simon, glared at him. Simon gave a sheepish grin and was about to look away, not before he noticed the white t-shirt the boy was wearing. The shirt had a saying that stood out to Simon. The shirt was stained and worn, like the baggy jeans he had on

On young man's white t-shirt was a phrase. It was obvious he wrote it on the shirt himself with a black marker.

He ran the phrase from the t-shirt through his mind over and over again.

"What are we going to do?"

This was a new time. Not a time to fret over phrases on the filthy t-shirts of strangers. The flashing red hand finally turned green. It was simply time to cross the street. But still, he couldn't help but to run that phrase through his mind.

"What are we going to do?"

The crowd moved across the street, their silhouettes breaking the misty headlight beams of the cars, waiting impatiently for them to cross the road. Upon reaching the other side of the street, the crowd of strangers split to the four wet winds. He hadn't noticed which way the kid with no coat had gone. It seems one minute he was there, the next he had disappeared. He had such a terrible scowl on his face. Simon saw the grit under his fingernails. The fuzz on his chin. He wondered if that kid would ever smile again. He hoped the boy had something to live for.

The headlights from the passing cars reflected in Simon's eyes and their tires hissed as they spun by him. The leaves rustling in the wind. The heartbeat of the city. For once, he didn't mind. Didn't mind all of the people. All of the cars. All of the motion.

And the hiss of the cars. He never thought he would like the sound of hissing. But now he did.

And again, the sound of the rain hitting the streets.

And the constant heartbeat of the city.

The further he walked, the better the view of the New York City skyline. Thoughts of the innocent victims of this city flashed through his head. The firemen, the cops, the loss of thousands of innocent lives on that terrible day. Simon thought of the heartbroken victims that were left behind. This town looked so different without the two massive, gentle giants keeping a watchful eye on the city. Like New York City, he missed those two old friends. And yet, this town was a lot like Simon. It endured a terrible ordeal, and yet it emerged from the dust clouds and rubble alive. Still feeling its heartbeat.

Able to once more, find it's rhythm. It was reborn.

Simon stood admiring the new building, standing in their place. A proud vision of a great country. The new building reminded Simon of the church steeple in Beuern. Like the houses in that tiny village, the new Freedom Tower also looked as if it were reaching up to shake hands with the heavens. He felt so much pride in his country.

"I'm alive."

"We're alive."

"We're all alive."

A couple burst out of a lounge on his right side and they were drunk. Both wearing leather coats, wrapped up in one another for warmth and companionship. Both laughed in a laugh that only six or seven strong martinis apiece could generate. Simon jumped back, startled, only to find that they were only people. That's all. Just people. A screech sounded from the street, getting Simon's quick attention. One cabbie nearly rear ended another. In typical New York cabbie form, they both leaned out of their windows yelling obscenities at one another. The passengers in both cars chatted away on their cell phones, oblivious to the commotion they were a part of.

Yes, New York City had definitely found its rhythm again.

Simon, standing at the curb watching all of the commotion, couldn't help but to smile. He somehow drew comfort from those two men yelling at each other.

Stepping back onto the sidewalk, he spun around and

immediately ran into a man. A bald man with dark eyes. He wore a white suit.

He froze.

His heart went into his throat.

The man stood there, staring at Simon with dark eyes. Simon felt the sweat bubbles surface on his forehead. His mouth went dry. His legs knotted up.

He couldn't move. Still the man stood there before him. The awkwardness had gotten the best of this stranger, in his white suit, the rain beating down on his bald head.

"So are you gonna do something or just stand there like a bonehead?" His Brooklyn accent was thick, harsh, and sounded weathered. He eyed Simon from head to toe. Stuck his nose out at him.

"So we got a problem?" the man spat.

"I, uh-" Simon muttered.

The man shrugged and walked around Simon as he stood frozen in place.

"Oh, sorry." Simon, still in a bit of shock, said a little too late. He had to make an extra effort to get his legs to work. The stranger was not one of Them.

"He wasn't one of Them. He wasn't one of Them. He was just a man. Just a mean looking man in a white suit. I'm fine."

"I'm alive."

"Hey buddy. You're alive? Great. Now are you sure about that? You're really alive?" The man had a thick layer of sarcasm in his voice. Apparently, Simon had been standing on the sidewalk, yelling "I'm alive!," and was not even aware of it. Once his attention was brought back down to Earth, he looked around and saw a small crowd of people gathered around him, staring at him with amused looks on their faces. The man who spoke to him looked up at Simon's arms, which were outstretched into the night sky. He looked back at the little old man with the smirk on his face and sarcastic voice. He dropped his arms. Simon just turned and walked away, laughing to himself.

Another block later, Simon had reached the parking lot of his destination. The convenience store was open twenty four hours a day and according to the sign, had the best coffee in New York City. He noticed no one recognized him. However, he felt no need to question it. He enjoyed the anonymity. And this was where he was supposed to meet Bailey. He'd stay right here. She would be here right at the agreed upon time. She was always punctual. This was the very first time Simon was on time for anything. He would make a note of the date in his calendar when he got back to his hotel room. Perhaps he would even put a smiley face next to it.

At eleven o'clock at night, the parking lot of the convenience store had a full complement of cars of every shape and size. BMWs, Cadillacs trimmed in gold, low riders. A Ford Pinto covered in primer and a limousine.

The girl on the payphone was crying, the girl sitting on the hood of the low rider with long hair extensions was laughing into a cell phone. One old wino sat at one side of the building with a cheap bottle of wine covered by a ratty paper bag. In a rusty compact, a mother tapped out a text message on her phone, a lit cigarette in her mouth. She ignored the cries of her two children in the back seat. At the other end of the building were two youths wearing baggy pants, skateboards resting under their legs. They had a boom box blaring Packmule.

Simon rolled his eyes and went into the building.

The inside of the Manhattan Fuel Mart was inhabited by a bustling community of nighttime commuters, either on their way to a party or on their way home from a party. The man behind the cash register, an overworked Korean with bags under his eyes, had a half-burned cigarette hanging perilously from his bottom lip. Simon stopped at a magazine stand to scan the periodicals. Occasionally looking up to view the never ending exchange of crumpled up dollar bills for snack cakes and beer. The peacefulness of anonymity made it hard for Simon to keep the smile off of his face.

He pictured Valletta, in his mind, still pacing the floor waiting anxiously for his safe return. He smiled again. How would he have gotten this far in life without Valletta? The doors into the store saw no rest as they fanned in and out as the constant stream of customers came and went at a furious pace. It had been years since Simon could just observe people again. That was something he always enjoyed. The heartbeat of life. The lively flow of people. To be allowed to just watch mankind in action again was a dream come true. It had been Simon who for years was the spectacle. The person everybody else wanted to watch. He finally felt like just another face in the crowd again. Glancing down, Simon saw the cover of a naturalist's magazine. The cover had a picture of a large buck deer. Its impressive rack reached far and wide. Simon thought of the deer in the forest of Beuern.

He wondered to himself how Valletta would adapt to life in a smaller city. How would the Italian fit in?

Upon further consideration, Simon realized that Valletta would not adjust to Kansas City. Kansas City would have to adjust to Valletta.

He thought about his time on a farm. A short burst of glorious musical activity for Simon. All of the band rehearsals and song writing sessions on that farm years ago. Jamming with his friends in the barn as hogs snorted and groaned right outside the opened window. He thought about the long walks in the open fields. He remembered listening to the wind blow through the grass. He remembered the wide open skies. He thought of the family who lived on that farm. And how kind they were to open their home to him. It was on that farm that he decided he could try to make it work back in The States given the culture shock he had experienced being moved to his own country. And it was there that Simon decided he wanted to pursue music. Simon thought about that old abandoned house at the top of the high cliff that, when armed with a guitar and pad of paper and pen, always came back down with a great song. The hiking trips down in Jasper, Arkansas with Bailey.

"What a great time." He was excited that he had managed to find her again.

Valletta hardly understood why Simon wanted to go to the convenience store alone. This was something Simon wanted to do himself. He thought again about the hiking trip with Bailey. The camping out. The acoustic jam session in Jasper that the entire town took part in, at that old soda fountain shop. He thought about the love they made in that tiny little tent. How small the tent was, how hard the ground was and how it didn't matter because they were together.

He'd yearned for years to hold Bailey's hand again. Just unwind. Live again. But there always seemed to be something in his way that prevented this. Talk shows. Radio interviews. Those damned tours. His own paralyzing fear of speaking to her again.

Not anymore.

"It's time to go home. I want to go home now."

"Home" was where his heart was. And his heart was with Bailey Eden Piper. Tonight, if she would allow him, he would finally return home. For good.

Simon was snapped back to the here and now when he heard a gaggle of change clang on the floor.

"Crap!"

The Korean man behind the register bent down to pick up the change that had burst everywhere when he tried to open the fresh roll of coins. He hit his head on the open register as he came back up from the floor.

"Ouch!"

Simon chuckled at the man's accent as he cursed. "I'm alive."

He turned away from the cursing Korean and made his way to the coffee.

"Good grief" Simon said aloud. "That's a lot of coffee. "

The coffee section was crowded with coffees of every type and origin. Colombian. Vanilla. French Roast. Cinnamon. Decaf. Cappuccino.

"Now that's a lot of coffee."

Simon eyed the entire lot from one side to another, finally settling on the least threatening of the group. He grabbed the pot labeled "French Roast Coffee- Le Paris" and poured the steaming black concoction into a styrofoam cup. Shuffling over to the creamers, Simon stood for a moment laughing.

"Aaaand, that's a lot of creamers."

The shelf was stocked with creamers of every flavor known to this side of the universe.

All Simon could do was stand there and laugh at himself. How helpless he had been all these years. He just wanted a cup of coffee and he could hardly muster the know-how to pull it off.

Simon's cell phone vibrated and the words on the screen made his heart flutter. "Almost there. Can't wait to see you!" Bailey was almost here. He placed the magazine back on the rack, knocking several more onto the floor. He bent over, feverishly picking up the magazines and dropping them again as the slick covered periodicals slid from his hands. A group of teenagers laughed at his clumsiness as they walked by.

CHAPTER 55

Bailey sprang from the cab and paid the driver without even looking in his direction. Her eyes were locked on the convenience store. Somewhere in all the bustle of that busy little building was the man she had always loved. On the ride over she envisioned two different scenarios and both made her laugh: Either Simon was already standing in there waiting for her, fidgeting and making a nervous fool of himself in public as well as seriously contemplating making an escape through a back door, or he was running towards the meeting spot at a furious pace because he was running late. It was a classic Simon Glenayre trait. The cab pulled out of the parking lot, leaving Bailey standing there. As always, she would survey the place before she proceeded, making herself aware of her surroundings.

Someone stood out to her like a sore thumb. He was a boy, about fifteen. Something about him grabbed her attention. The youth had writing on the front of his shirt. It was sloppy, but she could read it. "What are we going to do?"

But it wasn't the boy's appearance she found alarming. It was the look on his face. It frightened her. No, it was not an expression of anger. It was far worse than anger. It was a look of hopelessness. Bailey knew that look far too well from her countless nights in the E.R. It wasn't the angry kids who shot one another. It was those who felt they had no hope. She watched him clutch at his left hip pocket. He took a deep breath and entered. Bailey shook it off. No, she was reflecting the gloom of her work on this glorious moment. She knew she had to play it cool. Simon would flee if she didn't play this right. Not because he was selfish or cowardly, but Bailey knew of the guilt Simon felt. She thought of Lily and the love they shared for her. She hoped for something simple. To hold his hand. To listen to him talk about his music. She hoped he had gotten in touch with his old sponsor from AA. She hoped.

Bailey gave the door a couple of tugs before she spotted the sticker on the glass that said "Push."

"Oh good grief," Bailey said, embarrassed as she looked around to see if any of these strangers saw her pulling on the door like a fool. Now up to speed on the proper method of opening the door, she still found no success because on the inside a man was leaning against it. Bailey thumped on the glass, just behind the large man's head. He turned around, glaring at the lean blonde. "Hey!" she spouted. "Move it!" His face went blank, she could tell he was shocked a woman talked to him in such a firm and commanding way. His instinct, honed from many years on rough streets told him to get out of her way. And quick.

Bailey leapt through the door at a man.

He was large, too large for that kid to handle. The man was taking something from the kid. It was that kid with the t-shirt. She could tell it was fast developing into a scuffle. Someone in the crowded store spotted the gun between the man and the boy and screamed. The crowd inside the door rushed towards Bailey.

Bailey's instinct was not to flee through the door she'd just entered. It was to find Simon. To be certain he was ok. Through the rush of the crowd, she spotted him. Frozen in place with a cup of coffee in one hand and an open magazine in the other. He was aware of what was happening, she could tell immediately. He was looking at the two scuffle over the gun. She noticed the boy. He had the writing on his shirt. It said "What are we going to do?" But this time the expression on his face was a far cry from the one he wore when she watched him enter the store. This was not an expression of hopelessness, but one of determination. She saw something.

The boy wasn't trying to rob the place. He wasn't trying to shoot someone. He was trying to keep the gun from the large man who was flinging him about like a rag doll. She looked at Simon who by then had spotted her. He smiled. She couldn't believe it. The crazy bastard smiled at her. He appeared warm that moment, like what was going on mattered little to him. This was because he saw her, for the first time in years, and at that very moment he had no fear. This was regardless of what was happening only a few feet away. She turned her attention back to the large man and the boy. His name was "Grimm." She knew this because she heard the boy shouting his name. The boy tussled with the burly man as best he could. She would help him. It was what she did. When someone was in need, she would be there.

Trying to work her way through the crowd she watched as the large man broke two of the boy's fingers. He cried out as she heard them crack. She had to get there. Quick. No one else was going to help that kid. No one. If she didn't get there in time he was sure to shoot that boy, though she couldn't comprehend why he would want to. What would he gain from it? All the cash was behind the counter. She didn't understand why he wasn't fighting to point the gun at the Korean man standing at the register.

What kind of convenience store robbery was this?

The boy shouted the name again. He screamed it aloud. "Grimm! No!" She watched him yank the gun from the hysterical boy and raise it towards somebody. But his back, it was against the counter. Grimm held the gun in the direction of somebody. And then the realization struck Bailey in one single, mortifying moment: That man, "Grimm," he wasn't trying to rob anybody. He was trying to kill somebody. And the gun in his hand was pointed at Simon. Her Simon. Bailey was knocked to the ground by a man in a hardhat as he sped over her towards the door. She looked at Simon to find his eyes never left her. And the expression on his face. It was serene. That bastard. He wouldn't. He couldn't just stand there. She wouldn't lose him again. Simon mouthed words to her. He said "I love you." Words she had hoped to hear again, and after all these years she would only get to see him mouth it before he died? She popped her knuckles. "Over my dead body…"

She leapt towards Grimm just as he struck the boy in the face, sending him spiraling to the floor.

Grimm raised the gun back to Simon who stood frozen, but unafraid. The distance between Bailey and Grimm was too far. He already had pressure on the trigger. As she sailed through the air towards the thug, the kid in the shabby white t-shirt jumped up, grabbing the man's wrist, flinging the gun downward as it popped. It would not be the headshot that Grimm was so famous for effortlessly pulling off. But he did make a hit. He could tell that much before Bailey Eden Piper gave him an elbow to the side of his head. He laughed as he blacked out. The boy made it to Simon nearly as fast as Bailey. Blood from the wound sprayed on Izzy's shirt. "I'm so sorry," he cried." I tried to stop him."

The instincts and speed of an experienced E.R. nurse kicked in. Bailey had experienced this many times, and in varying degrees of intensity. She tore open Simon's shirt and gasped. She had never done that before. Bailey actually gasped. Of all the gunshot wounds she had worked, none of them belonged to the man she loved. Simon's hand was bloody, it slid over hers as he tried to take hold of her. "Bail" he gasped. Bailey didn't answer. She knew that time was of the essence. And in this case, time was not on her side. "Bail, we almost made it, didn't we?"

Bailey ripped a large piece from Simon's bloody shirt, wadded it up and applied fierce pressure to his wound. The bullet missed his heart, somehow, though Bailey couldn't imagine how. The entry wound was right over his heart. "Get an ambulance!" The man behind the counter jerked. Through all of the horror of what he was witnessing, it hadn't occurred to him to call an ambulance. He fumbled for the phone and dropped it.

"Hurry up!" she screamed. She snapped her attention back to Simon. He was bleeding out. Quick.

The kid in the white t-shirt wept at her side. "I tried to stop him…"

Simon looked at the kid. "I know you," he whispered, "You were the kid at the crosswalk." He patted the boys hand and reached for his shirt, grabbing it. "I'll tell you what you're going to do" he said. "You're gonna be ok…"

Simon's vision was getting blurry. He could feel his lips getting numb. "Bail," he said. "Just stop." Bailey froze, and screamed for the ambulance. "Bail" Simon whispered to her in what little strength he had left. "I'm sorry. I'm so sorry for what I did."

In all of her years fighting to save lives, sometimes with success, and sometimes ending in failure, Bailey Eden Piper never cried. Her strength was always there. Always unshakeable, like her sense of right and wrong. "I know, baby" Bailey cried. "Simon, it wasn't your fault."

Simon pulled her down to his face. She could hardly make out what he said. But the words were there. "I'm not only sorry about Lily anymore" he sputtered. "I'm sorry I left you when you needed me the most. You were always the strong one. But you needed me and I ran." Simon coughed. "I left when you needed me to be the strong one for a change."

"I ran away, Bail," he cried.

"I'm so sorry." He coughed again.

Bailey leaned back up, looking at the blood pool on his chest. She could feel Izzy's arm around her. Simon Glenayre was fading. She could hear the sirens wail. Izzy turned to see police burst through the door towards Grimm who was regaining consciousness. It looked like the events from that moment on, passed in slow motion. Grimm raised the gun towards the police. He immediately took two slugs to the chest and one to his neck. He dropped like a stone. Izzy heard his skull crack on the tiled floor.

"No!" Bailey screamed. "Not like this!"

Izzy slid in the blood on the floor. Bailey screamed for an ambulance again. Izzy could hear the sirens blaring. They were drawing closer. He watched as Simon's eyes rolled to the back of his head. "I've waited too long!" Izzy watched Bailey as she frantically worked to save this man's life.

The spirit of Simon watched Bailey work his wound with frantic precision from over her shoulder. He looked down at the boy beside her weep. He realized he felt no pain, and he had regained feeling in his lips. He watched calmly from above as medics burst into the building and raced over to him. Simon listened as Bailey told them his situation.

Things turned white.

He felt so peaceful.

CHAPTER 56

The medic yanked Izzy out of the way.

He stood up and looked over to see Grimm lying just as he had fallen. The grimace was still frozen on his face. The gun was still in his giant, cinderblock hand. More police poured through the door. Others, wanting to fulfill their own morbid curiosity, tried to get in hoping to see blood or even a body. None stood a chance because the door was now filled with police. No one other than those on official duty was going to get in. As Izzy looked over the medic's shoulder and then back at the door, something peculiar happened. It was a man. He was old, and his clothes were shabby. He walked past the police and through the door as if they couldn't even see him. He wore gloves. The fingers were cut out of them. How did this man manage to get in? He walked right in like he owned the place.

He looked right at Izzy and motioned for him to come to him.

"Hello Izzy," the old man said. His voice sounded so calm. How could it be calm, given what was happening? He'd just watched what appeared to be Simon Glenayre dying. The old man looked at Simon. His face had no expression. He looked back to Izzy. "You just couldn't do it, could you, boy?" Izzy tried to lie to the man. He failed terribly. "Yeah," Ager said, "and that's why you pocketed that gun. And that's why you tried to keep it from Grimm. And that's why you risked your own life trying to save another person."

They both turned when they heard Bailey scream. "No!" she burst out when the EKG beeps turned to a steady drone.

"I'm not done" she yelled to the medics. "*I still have one last stone to throw."*

The medics looked at one-another, puzzled. "She's gonna throw a stone?" one said to the other.

And she went to work. Furiously, Bailey Eden Piper fought for the life of her man.

Izzy looked back at Ager, who looked so sad. "That girl, she doesn't know the meaning of the word 'quit'." Izzy shook his head. "Izzy, I got a job for you, son."

Izzy was scared to ask. The last time he heard words such as those he was asked to kill another person.

"No, boy" Ager said. "It ain't nothin' like that." Ager shared with Izzy what he wanted him to do. It would be his job, Ager said, to share this story. This was an important story because it was about the rediscovery of faith. "One of the most important messages," he said, "was that mankind always know that they can come back home," he said. "Back to God." A promise that this night, and the story that led up to this night would not all have been in vain. It would not be in vain he said, "if someone were brave enough to share this story." He asked Izzy to promise to remember this night. To remember the tale of Simon Glenayre, and all the people involved. Others would someday draw inspiration from it, he said. Simon's story had to be remembered, and passed on, so all that happened, and all those who were lost would not have been for nothing. "Promise?"

In her fight for Simon's life, Bailey glanced at Izzy. She saw the boy nod his head at the old man who was talking to him. The old man had his hand on the boy's shoulder. They both looked at her. She looked back down at Simon. His face was white. He nearly looked as if he would break out in a smile at any moment.

Ager looked directly up and closed his eyes. Izzy looked at the old man, who appeared as if he had just heard bad news. "I'm sorry boy, but you need to get home to your baby sister" he said. "Your momma just died in her bed, and Samantha is home all alone." Izzy gasped. He knew this day was coming, but still he was in shock. He moved towards the door when Ager took him by the arm. "Now you listen to me and you listen good" Ager said urgently. "I know you are scared, but don't you pray for what you think is best for your baby sister, but pray for what *He* thinks is best for her," Ager said. "And pray for what He thinks is best for *you*."

Izzy was too frantic to acknowledge anything. But he would remember. He made for the door, hoping the police wouldn't stop him from leaving. He was certain they would, after all, he was the witness to a crime: Murder. Izzy moved towards the door anyway, and the police seemed as if they didn't even see him. Before walking out, Izzy took one last glance at Bailey.

She was fighting so hard.

AFTER

Reverend Isaac "Izzy" Lighthouse opened his eyes. The dark spot on his opened Bible was now dried. He turned his face to his congregation. They were silent. During that, Samantha stood up from her piano and walked over to her brother and put her arms around him. She whispered into her brother's ear. "Good job." The congregation would not ask any questions about the story past what was shared with them. They could tell Lighthouse was spent.

As Samantha sat back down at her piano, Reverend Lighthouse spoke.

"You see, we all have a name" he said. "And we all have a purpose." He looked down to see Orpha Mae nodding in agreement. He smiled to her.

Lighthouse spotted a teenager sitting in the front row with his mother. "What's your purpose?" he asked. The youth looked away for a moment, as if to consider the question for the first time in his life. Then he looked at Reverent Lighthouse and nodded, as if he had the answer.

"Yes, my friends. What a beautiful day it is. Twenty years later" he said. "Twenty years after that horrible night and it's a beautiful day!"

"In closing, just know what the good Lord wants you to understand: He is there." He said. "And redemption is there. All he asks is that you reach out for it."

"Because He's always reaching out for you."

The congregation sang "Power in The Blood" as they stood up and worked their way out of the pews. Reverend Lighthouse stood at the exit, shaking hands and smiling for everyone on their way out. More than once he had to gracefully break off a prolonged handshake with a single lady of the congregation. He had become good at doing this, without hurting their feelings or embarrassing them. He sang along with the choir.

"Would you be free from the burden of sin/There's pow'r in the blood, pow'r in the blood..."

Sitting in the back of the sanctuary, a family. They looked out of place here, but they were treated very well, as if they had been regulars in this church for years. After the church had all but emptied, they stood up and walked over to Reverend Lighthouse. The man, with shoulder-length hair speckled with strands of grey, held out his hand to Lighthouse. They shook hands and shared a warm embrace. The man's wife was long, graceful and excessively beautiful. She stood lovingly by her husband's side. It was obvious the feeling was mutual. The woman spoke to Lighthouse. "Izzy, I want you to meet our children." She motioned to a boy and a girl, twins. The boy, very passive, and the girl, very much an alpha personality.

The mother of the twins had to separate them but it proved difficult. The little girl had her brother in a firm headlock. The father pulled his hair behind an ear and shook his head. "Good grief," he moaned. "They never learn, do they?" Lighthouse gave a laugh. "No, they don't" Lighthouse laughed. "And we didn't either, till the time was right." Soon, Samantha joined her brother at his side. She hugged the woman and her husband and knelt down to visit with the children. The little girl calmed when she saw Samantha's smile. "Well there you go, Daisy," she beamed. "I haven't seen you and your brother since the day you were born." She stood up, crossing her arms and smiling. "My how you two have grown!" The little girl sprang up into Samantha's arms, hugging her tightly around her neck. Samantha looked to little Sascha, who seemed far too shy at the prospect of approaching Samantha. "It's ok" she smiled. "Come here and give me a hug, boy!"

The little boy never allowed anyone to hug him other than his father and mother. But for reasons he did not understand, he eased into the outstretched arms of Samantha.

Off in the distance, two men watched from a tree line as Reverend Lighthouse, his sister and the family emerged from the church. The man with long hair looked up to the sky. He enjoyed the warmth of the sun on his face. He smiled. The lady he was with, kept her eyes on him. She seemed to enjoy the moment. Reverend Lighthouse and his sister, the lovely Samantha remained in the doorway of the church. They waved at the family as they climbed into their car and pulled off onto the small gravel road, disappearing around a bend of woods. Then together, they waved at two figures standing at the tree line.

Valletta slapped Ager on the shoulder. Dust poofed up into the air. "Fer cryin' out loud, Ager" Valletta complained, "don't you think it's time we get you some new duds?" Ager smacked Valletta's hand away.

"Hey now! If something ain't broke-"

"Don't fix it, right?" Valletta interrupted.

"That's right. Don't fix it!" Walking into the woods, Ager started to sing.

"Sometimes I wonder/ If my tomorrow will ever come/ Show me where to look/ Show me where to look…"

Valletta rolled his eyes. "Again, with that song?" Valletta urged. "You been singin' that same song for almost fifty years!"

"Show me where to look/show me where to look."

"You need to look for a new shirt because that thing is disgusting." Valletta cracked.

"You just leave my shirt out of this" Ager barked. "Heck, it's a warm spring day and what you wearin'?" he asked. "A black leather coat!"

"Two thousand years, and you're still picking on my fashion sense." Valletta argued.

"It's been two thousand years of your big mouth!" Ager laughed.

The two men could be heard bickering as they disappeared into the woods.

And from the heavens Lily giggled and smiled with her eyes.

JAMINKSHTABOB! ™

ABOUT THE AUTHOR

Author D. Aaron Smith is a father, avid fan of The Beatles and author of the soon to be released companion novel to "Simon's Bridge," called "The Journal of Simon Glenayre."
He and his daughter live in Kansas City, MO.
So there.

"We are the music makers, and we are the dreamers of dreams."
-Arthur O'Shaughnessy

WHO'S INTERVIEWING WHO HERE: VALLETTA, AGER AND ME

Valetta yanked a handful of napkins from the dispenser.

In his irritation, he stirred his drink so fast, the coffee leapt over the brim and onto the table. Worst of all, it splattered upon his white as the fallen snow and flawlessly-pressed new shirt.

"That has to be the stupidest thing I've ever heard," he grumbled, rubbing at the coffee stain with a wet napkin. The flimsy paper soon broke apart, leaving white bits of rolled up debris all over his stomach. Valetta grumbled again and tossed the pile of white mush into a nearby ashtray.

Ager smiled without looking up from his waffles. "He asked us meet him here," he laughed, "I'm not too big on the idea either, but he's the guy who wrote the book and it should only take a few minutes of our time."

The lines in Valletta's forehead deepened. "I hear he's a bit of a jerk."

"I heard that too," Ager said as he successfully got the attention of their waitress. Without missing a beat, the woman behind the counter ordered up more waffles for the man in the dusty clothes, who seemed to have more money for breakfast than what he appeared he should. She expected the Italian he was with to have the bigger of the two appetites, but he seemed more focused on his coffee than the enticing scent of sausage and eggs. A plate of hot waffles soon scraped their way across the stainless steel window ledge, separating the kitchen from the eating area. She gripped the hot plate with a moist rag, and grabbed a pot of coffee to take on her way.

Ager smiled when she arrived, his fork and bottle of syrup at the ready. "How'd you know I wanted more waffles?"

"Just call it precognition, honey" the waitress said as she sat the third serving of waffles in front of the less fashionable of her two patrons.

Valetta gave up wishing his shirt clean and leaned back in his seat. "Thank you, Jenny," he said, watching her fill his coffee cup. The waitress couldn't hide her curiosity about this stranger who knew her name. She didn't get the chance to ask.

"I've been here before," Valletta shared before he knocked back the remainder of his cup with a loud slurp. He held out his cup and Jenny filled it again.

"Oh yeah?" she said. "When where you here last?"

Valletta gave pause, quickly shuffling the dates around to a more believable time span. "Oh" he mumbled, "I think it was last week."

The waitress spotted another empty coffee cup, held high. She turned on a heel slower than in years past. The decades of balancing on greasy diner floors had taken their toll on her knees and one of her hips. Still, Jenny managed a smile for everyone she saw. The patrons of this old Seattle eatery always stepped out into the rain with a smile on their faces because of her demeanor. She'd inherited her cheerful ways from her truck-driving father, long since passed away, the thought of the old man brought a sparkle to her eye.

"I think that's him," Valletta said looking toward the door.

"Not very impressive, is he?" Ager snickered as he turned around. Ager began hacking up his waffles. "Is he coming over here? Is it him?"

Valletta leaned to a side, looking over Ager's shoulder. "Oh" Valletta said, embarrassed. "He saw me."

"It's him?" Ager's fork froze in his waffles. Valletta rubbed at the base of his nose, shaking his head. Again.

"You can stop talking about him, Ager. He's standing right beside you."

D. Aaron Smith: Hi guys. Guys?
(Valletta and Ager nod their heads, only.)
DAS: Thanks for coming. I've always wanted to meet you both.
Ager: What do you mean, "Always wanted to meet us?" You made us up, you big dummy.
DAS: Well, I'm just saying I always thought it would be cook to meet you.
Valletta: "Cook" to meet us? "Cook?" And you call yourself a writer.

DAS: Hey, that was a typo. The k is right by the l. Cut me some slack. You didn't even give me a chance to correct it before you said something.

Ager: Oh yeah. We've heard all about your typos.

DAS: Ok. Fine. Elephant in the room. So I had some typos. I'm done revising the book now. Now can we please move on?

Valletta: So did you get them all?

DAS: All of what?

Ager: All the typos. Hello?

DAS: I'm confident. I've had some fresh eyes read through it for me. And that's part of what brings us all together.

Valletta: What do you mean, "brings us all together?"

DAS: Well, I thought as a "thank you" to my readers, I'd give them a little something extra. I'm talking about this interview, guys. With you. Get it?

Valletta: Oh, I see. What's that thing you say, Ager?

Ager: "Whoopie-doo."

Valletta: That's it. Whoopie-doo.

DAS: Wow. Ok then. So let's get started. How long have you two known each other?

Ager: You know the answer to that. Again, you made us up.

DAS: Ok. Can you just go along with this?

(Valletta looks at Ager who looks back at him. I can tell they're having a conversation without even opening their mouths. Certainly a perk of being angels, the whole talking without talking bit. It's about me. I just know it. Really, I don't think they care for me all that much.)

Ager: We've known each other for just over two-thousand years.

Valletta: Give or take a century or two.

DAS: You guys are only two-thousand years old? I thought angels were around close to the beginning of it all.

Valletta: Well we were. But we didn't know each other at first.

DAS: Didn't know each other at first? I don't understand.

Valletta: We passed each other in the halls, but never spoke. He had his crowd he hung out with, I had mine. I think we played each other in a checkers tournament once, though.

DAS: Checkers? They have checkers where you guys are from?

Ager: What were you expecting? Can you envision Valletta sitting around on a cloud all day, playing a lyre harp? Gimme a break.

DAS: Alright then. I get your point. So, let's talk about Simon Glenayre.

Valletta: Simon Glenayre. Simon Glenayre. Yeah, ummm. I think

I've heard of 'em.

Ager: Yeah, long-haired dude, self-loathing, musical genius. Looks at his feet a lot.

DAS: Right, that's him. Have you checked in on him and Bailey lately?

Ager: We see them every day. In fact, he's sitting right over there, with Bailey.

Valletta: He's right. Just look, they're sitting in the corner, looking all gooey-eyed at each other.

DAS: Well I'll be darned. It is them. Man, they're really getting up there, aren't they?

Ager: You all do. That's how it works. You're born, you age, you pass away.

DAS: It's just that I'm kinda surprised is all. I never imagined Simon and Bailey as an older couple.

Valletta: How did you envision them?

DAS: I dunno. Never really gave it much thought. Well, Simon anyway. I didn't think he'd last.

Ager: What do you mean, "didn't think he'd last?" You wrote the book.

DAS: Sure, I know I wrote the book. But while I was writing it, I had my doubts about his survival. So I never gave any thought to what he'd look like as an older man. I see he cut his hair.

Valletta: Look at that. After all these years. They're still in love.

Ager: Does a heart good, doesn't it?

DAS: She's still pretty. After all these years she still turns heads. See that guy as he walked out the door?

Valletta: Yeah. I thought his head was gonna twist clean off his neck looking at her.

DAS: I'm surprised they haven't spotted us. Wouldn't that be awkward.

Valletta: They can't see us.

DAS: They can't see us? How's that?

Ager: Well, that's how it works. We gotta give 'em their space. It might be kind of a shock for them to see us. It's been another twenty years since the incident at the Manhattan convenience store.

DAS: I guess you're right. You guys haven't aged a day, though.

Ager: That's how you wrote us. Eternal. We're angels, you know.

Valletta: And you?

DAS: No, I'm not an angel.

Ager: No. He wanted to know what you've been up to.

DAS: Me?

Valletta: No. We mean all the other guys wearing that ugly shirt. We'll try again: What have *you* been up to? I almost regret even asking the question now.

DAS: Well right now, I'm talking with you guys, and I'm making brownies too.

Ager: Brownies? What do you mean? You're sitting here in this diner talking to us right now.

DAS: Sure I am. But in reality, I'm sitting at my desk, tapping on my laptop. And at this very moment I've just returned from the kitchen from checking on the brownies.

Valletta: Oh, so you're a multi-tasker.

DAS: Wait a minute. Something just dawned on me. We're in Seattle. Simon and Bailey live in Missouri. What are they doing here?

Ager: Yeah, well you should know this. You wrote the scene.

Valletta: It was Chapter 30.

DAS: Chapter 30. Chapter 30. Refresh my memory.

Valletta: Sy always told Bailey he wanted to take her here. Rainy Seattle, I know. But two important things happened here. They were important moments for Simon.

DAS: And what were they?

Ager: Really? You don't recall? Guy who wrote Simon's Bridge?

DAS: Will you cut me a little slack, for crying out loud? I write a lot. And now I think I smell my brownies. Ok. I'm back.

Ager: Back from checking on your brownies? You just finished that very sentence, and now you say you're back from checking on your brownies? Chapter 30. Now do you remember?

DAS: Oh. That. Ok, I remember now.

Ager: "That?" That's all you have to say? "That" was a pivotal moment for Simon, meeting that couple in the elevator. They spoke to him. Really, they were a compass for him.

Valletta: He's right. They showed Simon something. They were a fine example.

DAS: A fine example of what?

Ager: They showed him, ever so briefly, that a healthy, loving and blessed relationship could still be had in this day and age-

Valletta: And that everyone was worthy of love. And the journey to love was part of becoming worthy of it.

DAS: Worthy of what?

Ager: Love, you big dummy.

DAS: There you go. Calling me "big dummy" again.

Valletta: I think it's kinda funny. He's been calling me "big dummy" for two thousand years-

Ager: Give or take a century or two-
Valletta: In one language or another.
DAS: You guys have been hanging out way too long. But wait a minute. You said two things happened to Simon here in Seattle. That was only one.
Valletta: You're right. The other was him. (Motions to Ager)
Ager: That's right, man. It was me.
DAS: Yeah! I remember that! He wasn't the nicest person in the world when you met.
Ager: Right you are. He did bark at me, kinda. I was expecting it, though. I was aware of what he was going through. Val was too. Wanna know a secret? (Looks over at Valletta)
Valletta: That wasn't the first Ager had been around Simon.
DAS: Been around him?
Ager: That's right. We were both there, with him, when he lost his parents. We were right there in the room when he got the news. He couldn't see us, but we wept with him.
DAS: Right there with him?
Ager: That's right.
DAS: Did he ever go back home to see his grandfather and cousin?
Ager: Oh yeah. (Looks over, sees Valletta smiling)
Valletta: It was a sob-fest! He brought Bailey with him. She saw his family for the first time in years and years.
Ager: And they discussed what happened to Simon's parents, but not too much. There weren't a lot of answers available to them, so what's the point? That's what they said. "What's the point?"
DAS: So that's it? Simon's just going to let the mystery of his parent's deaths go unanswered? That's crazy.
Ager: Well, calm down there, hot rod. They aren't just sweeping it under the rug. What can be done sitting around a kitchen table in the middle of the night? Those folks love sitting around the kitchen table all night, visiting over coffee. It's a good time.
Valletta: So, have you told them about Simon's parents yet?
DAS: What? Simon's parents? You're asking me? Tell who?
Ager: Your readers, you big-
DAS: Dummy. I saw that one coming. I've given it some thought. I've touched on it some in the companion novel to Simon's Bridge. Dropped a few hints.
Ager: And what's the companion novel to Simon's Bridge called?
DAS: I've decided to call it "The Journal of Simon Glenayre." It's kind of a prequel. It's selected diary entries from the time Simon was twelve and concludes at the end of his marriage to

Bailey Eden Piper. It's much darker-

Valletta: Groan.

DAS: What?

Ager: Plugging your book during *our* interview. How classy.

DAS: Well you asked!

Valletta: So you're working on the second. Will there be a third?

Ager: Yeah. People love trilogies.

DAS: Dunno. It's kind of hard to say. The first two really took a lot out of me. How I'd love to write something humorous for a change.

Valletta: Are we gonna be in it?

DAS: Not if I can help it! You two have been a handful as it is. Val, why aren't you eating?

Valletta: Na. Not hungry. I had a nice breakfast.

Ager: A big breakfast. Tell 'em what you had.

DAS: What'd you have for breakfast?

Valletta: It was nothing! A steak sandwich, ok?

Ager: Four steak sandwiches.

Valletta: Yea, thanks Ager.

Ager: And the rest of the potato salad.

Valletta: Thanks, Ager.

Ager: Don't forget the ice cream.

Valletta: Shut up, Ager.

DAS: What kind of ice cream do you like?

Valletta: Don't remember (Looks at Ager, glaring).

Ager: It was Neapolitan!

DAS: Neapolitan? Nobody likes Neapolitan! You like Neapolitan?

Valletta: Miss? Coffee, please.

DAS: Don't change the subject, Val.

Valletta: You don't call me "Val". Only Sy calls me "Val". And it wasn't Neapolitan.

Ager: (Whispering) It was Neapolitan.

DAS: Neapolitan.

Valletta: Stop saying that.

DAS: Neapolitan, Neapolitan, Neapolitan.

Ager: (Attempts to speak, can't. Laughing.)

DAS: Oh, don't want anyone to know big, tough Valletta likes Neapolitan?

Valletta: It was chocolate.

Ager: It was Neapolitan!

Valletta: Oh! So let's talk about your embarrassing little factoid! I bet there's something…

DAS: I don't have anything embarrassing to hide.
Ager: Oh, now that's a line and a half! Fibber!
Valletta: Spill it, Smith.
Ager: Or I will.
DAS: Ok. So my mom has a nickname for me, alright? And I hate it.
Valletta: So what is it? "Snooky-wookikins?"
DAS: Nope.
Valletta: C'mon! What is it?
DAS: Yea, hold your breath. It'll come out, in like a million years or so. You'll be tossing snowballs in-
Ager: Puddin'-Pops!
DAS: Put a cork in it, stinky. Good grief.
Valletta: Puddin'-Pops? Your mother's nickname for you is Puddin'-Pops? Oh. That's sweet!
DAS: Shut up, will ya?
Valletta: Ok, Puddin'-Pops!
Ager: (Laughing) Oh man, can't talk…gut hurts.
DAS: Oh, yea. Sure. Laugh it up, Ager. Why don't you hop the next head of a pin out of here.
Ager: (Still laughing) Aaaw! Poor feller. Did I offend you?
DAS: No. I think it's comical. Hardy-har-har.
Ager: (Elbowing Valletta) Look at 'em. He's mad now. I offended him!
DAS: How funny. And what offends you? Soap?
Ager: Hey now. That ain't funny. I just bathed. Recently. When was it? Nineteen-
Valletta: Sixty-seven, I think.
Ager: Yea. It was nineteen sixty-seven.
DAS: Please, can we change the subject? Please?
Ager: Sure. We can change the subject.
Valletta: Hey, wanna know something interesting about Ager? He can name the capitol of any country. Try 'em.
DAS: Oh really?
Ager: I sure can. Hit me with your best shot.
DAS: Alright then. What's the capitol of Denmark?
Ager: That's easy. The capitol of Denmark is Puddin'-Pops.
DAS: Alright. That wasn't funny.
Valletta: Sorry. Ager's been giddy today. He just bought a car.
DAS: A car, eh?
Ager: Yep. I bought a car. They even threw in the steering wheel.
DAS: Alright! Let's talk about *that*. What kind of car did you buy?
Ager: It's a nineteen seventy-two Ford Puddin'-Pops.

DAS: That's enough! Waitress? Valletta, sit up. You look ridiculous. Can't you help him up?

Ager: I can't do anything about it. He's doubled over! Man, I've never seen him laugh so hard. Tears are streaming down his face. He can't breathe.

DAS: Yes, hi there. Please excuse my friends. Can I get a refill?

Jenny The Waitress: Sure, hon. (Pours coffee) There you go. Anything else?

DAS: No. That's all. Thank you.

Jenny The Waitress: You're welcome, Puddin'-Pops.

DAS: Right. Well, it's obvious this has gotten out of control. That's what I get for coming up with this idea.

Valletta: So whatcha sayin', Puddin'-Pops?

DAS: I'm saying this interview is done. Just give me a second to get my stuff together.

Valletta: So what's next for you?

DAS: Brownies. I'm going to eat a pile of brownies and try to forget this interview was my stupid idea.

Ager: Brownies. Man, I sure like brownies.

DAS: You like brownies, do you?

Ager: Oh, yea. I love 'em.

Valletta: Yea. He loves 'em. We both love brownies.

DAS: Well, I make excellent brownies. You guys want one?

Ager and Valletta: Yes!

DAS: Well tough. I'm not giving you any.

Ager: That's terrible!

DAS: Terrible? You're lucky I don't turn you guys into a couple of mimes, just out of spite.

Valletta: Can I ask *you* a question?

DAS: Does it have the name "Puddin'-Pops" in it?

Valletta: Nope. It's a straight question.

DAS: Alright then. Ask away.

Valletta: Did you put any of yourself into the characters in your book?

DAS: Yes. I did, kinda. Sorta. Whatever.

Ager: So, who did you put yourself into?

DAS: Much of my self-doubt, misplaced pride and apathy went into Simon, much of what I want to be went into What's-his-name, and much of what I desire went into Bailey Eden Piper.

Valletta: And us? Who did you put into us?

Ager: Yea. Who did you put into us?

DAS: My family. My mom and dad, my brothers. The humor of my grandparents and uncles, the caring, the love. The admiration

I have for my own daughter. All that I hold dearest. Except for that silly nickname.

Ager: So that's it? You just gonna up and leave now?

DAS: Yep. Just like that. Hey, thanks for the visit, guys. It was fun. Well, to a point anyway.

Valletta: You take care of yourself, now.

Ager: Yea. We'll be around, checkin' in on you every now and then.

DAS: Uh, yea. Like I find that comforting.

Ager: I bet you do, Puddin'-Pops.

DAS: I think I have everything together now. Before I go, what's next for you guys?

Ager: Us? We're goin' to one of our favorite places.

DAS: Oh yea? And where's that?

Valletta: Big Charlie's Saloon.

Ager: That's right. We go there sometimes to watch our favorite football team. You should visit the place, man. It's red. Everywhere.

Valletta: Arrowheads. Everywhere.

DAS: Where's it at? I don't think I've been there.

Valletta: Of course you haven't. It ain't in Kansas City.

Ager: Nope. It ain't in Kansas City. But it very well could be. Full of good people. Just like in Kansas City.

DAS: So where is it?

Valletta: Philly!

DAS: Philly?

Ager: Philly.

Valletta: My kinda people.

DAS: So you're saying they like Neapolitan ice cream too?

Valletta: No, smarty-pants. Look, they love our football team. Just like Kansas City does.

Ager: Do they ever. Our football team is their football team.

Valletta: Love that red.

Ager: Flame on, baby.

DAS: Now I'm going crazy. I have to go there. Sounds like my kind of place. Alright. Take care, guys. And try to get along, will ya?

Ager: It's been two thousand years. If we ain't learned by now-

Valletta: Where'd he go?

Ager: Man. When that boy says it's time to go, he don't screw around. It's time to *go*.

Valletta: Yea. He disappeared just like that.

Ager: You can do that when you're the writer. Heck, he wasn't

that bad of a guy, was he?

Valletta: Maybe. But I still think his typing sucks.

Ager and Valletta stood up, each freed their coat from the coat rack with a tug. Ager noticed Simon and Bailey rising from their booth too. Both watched Simon helped Bailey on with her overcoat. He eased her around, buttoning her coat from the bottom up, smiling. Bailey put her hand on his face and smiled back.

"Aaaw", Ager gushed. "Will ya look at that? He pulled her collar up to keep her neck warm."

Valletta turned to see. "Man I sure wish I could go up and talk to 'em."

"Me too," Ager said. "I miss rattling his cage, making him think." He buttoned up his raggedy coat. "Inside all that fear and sadness, buried in all that sin was a good man, just tryin' to get out."

Valletta gave a sigh. "I'd wave, but he can't see me."

"Direct interaction with him isn't allowed anymore," Ager said softly to his friend. "He has to take it from here, Valletta."

Ager gave Valletta a pat on the back, motioning him forward. Valletta paused when he saw Simon and Bailey nearing the exit as well. "C'mon, man" Ager said. "They can't see us. Let's be on our way."

Both watched the grey-haired Simon walk with Bailey to the door, his arm entwined with hers. Simon reached from behind Bailey and pushed open the door. A gust of cold, damp air blew Bailey Eden Piper's hair in his face. He laughed as he pulled strands of hair from his mouth.

Valletta and Ager watched Simon stop in the doorway. And then to their shock, he turned, looked directly at them and smiled.

The wind groaned and slammed the door shut behind Simon and Bailey as they stepped into the chilly, dark night. Ager and Valletta stood with joy in their hearts, watching Simon and Bailey as they strolled arm in arm past the window.

Yes, it was another cold and rainy night. The wind was blowing, and it was dark. But within the darkness there was still a light.

And the darkness could not overcome it.

THE JOURNAL OF SIMON GLENAYRE: EXCERPTS
BOOK 2 OF 3 IN THE TRILOGY

Man, do I ever love packing books with all kinds of extras. This is the last thing I'm packing into this book because I've got a sink full of dishes to tend to and they aren't gonna wash themselves.

Below are a few excerpts from the second book in the Simon Glenayre Trilogy, called The Journal of Simon Glenayre. It's exactly what it says it is: It's Simon's Journal.

Bailey Eden Piper provides the Foreword, shared below. Also included are few entries from Simon's journal. So-

Have a good read and enjoy these selected excerpts from my second book, The Journal of Simon Glenayre. Off I go now, to do those dishes.

How I wish they'd just learn to wash themselves.

Peace and Light,
D. Aaron Smith

FROM BAILEY EDEN PIPER

"His name was Simon Glenayre, but you can just call him Simon."
Those were the words of our dear friend, Isaac "Izzy" Lighthouse as he introduced you to my husband, the musician and poet Simon Glenayre.

Simon Glenayre. To this day he is shy about my love and commitment to him because in the years before our reunion, he came to believe nobody really cared about him at all, except for Valletta, of course. I truly love him unconditionally and I think my sincerity is still new to him.

Sincerity is like a foreign language to Simon. He still seems puzzled when I share my feelings for him. He still harbors a great deal of guilt for what happened all those years ago, like the way he ended our friendship and our marriage. "I love you Bails and I'm sorry I set you adrift that day," he whispered while looking out the window as he did the dishes. "Never again" *he said.* "Never again."

That's Simon for you. He's the only man I've ever heard use the word "adrift." I often wonder where he came up with that analogy, as if I were a ship on the ocean or something.

And that's right. I said it: Simon Glenayre does the dishes. I think he feels as if that simple chore anchors him to his new life. When he washes the dishes, it keeps him anchored to reality. I think that by staying busy, he keeps the current of his past from catching up and sweeping him away to the life he had before. He turns on the radio, listens to NPR and just scrubs away at those dishes and pans. I've never witnessed anybody enjoy one of the most hated household chores the way Simon does. He could use the dishwasher instead, but he actually enjoys washing the dishes himself. Washing the dishes!

My friends have asked me why I've allowed a reunion with Simon and I understand. Look, everybody has their flaws. My flaw is the weak knees I have for my man. My friends say he doesn't deserve me and I say they're right. Simon doesn't deserve me. But everyone deserves love. I have a better idea of what Simon is now and I'm not trying to convince myself otherwise. He's an alcoholic. He's an addict. But don't judge me too harshly. If you insist I'm wrong in forgiving Simon and forging a renewed path with him, try this: Look into the mirror and picture the person you love most in the whole world and then imagine turning your back on that person when he or she needs you the most. He isn't worthy of my love, you say? Well if I don't love and care about him, who will? So yes, I've given him another chance. I've given us another chance. I have no regrets because life and love are always worth fighting for. Always.

So I'm sure you're asking how I came to be in possession of Simon's journal. It's very simple. One morning after work I stopped to check the mail and found it in my mailbox. It happened just like that. Simon, before he hopped that flight to Germany and off to an uncertain future, put his journal in the mail to me. I believe he thought there was a chance he wasn't going to come back. It makes sense: he'd already attempted suicide twice and had an assassination attempt on his life as well. There would be another attempt on his life to come.

I wonder if he felt it coming on, as if through precognition. So he popped his journal in the mail to me and it's been in my possession ever since. I think he wanted people to know what was going on in case something happened to him. I think he wanted me to understand him better in case he never got the chance to explain it himself. Sure he knows I have his journal. He's the one who mailed it to me. But he's never asked for it back. Not once has he asked to see it. And yes, I have his support to do this project.

This book is Simon's life. It is a collection of his thoughts. It's a collection of his hopes and fears and dreams and pain and anguish and more dreams and…well again, I'm sure you get my point. To add a little bit of structure to it, I've divided it into three sections, starting with "The Beginning." It just seemed an appropriate title for the start of his journal. He was twelve years old.

At this very moment, Simon is sitting in a lone chair at the picture frame window, looking out over the meadows and of course, he's lost in thought. I'll know when he's done because I'll hear him sigh, then he'll stand up and cheerfully continue on about his day. He always does his best to keep busy with chores on our farm. He won't mention what he was thinking about, sitting there for an hour or so. However, once curiosity got the best of me and I asked him what he thought about when he sat there, looking out the window. "I saw hummingbirds," he answered before his voice trailed off and that was it.

Simon was a very prolific writer at a young age. And his journal, I mean really, this thing is thick! So I read through the whole thing from cover to cover (it took forever) making selections I thought you, the reader, would find *the most interesting, inspiring and yes- even frightening. Some of this book you will find enjoyable. Much of it is a sort of "Simon Glenayre Trivia." Some of it is a little funny, some of it inspiring and other parts...well, they're just terrible. It's the entries about the end of our relationship that I found most difficult to read. He knew what he was doing and yet he didn't. It was a very difficult time for Simon, for me and for all who loved and knew us as "Simon and Bailey."*

Also, I've included some of his drawings and sketches. They are in pencil, pen or charcoal. Some of them are kind of hard to describe. You'll just have to see them, I guess. I also found some pictures of historical figures and such that for some reason, he stuffed in his journal. He has a thing for numbers too. What they're about I have no idea. I never really gave it much thought but included them with the batch of sketches they were found with. Maybe you can figure them out.

In The Journal of Simon Glenayre, some of Simon's entries are followed by comments from me. I only insert my input in those places because I may be able to elaborate on something that's worth sharing. It's only to give you the reader, a better understanding of what Simon is trying to say. Some of my entries are written from pure shock because I had no idea of what was going on.

Simon did give his permission to use his journal for this project. He thinks someone may draw some strength and inspiration from it. A kind of "if I can survive this, you can survive that" metaphorical read. You will find some of Simon's entries to be difficult to understand. I did my best to translate, but some of it was nearly impossible. So why would I include an entry hard to understand and at times very disturbing? Because it's an important reflection of where Simon was at that particular moment. I saw that particular journal entry as a relevant ticket onto the subway of his soul, for better or worse.

So open a bottle of wine and let it breathe for a bit. Maybe the wind is groaning outside as you read this. Go ahead, light a candle and open the window. Can you see the moon up there? It's watching you now.

I present to you, The Journal of Simon Glenayre.

-Bailey Eden Piper

<u>March 17th, 1982 *(Age 12)*</u>

Today Mom and Dad told me to come into the living room because they had something really important they wanted to tell me. I thought it was going to be bad news cause this sort of thing always means bad news. Usually it means I have been caught doing something I shouldn't have done and I'm in really big, big trouble. But it wasn't that. I sat down and Dad said we were moving back to the states. The good old U.S. of A. I think that's pretty cool, or at least I *think* it's pretty cool. OK. I'm really not too sure what to make of it. I haven't been back to America since I was little and I don't want to leave my friends here in Beuern. I know Karl is going to cry. I'm about to cry right now. Darn it. I think I don't want to go. It scares me going back. This is my home now. No, I don't want to go back to the states. I want to stay here. I'm so scared.

<u>June 8th, 1982 *(Age 12)*</u>

Today I said goodbye to my best friend ever, Karl. I was right when I said he would cry because he did. I think I cried more. Karl's Mom cried and so did my Mom. If all of us are crying, then why don't we just stay?

Yesterday I got all my stuff packed up. All my clothes and toys. Mom helped me. I think she kinda wonders if this was the right move. She helped me to pack my guitar so it would be safe for the trip over. We were gonna wrap it in a blanket and put it in the case. Before she wrapped it up I asked if I could play it one more time cause it's gonna be a long time before I get my hands on it again. I played her my newest song and when I finished she just kinda sat there without saying anything. I thought she was gonna cry and I didn't know how to feel about it. She took the guitar out of my hands and looked at it. After she laid down the guitar she reached out and put her hand on my face. She said *"You are a prince, my Simon, for you are a son of The King."* Mom looked so sad and it doesn't make any sense to me because what she said was really nice.

After that, I followed Mom to her and Dad's bedroom. Mom went to Dad's closet and pulled something down. It was wrapped in an old blanket and tied up with a rope. She carefully put it in a large crate with my guitar. I asked her what it was and she said it was a really old instrument from Germany. I asked her if I could see it but she said I couldn't. She did say that someday I would get it but now wasn't the right time. I was supposed to pass it on to someone else. I asked her who I was supposed to pass it on to and she didn't answer. Sometimes being in this family is like being in a mystery novel. So I just agreed and that was it.

I watched her close the crate with my guitar in it and this made me kinda sad. Goodbye guitar. I'll see you in America.

<u>September 3rd, 1989 (Age 19)</u>
Hello, journal. Remember me?

Sorry it's been so long since I've been by for a visit. I know I've dipped in here and there over the past couple of years, mostly to whine about my dreams and such, but I'm here to just say hello.

So from the bottom of my heart, my dear old friend, I warmly greet you with an open heart and a brand-new pen.

I'm sure you have noticed I haven't made any entries on my birthdays or for New Year's Day. I've just decided not to on those days. It's just too tough to talk about. But I promised I wouldn't whine!

The band has been out on the road a lot the past year. We started out playing bars and clubs but have moved up to small theatres and we're filling them up without the support of a record. We're doing it all on our own. We'll play any place that will have us. Valletta said we'd play at the opening of an outhouse if we were asked! Valletta, ever-present and of course only an arm's-length away from me at all times.

NOTE: At this point, word was spreading about Simon and it was spreading quickly. He told me that by this point, their small, clunky bus was being followed from town to town by fans and shows were selling out everywhere. Every place they played, they packed it, shoulder to shoulder.

-B.E.P.

www.ingramcontent.com/pod-product-compliance
Lightning Source LLC
Chambersburg PA
CBHW020258200626
46816CB00001BA/362